careering

DAISY BUCHANAN

SPHERE

SPHERE

First published in Great Britain in 2022 by Sphere

1 3 5 7 9 10 8 6 4 2

A CIP catalogue record for this book
is available from the British Library.

Hardback ISBN 978-0-7515-8020-4
Trade Paperback ISBN 978-0-7515-8021-1

Typeset in Sabon by M Rules
Printed and bound in Great Britain by
Clays Ltd, Elcograf S.p.A.

Papers used by Sphere are from well-managed forests
and other responsible sources.

Sphere
An imprint of
Little, Brown Book Group
Carmelite House
50 Victoria Embankment
London EC4Y 0DZ

An Hachette UK Company
www.hachette.co.uk

www.littlebrown.co.uk

This story is for every person who has ever messaged me and asked me if they should quit their job.

Our jobs are our private fantasies,
our disguises, the cloak we can creep
inside to hide.

A Month In The Country,
JL CARR

Chapter One

Cupboard love

Imogen

'Through sharing my most audacious desires . . .' Audacious, or outrageous? '. . . outrageous desires with my rapidly growing readership, I am confident . . .' Oh. Is that too much? It's such a thin line, with job applications. How do I convey that I'm dazzlingly and uniquely talented, while sounding just the right amount of desperate, available and cheap?

I'm writing this, sitting on an upturned bin. Well, my left cheek is on there, anyway. The right one went numb some time ago. The best thing about being exiled to the fashion cupboard is that it guarantees a little privacy for 'personal admin'. (The worst thing is that an intern can occasionally get forgotten about, locked in and sometimes get left overnight. Rumour has it that this happened to a girl called Bella when she was working on a posh lifestyle mag called *Trunk*.)

1

For all of my efforts, it's possible that no one in the *Flair* HR department will even read this letter. I know, from bitter experience, that CVs do not hold any weight. No one can be bothered to read beyond 'Imogen Mounce, 26'. Even though I've made up a Duke of Edinburgh Bronze Award, purely as a creative writing exercise.

There's probably another intern, a Millicent or an Isobel who is already *in situ*, lined up for the role with all the right qualifications – uncles on the board, old school friends on the Beauty desk. I got very lucky when Mum named me after her favourite Jilly Cooper book.

On paper, I can pretend to fit in. I don't think my CV would even grant me access to this cupboard if my dad had got his way and called me after Michelle from EastEnders.

I'm inches from the clothes rail, and I can see a pair of cobalt blue, neoprene hotpants. That's what confident looks like. Out of habit, I squint for the label. Alexandre Vauthier. Nine hundred quid, minimum, although press samples don't really have a price. Imagine having a grand to spend on Net-a-Porter and blowing it on shorts! What would I do with a grand? I permit myself a brief fantasy of fancy skincare and estate jewellery, until reality bites. I'd pay my rent, wouldn't I?

Squinting at my cracked phone screen, I check the time. Oh fuck. Oh help. The deadline for this application is in twelve minutes. And I should have left twelve minutes ago, I'm going to be late for my shift, again. I'm going to get my wages docked, again.

Maybe I should go for broke and tell the truth. If nothing else it would make the application stand out. 'Through setting up a sex blog and describing some of the most intimate and embarrassing details of my life, I've gained writing experience, even though no bloody newspapers or magazines will let my words anywhere near their pages. I'm desperate for a day job, I'm very, very tired, and I'm fed up with supplementing my casual part-time bar work with odd shifts at the pen factory. Tonight I'm on lids, which means I won't be able to feel my thumbs for a week.'

Without warning, the Acting Editor sticks her head around the door. 'Everything OK in there, Imogen? You all right? How are you getting on with the Box of Doom?'

Arghhhh! 'Hello, Harri! Yes. Sorry!' I throw my phone behind me and lunge for the box.

I'm supposed to be untangling necklaces and returning them to their rightful press offices – not applying for magazine jobs on *Panache* time. Still, it's not as if *Panache* are paying me. Also the Box of Doom is busywork, it's something to do when the server goes down, or when Rosa, the old editor, was having a major tantrum and Harri, her deputy, had to come up with a scheme to get the interns out of the way and keep them quiet.

The fashion cupboard is a sort of rarefied priest hole. Sometimes, you come back from lunch and there's a real atmosphere in the office – it's obvious that Something Has Happened, and it feels as though it must be your fault. (As if I had that kind of power! Usually, it's a brand pulling the ad that's paying for the rest of the mag that week. Once, it was because someone microwaved some leftover fish curry, and no one would own up to stinking out the kitchen.)

Harri smiles. 'I've got to pop upstairs for a bit, I've been summoned by the boss man.' She dusts herself down for invisible lint, non-existent wrinkles. 'Actually, I've just realised what the time is, you can probably get going.'

How does she do it? Harri is one of those magical people who always gives the impression of having showered no more than thirty minutes ago. After about 4 p.m., I start to feel stale. Biscuit crumbs collect on my knees and elbows, regardless of what I've actually eaten. Harri is a human toothpaste advert. A riddle, wrapped in an enigma, wrapped in a heavenly cloud of Santal 33. She has her own Wikipedia entry, which I know off by heart – but even though I've been her eternal intern, on and off, for over two years, I know almost nothing about her life outside *Panache*. All I have are the rumours. Giles the fashion director has hinted that she had an affair with a famous movie star, back in the nineties. Araminta, my old boss at *Splash!*, sniffed that the movie star was on the fringes of the Brit Pack, and now only gets work popping up in home insurance adverts – but then, Araminta put most of the budget up her nose and the magazine got shut down after six months, and I don't think she enjoyed watching Harri's star soar as hers descended. Poppy, a woman I interned with at *Sleek* a while back, reckons that Anna Wintour herself tried to headhunt Harri, and Harri turned her down.

I believe a three-year-old child could identify Harri as the editor of a fashion magazine. I have absolutely no idea how old she is. There's a whisper of a wrinkle in the corner of her eyes, and I can't work out whether she has perfect skin, or access to the most expensive, subtle Botox going. Probably both. I've never seen another person with hair as shiny as hers in my life. Not even on TV. Not even on Instagram. But sometimes she twists it up and pins it with a chewed

4

Biro. And when she pulls the Biro out, it falls perfectly into place. (I tried it once on a night shift – bad idea – and I had to cut the lid out with nail scissors.) Harri has eyebrows like Elizabeth Taylor. Once, I asked her what she used to get the perfect arch, and she said 'Vaseline.'

Yet, she's warm. It might be her accent – I think Yorkshire, maybe Sheffield? Harri expects excellence from everyone, but she's fair. She sees people. She says hello, she asks how I am, she has never once addressed me as 'oat latte' unlike most of the fashion team. I suppose she had to put out plenty of fires started by Rosa, but Harri is decent. It's not a quality I encounter very often in this industry. She's always in immaculate black, never greying, never bobbly. Although – not today. She's in a fitted flowery dress, splodged with pink and green. It looks odd on her. She doesn't look like a media star, she looks as though she's going to the wedding of someone she doesn't like very much. Still, she's probably ahead of a curve, and the rest of us will all be in the Zara version in a month.

'Thanks Harri, see you tomorrow! I hope it ...' Can I say I hope it goes well, when I'm not sure I'm allowed to know what 'it' is? The funny thing about being the most junior, least important person in any office is that you're not supposed to let on that you know about anything. Even though your invisibility invites indiscretion – people will say anything in front of you. I am omniscient, and sad proof that knowledge is not always power. 'I hope it's a lovely evening! For you! Um ...' Urghhh.

Harri chooses not to respond to the fact that I sound as though I started learning English after lunch. 'Thanks for today, you've been ace, as always. See you tomorrow.'

Ace. Harri Kemp, industry legend, thinks I'm 'always ace'. That will keep me warm at midnight, when my numb, inky fingers are wrapped around a polystyrene cup of Nescafé. That will soothe me when I've been on my feet for eight solid hours, and every tiny bone in my body is aching so acutely that I feel like a skeleton in a wig. That's enough to make me smile when my alarm goes off after three hours' sleep and I haul myself out of bed to the bus to the train to the tube and do it all over again.

If I was even 10 per cent less broke, I'd call in sick, skip my shift at the factory and hang around the office for a little longer to see what happens. Perhaps that would be tempting fate. I've been letting myself nurse a secret hope. It's the hope that kills you, I know. But I'm crossing my fingers and holding my thumbs, all the same.

I'm not an idiot – I know that I've been sent to the cupboard because Something Has Happened. But today, I think it might be something good. Rosa left *Panache* a month ago, leaving Harri as acting editor. The new editor is about to be announced, and it's going to be Harri. It has to be.

And if Harri is made editor-in-chief, I think she might give me a real job.

Still, it's a big If, so I start putting one arm through a coat sleeve while rereading the *Flair* application in my Notes app. I apply for at least eight jobs a week, no matter how much they challenge and stretch the definition of 'journalism'. Or indeed, 'paid employment' – so I can copy and paste the final paras, the excited for the opportunitys and the look forward to hearing from you soons. My screen is so knackered I can barely see what I've typed any more so it helps to have something I made earlier.

Twenty minutes later, sitting on the bus, I realise just how badly I've fucked up.

It occurred to me that the internet in the fashion cupboard can be a little patchy, and I should check to make sure that my *Flair* application letter is in my Sent folder.

It's there, all right. Well, half of it.

The other half is a paragraph from a blog post I've been working on. One I wasn't sure I was ready to publish.

The sound that emerges from my throat is something between a death rattle and a moo. Sweating under my coat, I read the words I'd written, furiously in the dark, a couple of nights ago, as Sam Strong snored beside me. 'There's an art to the hate fuck. You have to go all in. It's not just about releasing your inhibitions – you're dissolving them, in your acid rage. I didn't know my pussy could grip a cock so tightly, as though I was trying to break it, until I'd completely let go of the notion that I was trying to make him fall in love with me. I know he's a bad man. Does hate fucking make me a bad feminist? Maybe. Does it make me come? In a way I didn't even know I was capable of. I'm embarrassed to admit to the number of times I've cried over S— but the orgasms are making me so much wetter than any tears could.'

Those words are preceded by these: 'Here are the ways in which I've demonstrated strong attention to detail.'

Chapter Two

Something Has Happened

Harri

Neither of them will sit down. Harri knows he is waiting for her to go first. It's absurd; sexism, disguised as chivalry. She will not play the game – partly because by staying standing, she is able to retain what little power she has. Mostly because she has worn uncomfortable shoes, in honour of the announcement, and she needs to stay on her feet. If she sits, she may never be able to get back up again. She tips the heavy chrome chair against the big table, surreptitiously stretching a sore calf, like a runner. Will has been speaking without stopping for seven minutes now. He's rambling, mumbling pointless professional platitudes. When will he get to the point? Why does he have to make such a ceremony out of everything? Well, because his job is dull, and his life is dull, and dullness is his MO. The first rule of media. The glamour of the company is always inversely proportional to the glamour of the person in charge of the operation. Officially, *Panache* is very much the jewel in Hudson's crown. The truth is that the whole company is mostly profitable thanks to the steady, consistent demand for *Construction & Scaffolding Weekly*.

Will is looking at her now. What is he saying? His monotone makes it difficult to concentrate. The man is an utter charisma vacuum, '... long term service to the company. In recognition of your talent, and considerable ability, we think ... ' *Please get on with it.* Harri wants to savour this moment, but she can barely concentrate. Downstairs, chaos reigns. The cover interview hasn't been confirmed, seven suitcases of couture gowns are stuck in Customs and she has just learned that the new girl in Classifieds is taking make-up from the Beauty cupboard and selling it on eBay. She wonders whether she can sneak a look at her emails, by peering into her pocket. But she has no pockets today. She is wearing The Dress, bought the very second she felt sure of her promotion, once Rosa had assured her she was not tempting fate. Most editors wear black, black, black. But the editor-in-chief wears Erdem.

Harri has fetishised the floral dresses, ever since she saw Alexandra Shulman wearing one to the *Vogue* anniversary party. Harri is usually careful with her clothes. She is a pragmatic dresser and her outfit choices are dictated by necessity before aesthetics. She is required to move through the world at twice the speed of everyone else. But when all of your dreams come true, you can justify a dream of a dress to match. The birds of paradise and hot house flower print make Harri yearn for the tropical, the botanical, a land of warm nights and soft breezes, free from all cares and MacBooks. Now, Harri wishes her warm thoughts would provide some actual heat. She feels shivery, exposed, angry with herself for every 'right to bare arms' pun she has ever let the subeditors sign off. The Regent Street Christmas decorations have just gone up. What was she thinking?

'So we're pleased to offer you an exciting new challenge,' says Will, who is now staring at the table, not making eye contact.

Harri smiles. She has known Will for over ten years, and he has never become any more open, any less awkward. 'Well, it's not *too* new. I know *Panache* inside out. You're in very good hands.' She laughs, because she knows how to play the game, make nice. *Come on, Will. Please wrap this up. Let me get back to my magazine.*

'Hnnnnnn,' says Will, clasping his hands in front of him, like a little boy on a school trip, anxious about straying from the crocodile formation. 'That's the thing. We think you need a change. We've run the numbers and decided we want to go ahead with the new product idea. The online magazine, for younger women. Everyone was very impressed with the research you did last year. We want you to be at the helm of the new launch.'

'Right. Right.' Harri can feel the cogs and cells of her brain whirring, expanding, trying to absorb this information. 'So – a lot of work. Exciting work! But how would that fit with my role at *Panache*? Because I have so many ideas and ongoing projects that I was working on with Rosa, and as an editor-in-chief I'd expect to—'

'Harri,' Will cuts her off, with something akin to tenderness. 'You're not the new editor-in-chief of *Panache*.'

'I see.' Harri will never, ever cry at work. But she may

puke. What has she eaten today? She remembers the first three quarters of a banana, abandoned as she left the tube upon encountering its final mushy, brown inch. Then ... coffee. More coffee. A cheese sandwich, still in its wrapper, that has been resting on her desk for the last two hours. Every time she has picked it up and started to open it, her phone has rung or an urgent email has come in, or someone has rushed over with an emergency (one was legitimate, a major fuck up with a mascara ad – one was a meme starring a penguin in a party hat). She does not have the energy to throw up. There is nothing in the tank. The sensation is similar to falling in the playground. Running, flying, throwing yourself into a fantasy world, and then having the ground rise up to meet you, sudden and hard. The shock. The pain. Harri does not consider herself to be much of a reader of poetry, but as she feels her soul fly from the room, seeping through the glued shut windows, she finds herself remembering a fragment of Audre Lorde. Something about being non-essential. Wrong. Worn thin.

'Will that be all?' No, that isn't right. Ask a normal question. Ask a human question. 'I mean, who will the editor be? The new launch – when will that start? How will I transition from my deputy role to the new project?'

Will gulps and looks relieved. Harri is letting him off the hook, asking questions, comfortable, answerable questions, and not the screamingly obvious one, 'How could you do this to me?'

'It's Mackenzie Whittaker, from Hudson US.'

Is that a person, or another company? thinks Harri, for a stupid second. 'Um, I don't think I know ...'

'Her background is very much management, not

editorial, she's been overseeing various US titles, and she's turned them around, profit-wise.'

'Oh, was she on *Glamor*? Or *Mademoiselle*? *Lucky*? I never came across ...'

'No, no, things with a different profile. *Go Fish. The Racing Hound.*'

'But *Panache* is a women's lifestyle title. And I would have thought you'd want someone with experience in the sector ...'

'Harri, we both know that things are changing, it's becoming increasingly difficult to sell a premium print product.' Against her will, Harri imagines Will screaming the words 'PREMIUM PRINT PRODUCT' at the point of ejaculation. 'We need to make significant changes in terms of how we cost the magazine. And Mackenzie knows money. Don't worry, I'm sure she'll still want your editorial expertise.'

Yeah, that bitch can whistle for it, thinks Harri, as she says 'Of course. You know how much I care about *Panache*. After all, it's been my life for ten years!'

Another polite, tinkling laugh. This time, she is laughing at herself. Because what kind of fool, what kind of idiot, what kind of woman reaches the end of her forties with so little to show for herself? No big job. No personal life, to speak of. A tiny flat that still feels far too big. And a mortgage that is definitely too big to permit Harri to speak what's truly in her heart and tell Will to go fuck himself.

Will still has the audacity to look relieved. 'So, the plan is to launch towards the end of January. That gives you about eight weeks. You'll need to start research and assemble your team, while you're phased out of your role at *Panache*.'

12

Harri imagines herself fading from high to low definition, her outline flickering and blurring, leaving the office a ghost.

'Anyway, lots to do, best get back to work!' Once again, Will looks at Harri as though he is waiting for her to move. It is polite to let her leave first. It also gives Will an opportunity to have a good look at her arse. On the scale of terrible Hudson letches, he barely registers, but Harri trusts no one. Especially because now the meeting is over, Will has stopped looking at her like a senior employee, and started looking at her like a girl in a dress.

'By the way, you, ah, you look, um, really nice. Doing something after work? Special occasion?'

Harri tugs at the skirt of her treacherous, overpriced editor-in-chief dress. 'No, not at all. Just fancied a change.'

Chapter Three

The Wake

Harri

'Where's the champagne? Did we get a cake in the end, or ...'

Hiding behind the door, Harri can picture Giles, her fashion director, scampering about. This would have been his victory too. He likes to call himself her Girl Friday, or the Lieutenant of her Heart. He can be glib, he can be bitchy, but he's secretly incredibly kind, and volubly, noisily, proudly Team Harri. She knew he'd be organising the straggling staffers who were sticking around after six, desperate to celebrate her good news.

There is no way she can go back into her own office. Not tonight.

She has failed, she has fucked up, and she can't face anyone, ever again. She will have to run away. For three minutes, Harri considers her options. A suite at Soho House? Absolutely not, far too many concerned friends, and crowing enemies. She is quite near St Pancras – she could get a train to anywhere, perhaps she can start a new life in Paris? No, she might bump into someone. Belgium? She is being ridiculous, she really needs to sit down with a glass of water – but in this moment she doesn't feel strong enough to visit the kitchen.

In truth, Harri knows she is all out of fight *and* flight. Every single drop of adrenaline has evaporated through her pores. She might cry now. She'd have to go to the disabled toilet in the basement. The toilet reserved for weeping juniors, rats and – apparently – ghosts. And once Keith Richards during a legendary interview for the now defunct Rock Show. (A title that was unsuccessfully relaunched as a geologists' periodical.)

Harri knows that if she goes to the basement, she will never leave.

Blinking hard, she sends Giles a message. Then, eyes screwed shut to keep the tears at bay, not caring whether she gets run over, she stumbles all the way over the road to the Angel, and waits.

Harri and Giles have seen out many a crisis upstairs in the Angel. It is their War Room – the sticky, stinky antithesis of Media London. Too grubby for a gossip columnist to bother with. As a young, ambitious hack, Harri would go out of her way to be seen in the smartest bars. Now she can only really relax in a pub where nobody knows her name.

'All right, Kev!' Giles nods at the elderly regular, as he dumps four bags of crisps on the table. And, to Harri, sotto voce, 'It's a shame. Acid, they say. The old fella used to be such a raver, down the Blitz every Tuesday night in his

15

leather vest.' Kev gave nothing away but Giles was always full of theories.

Harri tears into the cheese and onion. 'Careful with your references, Giles. Blitz was before you say you were born. If word gets out that you're a day over thirty-five, they'll fire you too.'

'Ah, I've always been precocious! What did I hear some-one saying the other day? We're all convinced the nineties happened ten years ago, and no one is willing to accept that they were actually thirty years ago.' He leans forward conspiratorially, 'Anyway, to catch me out you have to be really good at maths. Never a mag hag's strong suit. You think anyone spends two grand on a Balenciaga blazer if they're good at maths?'

'This Mackenzie is, apparently,' Harri mutters gloomily, before she slurps her white wine, 'a real pound buster. Or dollar buster. But then, she's not one of us, is she?' She bites her lip, hard. 'It's humiliating, so humiliating, to be ditched for someone whose biggest career achievement is a stint at *The Racing Hound.*'

Giles pats Harri's forearm. 'But that's the thing, surely? It would be awful if they brought in an Anna, a Carine. You're not being replaced by an icon. You're the icon, and they want a . . . what? Look at Diana Vreeland! Being fired by *Vogue* only made her legend greater. Anyway, you've not been fired,' Giles punctuates his point by crunching a fistful of crisps.

'I've been sidelined. Which is somehow worse. If they'd properly sacked me, they'd have to give me some money, and I could slink away with a little dignity.' Harri silently admits to herself that if dignity is what she really wants, she

16

ought to stop submitting to the cheap thrills of the Angel's pot pourri flavoured Sauvignon.

'Anyway, you told me you enjoyed the research for the new launch. And we both know *Panache* is on the outs,' says Giles. Harri rolls her eyes. Giles has been predicting the end of *Panache* for the last five years, usually whenever his expense forms are queried. She's never worked on a magazine that hasn't lurched unpredictably and uncertainly from month to month. 'Still,' he adds, 'I think this online thing might be a really smart move for you. After a couple of months with this horse and pound of flesh lady, I'll probably be begging you to hire me.'

'It's just ... GOD. Twenty-somethings, Giles? What do they like? What do they know? Who do they fancy? I'd be arrested for lusting after the people they're into. Their vintage isn't just the stuff we wore first time around – you shot and styled it. If they know who Kate Moss is, it's because she's Lila Grace's mum. They wear *Friends* shirts, but they were actual *babies* when *Friends* was on TV. I can't do it. Maybe I can get a job writing for *The People's Friend* and edit cosy stories about grumpy grannies teaming up with troublesome grandsons to defeat the school bully.'

Giles raises his eyebrows fractionally. Harri has known him well enough, for long enough, to predict that he is approximately three weeks away from his next Restylane top-up. 'How do you know so much about *The People's Friend*?'

'Oh, my nan used to get it; sometimes they have it at the dentist and I have a read for nostalgia's sake. And it's taught me about all sorts of clever tricks with a stock cube.'

'You need to get laid,' says Giles.

'You always say that. So do you.'

'Let's see if Kev fancies a threesome.'

Harri is not really in the mood for Giles' nonsense. 'Sure, if he's up for it, you can take his trousers off and I'll hold your poppers.'

Giles will not let it lie. 'Seriously, when did you last ... I mean, it's been a while, yes? A date? Why not? A teeny tiny trip out for an itsy bitsy cocktail, avec un handsome man? When did you last wax, even? I shudder, Harri. I bet it looks like all of the Marx brothers, down there. You were the one who told me that if you don't stay on top of the grooming, your fanny looks like the face of a man who brings his own cider to a folk festival.'

Harri thinks briefly of the last time she'd been waxed, of the man she'd waxed for, and decides she would feel slightly more comfortable considering Giles' pubic topiary instead. 'What are you doing, down there, right now? What are the current styles?'

'Actually, I'm experimenting. Growing it out. It's a bit stubbly now, but in a few months it will be luscious. The seventies are back, and I'm going to have me a summer of love.'

'But first, I suspect, a winter of discontent.' Harri allows herself to smile.

'This is the trouble, though, with you. You've always been married to the job. And now the job wants a divorce and maybe it's time to go out and meet, you know, a human person. After Andy ...'

Harri shakes her head vigorously and splashes her cheap wine down the front of her expensive dress. 'No, Giles, really – it's been a long day. It's been a lot. I can't – I've only got room for this. You can buy me another drink and we can talk about anything but that. Then I'm going to go home, and put my best pyjamas on, and have my last early night for a while. I'm giving myself twelve hours to wallow. Then I'm going to work.'

Chapter Four

The triumph of hope over work experience

Imogen

'What was the most challenging aspect of the role?'

'Well, as you know, my character, Jennifer, falls in love with the village baker, and I haven't actually eaten anything containing flour since 2006, so . . . '

I'd never even heard of this actress before I was asked to transcribe this interview, but I already hate her. An hour ago, I was in such a good mood. I'd raced into the office, having convinced myself that Harri would be offering me a real job before I sat down. But everything seems tense and strained today, and I feel more ignored than ever. Why do I bother? Why do I keep coming in? I think about it for twenty seconds and come to the depressing realisation that being an unpaid intern on a major magazine is really all I have going for me. It feels like more of a career than 'casual bar worker' and 'temporary factory operative'.

I am so, so hungry. I could eat a bag of flour on its own.

Breakfast was, as always, crappy instant coffee from the office kitchen, and I'm not entirely sure what I'm going to do about lunch. I think I can rustle up just enough change for a banana and some instant noodles, but I really ought to do a bit more work before I go outside.

On the other side of the office, a giant gingerbread sculpture is being erected. Some company has invented a new festive hand soap, and in order to 'celebrate the launch', they have sent *Panache* a gingerbread Twelve Days of Christmas. It's the end of November, so that partridge is going to be very stale by the twenty-fifth.

Would anyone notice if I sneaked over and stole a Lord a-Leaping?

A soap and moisturiser set has been dumped on everyone's desks, regardless of status and hierarchy. The press release tells me it retails at £49.95. Do I a) Sell it, b) Give it to my mum for Christmas or c) Use it for shower gel?

I will never, ever become blasé about free stuff. In fact, all of my stuff is free stuff. Everywhere I look, I see piles of books, chocolate, perfume, T-shirts, stickers, phone covers. The *Panache* staffers open their post, sigh with irritation about the fact that another publicist has dared to send them yet more clutter, shoving the treasure to the side of their desks. I am constitutionally unable to say no to anything that I don't have to pay for – even though sex bloggers get sent some seedy packages. Blow-up dolls. Penis shaped soap (which gave me a rash under my armpits). Edible underwear.

Edible underwear!

I might have some on me. I bumped into the postman on my way home from work last week and shoved my weird packages into the bottom of my bag for safekeeping. I don't think I ever took them out.

In desperation, I look over at the gingerbread. There is so much gingerbread. It's still under construction, and it's already covering every conceivable surface. It smells like treacle. Like Christmas. I'm desperate for it.

But there are unspoken rules in the *Panache* office. Maybe, in an hour or two, one of the senior Sales girls will say 'Oooh, I'm so naughty!' and start nibbling on a turtle dove feather, or half a golden ring. Over the course of the afternoon, 'the boys' from various other bits of the building will be invited to come in and demolish it.

But the work experience is the lowest of the low. If I were to eat my fill of gingerbread right now – even though there's enough here to feed an orphanage – no one would say anything. But I'd never, ever be asked back. And I'd be talked about. 'Do you remember the weird intern who just helped herself to a load of biscuits?' Eventually I'd pass into legend, they'd say I'd devoured an entire traybake, or a vast Victoria sponge, fistfuls at a time. It would be less embarrassing if I fainted at my desk.

So, after checking that no one is looking, I reach under my desk, and rummage in my bag for a handful of edible panty.

I'm not sure what I was expecting, but it's surprisingly chewy. Extremely sweet, sort of apple-y, not unpleasant – but it really sticks to the roof of your mouth. I put my headphones back in, typing out the actress's words as I try to uncoat my tongue and teeth.

'So I researched the role by trying to make toast, and seeing if the smell would . . . '

'Imogen, hey! Can I have a quick word?'

Harri is at my side, by my desk, with one hand on my shoulder. I squeak in panic. She knows. She knows I am eating edible underwear. I freeze. She tugs delicately at the wire of my headphones, and I swallow hard.

'Harri, sorry, yes, yes of course, I was in the muh of a . . . nuhhhh . . . ' My tongue feels thick and furry and I chew at it, trying and failing to scrape off the panty coating. 'What can I do? How can I help?'

'Can you come out for a chat? We can go to Soho H . . . ' she glances at her watch. 'Actually, sorry, best go to Pret, I've got the visuals meeting in an hour. This shouldn't take long.' Treacherous, dangerous hope blooms again. My gut starts to untwist itself. I think this might mean that Something Has Happened.

Chapter Five

The Quick Chat

Imogen

A paradox. A good intern is an invisible intern. But we only give away our labour, for free, because we hope to be noticed. There are two alternative definitions for 'intern'. One is 'work experience'. The other is 'political prisoner'.

For some reason, I don't mind being called 'the intern' but I hate it when I'm referred to as 'the work experience'. Or 'the workie'.

If I'm not getting paid, surely I'm the only person in the room who is not a workie.

It would be in shockingly poor taste to consider myself a political prisoner. Wouldn't it?

These are the machinations my brain runs through, as Harri orders a macchiato, takes a table and establishes that I would not like 'a bun, or something' to go with my filter coffee.

Obviously I long for a bun or something. If I'd had my

wits about me, I'd have ordered the fanciest, foamiest, most elaborate drink on the menu, and a triple decker sandwich. But then, that's another trap, another trick. Plenty of companies have told me that they have a role for someone who is hungry. They don't really mean it.

'... I'd get you to sign an NDA or something, but ...' Harri shrugs, and I clamp my lips into a tight, silent smile.

'Anyway, we're launching a brand new online title for younger women, and I'd love to hear your thoughts. You're, what, twenty-five?'

I'm panicking. 'Um, twenty-six.' Is that the wrong answer? I should have lied! I've missed something vital. Am I being hired, or fired? (Once more for the people at the back, says my brain, You can't get fired if they aren't paying you.) 'Um, right, of course. What sort of thoughts?'

'We're looking to launch early next year, we're coming up with a content plan, our key demographic is a woman who is a little younger than the typical *Panache* reader, 18–34 although we're focusing on the twenties, obviously ... she's dynamic, ambitious, politically engaged, sexually confident – in fact, that's where you come in. I really love your blog, and it came up quite a few times when we started our research last year. Your readers are the readers we want.'

My readers? 'Right! Great!'

Another paradox. I am happy to share my innermost, intimate thoughts and feelings with total strangers, but I baulk at sharing them with Harri.

'Your tone is perfect, funny, frank, insightful, raw. Exactly what we have in mind.'

'Thank you.' I've forgotten how to be this person Harri is describing. Panic is making me feel prim, uptight. I find myself momentarily unable to perform the role of funny, frank sex blogger. Scrambling, I try to keep the conversational ball in the air. 'Do you have a name for it yet?'

Harri shakes her head. 'That's always the hardest part. We need something that sounds very sharp and smart, not overly feminine, something about knowledge, being connected ... we're working on it. If you have any thoughts, I'd love to hear them.'

I have no thoughts at all. Not 'no thoughts about what to call the glamorous new start-up' – just no *actual* thoughts. 'Erm, *Savvy*?' I say, a little too loudly, and make a face. 'No, that's awful. Something about knowledge ... power ... being in the know ... ' Shit. Looking at Harri's frozen face, I suspect she is seeing my potential drain away faster than she can drink her coffee.

'*In the Know* – there's something there, maybe? Anyway, basically, I wanted to sound you out. Hypothetically, would you be interested in a full time contract for this website? And available to start early in the new year? I'm still working out final details and numbers, so I can't confirm anything yet.' Harri shrugs. Just like everyone else I've met who is in a position to offer me a life-changing job, she is oddly reluctant to admit whether or not there actually *is* a job. 'Anyway, tell me, what are you working on at the moment?'

'Pegging,' I say, before I have a chance to decide whether or not it's a good idea to do so. Harri looks blank so I blunder on. 'It's, ah, female led penetration, that is a woman, a cis woman usually, wears a strap on dildo and penetrates her partner's anus. Well, it doesn't have to be a male partner but it's often the case, it's all about subverting traditional, het power dynamics, and I'm exploring the complicated feminist perspective – I mean, I've found that pegging brings out something quite aggressive, when I do it, and I love it, but I worry that it's quite problematic ... '

Harri nods. 'Imogen, I know what pegging is,' she says quietly. 'I meant, what are you working on today? At *Panache*.'

We walk back to the office in near silence. 'Not so cold today,' I offer. Harri nods.

It is entirely possible that I have just been almost hired, then fired.

Christmas comes and goes. Every phone call, every email, every mysterious sound fills me with brief, tremulous joy, and then instant, crushing despair. *This* is the worst thing about wanting to be part of this world. Every professional rejection is simply a ghosting. No one ever tells you where you stand, or gives you a straightforward refusal. No one lets you know when to stop hoping, and because hope is all you have, you hang onto it, in vain.

At home, I reassure Mum by telling her that I might have some exciting opportunities coming up in the new year. Hope flickers, and fades. It's the hope that kills you. I should know that, by now.

I apply to be a social media executive on *Kites and Dirigibles* and hear nothing. I apply to be a coordination assistant on *Modern Ferret* and get a form email telling me I have not got the job 'owing to the high volume of applications from many strong candidates'. I write a blog post about whether masturbation is an effective antidote to loneliness and feel too depressed to publish it. And then, after a long, bleak bar shift (during which I both have my arse pinched and am declared, loudly, to be 'ENTIRELY UNFUCKABLE' by the same customer), I take my phone out of my bag and check my emails, out of habit, expecting little.

Imogen, can you call me first thing tomorrow? We're on. Btw we really liked your name. It's *The Know*. Hx
Harriet Kemp
Editor-in-chief, *The Know*

Chapter Six

Imogen phones home

Imogen

'Mum? Mum, it's me. I got the job!'

'Imogen?' A heavy, wheezing, Tramadol breath. Another, longer, deeper, worse. It's as if the simple respiratory act exhausts him. 'Hi, Dad. How are you?' Fuck. He almost never picks up the phone. 'I was just ringing to tell Mum – and you! I got that job. The website one.'

'Right. I'll get your mother.'

Well done Imogen, I mutter, sourly and probably not silently enough. Dad hears only what he wants to, but he is tuned into any and all expressions of bitterness. It's his factory setting.

'Love! How are you, sweetheart?' She loves me so hard, she loves me from so far away.

'Mum, I've just got a job, I spoke to the editor this morning. I'm going to be a writer! A staff writer!' I can't get enough of those words, the weight of them, the rhythm of them. Solid sounding, after all of that fear and floating. 'In fact, they're using the name I suggested.'

'Oh, Im, that's great news! I'm so proud of you. And you'll be working on a magazine, a proper job at last. Good girl! We've been worrying, you know. Are they paying you well? Do they pay you extra for coming up with the name? You'll have a pension!'

No, no and no.

'Um ... for the first few months I'm on a contract, it's sort of a start-up, it's connected to the magazine. I thought I explained it at Christmas, don't you remember?' Panic makes me exasperated, cruel. 'It's early days, but the editor really likes me. I met her doing work experience.' Also, Harri is a big fan of my sex blog. Still, as long as Mum remains resistant to online banking, I think it's fine to let the rest of the internet remain a mystery. 'So, I think they want me to start in about a week. It's good, isn't it?'

A pause. 'You can always come home, love, if it doesn't work out.'

Home, where it's perennially cold, even though the plastic logs are lit up in the gas fire grate on a July day. Home, sleeping in a single bed mounted on castors, where you can't masturbate yourself back to sleep without bumping and squeaking and being forced to explain over breakfast why you were making so much noise in the night. Home, where the sweet, bright, fake air freshener smells curdle with the smells they are trying to mask – the cigarette smoke, the drink, the damp, the litany of issues that we've always been a little too poor to fix. Home, where I dare not go, where love is limited, and no one lives out loud.

'I saw Su, you know, Jen's mum, the other day, they're

delighted that she's home. She's thinking about teacher training, did she tell you?'

'Yeah, she said she might be able to start early, in the spring term.' Technically Jen said 'If I have to wait until September I will kill. I need to be out of the house.'

'You'd both be together, if you did come home. You girls have always done things together.'

'Mmmm, well, let's see, shall we?'

'Are you OK for money? We're a bit … well, you know it's not easy with your dad, they keep changing his benefits. But I'll pop something in the post for you, you can get yourself a new outfit for your first day!'

'No, no, Mum, honestly. I'm fine. There's actually a … dress code, I'm just wearing black, like I do at the bar! So I've got everything I need, save it. Take Dad out for a cup of tea and a cake or something.'

'Oh, love, you are thoughtful. Me and your dad – we're very proud of you, you know that.' Sure.

'I know you are, Mum.' She is proud for both of them. Dad wouldn't be proud of me if I appeared before him on TV in the middle of a *Storage Wars* marathon. I'm not entirely sure he would recognise me.

'Anyway, love, better go. Got to get dinner on.'

'It's not 5 p.m. yet!'

'You know we like to eat early. Anyway, you should go and celebrate! Go out for a drink with those girls you live with. And come home soon. We miss you!'

What can I say? 'Love you, Mum. Love to Dad, too.'

I shouldn't feel so low, after all this time. I should have known exactly what to expect. The cold is biting into my bones, and my knuckles ache. I ought to put my phone back in my pocket, and put my gloves back on, but I check my messages. Blue ticks indicate that Jen has listened to my squealing voice note, but she has yet to reply. That is even harder to bear. She's probably busy. But I can only picture her sitting on a stool at the breakfast bar, watching her mum watching the kettle, staring into space.

Putting my phone back in my bag, I feel for my keys, and start the dull, grey, windy walk home. It's a little like planning a military defence strategy, returning to my flat. The lock gets very stiff in the winter, so I need to approach it with a running start, lifting the heavy door in the frame to tessellate everything into place. However, if I make too much noise, Downstairs Colin will come out in his dressing gown to shout at me about how I need to stop going to the toilet in the night because the gurgling pipes wake him up. (I don't. And I would wet the bed and sleep in it every night for the rest of my life if it meant I could avoid any and all interactions with Downstairs Colin.) Holding my breath and making a wish, I shoulder-barge the door and scurry up the stairs, sprinting and leaping up the squeaky steps.

I have a tiny bit of luck left. I appear to have the place to myself. The pile of post indicates that neither Gemma nor Emma is home yet.

I gather up the envelopes, wincing when I see a couple of brown ones with my name on. No. Not today, not when the world is working for me, for once. I know I'm broke, the bank knows I'm broke, the Visa people know I'm broke. We're locked in this endless, pointless détente: they write, they call, they say 'we've noticed you don't have any money and we'd like to know what you're planning to do about that'. I say 'Well, nothing, because I don't have any money.' It's like a Beckett play about administration. I don't understand how something so dull gives me so many nightmares.

Holding my breath, rolling up on the balls of my feet, I enter the kitchen as though I'm taking to the stage in Covent Garden wearing satin slippers, rather than taking to the floor in grubby Converse, hoping to steal some toast. Yes! I see bread. Thick, white, carb cushions, hope and heat and home. Will there be butter? Gemma has some sort of terrible flax spread, bought ostensibly because she has high cholesterol, but almost certainly because it tastes so revolting that even I won't nick it. Emma alternates. Three weeks out of four she's on the tiny tubs of coconut and hemp and things that cost fourteen pounds from Whole Foods. But if she's had a bad date or a worse hangover, she hits the hard stuff – super salty Lurpak Spreadable. And here it is, emblazoned with her name, Sharpie'd in letters two inches high, bedecked with black, cartoon daisies, as if she's some sweet-natured, giving hippy child, and not the sort of woman who would burst into your bedroom without knocking and accuse you of nicking a spray of her Carolina Herrera. (Firstly, I like to think of myself as a sort of Marxist Robin Hood, stealing only according to my needs, taking from the rich and giving to the poor. The poor is me. Secondly, I would never intentionally smell of anything that comes out of a bottle shaped like a high heeled shoe.)

I'm halfway through my first slice, standing up, butter sliding off my chin, onto my coat lapels, moaning like a Catholic martyr in the throes of an ecstatic vision, when I hear footsteps. Shit. Shit shit shit. Have I got time to run to my room and lock the door? I am frozen to the spot, my treacherous toes curled tight and rooting me to the ground. Somewhere, David Attenborough is gently warning an invisible audience that my survival skills are insufficient, and that they should prepare for bloodshed.

Gemma or Emma? Gemma or Emma? Gemma is always absolutely horrible to everyone. Emma is occasionally nice to me. However, I'm pretty sure I'm eating her bread. She catches me just before I return her decorated butter tub to the safety of the fridge.

'Imogen, hi ... oh. You're eating my food again.'

She's not angry, she's just disappointed. Although previous experience suggests that disappointment is the warm-up act for the headliner, a hair metal rage set.

I swallow too quickly to taste the toast. What a waste. 'I'm sorry. I'm really sorry. I'll replace it. I just got in, and ... yeah. Anyway, how are you? How was your day?'

Emma is briskly flicking through the pile of envelopes. She has never had cause to be frightened of her own post. 'Fine, fine, the usual, really busy, brokers playing me up, lot of first time buyers at the moment. It's amazing, you'd think that the banks being such cautious lenders would mean that demand really dropped off, especially now the minimum deposit is so much higher. You really need at least 20 per cent of the property price to get your mortgage approved.'

Whenever Emma tells me about her job, I feel a bit sick. Then I remember that she owns and rents out two flats in Birmingham, and she's slumming it here, while she 'saves up' for another property for her portfolio, and I can feel the vomit rising in the back of my throat, lumpy and acrid.

34

You'd think she could spare a slice of fucking bread.

I wait for her to ask me about my day, and when I can wait no longer, I blurt it out. 'I just heard that I got a job! I think I told you that Harri from *Panache* mentioned something just before Christmas? I'm going to be a staff writer on a new website.'

Emma looks blank. She doesn't remember. 'Ah, right, well done. Is it full time? You'll have regular money coming in? You know rent day is next week?'

I do know, Emma. I know that if I don't buy anything, or breathe out, and make some creative, less than moral meal choices, and buy my train tickets on my credit card, as long as I get paid for this week's shifts on time I can just cover the cost of my windowless box room.

'Of course, I'm on it,' I say, smiling, doing a half-hearted impression of scatty old Imogen, forgetting to pay her rent and do her food shopping! 'That girl would forget her head if it wasn't screwed on,' I'd heard Emma tell Gemma, with a little affection, and no imagination. That girl – me – would sell her own hair if the man at the shop hadn't told her it was too dry and damaged. In fact, she's broke enough and scared enough to have thought about stealing your hair while you're sleeping and trying to sell that too.

Someone, somewhere must want to celebrate with me. Sitting on the edge of my bed, I stare at my phone, and the space where a message from Jen ought to be. I try calling her – a bat signal of urgency, an act so audacious that it can only suggest wonderful or terrible news – but she does not pick up. Eventually, the little dots begin to flicker. Sorry, out with Mum, will call back when not busy. Gr8 news x

The single kiss and lack of exclamation mark make it

very clear that she does not think the news is Gr8, at all. *Be kind,* I remind myself. *This can't be easy for her.* Jen is always the first in line when I need someone to support me during a disaster. But for once, I've triumphed. I have something she really wants. If she'd got this job, I'm not sure how I'd handle it.

Sighing heavily, I realise there is one person I can call. I vowed I'd try to stop doing this, unless there was an emergency. I think this counts. I reply to Jen. Call me or I'm going to see Old Man Strong. Dot dot dot. Dot dot dot. Dot dot. The flickering fades, and she stops trying to think of a reply.

If I look away from my screen I can pretend I'm not responsible for what my fingers are doing. Can I come over? I can. It's fine, it's fine. One last hurrah. It's the final orgiastic day before a self-imposed, sexual Lent. I should shower, I should shave, but when I shove my hand under my armpit, I don't feel too stubbly. A quick spray of deodorant, the last drop of a Diptyque Do Son sample stretched all the way from ear to wrist to elbow to knee. A hunt for a better bra and almost matching knickers – black mesh buttock burrowers, but *il faut souffrir pour être belle,* or rather *pour faire l'amour avec un homme mauvais.* A fist, shaken at my wardrobe, and then at the sky, before a slightly bobbly, faded, fitted black Lycra dress is unrolled from my washing basket, plucked of bits of tissue, and rolled onto my body. A pair of opaque tights receives the same treatment. I gave up wearing stockings for Sam Strong some time ago.

I throw make-up on my face as fast as I can manage, before I can change my mind. Then it's the same old routine, down the stairs and out-the-door and into the cold, onto the train, into the city, then inside a taxi somebody else is paying for, London grey but glittering, lighting itself up as I speed over the river, towards a place where I am a plaything, not a problem.

Chapter Seven

Some enchanted evening

Imogen

I don't actually mind much when Sam Strong smokes in bed. Sometimes I worry that it's faintly Oedipal – or Electracal, I suppose. Mmmm, just had sex with a middle-aged man who smells like my dad! But there is something profoundly comforting about the urban, social stink of it. I'm not above taking the odd, delicious drag. With him, I can pretend I'm in a French play. More to the point, when Sam Strong lights a cigarette it's difficult for him to ignore me because it's hard for him to smoke and scroll through his phone at the same time.

'So, new job, is it?' He is leaning up on one elbow and smirking at me through a blue tinged cloud. 'I think there's some Mumm in the fridge.' Almost courteously, he pulls my knickers off from where they've fallen, halfway down my right leg, and waves me away towards the kitchen. I'm still wearing my bra, and even though I don't think anyone can see in, at least not this high up, I feel a little self-conscious. 'Hope your neighbours don't catch me Donald Ducking it,' I call, returning to the bedroom still knickerless, holding the bottle and the glasses. He's managed to get his phone out anyway, the cigarette is stuck in the side of his mouth now, and he does not look up when he replies 'You're Porky Pigging it. Donald Duck wears a hat.'

'Would you open it?' I catch the whine in my voice and hate myself for it.

'Fuck's sake, Imogen, you work in a bar! Mind you, I suppose there's not much call for champagne at The Grill. Pinot Greej for the suburban crowd.'

I roll my eyes, but he's not wrong. I open my mouth to call him a snob, but he's interrupted me before I start speaking. 'Oh, give it here. No, actually, you should do it. Otherwise you'll never learn. Twist the bottle, not the cork.'

I know, I know, you paternalistic fuckhead. I brace for the pop, and I'm eight years old, trembling and weeping my way through a noisy firework display, but this is Sam Strong's apartment, where everything is engineered to work perfectly. The cork release is signalled by a sound both full and low, it's the toot of a bass clarinet. Pouring the drinks, I allow myself the luxury of looking at him directly in the eyes with full, unflinching contempt. I glance down. His dick twitches.

'So, cheers! Here's to your new job. To publishing! To your touching and baffling faith in a declining industry!'

'It's your industry too,' I point out. 'And we'll be online. Everyone loves the internet!'

'Well, these days, new launches are usually over before they start. I'd keep your eye out for other stuff, just in case.

Why don't I try to get you a job at the *Guardian*, with me?' says Sam.

I will not rise to it. Approximately every six months, Sam Strong likes to raise my hopes and break my heart by offering me an imaginary job at the *Guardian*. In fact, that's how this nonsense began. He found my blog, he slid into my DMs, he declared himself a fanboy – given his proximity to fifty, the 'boy' should have been a red flag – and suggested that his editors might want to meet me. There were never any editors. There was a blackout boozy lunch at the Soho Hotel, and then bed. I fell for him, he ignored me, I got over him, I ignored him. The second he sensed my interest was waning, he was back in hot pursuit. I resisted, then remembered the well stocked fridge, the underfloor heating, the Addison Lee account. The reliable orgasms. As long as I focus on what a detestable twat he is, I'm safe, and I can treat my trips to Docklands as a sort of luxury mini break.

Still, I'm so tired of doing this dance. Sam's excuses for the lack of this imaginary job have been so creative, inventive and impressively consistent that it's almost baffling that he's failed to find any critical acclaim as a novelist. (I took a screenshot of his worst Amazon review, and I reread it when he is being especially distant and dismissive. The schadenfreude soothes me like a prescription tranquilliser.) First, there was no budget. Then Sam started sleeping with his editor and would only be seen with me under cover of darkness. Then there was a job – classified ad sales trainee, commission only. 'It's a great way to get into the building!' he'd enthused. If that was all I'd wanted, I would have nicked his pass and swiped myself through the barriers.

But now I have the upper hand. 'I don't want a job at the

Guardian, I want to work at *The Know*. It feels really timely and exciting. Harri says she loves my irreverent tone, she thinks it's "perfect for the brand".' I can't resist making air quotes. 'Everything else for women seems so earnest and po-faced, this is supposed to be feminist and funny. And you know, working for Harri is a big deal.'

Sam looks thoughtful. 'Harri Kemp, right? I think we used to ... I mean, everyone just assumed she'd take over at *Panache*, after Rosa Calder left. Wonder what happened there?'

'Well, it's still all Hudson Media, I think.' I wish I had a story to shut him up with. Sam likes to position himself as the fount of all media gossip. It's very, very irritating. I yawn, stretch and wiggle, relishing the soft, warm cotton beneath me, the mattress stretching above and below me, endless, a happy horizon of memory foam. The one at home can't accommodate my head and heels at the same time. Sam Strong looks at me with some alarm. 'I've got to go out, this artisanal gin awards thing. You're welcome to stay the night ...'

'Great, thanks. Will do!'

I have designs on his power shower, the Aesop soap, the drinks trolley, any edible delights his cupboards might yield. Netflix on his big TV, not my crappy old laptop. Sleep.

'I'm not sure when I'll be back ... if I'll be back. My sister is in town, so ...'

Ah, the sister, a sexual Bunbury, a suspected invention, a mythical woman evoked to ensure that Sam Strong never has to be entirely honest about the whereabouts of his penis.

'Cool, cool. Well, I can let myself out in the morning.' Hurry up and go already.

Sam Strong takes his time, waffling away about the celebrities he expects to encounter (maybe Sienna, possibly Cate, definitely the woman from *Love Island* who became famous for coining the expression 'nipple o'clock'.) He makes me pick a shirt for him, and I eschew an ink dark, velvety navy in favour of a pale, sickly green that makes him look like he's off to his job at the prison morgue. Eventually he leaves, and I spend thirty seconds nursing an existential crisis, wondering why I'm here, and why I keep coming back. Then I look at the fridge again, crack open a beer and remember. My options are limited. I could be at Sam's, or sitting at home in my room, where the energy-saving bulb acts as a light-sucking black hole, and I can't see my hand in front of my face, all the better to tolerate the squalor. There's sitting at home in front of the TV, where Gemma will provide an unsolicited audio description of everything including the adverts, and shout at me for making too much noise if I cough or cross my legs. There's the vagaries of Tinder, et cetera, and buying bad wine I can't really afford, while someone I don't fancy tells me about their obsessive passion for bukkake, or sky-diving. Sam Strong is awful, but at least he is dependably awful. He doesn't treat me any more terribly than anyone else I know. Apart from Jen, who has been a neglectful friend today. But Jen doesn't have an apartment like this.

I call her again, ruminating my way through the rings, rehearsing a passive aggressive voicemail, and I'm taken aback when she picks up.

'Imogen! Sorry, I know, I've just been a bit ... ' she exhales. 'I've had an awful day. Well, not awful at all, really, that's the problem. Just ... I suppose it's hitting me that this is my life now. I'm stuck here, and I miss you.'

'No, no, you're not stuck, you're just,' panicking, I reach for something – anything – that might comfort her. 'You're assessing your options. You won't be there for ever, you'll figure out a plan.'

'I wish you'd come back with me.'

'Well, I'd do it if I could live at yours. Do you think Su would adopt me? Can you be legally adopted, at twenty-six?'

'Mum would sign the papers in half a heartbeat, you know that. But if you lived in this house, you too would be drowning in teacher training brochures. You'd be getting them on toast. You'd go to wipe your bum and instead of tissue, you'd find a course syllabus. I'm expecting to wake up and discover that Mum has papered my room with them in the night. Anyway – oh my God, new job! I'm really proud of you!'

In most people's mouths, that phrase makes me bristle. Dad is – Mum claims – proud. Strangers on the internet are 'so proud of u, hun' when I'm 'brave' and share sex toy reviews and unfiltered accounts of my quest for multiple orgasms. Whenever I go on Facebook, Leanne Patterson, who once stamped on my foot so hard that she broke my little toe, is posting and boasting about her pride, because her old 'bff' (HA!) appears to be doing so well.

If any of these people have earned a whisper of a right to pride, it's because their cruelty, their obstructiveness, their lack of faith forced me to double down. I might have given up, had they not made it clear that was exactly what they wanted.

I don't really know how to say what I'm feeling. That I need Jen to celebrate me. This opportunity is so hard won. Jen knows better than anyone about the grinding anxiety, the night shifts, the sketchy bars, the factories, the unpaid hours in fashion cupboards all over Soho and Mayfair. Because Jen has lived it too. And I know she has wanted this just as much as me. It's only luck and circumstance that means that I'm still in London – just – and she's down in Devon.

I try. 'I've been missing you so much, today. You're the only one who gets it. Mum basically told me to come home when it inevitably goes to shit – because everything she's ever known has gone to shit. Not that I ever could. Even Sam Strong hardly reacted – you'd think he'd have some professional curiosity.'

Jen snorts. 'Oh, love, I'm sorry, you're in a bad way if you're expecting Sam Strong to feign an interest in any aspect of your life where you keep your knickers on. Look, why do you think I'm so miserable about this? It's because it's so exciting! It's because you've tried so hard and worked so hard. You're going to be a huge, huge success. And I will be an English teacher, living with my mum, inspiring fresh generations of young women to become journalists until my resentment and frustration move me to violence, and I get struck off.'

What can I say? How do I comfort her? 'The odds are never in our favour, and if they favoured me, they could favour you too. It's really hard for girls like us.' Because girls like us don't get to be writers. We read, sure. We're quiet, we're studious, and if we're really lucky, we encounter an encouraging teacher and discover that we love to invent stories just as much as we love to hear them. We might rise through the ranks of the school newspaper, or sometimes we meet someone more confident than us, or more comfortable in their ambition, who is putting together a student blog, a fanzine, a journal, and they want gig reviews or recipes or poems. We write, and write, and frustrate ourselves because we cannot find words accurate enough to explain why the writing itself is nourishing us, why this is the first thing we have ever done that fits around our fractured understanding of who we are. Because in writing, we are able to lose ourselves, and then find ourselves again. The work is nourishing, it drains but then restores more than it has taken. We think 'my heart is singing when I do this' and we mean it. We build our own foundations. Then, others come to build their walls.

It's a nice hobby, isn't it? But not a *proper* job. Something for your spare time. Something that, if you're any good at it you'll still really want to do when you've staggered off the bus at the end of your fourteen-hour day, and your eyeballs ache, and your feet are bleeding. Something that you have to earn the right to want. Something you have to earn the right to do, in shift work at eight pounds an hour, shoes sticky with ink, or glue, or generic cola syrup, anyone's 'darling', then anyone's 'stuck-up cunt', measuring your life in two-minute toilet breaks, always smiling, always tired, so tired, coming to in the shower in the morning and wondering whether it was all a bad dream.

Because eventually we realise that the writers aren't broke girls from Bumfuck, Nowhereshire. Writers need supportive families. Not just families who love you, or families who believe in you. But families with money. Fathers who own mews properties in West London. Aunties with columns in the *Daily Mail* and pals at *Tatler*, who will put money in your bank account while you come in and answer the

45

phone in the Easter holidays. Mums with handbags that cost more than most second-hand cars, who will truss you up in their cast-off Chanel, to make sure that you look the part in the office. If I was a real writer, perhaps I wouldn't feel quite so alone, and abandoned. I'd never look at the people who live their lives in daylight and feel like the one left out in the cold.

I reach for something positive – I feel as though I owe it to her. 'Honestly though, Jen, I think teaching English will inspire you to write your novel. Sure, my grubby, sexy stuff seems exciting now – but by the time we're forty, I'll be barely making a living and you'll have won the Booker Prize!'

'I am rolling my eyes down the phone at you.' Still, I can hear the smile in her voice. We're good.

Chapter Eight

Nothing But The Girl

Harri

It's the third Sunday night in January, the eve of that magical, melancholy Monday that has been labelled 'blue' by scores of desperate and inventive public relations teams. The day that all sparkling Christmas memories have faded and tarnished, the only evidence of any festivities being a reminder to make an eye-watering minimum payment on a billowing credit card balance. The day before the chicken, chocolate and turkey come home to roost, and women all over the world lie on their beds, tense their biceps and feel beads of sweat jewelling their foreheads, as they force zips and button-holes to defy all known laws of physics. The night before the Day of Grey, when you're statistically most likely to pour coffee down your white shirt, somewhere between your front door and your office. A day when you don't just miss the bus, but you'll be caught in its splashy, filthy trail as it drives through puddles at 70 miles an hour. Harri reckons that any bleak

Blue Monday would have to go a long way to beat the one when she leapt out of an Uber only for her right foot to crunch against the bones of a still warm, near dead pigeon.

But this Sunday is special. Harri knows she needs to stay calm, relax, and get a good night's sleep. She's meditated – well, she's downloaded an app – she's changed her sheets, and she's grimacing her way through a mug of camomile tea. Why don't I just throw it out? she thinks, between odd, floral sips. Why do I always forget that it tastes so horrible? She is wearing her best pyjamas – black, soft cotton, emblazoned with fuchsia pink dancing leopards. When she really needs to screw her courage to the sticking place, she likes to summon a leopard or two. She has collected them ever since she heard that Marchesa Luisa Casati liked to wander around Rome with a pair of leopards on leads, in diamond collars. Briefly, she allows herself a short fantasy in which she turns up at the office and sets her own leopards on Will, and then decides that wouldn't be fair. He's too boring to be an enemy. It isn't fair to subject him to an imaginary blood-bath when he has absolutely no imagination whatsoever.

For the past few weeks, Harri's own imagination has been getting to work.

Hilariously, Giles thinks she's having sex. 'Where are you? Who is he?' he laughed, as he waved his hand in front of Harri's face, in order to get her to sign off on her final flatplans at *Panache*. 'You're wearing too much perfume. I caught you singing to the radio.' Giles is a little far off the mark, but Harri does feel as though she's having an affair. She's fallen in love with The Girl.

The Girl is her new reader, and Harri has been spending every second getting to know her. She even secretly brought

The Girl back to her mum and dad's for Christmas – picturing a 25-year-old reconciling her piercings with a paper party hat, sneaking glances at Instagram under the table. (Her new reader either was out raving in a frozen field, or live tweeting along with the Muppets and shrieking with glee as Gonzo cleaned a frosty window with Rizzo the Rat.)

When alone, muttering over her lists and notes, she feels like a Raymond Chandler character, searching for clues within clues. (In her wilder moments, she's thought about purchasing an antique pipe.) Harri had not realised that the *Panache* woman had become boring to her. But the new Girl was a thrilling blank space. Was she pretty? Was she punk? Was she a pirate priestess with a power brow who always ate vegan, except on weekends? Did she read *Co-Star* or *Astrology Zone*? Was she living with her parents and saving up a tiny deposit for her first tiny house? Was she planning to sack it all off and run away to Berlin? Did she collect vinyl, but own no record player? Had she just heard the Beatles for the very first time on Spotify? Which vibrator did she use? Harri visited so many corners of the internet that she diagnosed herself with carpal Tumblr syndrome.

Harri knew that she needed to set a Girl to catch a Girl – that her writers needed to be her readers. Most magazines usually operate on a sort of washing cycle, with a posse of Posys-from-*Vogue* rotating their way through the glossies, becoming junior, then senior, depending on how long they were able to finance indefinite, unpaid stints in the fashion cupboard. *The Know* needed to be, as much as possible, a Posy free zone. She needed tone. She needed writers who could be funny, raw and honest. The trouble was that the potential pool of new hires was flooded with

Posys. Looking for writers who could afford to live within commuting distance of Central London limited things a little – but not as much as her budget. 'Will, am I missing a zero? Rosa used to spend more than this on taxis,' she'd complained.

Will shook his head at her. 'We're cost-cutting. And you can hire kids for next to nothing these days, they're just glad of the opportunity. It's market rate.'

Harri thought of Will's three children, all at private day schools, and wondered how the fees compared with these proposed annual salaries. Then she walked away, wordlessly, because she could not trust herself not to hurl a stapler at his head.

The team that Harri has assembled is scrappy, and tiny, and still a bit too posh for her liking. They have been allocated the worst corner of the building, and Hudson's marketing department seems to think that *The Know* will get all the exposure it needs if Harri just keeps tweeting about it. Still, Harri is excited. Giddy, even. And now, it's the night before her big day, and she's setting her alarm, and turning off her bedside light, and trying to slow her breathing and wondering whether this is going to mark the end of her career, or the beginning . . .

Chapter Nine

Left out of office

Imogen

The worst thing about landing a brand new job, even one as shiny as this, is that you actually have to get up and go to it. Finding out that you have it, telling everyone you know about it and planning what you will buy when you get paid – well, that's better than most drugs. But the reality of waking up when it's dark, finding clean tights, clean knickers, standing in the shower that's never quite strong enough or quite hot enough, banging Emma's almost empty Original Source bottle against the sink ... the novelty has worn off before my eyes are fully open. I'm still stumbling in the soft, nebulous space between my getting-the-job fantasy and the doing-the-job reality. When I started dreaming about working for the mystery website, I had a vision of what I'd wear, and by that, I mean who I'd become. The confident, capable woman I hoped I might magically be able to transform myself into the moment I was making regular

National Insurance contributions. Now, the thought of choosing actual clothes makes me feel tender and defenceless – if I want confident and capable, I'm going to have to roll my body up into my duvet, and leave my head sticking out of the top.

From deep inside my brain, I hear the voice of a thousand Women's Magazines Past, a swelling, harmonic choir. 'Before a big day, always put your outfit together the night before. It's one less thing to do in the mo-oooor-ninng!' Oh, fuck off. It's not as if I've never dressed myself. Still, this feels like I'm failing to answer the £100 question on *Who Wants to Be a Millionaire*. In another reality, someone is screaming at me through a screen while I think stupid thoughts like 'Mum's old Dorothy Perkins skirt suit with the button from the jacket missing! A pair of workout leggings with a fluorescent yellow polo neck! A straw hat!' Eventually I go for the tried and tested – a sober, sedate, neutral frock and boot combo. (About a year ago, I got three weeks of lucrative temping work and I only really had two outfits that were up to office scrutiny. Now almost all of my smart clothes are second-hand midi dresses, chosen to allow me to sit behind a reception desk without alarming anyone.)

The email from HR told me to make sure that I arrived before ten. Obviously I'm outside the Hudson Media building at 8.27, hollow boned from the evening's relaxing four-hour sleep, drenched in a cloud of caffeine, eyelids vibrating. *Today is the first day of the rest of my life*, I think, trying to stride and glide through the revolving doors, before chinning myself on heavy glass, looking up and seeing one of the security guys shaking his head, waving his hands and gesturing to the 'Emergency Access' door on the right. The one that's already open. Ah. Keeping my head down, I plod through reception. Did he just mutter 'fucking idiot'? Surely not, it must have been the wind.

The next disappointment is the office itself. It's silly, really, what else could I have been expecting? I've been into this building so many times – not just to make coffee and hand out the post at *Panache*, but to steam clothes, answer phones and get shouted at by staffers at *Women's Monthly*, *Steam*, *Fizz*, *Clutch*, *Nearer* and *You and Your Yacht*.

Anyway, I know the 'fading Edwardian grandeur' of the Hudson building is now invisible to the naked eye. In places, it's quite sad and shabby, draughty and drab. But I thought Harri would have worked a little magic on our corner of it, or at least bagged a half decent space for us. This is a nook. An anti-fashion cupboard. I would bet my brand new salary on it being the place where brooms used to be kept.

There's a long, thin window, in the farthest corner from the door. It seems to look out onto a murky stairwell. If I lean and squint, I can almost see the ankles of the people passing the building – you'd have to get up and press your face against it in order to actually see anything of the outside world. We're above ground, but barely. Still, someone has tried their best with the neon signage. HEY, SEXY! screams the space over the door. GOOD VIBES ONLY blurs blue, opposite. And most chillingly of all, in the space beside what I assume is Harri's desk – it has the biggest, shiniest computer on it – you're invited to CREATE YOUR OWN REALITY. I think this is how cults start. A few nights ago, I got caught in a sleepless YouTube hole and watched a truly creepy documentary about the Peoples Temple and the Jonestown massacre. That's what happens when someone thinks they can create their own reality.

Compliant vibes only.

I don't know if we'll be told where to sit, so I pick a desk in a cosy-looking corner where there is minimal neon glare. I sit down, and spin around on my chair – oooh, these are fun! Although I'm not sure the seat was always this close to the floor. As I stop spinning, a wheel falls off and I'm tipped onto the floor. Shit. The chair next to me only appears to have one wheel out of three. Will the chair beside that one be just right? As I lug it to my corner, it wobbles and rattles alarmingly, but it does not appear to be broken. Against my better judgement, I'm thinking about doing an experimental spin when I hear a 'Hello?'

I look over my shoulder. A girl's head is peeking around the door frame. I can see wisps of coppery brown hair flopping forward, and a bit of green and white shirt, speckled and swirled. She radiates extreme poshness, and extreme nervousness. Is she here for work experience? It seems a little bit weird to get an intern to come in on the first day.

Carefully, I get up, holding my breath until I'm certain that my new chair can survive such vigorous motion. I walk to the door beaming, palms outstretched. Poor thing. If I'm nervous, she must be terrified. If this is a cult, I can do a decent impression of cult leader before everyone else arrives.

'Hello. Welcome! Did you find us OK? I'm Imogen, I'm the first here! No one knows what we're doing yet, hahahahaha. Um, er, would you like a coffee? We could go up to the kitchen, but it's just crappy Nescafé. Or Pret? It's early, we've got loads of time.'

'I'm Louise. I'm the, um, culture and entertainment editor,' she tells her shirt collar.

Ah.

Louise might be taller than me, but her posture is even worse than mine. There's something about the way that her face is arranged that puts me in mind of friendly woodland creatures, and *The Wind in the Willows*. (I'm Louise, and I'm here today to play the Nervous Vole.)

'Oh, God! I'm so sorry, I thought you were the ... ' I cannot tell her I'd mistaken her for an intern. 'I wasn't sure you had the right room,' I finish, lamely.

'I'd love a coffee, actually,' she pronounces it 'uckshully', 'but we should probably stay in the office, just in case Harri comes? I'd hate to get into trouble on day one – I mean,' her face is very pink now. The green shirt really brings it out. 'Not trouble, but, best to be on the safe side, eh?' Well, this is a surprise. I think I might be the naughty one.

'What was your journey like?' I ask. 'Do you have far to come?' I mean, this woman pretty much has a thought bubble suspended above her head that reads 'I live in Fulham, if anything is ever going to make me late, it's the constant pressure to stop for Pilates and brunch.'

'Oh, not too bad, I'm in Parsons Green,' Knew it! 'So it's just dealing with the District Line, bit of a nut mar.'

'A what? Oh, *nightmare*. Right, right.'

'How about you?' Oh, lord. If I tell Louise about where I live, she'll be horrified. She might start some sort of fundraising rescue campaign on my behalf. *For just three pounds a month, girls like Imogen can be moved to safe housing, where they are no more than ten minutes' walk from a cafe that does organic almond cortados.*

'It's a place called Mitcham, it's south of London really, kind of between Wimbledon and Croydon.'

Louise smiles. 'Oh, that sounds lovely. Is it very green? It's so nice to get out of London!'

Louise has definitely never been to Mitcham. I make vague noises of assent, and we start chatting about our favourite bits of London – Louise has a surprisingly extensive knowledge of cake shops – before we hear voices. Harri is here, in her trademark camel coat.

I have many questions about this coat. *Panache*, without a trace of irony, regularly runs features on 'this season's Forever coat'. I now realise that 'Forever' does not mean that you wear it for ever, just that it costs upwards of a thousand pounds. Yet, this is the coat Harri was pulling close to her body when we walked to Pret, just before Christmas – and the coat I've seen draped on the back of her chair, or over her shoulders when she's stuck her head into the cupboard to ask me if I'd mind doing a coffee run. It's lustrous; the depth of the colour and the thickness of the wool give it a golden glow, it seems to come with its own secret lighting system. It's plain, but it's perfect, and it might have been made for Harri. A visibility cloak, I guess.

My dad – when he deigns to talk to me about what I do – likes to start fights about fashion magazines. He doesn't understand why I'd 'work for free' for 'a load of stuck-up cows' when I could be doing something 'worthwhile'. (He has many strong opinions about 'honest' work, even though a range of various, mysterious ailments have kept him out of full time employment since I was a baby.) It's easier to pretend that I'm an idiot airhead than it is to tell him the truth; when you have always felt that the world excludes you, there is a perverse and complicated pleasure to be taken from pursuing a place in one of the most exclusive industries in the world. The more I work, and the harder I try, the greater my chance of belonging becomes, and if I can belong in fashion, I can belong anywhere. Yes, it's weird that I spend so much time thinking about Harri's coat. But I'm not considering it in any greater depth than my bullies spent considering my trainers.

Literally riding Harri's coat tails, which are flying out behind her, I see a group of women being swept along in her wake. Goodness, that one is tall. She seems much older than Louise and me. Maybe she's come over from *Panache* – but, I realise with guilty horror, I think she might be the only black woman I've ever seen in the Hudson building. She moves like a model. Immediately I'm aware that I'm slumping, my spine tilted like a Tyrannosaurus rex's. I sit up a little straighter. She's smiling and laughing at something Harri said. Could she be management? Does Harri have a boss?

This ray of sunshine is followed by a pair of scowling dark clouds. One is tall, in jeans and a white shirt, hair in a Grand Old Duke of York special, neither up nor down. You'd brush it, wouldn't you, for the first day? The other is shorter, boring trousers, even more boring grey jumper, angry eyebrows that start full and dark and arched, but become straighter and skinnier, like a sperm. These two don't look very magaziney. Maybe they're just setting us all up on Payroll.

'Goodness, you're early! We've just had a management meeting, we didn't expect to see you – we didn't think anyone would be quite so keen,' says Harri, sounding a lot less friendly than she had when we'd talked before.

This is already awful. I have been weighed, measured and found keen. I'd completely forgotten about the hell of the first day of a new job. You're being judged every time you breathe out. You realise that what you eat for lunch is weird. The way you eat it is weird. The number of times you need to go to the toilet is definitely weird. You stop being convinced of your own status as a human being.

Gingerly, I spring to my feet to greet Harri. My chair shrieks with distress, and Harri shakes her head. 'You know what, stay there, we might as well get started. I'll let these guys quickly introduce themselves and then we'll get going.' Harri already looks quite stressed. I hate myself for noticing that she seems to have aged over Christmas. I can see her elevens. I just read an article in one of the Sunday supplements about these elevens, the pair of short, vertical frown lines that form in the gap between our eyebrows, which apparently must be Botoxed into oblivion before they start to multiply into other numbers. This new knowledge has ruined faces for me, for ever.

I'm relieved when a voice cuts in and throws me off my own terrible train of thought. 'I'm Akila,' says Model Woman. I still can't quite work out how old she is, she might be in her mid thirties. She has cropped, close-cut hair, and huge, round spectacles with expensive-looking, dark jade green frames. The flickering neon is draining most of us, but it makes Akila luminous, throwing her cheekbones into sharp relief. That woman is really well dressed, I think, even though she's simply wearing jeans and a jumper. The jeans are a perfect inky indigo, and they look as though they are soft to the touch. Her electric blue jumper – cashmere? – is stitched, in shocking pink cursive, with the words 'Queen of Queens'. The word regal has already formed in my mind before I've started reading the slogan. Immediately, I know I want to be Akila when I grow up.

'I'm the audience and engagement manager. I've worked here and in the US, developing brand strategy at Glossier, MTV, Nordstrom – a lot of e-commerce, mostly beauty and fashion with some entertainment brands. We're going to be evolving *The Know* into a brand too. It's a big part of Harri's strategy. This isn't just a website. We want to build ourselves into our audience's lives and it's my job to make sure we're delivering from Day One.'

This is the sort of speech that would usually make me hysterical with laughter or nerves. But Akila's voice is so soothing to listen to – deep, smooth, but a little unpolished. It's the sound of Mitcham High Street, but dry cleaned and ironed.

Harri smiles at Akila, and I see the chemistry between them. Game recognising game. 'We're thrilled to have Akila at *The Know*, we're incredibly fortunate to be able to hire her. It's not just that her level of experience is so impressive – but she's a real future thinker. I've worked with her before on a few campaigns and this woman, well.' Harri grins again. 'This isn't a battle, exactly, but she's going to lead us to victory.'

Sperm-eyebrows clears her throat. 'I'm Lily, I'll be interim assistant editor, and I'll be job sharing with Katie, here. We work across several titles at Hudson, we're going to be here for a few months assessing the viability of the title, ensuring all editorial decisions are consistent within the overall Hudson brand and reach the right audience, and crucially keeping costs down.'

Katie with the Bad Hair cuts in. 'We're going to be working closely with Mackenzie Whittaker, the new editor-in-chief at *Panache* and directing editor across all titles. Mackenzie is joining us from New York. She's flying in later this week. We're really lucky – her background is corporate, and she's very financially savvy. Our new investors recommended her specifically, she's going to be getting Hudson back on track. So we'll be supporting her, closely monitoring your budget. But it's not all doom and gloom!' Katie's laugh sounds like dial up internet. 'We know that we've got a young team, and a productive workspace is a fun workspace. So we bought you these signs!' She gestures to CREATE YOUR OWN REALITY. 'Actually, Harri, that reminds me, I've got the receipts, you need to sign them so I can get the reimbursements from Petty Cash.'

The office feels even smaller, stuffier. Louise looks at her feet. Akila looks at the patch of wall where a less sadistic architect would have placed a window. I'm certain that, for the briefest fraction of a moment, Harri looks at Katie with unfiltered, unconcealed hatred. But she shakes the look off her face – before it has a second to settle, she's blank as a brand new Etch A Sketch.

Harri adds, 'On the cash front, I have some great news. I'm in the process of securing some sponsorship for our launch with a new mobile viewing platform. Louise, we need to have a chat about some entertainment content. I think the big boardroom is free, shall we all go up and talk ideas? In fact, Lily, it would be really good to go over the proposed numbers with you, this should leave us with much more space in our budget.'

Everyone else seems to be gathering bags and jackets,

preparing to move, so I stand up, a little too quickly. My chair makes a rumbling noise. 'No, not you,' says Lily. 'Just the other girl. You're not necessary for this.'

My skin reacts before my brain does, blood burning up on the surface. I am not necessary. I don't belong. I'm on my own, at the very edge of the playground, again. Now I'm looking at the space where the window should be, unable to meet anyone's eyes.

Harri really tries. 'Imogen, can you start working on some features ideas? You've sent me some really strong pitches for *Panache* in the past, maybe have a look at those again – but see if you can make them completely fresh, original, unique.' My *ears* would blink, if they could. What does that even mean? Before I can beg for clarification, Harri is backing out of the room, saying 'You should have the Brand Bible on an email. And the rest of the team will be in soon, you can hold the fort while we're upstairs.'

The rest of the team? Great. They'll arrive, they'll see me on my own and they will immediately know I'm a total loser, already excluded from Harri's main gang. I force a smile, using my cheek muscles to force the prickle of tears back into my eyes, and open a Word document, typing frantically. My first feature idea is 'HIHIHIFWFBFIBIUBUBUBUBUA;OHBBUUG,'

As soon as I know I'm alone, I message Jen. First day is shit. They're all bitches. How's your day going?

She rings immediately. 'Im, it sounds awful. Come home! Be a teacher with me.'

I can hear muffled chatter, familiar rhythms, the notes of conversation ascending. 'Where are you? It sounds like you're in a bar.'

The sound stops. 'Sorry, I've muted it. Not a bar, the telly. They're interviewing a dog who is launching a political party.'

'Who is?'

'Who is interviewing the dog? Holly and Phil. They have just established that it's pro Brexit. Which surprised me, because it's a German Shepherd.'

'Jen, I don't know what to do. I've been here for an hour, and I'm already the only one not allowed to go to this big important meeting. How bad will things get by lunchtime? I already want to go home.'

'Home here?' Jen sounds excited, and I resent her for it.

'I meant, you know, back to my flat, back to bed for the day. It's early. I'm sure it will get better, I'm sure I'll get used to it.' If I say it out loud, I can make it come true.

'Well, rather you than me. I'm having a lovely day. I'm going to have an afternoon nap, and watch Food Network – and Mum's promised she'll pick up fish and chips after work. I should have come home years ago!' I have to put the phone down, I cannot trust myself to say anything else. 'Listen, I better get on. Enjoy your chips.'

Six months ago, Jen was weeping into her pillow – our pillow, really – after a bad day during her internship at the *Independent*.

'The cheapest mattress I was allowed to include in the round-up was nine hundred pounds, Im. And it hit me – if I carry on like this, I will never, ever have nine hundred pounds to spend at once, on anything.'

I felt a familiar, gnawing tightness in my shoulders, in my chest. My constant money anxiety. 'Does anyone, really?

And mattresses last for ages, at least ten years. So that's ninety pounds a year, or ... ' I try, and fail, to do some fast maths, 'less than two pounds a week. I'm sure people are all buying their mattresses on credit cards, it's all going in the big black hole. Well, I guess it would be a red hole ... '

'No, Imogen, listen,' said Jen, through tears. 'I think most people don't live like us. I don't think it's normal to not have nine hundred pounds saved up somewhere for a mattress, or a holiday, or ... Leanne from school has bought a house.'

'We hate Leanne. We're not friends with her.'

'That's not the point. Leanne, who grew up in the same shitty town as us, with absolutely nothing going for her, is now a recruitment consultant with two children and a three bed semi. She's building a life. Maybe it's not a life we'd want to live, but ... Mum was telling me that if I came back and trained to be a teacher, I'd probably be eligible for a key worker mortgage. I might be able to buy somewhere to live in a few years.'

'In Devon, though? You'd give this up for that?' I was crying too, now.

Jen looked away. 'Yeah. "This" isn't ... it's not really working, is it?'

'Maybe we're still paying our dues.'

'No. We're broke, we're burned out, I'm not even getting interviews any more. I just tried for a staff writer job for *Mortgage* magazine, they wanted someone with "extensive experience" and the annual salary was about the same as I'd get if I went home and worked as a teaching assistant. I applied anyway, and got an email back saying sorry, no thank you, they had been "inundated with applications".

Inundated. Overwhelmed by the number of people who want to write about mortgages all day long, for hardly any money. Mum says that they're so desperate for teachers at the moment that I'd get a bursary to train – and probably walk into a job as soon as I'd qualified.'

The most awful thing was hearing the lightness in Jen's voice. Knowing that at some imperceptible point in her speech, she had made up her mind. And I'd missed the chance to derail her train of thought, to pull the emergency lever that might bring this to a screeching halt, and now she is gathering speed.

'But if you go home ...' The thought was fully formulated, filling my mouth like blood, and I had to swallow my raw need back down. If you go home, I will have no one. No one to wonder and worry when I'm late or lost. The little light in my world will die, and I will fade away. I will be a ghost. I squeezed my eyes tightly against the saltwater sting and tried again. 'It's different for you. I can't go home.'

'But surely ... maybe ... it might be OK, just for a few months? Or maybe you could come and live with us?'

I shook my head. 'I don't think I can. You'd be a great teacher, but what would I do? Mum would worry, Dad would be unbearable, I'd just be another mouth to feed. And if I stayed with you – I'd worry about wearing out my welcome. Mum would be heartbroken that I'd rather live with you and Su, Dad – if he noticed – would be furious with me about it, Mum would want to give Su some money for my keep and she doesn't have ... it,' I was crying now, I couldn't stop it. 'Jen, I'm trapped. Going back to Devon might be your nuclear option, but it's an option. And if you go, how will I ... will I ...'

'Maybe I can keep paying my share of the rent for a couple of months?'

'NO! I mean – how will I do any of this? I'm going to be so ... lonely.'

We both cried ourselves to sleep. When I woke up, I nursed the faintest hope that Jen would have changed her mind, blaming an especially bad day, or that the *Independent* would immediately hire her on a full salary with a mattress allowance. But over the next few days, we gave our notice on our room. We looked through the bowels of the internet, I seriously contemplated going to Archway to meet a man who was advertising for a woman who would live with him for free 'in exchange for nightly visits', until Jen said the Sam Strong thing was bad enough. (I'd have moved in with Sam Strong in half a heartbeat if he hadn't made it very clear that I wasn't allowed to entertain that thought.)

Perhaps motivated by guilt, Jen combed Gumtree for days, and eventually found me a room of my own in a flat with two other girls, and I was so grateful and relieved that I didn't mind that the girls were awful, that the room had no windows, that it was a forty minute walk from the tube, and technically not even in London at all.

I don't want to look at my phone any more. I place it face down on the desk, and return to my Word doc.

Features ideas:
Can your best friend break your heart?

Chapter Ten

Battle lines are drawn

Harri

Harri truly hates this boardroom. Harri blames this board-room for everything that has gone wrong for her over the last few weeks. Here, the fault lines lie. This is where all she'd ever worked for, all she'd ever hoped for, careered away from her, out of her grasp. This is where she learned that control is an illusion, that loyalty is for losers and that her whole world could be destroyed by a man who buys multipack shirts with the ties attached.

'Today is a special day, and I'm so glad we're all here together,' she lies. 'I've got some notes on the campaign, we're waiting for final sign off from the platform, but the money is excellent, and the profile of the product is a great fit. Now, you've all read the Brand Bible, and we've identi-fied our key reader ... yes?'

Lily is frowning at her with undisguised irritation, keen to cut in. 'We need Mackenzie's sign off, and she's not going to agree to this. Firstly, we haven't approved the Brand Bible demographics yet. The reader's projected annual earnings are far too low. We're not going to get any advertisers unless we can prove that our reader earns at least 80–100k.'

Akila starts to speak. 'But that's a crazy figure! Even if we were targeting an older audience, that number is twice as high as I'd expect it to be. And Harri has interested advertisers based on these very—'

Lily interrupts her. 'And we've got major concerns about the sexual health and wellness section. It says here that our key reader is "more likely than previous generations to identify as LGBTQI+ and keen to invest her disposable income in sexual pleasure". I mean, Harri, really? Just where do you think you're going to find these girls?' She bleats a half laugh.

Katie nods. 'Mackenzie is extremely conservative, she will have serious concerns about alienating our potential American audience with these content proposals.'

Harri digs her nails into the flesh of her left palm, and counts to five. It doesn't hurt enough. She squeezes harder. Harder still. Just in time, the pain comes and jolts her back into the room. 'This platform wants to advertise their launch programme, Confessions, which is an interactive sexual health chat show. They're very keen for us to think of some features to promote it. Actually, we really should have Imogen up here. I showed the team her blog, and that's the sort of content they want. Their proposed budget would cover most of our expenses for three months, this is good business.'

Lily wrinkles her nose. 'Well, we can't do anything without Mackenzie's say so, but ...' Katie smirks. 'She'll probably say no.'

Akila and Louise are staring, open mouthed. Harri feels her own jaw falling, and snaps it back. She's got to take control of the situation. She's the editor. This Mackenzie woman isn't even here yet.

'OK, well, we can come back to this. Lily, Katie, thank you for your time. Akila, Louise – do you mind staying for five? We can do a quick entertainment debrief.' Harri folds her arms, musters her sweetest smile, and stares, unblinking, at Lily and Katie, while fantasising that she is watching them both being fed into an industrial woodchipper, one limb at a time. They try, and fail, to stare her down, before shuffling out.

Harri sighs heavily. 'You know what? Ask for forgiveness, not permission. I'm going to get this signed off with the brand before Mackenzie turns up. Louise, could you have a chat with Imogen about some sexy content ideas? Akila, we can definitely use this as bait – talk to some sexual wellness brands and see if they want to follow with their ad dollars.'

Akila looks nervous. 'Maybe we should wait until ...' Harri shakes her head. 'No, no, it's always like this at the beginning of a new project. Hudson are freaking out now – but we just need to hold our nerve.' Harri notices that her palm still feels tender as she crosses her fingers behind her back.

Chapter Eleven

Who's that Girl?

Imogen

Features ideas

Can your best friend break your heart?

Teledildonics – the hottest thing in digital intimacy or a
  privacy problem?

Would YOU have a threesome with a Real Doll?

Is social media giving you compassion fatigue?

Meet the new influencers who will make you . . . something

Is 'Gen Z' an offensive label?

How to be a grown up

How not to be lonely

How to survive until pay day on . . .

The Girl is giving me an identity crisis. 'For the first time
in new media, *The Know* will not dictate trends or styles
to its reader. *The Know* Girl herself will lead the way.' This

statement is made at the very start of the Brand Bible, which proceeds to tell me all the ways in which I, the 26-year-old key reader, am doing it wrong. This is why my list of features ideas now reads like a cry for help.

I'm not The Girl. I don't think I even know any Girls. She's an insane riddle of an imaginary young woman, who takes drugs, but never talks about them, who buys rare vinyl but listens to everything on Spotify, who makes her own packed lunches yet has a mysterious amount of money to spend on clothes, who has a sex life that would make Cardi B blush, who lives in Margate, and Berlin, and up a tree, simultaneously. 'Her first is in hipster, but never in "hip" ...' The only thing I'm sure about is that this Girl has never, ever had to go to the toilet at work and put half a wadded loo roll into the bowl in order to muffle the splash of an unexpected poo.

I wonder how widely *The Know* will be read in Devon. It seems strange to think of my old school friends setting the tone. I imagine Akila rushing in, saying 'OK, we need more content about embellished Ted Baker dresses, how to find jobs that come with company cars, and the case for lobbying the government to get them to bring back Jello shot night at Club Rococo.'

I'm sighing and deleting the word 'lonely' just as a living, breathing embodiment of The Girl walks through the door.

'Are you *The Know*?'

'They're in a meeting ...' I mutter lamely. 'I'm Imogen.'

Standing, smiling, I stretch out my forearm and extend my right hand – which she ignores as she walks past me, and takes the seat farthest from mine.

I try again.

'So, I'm a staff writer, I think mostly features but Harri said we'd all be mucking in on everything, at the beginning . . . you?'

'I'm Tabitha. In fashion?' The inflection at the end of her sentence does not indicate her own uncertainty – just her outrage that I had to ask.

To be fair, Tabitha should not have to explain herself when her outfit works as a sort of living CV. There is so much to take in, my brain didn't fully process it all as she walked through the door. From the waist up, she's dressed as Gene Kelly in *On the Town*, in a puffy white sailor blouse, with a navy blue collar. But everything literally pales into comparison against her luminous trousers. I can see portions of neon green tweed leg glowing under the desk, in a Prince of Wales check. (I can identify that check at twenty paces, after working on *Panache*'s hellacious Diana Fashion Special double issue.) She is also wearing a sailor's cap over her white blonde Lord Farquaad bob. Her fringe is a work of art – edged in turquoise, which is edged in silver. Seafoam is the word my brain surprises me with.

'Great. Fashion! I'm hoping to write some fashion features. I used to do some fashion things for *Panache*, so . . .'

'Fashion? You? Ha. Funny,' says Tabitha, mirthlessly.

I am wearing a dark blue Whistles jersey dress from Wimbledon Cancer Research, with black tights and my Christmas present from Mum – very plain, flat black ankle boots from New Look. No, Alessandro Michele isn't about to ask me to walk for him, but it isn't funny. It isn't fair. Who the fuck is this? Why do I ever bother to try with posh girls?

Perhaps she realises she's been rude. She leans towards

me, with maybe half a degree of warmth. 'Listen, we both know Hudson Media is a backwater. I can't believe I'm working for a company that makes a magazine about cranes, or whatever. And obviously something weird happened – I don't really rate Harri, but she should have been editor of *Panache*. There's a hiring freeze at Condé, so I'm just ... waiting. For now.' She doesn't say 'I didn't come here to make friends' out loud but I hear it.

For a few stupid seconds I open and shut my mouth, trying to formulate a response. *Harri isn't there for you to rate*, I want to scream. *You're lucky to be here. We all are.* I reach for the cheapest, snarkiest and most regrettable comeback. 'I was at Condé for a little while last summer, and I don't think I'd want to work there.' Tabitha does not need to know that it was for two days, on a new technology supplement, and I was asked to leave after I accidentally poured coffee into the internal monitor of an Oculus Quest.

Tabitha wrinkles her small, straight nose. 'Well, you wouldn't exactly fit in, would you?'

Chapter Twelve

It takes the cake

Imogen

I wake up just as I become aware of the drool pooling on my chin. I can't miss my stop, again. Why am I so tired?

I can actually sleep at night. I said I'd do some bar shifts this weekend, as payday is still far away, but my working week has halved to a manageable forty hours. I should be brimming with energy. I don't understand why I'm not leaping out of bed, raring to go, powering through the day and then doing an hour of yoga as soon as I get home. (Well, I suppose that the only pose I can do is the one where you pull your legs up into your chest and squeeze – I don't have the bedroom floor space for Downward Dog.) Why does my whole body feel as though it has been stuffed with damp sawdust? How can the gaps between my toes be aching?

I think it's Friday, but who knows? I wouldn't be at all surprised if The Girl observed some sort of eight day week, just to spite me. It has honestly felt like the longest week of my life. Harri hates three-quarters of my ideas, and expects me to come up with twenty, every hour. Tabitha won't even respond when I smile and say good morning – also she hates four quarters of my ideas and mutters every time I say something in a features meeting. At least Louise is nice. Akila is always running in and out of meetings, but she's great when she's there. And we have a new boy, Kim, on design, plucked from obscurity – well, *Wooden Flooring World* – by Harri.

Kim is brilliant fun – and filthy. I used to be filthy, I think, gazing out of the window, as suburbia speeds past. Maybe someone will have pinned some really great features ideas to a tree. Sex … sexy pylons … sexy fences … on the sexy fence? I really need to have sex with someone other than Sam Strong soon, if only for the content. The trouble is, he's so handy. Meeting someone, establishing some kind of chemistry with them, and finding a place to have sex with them other than my box room – there are just so many variables to worry about. Sam is an idiot, but he makes me come every single time and there are always sheets on his mattress.

Sighing, I look at my phone notes, and search for my lacklustre features list. Sex, sex, sex … oh! And work in progress.

I had almost forgotten about this piece. I've been on the brink of posting it to my blog, tweaking it, rewriting it, and wondering whether or not I could pitch it to an actual magazine. Strangely, it was Harri who inspired it. When she took me out for coffee before Christmas, and started talking about my blog, I kept thinking about her word, 'raw'. I wanted to write something really raw, for once, and be emotionally, as well as sexually, explicit.

That's the trouble. I *think* it's good. I think it might be one of the best things I've ever written. But I've never felt so exposed. I've tried so hard to be honest, and every time I try to edit it, and change a line, I feel differently. Sometimes, I am very proud of my words, and sometimes, seeing everything written down makes me feel extremely vulnerable.

Would Harri like it? Would it work for *The Know*? I reread it, hoping that it might at least inspire me to come up with some other ideas for the list.

My threesome fantasy got out of control – and I'm still slutshaming myself

It took me a long time to lose my virginity. Even after it happened, I felt very self-conscious about my lack of experience. Perhaps that's why I slept with two people at once. To get my numbers up. I was worried that I was failing grown-up sex education, and I didn't want to be bottom of the class.

At the very end of my first year of uni, my boyfriend – the only person I'd ever had sex with – broke up with me because he felt that our relationship was preventing him from 'fully focusing on studies'. I think his dad made him do it. Being dumped is humiliating but being dumped for Physics is exceptionally bleak. He could have cheated with my best friend – or his best friend – and it would have been a little bit easier to take.

I thought my heart was broken, but now I realise it was my pride that hurt the hardest. My friend Rachel told me that summer was the perfect time to be single. 'Go out, have a wild time without him, and when it gets back to him, he'll miss you so much that he'll beg you to get back together.' Rachel's idea seemed genius. The trouble was that it's hard to have a wild old time when you live with your parents in Devon. Rachel suggested we both apply to Summer School USA – and become camp counsellors for wayward American teens.

We both got through the application rounds by lying. 'Why do I want to be part of Summer School USA? I'm really passionate about the arts! As a British person I regularly read Shakespeare for fun! I can't wait to help these young people find a new meaning in Hamlet!' I couldn't tell you the old meaning of Hamlet – the only line I know comes from Clueless. But I wasn't going to say 'Please let me join your programme, I wish to have promiscuous revenge sex with many college boys.'

Lucky Rachel landed in California, but I got sent to Pennsylvania, which is practically next to New York. If 'practically' means 'four and a half hours on a very cramped bus'. I was put into a team with Alllison (three 'l's), Russ and Tyler. Alllison was a very active Christian. In fact, I'm pretty sure that she was a promising junior member of a small cult, and that she'd been sent to recruit.

I hated Russ and Tyler on sight. Tyler wore his naturally dark hair gelled into upward spikes. And I hope he'd bleached it himself, because if he had paid a person money to do that to him, they should be in prison. His jeans were cut like palazzo pants, with a wallet chain that looked like a skipping rope for S&M Barbie. At first, I assumed he had flown from afar and was TALKING LIKE THIS because his ears hadn't popped yet. He had driven in from

Connecticut. Russ, his best friend and sidekick, was a little more well mannered and moderate. But unforgivably, he'd punctuate every single one of Tyler's VERY LOUD OBSERVATIONS by slapping his knee and screaming 'That's what she said!'

We'd all arrived a day before the kids, to plan a programme of activities. Russ and Tyler were unbearable, and Alllison wasn't interested in making friends with me. Not when she already had her good friend Jesus.

By dinnertime, I'd managed to calm myself down. I needed to be kinder, more open minded. I was very, very jetlagged. This was all new. Everything would be easier after a decent night's sleep. That's when Tyler made his pitch. 'YO, BRITISH!' He gestured to me. He is still the only person I've ever known who is able to whisper in capital letters. 'DON'T TELL THE NUN, BUT WE'VE GOT SOME DECENT SCOTCH IN OUR CABIN. JOIN US AFTER LIGHTS OUT?' Alcohol was strictly forbidden at SS USA, but I thought that I could get away with pleading British confusion. We didn't properly start until tomorrow, anyway.

Tyler may have looked like he was in a Sum 41 tribute band but his father owned a village green's worth of hedge funds. He'd raided the family liquor cabinet and sneaked out a 30-year-old Glenlivet. It's still the nicest thing I've ever had to drink. 'It's older than you are!' he said, a little bit pervily. 'We're the same age,' I sniffed, and necked a shot.

Because we were all terrible clichés, we played a game of I Have Never. I hadn't really done anything, ever. So I lied, unconvincingly. I'd had sex … at Wimbledon. In the

Millennium Dome. I'd given a blow job in the gardens of Buckingham Palace! The more I drank, the madder my stories got. To be honest, it didn't help that I knew London less well than Tyler and Russ. They started winding me up. 'You think you're so fancy, British. You're a stuck-up bitch!' said Tyler, laughing at me. 'If she's British and a bitch ... she's a BRITCH!' Russ gasped. I remember Tyler looking at him approvingly, as though it was the cleverest thing he had ever said, and feeling strangely jealous. I wanted someone to look at me that way.

When Tyler started kissing me, I was confused, and a little disappointed. He was a bad kisser. He stabbed my mouth repeatedly, rapidly thrusting his tongue in and out of my mouth. I did what frustrated women have been doing for hundreds of thousands of years and attempted to use my own tongue to coax his to do something a little gentler. He pulled away for a moment and looked hurt. 'What are you doing?' he whined. As I searched for a polite answer, I felt my shorts sliding off my body. Russ's hands were on the inside of my thighs. They felt surprisingly warm, solid. I felt his fingers tracing the outline of my underwear. Ohhhhhh.

For a long time, I've tried to make sense of what happened next, the bad decisions I made, and whether I really made any decisions at all. I wasn't so drunk that I didn't have any control. But I was drunk enough to be fully numb, floating away from myself. I wanted to do this. I wanted to not want to do it. I was scared. I was horny. I didn't want to make the choice. I wasn't fully present.

Tyler yanked down my vest top, and started kneading my breasts, hard, while carrying on with the terrible kissing. But with surprising subtlety, Russ seemed to be pulling my knickers down, agonisingly slowly. I could feel myself getting hotter and wetter. This had never happened to me before – certainly not with Neal, my ex. I moaned, unable to control myself, as Russ brushed me with his fingertips. Tyler took this as encouragement and squeezed my right nipple extra hard.

The moment Russ pushed a finger inside me, I came. I know that sounds hard to believe – weirdly, I think Tyler's terrible technique was so distracting, that I was able to focus my anxieties on that, without worrying about making the right moves and the right noises. It was a little like being high. When I heard Russ unzipping his fly, I moaned again. I'd never wanted to be touched, to be fucked, so badly. It was as if I was starring in my own porn, in my head. I'd seen porn – never with Neal, who looked quite nervous when I'd once suggested it. But I'd fantasised, alone, about being objectified and desired, about men who would see me and be overwhelmed by the need to fuck me. I'd never felt this much pure lust, focused completely on me.

Nearly every man and boy I'd ever known had dismissed me (Dad) or teased me for being a nerd (school) or simply looked straight through me. Even Neal was disappointing. When I met him at an event early on in the term (forgive me, I think we called it Freshers Pre Lash!!!!!) I would have happily had mediocre sex in his single bed, and then been content to spend the rest of the year hiding behind a friend if ever I risked bumping into him in the library. After weeks of earnest courting, Neal took my chin into his hands and said 'I'm going to kiss you now.' At the time, I wanted to believe it was adorable. Too late, I realised that Neal used exactly the same intonation when he said things like 'This is how we will make the experiment a fair test.'

But Russ was behind me, inside me, grunting furiously, sounding how I felt and wanting, wanting, wanting. Then Tyler was cupping my face in his hands too. He didn't ask me anything or warn me of anything – he took his dick out and guided it straight into my mouth. I closed my eyes and wondered what this looked like from above, wondered about all of the people who would love to make themselves come with us, if only they could see us. I was wild. As I felt Tyler pressing hard against the back of my throat, I remember thinking something silly; I could marry a vicar next year, and I've still done something crazier and sluttier than most people. All my life, I've worried that I wasn't pretty enough, that I wasn't hot enough, that no men would want me. But in that moment, two men wanted me at once!

Tyler pulled away abruptly and made a pained face. 'Sorry, nearly came,' he explained. I wouldn't have minded but was strangely touched by his unexpected courtesy. Russ came to a stop. 'We could come on her tits,' he suggested. Only now do I realise he almost never addressed me directly.

I kneeled upright, knees as wide as an imaginary yoga mat, and started to touch myself. I think the boys thought it was for effect, but I was desperate to come again. Every part of me felt swollen. As I closed my eyes, wanting to stay in my filthy, outrageous fantasy for ever, I heard a gasp and a grunt and felt something hot and wet land on each breast. I started to feel disorientated, suddenly woken from a strange dream. 'We should take a picture!' said Tyler. As if it was a birthday party.

The tiniest mote of common sense entered my brain. 'I don't want my face in it!' Russ laughed, and Tyler said

'Yeah, well, we don't want your face in it, Britch.' The *iPhone autoflash gave it a* Blair Witch Project *quality, semen gleaming in the sudden, dazzling light.*

That's when I started to feel sober, and very afraid. Wiping my chest with some discarded underpants, I pulled my top up, and wriggled back into my shorts. 'I'm off to bed. See you guys in the morning!' I said. I tried to sound cheerful. I tried to sound as though I found myself in this sort of situation all the time, and that I was always able to retain my dignity.

Stumbling out into the dark, I attempted to put my feelings into some kind of order. I'd just had an adventure. I was getting over my break-up with crazy behaviour. I was drunk! If I felt a little sad, and a little freaked out, it was only jetlag, or a hangover. I was so used to being good, doing the right thing, trying so hard to be perfect. I couldn't work out how to get to the bathrooms, so I squatted down and peed in the grass. At least I wouldn't get cystitis. When I crept back into my cabin, Alllison sat up and shone a torch at me. 'Where were you?' she hissed. I'd prepared an alibi. 'I couldn't sleep, I went for a long walk around the lake. It's the time difference,' I explained. 'You're lying,' she replied. 'I'll pray for you.'

My memory plays tricks on me. Sometimes, I remember the way I shuddered with pleasure when Russ touched me, being overwhelmed with want, the sensation of being forced into my body and out of my mind. Sometimes I think about the uncertainty, the fear, the shame of not saying no and not knowing how to say yes. We never repeated the experience, and we didn't stay in touch. Russ was fired after he said something inappropriate to an underage student. Sometimes I see Tyler on Facebook. He has a baby on the way.

I don't think I regret what happened. But perhaps that's because I can't afford to let myself regret it. Since the threesome, I've learned how to get better at establishing my own wants, desires and boundaries. I have discovered that you can just ask for what you want, you don't need to wait for someone to give it to you. And labels aren't always helpful when we're trying to understand our sexuality, and our own desires. Ultimately, I've made peace with the fact that maybe we can only have the sex we want and crave by making a few mistakes. I'm not sure I'd have learned what my own boundaries were before I tested them. At the time, I thought I wanted to let Tyler and Russ objectify me. But maybe, in my memory and imagination, I have objectified them, too.

It's a decent piece, I think. But I still don't know what to do with it. Could I pitch something about the complications of consent, maybe? How to navigate a world in which yes must mean yes, and no must mean no, when your own nascent sexuality has been shaped by shame? How to feel and express desire independently, when you have never been granted the societal headspace to see yourself as subject, not object? I can already hear Harri. 'Imogen, this isn't an academic journal. Go away and write a round-up of the best Insta filters for fanny photos!' Still, I'm *certain* there must be something worth exploring.

I'm lost in thought for the rest of the journey. When I arrive at the office, only Louise is in, beaming sweetly behind a giant box of cupcakes. 'Hey, Immo, guess what?' Immo? I don't love it, but I don't want to sound mean. Still, if I don't say something now ... I clear my throat, but Louise is not leaving me any space to object, or indeed guess. 'These are from that new bakery, Piece of Me. Look! Congratulations to the team at *The Know*! Sending you something special from our oven to celebrate your upcoming launch.' The cupcakes look absurd. They are tiered. In fact, if they can be classed as cupcakes, then a BLT is just a slice of bread. One has a pink-and-white swirled lolly sticking out of the top. It looks as though a spoiled child has been using it to play moon landings. Another is crowned by a full-sized doughnut. Still, I'm breakfastless and starving, so I reach for the healthiest looking cake, which is decorated with a three inch tall foam banana.

'Immo, NO!' Ah, it's too late. I shall be Immo for ever. 'What are you doing?'

The cake is so close to my open mouth that I can tell the top of the banana has become sticky.

'Sorry, what? Did you want this one?'

'No!' Louise's lip is trembling slightly. At first, I thought that she always looked as though she was on the brink of tears because her mist-pale eyes are so enormous. Now, I realise that she is possibly just always on the brink of tears. 'These are ... for Instagram! We haven't done a picture with everyone yet. We need to wait until we're all here!'

I lower the cake until it is resting on the table. The banana is starting to wilt. I am really, really hungry. 'Yes. Instagram. Of course. I think I need to run out for some breakfast. Do you want anything?' Partly as a peace offering, I go out and buy Louise something made from raw cashew milk and cacao nibs. It costs seven pounds. When I hold my bank card against the reader, I hold my breath too. By the time I'm back, Tabitha is glowering, Harri is tapping, and everyone is ignoring Louise's mewing. We'll do the photo before lunch, then after the analytics meeting, then tomorrow, then never. Over the next few days, the strange and splendid cupcakes will fade and grow frowsty, Miss Haversham-sad. Eventually the cleaner will chuck them. Well, I hope that's what happens. I hope Louise doesn't take them home and eat them.

Chapter Thirteen

Putting the Oooof in Yoof

Harri

On Monday, Harri was hopeful. By Friday, she's exhausted. She's crashing out in the Cafe Cucina – again, terrible, but so handy for the office – and trying to listen to Giles' long list of woes, complaints and grudges, and how Giles has effectively been left to run *Panache* single handed. I'll just shut my eyes for ten seconds, she thinks. He won't notice. He hasn't drawn breath.

'And then she bawled Cam out, in front of everyone. Told her she had a month to up ad spend or she'd get fired! Poor Cam went for a quiet cry in the cupboard, and it was full of weeping interns. It's miserable, out there. Aliysha's trying to get a job on *Style*, she says she's going to quit.'

'Hmmmm? God, how awful. Do we need to order?' Harri tries, and fails, to suppress a yawn.

'Oh, I'm sorry, love, am I boring you? I know it's not as much fun as *Hot Lady Daily*, but this is my life,' says Giles, huffily. 'And it was your life too!' A waitress appears, bringing a Caesar salad and a bowl of chips that Harri has no memory of asking for. Still, though. Chips. She lifts one to her mouth, and then, distracted, waves it like a baton.

'It's . . . yeah. I am really sorry, I will try to pay attention, but – I've never been this tired in my life. In fact, the best thing about this lunch, other than seeing your fabulous face,' she says, quickly, 'is that when I sat down, I could say "oooof!" Every single bit of my body just wants to scream "oooof", all day long, and I can't get away with that in there. They would all laugh at me. I'm starting to worry I'm not . . . relevant, any more. I feel as though I've aged ten years this week.'

'But you're putting the oooof in yoof!' smiles Giles.

'I'm doing about nine jobs. It makes *Panache* feel like a fortnight in a spa. Usually, I could control the drama at *Panache*, because it would be about the actual magazine. Now, all day long, I hear "Is ibuprofen better than par-acetamol for period pains?" "What can the bank actually do once you've gone over your overdraft limit?" "I think I've got thrush, but maybe it's an STI, can I show you?" I feel like a teacher at a tiny boarding school for the bright-but-wayward. Miss Jean Br-overshare.'

'That reminds me,' says Giles. 'I think I spotted your fashion editor in the lift the other day. Unless you were hosting a panel for Comic-Con. Is that my competition? She made me feel about a thousand years old.'

Harri has been trying to work out what, if anything, to do about Tabitha. 'Today, she's in short shorts – black vinyl lederhosen and a matching harness over a silver sports bra. Obviously, she looks amazing. But not for the office. Certainly not before the leaves have returned to the trees, and the clocks have gone forward.'

'Did you take a picture?'

'Did I take a picture? Sure, creepshots of junior employees – totally normal.' Giles looks deflated, so Harri checks Tabitha's Instagram account. Sure enough, she's posted her #ootd. Harri holds her phone up, and Giles snatches it from her.

'Yowsa yowsa! That girl is going places. Naked places.'

Harri picks at a cuticle. 'It's not just me? It seems a little much – or rather, not enough. But *The Know* cannot be in the business of policing young women's bodies.'

Giles thinks for a minute. 'Just turn the heating off. Say the boiler's broken. That will get her clothes back on. Now, have you had your audience yet with she who must not be named?'

'This afternoon,' says Harri. She'd love a glass of wine – or methylated spirits – but she suspects it's best to keep a clear head. 'I'm not too worried, it can't be worse than having Lily and Katie hovering around and getting in the way all day long.'

'Always going where they are not needed.' Giles has never forgiven Lily and Katie for recommending that disciplinary action be taken when he tried to call in a free Louis Vuitton case, after his original got lost on the way back from a press trip to Marrakesh.

'It's very weird though, it's a lot of negative energy to have in the office. It unsettles my girls. It makes me think Hudson wants to see this fail – so why bother to launch?'

Giles steals a chip. 'I suppose you're much cheaper to fire, if you fuck this up. If they'd just made you redundant when Rosa left, it would have cost them loads.'

'GILES! Why would you say that? What's wrong with you?'

'Come on, you know that if you're going, I'm going.'

'You're so loyal.'

'No, I mean that if you're getting fired, everyone is getting fired eventually. There will be no *Panache*, none of the weeklies, nothing but mags for people who want gossip about bricks and building regulations. Will can cement – ha! See what I did there? – his empire of magazines for people who hate reading.' Harri shakes her head. Today she has even less tolerance than usual for Giles' Nostradamus impression. She reads the time upside down on his phone. 'I'd better get back.'

'But you barely touched your chips!' says Giles, reaching for another handful. 'Off you go, back to your young girls. I'll get this. Say it with me now, while you can. Oooof, old woman! OOOOF!'

Chapter Fourteen

Kitchen Confidential

Harri

As a child, Harri would sometimes be taken, for a treat, to a model village in which everything was scaled down by half. A kid could climb into a tiny house, and sit behind a tiny table, and feel like a giant. The first time Harri felt ashamed of her body, aged eleven, was when her widening hips trapped her behind the tiny table and the model village man had to be called to winch her out. ('You're a big girl, aren't you?')

Harri does not like this memory, but when she sees Mackenzie in the kitchen, it's all she can think about.

Miraculously, Mackenzie has folded herself behind the tiny table, and is somehow wedged between the cushions of the cheap, scratchy blue sofa. Her thoroughbred-puppy glossiness is tempered by her expression. If there was space for subtitles between her forehead and the sloping ceiling, they would read 'I can't wait for this to be over, so that I can go and shower in hand sanitiser.' Her white cashmere sweater has the freshness of a frozen lake, and as Harri follows her furious eyes, she sees that it's contrasting sharply with the dull, brown, flaky stain beside her. The stain has been at Hudson Media for longer than Harri has. It's possibly on a final salary pension. Harri had always assumed – hoped – it was soup.

'This is unacceptable,' says her new boss. She sounds just like Katharine Hepburn, if Katharine Hepburn had appeared in a prequel to *Robocop*. 'I was told my office would be refurbished and ready, ahead of my arrival. But the windows need replacing, it has carpet – carpet – when I asked for cherrywood parquet. Does nothing work in this country?'

And this is Harri's fault? 'I'll, ah, perch.' Balancing an inch of buttock on the table, Harri tries not to wince as the sharp corner slices into her thigh.

Mackenzie stares. The clock ticks. Harri's stomach rumbles, and she wishes she'd made more of an effort with the chips. She'd swear that she can hear crickets chirping in Soho Square, half a mile away.

'So! How are you settling in? Are you finding every . . . ?'

Mackenzie silences me with a wave of her hand. 'Harriet, *The Know*. I have little interest in new media, or the demographic that you will be serving. However, I understand the function of the product. Of course, you can't be expected to compete with American offerings, *The Cut*, *Jezebel* et cetera.'

She looks at Harri as if she's waiting for a yes, a nod. Harri settles for a non-committal, non-confrontational 'hnnnnn'. She's trying to seem collected, professional. Too late, she realises she sounds like Bugs Bunny tormenting Elmer Fudd with a tin whistle.

Mackenzie goes on. 'I have been warned that you're very ambitious. My job is to temper that. You, and *The Know*, are answerable to me. *Panache* is losing money because you and Rosa were given free rein. Editorial must be kept in check.'

Harri suddenly feels very hot. Even though Mackenzie's face is inches from hers, her voice sounds far away, as though a radio has been left on in another room. The words don't make sense. She concentrates hard, to hear Mackenzie saying '*The Know* is not a key growth project for Hudson. We're keeping advertisers happy with a product offering, but your main job is to keep costs down. I understand that you had a certain amount of freedom with *Panache*. You're not working on the flagship now, so I expect you to keep a low profile. From time to time, of course, you may be required to pick up elements of your old role at *Panache* while the team settles itself. My position will be more managerial than Rosa's. Eventually we'll need to hire more senior editorial staff, but for now our priority is cutting spend. It may take some time to find employees who will fit within our budget requirements.'

Wait, what? Harri recognises the words, she knows what they mean, but she doesn't understand how they fit together in that sentence. 'You'll be expected to step in, as and when. I trust *The Know* won't be so demanding that it will affect your availability to support *Panache* if it's required.'

There is no inflection at the end of the line, no space for Harri to say 'I have been asked to launch and run a completely new title and leave everything – and everyone – I've worked for. That includes my legacy, and everything I've achieved during over a decade of my career. I feel betrayed and humiliated and unsupported. Frankly, *Panache* can do one.' So she gets her tin whistle out again, sliding the notes out on a descending scale this time. 'Hnnnnn.'

'You can go,' says Mackenzie, having given Harri two whole minutes of her time. Easing herself off the table, Harri gathers her sheaf of notes and plans, thousands of words carefully handwritten on narrow lined notepaper, neon pink Post-its waving with incongruous cheer. Sleepless nights and gallons of ink and pages of Harri's best and most brilliant ideas. Mackenzie doesn't even want to glance at the first month's content plan. As sulkily as she dares, Harri shakes her books and papers, as if neatening the pile, when she really wants to smash it against Mackenzie's expensive nose. The room is far too small to flounce out of, but Harri bashes her heels against the tiles anyway.

Harri is able to gain a tiny scrap of satisfaction from understanding the real reason that she was dismissed so rudely. It's going to take Mackenzie at least twenty undignified minutes to wriggle out from behind the tiny table, and she does not want to concede any power to Harri by allowing her to bear witness to the indignity.

What just happened to me, in there? Harri is blinking, breathing through her mouth. She feels as though she's been mugged. *I'm a grown up*, she thinks. *I've negotiated seven-figure ad deals for this company. I've met Prince Charles. I've done a TED talk. I'm a homeowner. I carry an Hermès Constance.*

Then, three words, before she's able to stop them. *I miss Andy.*

If he were here, he would hold her, properly. He would pull her to his chest, and wrap his arms around her, and she'd feel safe enough to weep. He would soak up all of her tears, and rock her gently, and he wouldn't need to say anything, but he'd say it anyway. That she was the best, and anyone who made her feel like less than the best would have to answer to him, and that no one would ever, ever be allowed to hurt his girl.

No one but Andy himself, apparently.

Harri pushes her palms against her eyelids. She's not cried at work for years, she's not going to start now. Mackenzie is a bitch – no, she's a robot. In her time, Harri has been close to screaming with frustration over the Spinning Rainbow Wheel Of Death while elderly laptops have seized up on her, and she knows it's a waste of effort. Mackenzie is another.

She takes a breath, and sees Imogen coming out of the toilets. She's trying to regain her composure, she straightens her notes again, tries to imply bustle, but she hasn't organised her face fast enough. It's too late. Imogen is coming over, and she looks concerned.

'Hey, Harri, are you OK? Is everything all right?'

'What? Oh, fine, fine. Just been to see our big boss, Mackenzie. She's ...' Harri reaches for a word she doesn't know, a code word, something that sounds ultra professional while making it very clear that Mackenzie ought to die in a fire. (It wouldn't be a human death, she'd melt, like the Wicked Witch of the West.) '... very, um, different from anyone I've worked with before. Very American.'

Imogen laughs. 'I've seen her from afar, and she's so glossy! I mean, *Panache* was glossy, I used to peer out of the cupboard marvelling at how shiny everyone was, but she looks like she should be carefully arranged on a red velvet cushion, at all times.'

Harri nods. 'Yeah, I'm not sure how she's coping with London. Maybe she feels like Mary Poppins, surrounded by dancing chimney sweeps.'

Imogen is pulling something out of her pocket. 'Do you want a CBD lozenge? They just came in. They taste pretty vile, but they're supposed to be relaxing.' Imogen is not wrong. The proffered lozenge immediately evokes a strong sense memory that is initially hard to place. Harri sucks the revolting sweet until her brain cries 'Eureka! This is the inside of your mouth on the last day of Glastonbury, 1995.'

Sucking is strangely restorative, and even a bad taste is enough to shock Harri back to her body, back to the present. She's the boss. She's the captain of the ship. She's got to regain some composure, some control.

'Imogen, what I just said about Mackenzie – I was indiscreet. I want you to go through those features ideas with me at 4 o'clock.' Harri sees some life, some energy flicker in Imogen's face. The shoulders rise. The spine tilts. 'OK, I mean, of course.' Imogen turns back towards the office, and Harri has to pretend she is taking her papers on a tour of the building in order to avoid an awkward walk beside her. As she ascends the stairs, she feels the acid sting of failure. She's got it wrong, again. Imogen reached out kindly, bravely, generously. All Harri had to do was show up, respond, be human, but she blew it.

Oh, love. I'm sorry. I want to be friends. But I'm your boss, and I'm not sure I know how to do both.

Chapter Fifteen

Imogen tries to get her breath back

Imogen

Today is our official launch day, and I can't be late. We've all spent the last two weeks writing, preparing, cramming – I feel as though I'm about to sit an exam. So when my bag starts buzzing as I exit the tube, I'd like to ignore it, and concentrate on getting to the office as quickly as I can. But when I see the caller ID, my lungs are punctured by a stab of panic. I pick up, while walking at a half trot, half gallop.

'Mum! Is everything all right?'

'Oh, you know, same as always, we're rubbing along, your dad's trying some new tablets so he's sleeping better, so he's not been so ... anyway, I've just not heard from you in a little while.'

'I'm sorry. Just been a bit tired, getting used to the new commute! I think it's just hard now, because I'm still getting used to it. I'll be back to normal soon, I'm sorry.' How on earth can she make me feel so guilty, in a single sentence, from hundreds of miles away? It's a superpower.

'Maybe you could come home soon? Have a nice rest.' How would it be a rest? The moaning, the constant criticism, then the shouting. Hoping Mum doesn't cry. Just thinking about going back is exhausting.

'Maybe in a couple of weeks. Mum, I'm late for the morning meeting, can I call you back?'

'Love, I really think you're working too hard. Are you getting enough sleep?'

It's Mum's favourite question, and there is no good answer. Define 'enough', Mother. Technically I suppose I must be getting enough rest, otherwise I'd be clinically dead. 'I'll be fine, I've just got to get through these first few weeks. Can I ring you at lunch?'

'Of course, of course! I'm taking your dad to the doctor's but if I miss you, I'll call you straight back.'

'OK. Love you!'

With five minutes to spare, I've arrived at the Hudson building. I lean against the wall. All is well. I breathe in through my nose for four beats, hold my breath for another four beats, and slowly exhale. My heart is still buzzing, rather than beating. Quick. What are five things I can see? Um, bare brown branch, purple chocolate wrapper, striped cafe awning ... my own hand? Does that count?

My de-stressing techniques are mostly cobbled together from social media. I follow approximately seventy 'wellness practitioners', who are always urging me to keep calm, with slogans like 'Root yourself in reality'. 'Be present in the now'.

What is the now, though?

Is it work? Because sometimes, at my desk, I feel untethered, floating. I look up, and look around, and I can't find anything to fix me in the space. Less than a month ago, when this job was simply a thrilling idea, I thought I was finally being asked to the party, after years of hoping for an invitation. But now, there is no proof that I belong. I wish there was a word for this nameless dread. In fact, I wish Harri would fire me, so I don't feel quite so irrationally frightened every time she says my name. ('Imogen, would you like a coffee?' 'Imogen, do you reckon we should be covering audio erotica?' Never 'Imogen, why did I bother to hire you, you worthless piece of shit?' And yet ...)

When I'm in the office, I'm certain that I'll get sacked, sooner rather than later. But in there, at least that's the worst thing that could happen. Out here, beyond the glass doors, I'm tormented by the mights and maybes.

Being present in the now is a luxury. You don't choose to spend your hours breathlessly running through your terrifying future, you're forced into it out of necessity.

Still, even though I constantly anticipate despair, I live in hope. I have to. And I finally have exactly what I've been hoping for, after waiting so long. The dream job at the end of the rainbow.

And it felt so much better in the future than it does right now.

One day last week, when I was researching a dull idea Harri had suddenly got keen on ('Can white noise boost your orgasms? We ask the experts') I was startled by a burst of laughter beside me – Louise and Kim were giggling hysterically over something they had seen on Slack. I hate Slack – we're supposed to use it instead of emailing each other. It's like being in twenty hen party WhatsApp groups, all at once, and I've already got to the point where seeing the logo makes me feel as though my ribs are going to burst right out of my chest. Louise has been my office ally. Rationally, I knew I was being ridiculous. But seeing the two of them sharing a moment made me feel so excluded that bile began gathering at the back of my throat. The pressure shift, the sudden change in atmosphere and social altitude was so acute that I wondered whether my ears were about to pop.

Louise saw my face, put a hand on my shoulder, and started to explain, but I brushed her away. 'Sorry, just trying to get on with this,' I said, and then felt a thousand times more mortified than I had done a moment before. Never assume you're included. That's the only rule. Just when you think you're one of them, and you start to relax – that's when you get rejected, ejected. Never trust anyone. Never let your guard down.

I know what it is to be excluded. But sometimes being included is much worse. When it's done out of pity. When someone has intervened on your behalf. When you're some-one else's resented act of kindness. When tolerating you is someone's good deed for the day.

Lily's 'Not you, Imogen,' I can deal with. Because it's never me. And I'd rather hear someone saying it openly. What I can't shake is the paranoia. The idea that bullies will find me, everywhere I go, and they will whisper about me, and giggle about me.

Pushing my back against the wall, I concentrate on the rough texture of the bricks, which I can just feel through the fabric of my clothes. Like the Princess and the Pea.

The Princess and the Pavement that Smells Of Wee. This makes me smile.

Inhaling deeply, I look out at the road and smell city. Old things, fried things, fragrant things, pissy things. Traffic fumes laced with lilacs from the hanging baskets outside the bougie bar around the corner. It numbs me, just enough. I feel calmer, safer. Some people think you move to London because your ideas for your life are too big, because you're arrogant enough to believe you might get noticed, because you want to be somebody. They don't realise that most of us end up here because we need to feel like anybody – or nobody. We need to disappear. When I lean against this wall, I'm not a disappointing daughter, a disloyal friend, a failing writer. I'm just another girl in a winter coat, running a little late for work.

Chapter Sixteen

Failure to launch

Imogen

Kim is laughing. I can hear him the moment the lift doors start to creak open. Following the sound, I stand in the office doorway, and see he's bent double, and wheezing. He is holding a long, purple balloon in the air.

'Oh my God, is he OK? Do we need to call someone?' I ask Harri, who is standing beside him, her arms folded. She shakes her head, gravely. 'Only HR.'

'I mean ...' Kim tries to stand up, but another gale of laughter gets the better of him. 'I got to the office, and ...'

Harri cuts in. 'Imogen, I thought I'd decorate the office to celebrate our official launch day. I pretty much worked through the night, and I'm knackered. But I got here extra early, and found these nice balloons, in *The Know* colours ...'

Kim is crying now, his beautiful face folded in on itself,

his T-shirt rucked up and revealing a glimpse of very taut ab. He gulps, and pulls it over his head, wiping his eyes with it. Blimey. 'Sorry, sorry Harri, I know you worked very hard, I'll try to get it together, but …' he's gone again. 'A penis! It looks like a penis!'

Harri smiles, but a tiny sigh whistles out of the side of her mouth. She looks very, very tired.

'I think we're all feeling a little bit … bonkers, after the last fortnight. You've all worked so hard. I want today to be a celebration. Launching a brand new title is not easy, and we've made something really strong. We've got work to do, but I thought we'd knock off early, I've got some prosecco. I'm sure we'll do some speeches and things later, but we'll have the features meeting at ten o'clock, as usual.' Harri looks meaningfully at Kim, who whispers 'Sorry!' and straightens his shirt, so that Wonder Woman is now fully visible and flying across his chest.

When Harri is safely tucked away at her desk, in the grown-up end of the office, Kim sniggers again, and bops me on the head with the balloon. 'Penis!' he hisses. I squeak. Harri turns and gives me a sharp look. 'Um, sorry, just my … shoe.'

I have almost composed myself when Tabitha arrives. 'What happened in here? It looks like when you go into the bank and they're promoting pet insurance. Still, good news for dogs, I suppose,' she says, looking straight at me.

Her words always sting, but then, her outfits always provide a decent distraction from the pain. Today, she's in a pale green bowler hat, with a matching tie and a white collared shirt. Over the shirt, she's wearing a fawn coloured, thick woollen pinafore. Her tights are white, and her shoes are unusually conservative, for her – conker brown, shiny men's brogues. In fact, for Tabitha, the whole ensemble is relatively boring, sedate even. I'd wear the shoes and the shirt, it's really just the hat that makes it a little weird. I feel as though I've seen this look on someone before though. She reminds me of someone, I just can't put my finger on who it is. Edie Sedgwick? Jackie O? Who wears a green hat? In the middle of Conference, it comes to me, just as Tabitha is banging on about going to Estonia for Tallinn Fashion Week.

She's come to work dressed as Yogi Bear.

I have to bite my cheek so hard that blood fills my mouth, as Harri is saying 'At the moment we really don't have the budget, but I'm sure you can livestream it. Now, Imogen, what have you got for us?'

'Errrr ... let me have a look. There was something in the *Mail* about money saving tips, it's doing the rounds and it's awful, don't have coffee, maximise your tax allowance – and I was wondering about doing something on real, useful money saving tips, where to get decent samples of things like shower gel and shampoo, how to volunteer to test things out, finding good student hairdressers anywhere in the UK, student dentists when it's impossible to get an NHS appointment ...' I trail off. Louise is looking at me worriedly.

'Student dentist?' shrieks Tabitha. She makes the Dowager Countess sound like Danny Dyer. 'Is that why you talk like that? Is that what happened to you?'

Something flickers across Harri's face. She frowns, and the lines settle. Is she going to say something to Tabitha? 'Sorry, Imogen, it's like I keep saying. Think aspirational.'

She is not going to want my proposed guide to the best charity shops in the UK.

'Um ... um ... they've launched a new lube?'

'Who are "they"?' replies Harri, gentle but steely.

'It's an American brand. It has particles that conduct electricity, somehow, and it's supposed to enhance clitoral stimulation ...'

'OK, check out the science, but for now I've got some stuff from freelancers that I need you to read through, do a quick tweak and a copy edit.'

Even Kim, pushing his fingers into the corners of his mouth, lifting his face into a smile, and silently mouthing 'PENISSSSSSS' at me does not cheer me up.

I'm supposed to be a staff writer. All I want to do is write. Harri told me she loves my voice, she loves my ideas – so why am I hardly ever allowed to write anything? I've done one piece, and it wasn't even proper journalism. It was an advert. It was supposed to be promoting a show for a new TV app. Harri said 'make it outrageous', then told me the client had said all of my ideas were too outrageous, and I ended up having to write it as an 'as told to', interviewing a girl from *TOWIE* about the time she had sex in a bush.

It's not just me. I know Louise is losing her mind to the endless SEO-hell of writing articles called 'What time does the *Love Island* reunion start?' and 'Where can I watch *Selling Sunset*?'

'The Girl is supposed to be practically running Google, not barely capable of using Google,' she sniffed, after Harri turned down her proposed Nigella hagiography in favour of a glorified TV guide. 'I thought we were the team! I thought we were *The Know*! But I feel like we're just ... the admin.'

'I'm sure Harri has a plan for us,' I said – wanting to reassure myself, as much as her.

But when we go live, at midday – and we have a countdown, and a glass of warm prosecco, and a round of applause – the home page is dominated by Nella Stella, model, activist and influencer, writing about her insecurity, her lack of body confidence, and how she expressed her courage and bravery by posting a series of sponsored bikini photos. 'We negotiated it so that the brand paid her to write the piece, so we got it as a freebie,' I heard Harri telling Akila. 'Might be worth going back to them, I'm sure they'd be keen to do more content with us.' A writer I've never heard of has produced a round-up of the best CBD oils for anxiety, something I feel a sharp stab of when I see that the cheapest one costs eighty pounds. And Emily Forge, *Panache*'s tenured columnist, has produced something pretty ... clickbaity on whether a wolf whistle could ever be a compliment.

Ironically, the clicks aren't coming. Every so often, I get up, on the pretext of stretching my legs, getting a coffee, going to the toilet, so that I can sneak a look at the data on Harri's screen. Every time, I see a grey, flat line. I don't know what it means, but I can guess.

'Keep sharing on your socials!' urges Akila. 'The best way to spread the word is to do it organically.' There is nothing organic about this. Harri's shoulders are a bleak barometer of just how badly this is going. They're either up by her ears, or down by her nipples. At 6.03, Kim says 'Maybe we should go to the p ...'

He has misjudged the mood. Even Akila, the only person who always seems to be fairly cheerful, has a face longer than the purple balloon.

'... enis,' he finishes sadly, and starts to gather his things. He tugs at his T-shirt, distractedly. Wonder Woman seems to be sinking down to earth.

Chapter Seventeen

The success issue

Harri

As the deputy editor of *Panache*, one of Harri's greatest hits was the launch of the annual Success issue. It was framed as a feminist exercise – celebrating powerful women, singling out companies with a strong female presence on their boards, cheering for activism and ambition. But it was also effective advertiser bait, easy to compile (endless listicles – Most Influential Women On Twitter! Most Successful Women In Wellness! Biggest Women-Run Sustainable Homeware Brands!) and the cover was a no brainer. They just alternated photos of Beyoncé and Malala.

But Harri was haunted by an essay she had commissioned for last autumn's Success issue. She'd paid well over the odds to get an American megastar author and speaker to write about failure. 'Failure and success are part of the same weather system,' it began. 'Success is no cure for failure. To pursue success without being willing to entertain failure is a little like refusing to accept the seasons. It can't be August for ever. You can't go out in the snow in a sundress.'

It was the sort of thing the readers lapped up, but it made Harri itch. She did not believe in failure. She barely believed in winter, often buying herself long haul flights to the Caribbean for Christmas (and offsetting her guilt by giving friends little certificates telling them they had purified a village well or sponsored a goat for a family of four).

Not becoming the editor of *Panache* had been hideous, shocking, shaming, painful – but Harri had been able to staunch the acid despair by telling herself that *The Know* would dazzle everyone. It would restore her reputation and hopefully result in a broken and humiliated Will begging her to take her old job back. Not that she would give him the satisfaction of taking it. By that point, she thought she would be able to say something like 'Sorry, Will, I am leaving for the States, I have just been asked to oversee the launch of the *Millennial New Yorker.*' (Harri is aware that she thinks about work revenge far more often than she ever dreams about getting revenge on any of her terrible ex boyfriends.)

So far, *The Know* is dazzling no one. There had been a nice write up in *MediaGuardian*, largely thanks to Harri herself begging a favour from Ruby, an old mate on the main paper. But Lily and Katie claimed all publicity needed to be signed off 'by internal comms' – and then spent most of the Confessions sponsor money hiring a separate 'shit hot' agency to run the site's social media. The agency had tagged, variously, @u_know, @nono and @the_now. Harri had hoped Emily's wolf whistling piece would, at least, get a good bit of controversy going. There had been a very brief flurry of agitation, but no one was staying on the site.

It's the beginning of February, and spring should be on the horizon, but Harri is starting to worry that her professional winter is finally getting started. Still, she has Akila. Harri knows you're only as good as the people you work with, and Akila might be her best hire yet. She's known and admired her for years, and she's turning out to be a real ally. Akila can coax and calm Kim into producing his best work, nurturing his sense of fun while tempering the occasional all-out silliness. Akila does not buckle and weep in the face of Lily and Katie, who have excluded her from at least two meetings, and have turned down all of Akila's offers of tea. Harri knows that tea is what pumps blood, and love, around the office body. Tea is biblical. 'Would you like a cup of tea?' is working shorthand for 'I don't feel as though I have very much to offer, just now, but this is all of the energy I've got, and I want to share it with you.'

So when Akila arrives at 8.59, Harri pounces. 'Kitchen conflab? Cuppa? Apparently there's a packet of chocolate Hobnobs in the cupboard.'

Soundtracked by the drum-brush whisper of the boiling kettle, Harri jumps straight in. 'I'm worried. I know the numbers are really not good. Far below projections. And I don't understand why.'

Akila nods. 'Yeah, there's progress, but at the moment we're not quite strong enough to get much advertiser love. We need to pull something big out of the bag. The Confessions piece is actually doing quite well, the client is happy.'

The kettle boils, and as it clicks, Harri feels her synapses start to spark. Ignition. It's as if a faulty neural wire has been nudged back into place.

'Imogen had some brilliant ideas – they freaked the client right out. But I reckon we could revisit them, do more sex content. Have you seen her blog? She had a lot of engagement with her post on pegging.'

Akila wrinkles her brow, and nods, slowly, and Harri keeps talking. 'It's when a woman wears a strap on and penetrates ...'

Akila holds her hand up. 'Harri, I know what pegging is. But I think you're absolutely right. We've been cautious so far, I think we're ready to go bold. Women aren't really being served by what's already out there, it could be a real land grab for us. And every day there's a new brand or product launch, the sex tech people are really throwing their money around.'

Sex, thinks Harri. Sexy sex. Hot bodies, cool sheets, the sounds people make, someone else's sweat on your skin, earthquakes and tidal waves and losing yourself, finding yourself in someone's arms ... no. I can't remember. I cannot let myself remember. She shudders, involuntarily, freeing herself from the grasp of a ghost. 'That's a great point about advertising. And we have to remember that the joy of being so new, and being online, is we can try it, run the numbers, and if it doesn't work, we never have to do it again. We can respond, we can take risks. But the potential is untapped.'

'Let's have a sexy brainstorm – sorry, thought shower, at Conference,' says Akila, rummaging for a spoon. (Harri's generous offer of tea did not include the removal of the bag.) 'I reckon Mackenzie is going to hate this, though.'

Harri's brain fires sparks once more. 'Exactly.'

Chapter Eighteen

The rule of three

Imogen

I hate being late on a Monday. It feels like a terrible omen for the rest of the week. As I slide into my chair, mumbling vague apologies, I notice Harri seems more agitated than usual. 'Imogen, at last! Right, we're all meeting in an hour, bringing our best ideas. Our sexiest ideas.' I make a face at Louise, who looks a little alarmed. As soon as Harri leaves – to get coffee or go to the loo or go in search of sex in the rest of the building, I don't know – she whispers 'Help! I don't have any sexy ideas. I've not had sex in six months!'

'Pardon me?' whispers Kim. 'Not that it's any of my business, but, um, why? How?' Even before I've looked up, I notice there's an unusual sense of ease in the office. A borderline carnival atmosphere. Lily and Katie aren't here. I look over at sulky Tabitha, to see if she has any interest in making friends and joining the sex chat, but she's putting her massive headphones on in a manner I'd describe as pointed.

'Imogen, when did you last have sex?' asks Kim, slightly more loudly. 'If you don't mind me asking?!'

'Um ... oh, God, when was it?' I count on my fingers. 'Thursday night, I think? It wasn't very exciting, just this guy I sort of see in emergencies.' Sam Strong had lured me over with the promise of an Uber Eats from Park Chinois – I put out for the venison puffs.

Kim giggles. 'What counts as an emergency? Extreme horniness?'

'Honestly, it's because my flat is a bit of a dump and he's got this amazing rainforest shower.'

Kim nods. 'But what about, you know, lurve? Shouldn't you be looking for something exciting?'

I sigh heavily. 'I realise I should probably start dating properly, but God, it's no fun. You sort of know how awful the date would be before you swipe. I've tried being choosy, I've tried being open minded, and no matter what I do I'm choosing between a squadron of Ultimate Frisbee players, with a token wannabe freelance environmental campaigner who has strong and unsolicited opinions about why I need to stop using tampons.'

Kim nods. 'You're talking about hetero men. Nothing but plankton in the fish tank, baby. It's a total shit show. A bleak scene.'

'Well, I don't only date men, but, to be honest ... I'm not doing a great job of properly dating anyone, at the moment. When did you last have sex?' I ask. He's desperate to tell us, he's squirming in his seat.

'Oh, you know, about ...' he examines his wrist. He is not wearing a watch. 'Maybe four hours ago!'

'What? How do you look so ... well rested?'

'I got up really early to go to the gym, there's a guy on reception that I've been crushing on for months. A swimmer, right?! Anyway, after things ended with my ex, I was so, so low. I've had three months of just barely feeling it at all, barely feeling anything, and now ... you know those TV shows where they buy this rusty old car that doesn't even have an engine, and they fix it up and make it shiny?' I nod. 'Well, I feel shiny again.' Louise's mouth is open. She is gazing at Kim with undisguised envy.

'Kim, I am delighted for you!' I say. 'Louise, maybe you should join his gym?'

'Well, I,' poor Louise has gone pink, and I feel terrible. I'm trying to bond, I don't want her to feel awkward. 'When I say six months – does phone sex count?'

We're lit up with curiosity – Kim is as open mouthed and glowing as a Halloween pumpkin – but Harri has returned, and we fall silent. If we could keep gossiping for an hour, I'm sure we'd have some sexy ideas, but the pressure makes my face ache. I think about Kim at the gym, overwhelmed with lust. I think about Sam Strong, his teeth grazing a nipple, his 'you like that, don't you?' and how I hate myself a little bit for liking it, and for liking what he tells me to like. Then, I think about my threesome, and the fact that I have a sexy idea on my phone, written out and ready to go. Dare I share it?

Harri is in a state of high agitation. 'Imogen, come on!' I know you've been holding out on me.' I can see her chest, rising and falling rapidly under her cashmere polo neck. Louise looks scared, Akila looks encouraging, Kim looks hopeful and Tabitha looks out of the tiny window. 'We're thinking of your blog. Think sex. Desire! The Girl! What's she doing about sex?'

Over the last three weeks, Harri has not gone for most of my non sexy ideas. She hated Israeli teen soldiers ('So fucking done'), she hated Niksen, the 'hot new Dutch life-style concept' that was popping up in various online trend round ups ('Doing nothing? Nothing doing!') and she hated Growing Up in Grenfell ('Imogen, I know it's all very good and worthy but if I wanted to be depressed I'd throw my Sertraline out of the fucking window'). I'm proud of my blog – but I'm still not sure how I feel about writing about sex at work in such a personal way. I think I'd hoped to 'prove' myself with something serious. Something new. But then, I know the blog brought me here. It caught Harri's eye. Maybe it's time.

Still, the thing about the blog is that even though abso-lutely anyone can read it, it feels private. Intimate. Ninety per cent of it is me reviewing vibrators – and if I'm entirely honest, I'm so grateful to the publicists who send them that everything gets two thumbs up, as it were. As far as I can tell, most of my readers are sex bloggers themselves. It's a tiny, cosy, deviant community where I feel entirely safe to write and share what I want to share. I thought I was progressive and positive but the thought of writing about, say, touching myself, for *The Know* – well, this is starting to feel like those bad dreams when I look down and notice I'm naked. And I have to resit my A levels.

I peel off the last, lingering shard of ancient sparkling polish from a month-old DIY manicure, and speak to that. 'I, ah … had a threesome once. With two guys. I've been starting work on a piece about that.' Immediately, I wish

I could pull the words out of the air and stuff them back into my mouth. I'm still trying to decide how I feel about it, so I'm terrified about what the rest of the team will think. Was it the escapade of a wild adventuress who stops at nothing in her quest for multiple orgasms? Or was it not quite ... right?

'WHAT?' shouts Akila. 'Sorry, but – seriously? That's amazing!' Even Tabitha swivels around to stare at me. Lou gasps. Only Kim beams. 'Girlfriend, yes. Love your work!'

Tabitha frowns at me. 'Yeah, was it a proper threesome though? Or did she just kiss two guys on the same night at some backwater village disco?'

I'd been about to lose my nerve and try to back out of this but I'm fuelled by only one thought: Fuck you, Tabitha. It's easier to sell it to her than to Harri, because I have absolutely nothing to lose. I can't make her like me. Tabitha will never, ever support me, and I don't care what she thinks of me. No, that's a lie. I want to antagonise her. So I smile and keep going. 'It happened when I was working at Summer School USA in Pennsylvania. We were the only counsellors left up, we'd been drinking, and it got weird. But hot.'

As I try to order my thoughts, I'm gratified to notice that Tabitha's mouth is hanging open. I could throw a Tic Tac in there. Even Harri is leaning forward, smiling. 'That's more like it! The personal angle is really strong, I think. How do you see this working, as a piece? How did it get weird?'

'Um, I don't know ... I suppose ... I didn't want to, but I did want to. It happened a while ago, and I'm not even sure if I remember it right. Sometimes I think I liked it, but sometimes ...' I don't think I'm ready to simply present what I've written, and say 'Here's one I made earlier!' Maybe, if I keep fumbling and obfuscating, it will eventually get forgotten about.

Harri is exasperated. I am exasperated with myself. She clasps her hands under her chin and exhales sharply. 'Look, just write it up as though you're telling it to, say, Louise. Lou is your reader. A sympathetic listener, nosy, maybe slightly naive.' For a second, pain flashes across Lou's face, but she grins it into oblivion. 'Do not shy away from details, I want personal, but I want emotion, too. Because threesomes are a bit weird! With two men! I mean, if they weren't weird, we'd all be at it, wouldn't we, every night?' Akila nods at me with great enthusiasm. I force a smile in her direction. Clearly, I'm not going to get out of this.

Harri carries on. 'As you know, we're still in our launch stage and everyone is pitching in for everything, it's all hands on deck right now. Tabitha, I want Imogen to get cracking on this. Your diary is quiet at the moment, so I need you to take over some of her jobs. You can start by transcribing that interview with the hemp lingerie founder, or whatever she is. I need it done fast.' Aha! Ahahahahahahahahahaha! I bite my cheek in order to stop myself from smiling. I will cheerfully pitch a follow-up listicle called 'The Seventeen Penises I Have Known' if it means that Tabitha has to do my shitty chores.

After a quick chat at Harri's desk, I get to work, and attempt a final, thorough edit. Her brief had seemed a difficult one – but reading my work again, I realised I'd already fulfilled it. She wants detail, emotion, feelings. 'Imogen, it's got to be real. Make it as sexy as you like, be explicit, but this isn't the nineties. It's not *Red Shoe Diaries*. Capture the ambiguity of it. I love what you said in the meeting, really bring out that conflict. I'd rather we get it right and go long than force it into eight hundred words.'

This was radical, from Harri. I once saw her standing over Louise's shoulder and bellowing 'Stop writing! STOP WRITING. If anyone wanted to read that many words, they'd buy a book.' *The Know's* strapline is We Dare You – on the secret Slack channel, there's a running joke that it should be 800 Words Or Less. Harri is obsessed with brevity, and she's convinced that our readers are time starved, multitasking girl bosses who do not have time to blow their noses, let alone spend more than three minutes reading.

I think of all the time I've spent at various jobs, bored out of my gourd. If I were to add it all up, it would come to about a year. I've read entire ten-thousand-word Mumsnet threads discussing whether Center Parcs is code for a specific sex act. I've read every One Direction member's Wikipedia entry at least four times. I sometimes think Harri might be underestimating our readers. Or overestimating them.

But for once, I'm not procrastinating, distracting myself or checking the word count after every sentence I read. It feels fluid. I am engrossed, focused, entirely connected with the work. Still, I feel a bit sick when I press send. Because it's really long, far too long. What if Harri hates the jokes, or she thinks it's a bit waffly, or comes back frowning and tells me it's self-indulgent and badly written? I've forgotten that *The Know* Girl – Girls – are my audience. Harri is the only reader I care about. I just want her to think I'm a good writer. No, that's not quite it. She's the law. Any objective measure of my talent rests entirely in her hands. If she thinks it's shit, it's not an opinion I can dismiss. It means

I'm shit. I won't just have to find another job, but another life to dream about too.

Tabitha looks up. 'Imogen, are you ... grinding your teeth? Please stop, I can't hear my music over the sound of your mouth.'

Suddenly a bracketed (1) indicates a new email. It reads:

SUPERSTAR. This is perfect. No adds. I'll organise a legal read, then it's going straight up. HX

I commit the line to memory immediately. It's the chorus of my new favourite song. Superstar. Perfect. I have done it. I've climbed the only mountain that counts. Harri thinks I'm perfect, and I'm high. I could run up the wall and dance on the ceiling. I could phone up that old lecturer who once shamed me in front of a whole seminar group for confusing my Brontës. How do you like me now? I could fuck Heathcliff and Mr Rochester at the same time! Ha!

The euphoria lasts for about ninety seconds, until I stop and realise that Harri is not my only reader. This is about to go out into the world, for everyone to read, with my name on it. The anxiety buzzes and builds. I'm starting to feel as though I might be sick, not imminently but soon, if I don't go out and get some fresh air. I'm fine. I just need a glass of water. Then Harri comes over to check some details. 'Just had a thought – I'm assuming you've changed the names? If not, we'll need to swap those out, maybe add a line about the location, do a couple of tweaks – we're just making sure that there's no way anyone recognises themselves, or can be recognisable. But this is such a fantastic piece – it's so strong. I'm thrilled with it.'

117

Now the sick might be imminent. 'Is it likely that anyone will be able to recognise themselves?' I don't want to ask her my most pathetic question – am I going to get into trouble?

She smiles. 'Do not worry. It's my job to be really anal about this stuff,' she smirks. But even if you gave everyone's last names and birth dates, it's massively unlikely that they will come across it, in the giant internet sea. I think this is going to do well for us, but we're still pretty small fry at the moment. The Girl is gonna love it.' Not The bloody Girl, again. I'm starting to feel as though I've been landed with an imaginary nemesis. Harri misinterprets my frown, adding 'But it's OK, Tyler and Russ are not our Girl, and Alllison with three ls definitely isn't her. You're fine.'

Methodically, we work out a few tweaks and swaps, and after ten minutes I notice that my breathing has slowed back to normal, and I no longer feel the need to leap up from my desk and retch out of the window. We're small fry. If I'm lucky, this will be seen by a few hundred unfazed readers who attend weekly chemsex orgies. They'll get bored and stop reading before my knickers come off. Harri likes it. After days of waiting, hoping and desperately trying to impress Harri, I've finally proved to her that I can write! That's all I care about.

For the next hour or so, I wonder whether this will make me, or break me. In my imagination there is nothing in between, which is ridiculous.

My piece goes up and out into the world. I'm waiting for a thunderclap, or a metaphorical trumpet blast, announcing my work to the world. Of course, nothing happens.

*

For twenty minutes, I watch *The Know*'s social media accounts, refreshing the page every half a minute. Eventually, the tweet gets twelve likes, one from a company that makes hand sanitiser. (It's a coincidence but I wonder whether it's a passive aggressive sub-like, a cleaning brand calling me a dirty girl. But then, no one on Twitter is that subtle.) No drama, no fuss. I don't know what I expected. Strangely, I'm slightly disappointed. It's a little bit anti-climactic, after making myself so raw and exposed on the page. Well, the screen. I really wanted it to blow up, to piss off Tabitha. I suppose that does not say much for my journalistic integrity. This is the best case scenario, really. I mean, I feel a bit nervous about Louise reading it. I might just not mention it, and hope she's forgotten.

At 6.18, even though everyone else is still frowning furiously at their monitors, I decide it's home time. (It's only fair, I'm pretty sure my commute is three times longer than anyone else's.) With one arm through my coat, and my other hand clutching my phone, bag strap around my neck, pack-horse style, I burble a 'See you tomorrow' and make my escape. I'm perfect. I'm a superstar. I'm absolutely exhausted.

Chapter Nineteen

Good morning, Imogen

Imogen

I wake up the way that every wellness warrior says I shouldn't; alarm jangling, one eye open, hand under the pillow, feeling for my phone because I shoved it there last night after falling down a Reddit rabbit hole. ('AITA – I (M, 49) left my own wedding reception early to go surfing, and my new wife (F, 29) says she already wants a divorce?') Weather – rainy, rainy, rainy. News – awful, awful, awful. Twitter – formerly famous nineties gameshow host was racist on *Newsnight* ... but look! A bear is making friends with a kitten ... and oh. Oh. What's going on? I have more than twenty notifications, and everything is very slow to load. Maybe my Twitter is broken. I had that on Instagram, when it notified me about every follower I had gained in the last six months ... OH MY GOD.

Miley Cyrus has quote tweeted my threesome piece. 'Courageous, smart, relatable.' Sealed with a wink emoji, of course. And Emily Ratajkowski. 'THIS is the writing we need to read post #MeToo. Love @Imogen_Mou owning her complex sexuality.'

My heart is pounding. When I went to sleep I had about five thousand followers. OK, it's disingenuous for any woman on the internet to pretend like she doesn't know exactly how many social media followers she has at any given time. I had five thousand, two hundred and seventy-one followers, a slow to grow number that's had the odd bump from a couple of web pieces for *Panache* and a very silly viral joke about bees. My Twitter profile tells me that I now have 28.9 thousand followers. And counting. They've fallen onto Internet Me in the night, like fresh snow.

Another tweet that has been retweeted into oblivion just reads '*SLUT SLUT SLUT SLUT WHOR SULT SLUT.*' A celebrity dermatologist turned celebrity angry right-wing campaigner is taking aim at *The Know* – '*APPALLING example to set for young women*'. But some people are kind. '*So powerful!*' '*LOVE your writing*'. '*Thank you*'. '*Brave*'. It's 7.48 a.m. I should have got out of the shower nine minutes ago. I'm damp with sweat. My pyjamas are sticking to me. What. Does. It. Mean? Am I in trouble? Am I famous?

I decide to turn my phone off. It takes a little while to remember how to do this – and then I get into the shower. Ariana Grande knows who I am, and I live in a flat where the bathroom has a carpet. Somewhere out there, Emily Ratajkowski is drinking champagne on a marble plinth and thinking about something that happened to me seven years ago, while old shower water squelches between my toes.

As always, I do not have the right outfit for the day ahead.

I strongly suspect that all of us are shopping in an attempt to cosplay our own lives – and I can't ever get it right. Where are the bold, sexy, edgy clothes I need? Who took them and replaced them with this stuff? Ironically, that former celebrity crafter would approve. At least until she saw the safety pins holding up the hems. Anyway, as much as I want to look glamorous and assured and be the poster girl for twenty-first century sex-having, I would prefer to leave the house disguised, swaddled in blankets, with a false moustache and a crash helmet. Jeans and a jumper it is.

As I close the front door, I think about running back for a pair of sunglasses and then curse myself for being so vain. Twitter isn't the world, it's a tiny percentage of ranting lunatics. Only 14 per cent of people use it – I've memorised this statistic and I comfort myself with it when being online feels particularly toxic. Are people looking at me? I don't think anyone can recognise me from internet pictures with my glasses on and my hair up. Or can they? As I walk towards the centre of the train carriage, searching for a seat, a woman catches my eye and smiles. OH GOD. What do I do? 'Sorry to bother you,' she beams, 'I just wanted to let you know …' Oh, I'm going to be sick! 'that your flies are undone.'

When I make it into the office, I'm half expecting a hero's welcome. After all, this must have gone beyond anything that even Harri hoped for. Do I get a cake? But it's weirdly quiet. Only Akila gets up and gives me a hug, as I stand awkwardly in the doorway. 'Well bloody done,' she murmurs. 'This is huge! I was watching it last night, I couldn't sleep. I nearly called you.'

'I'm still in shock, I think,' I reply. I try to breathe in

slowly, but my lungs feel cramped in my chest. 'What do I do, now? What does it mean?'

Akila takes a step away from me, and frowns, thoughtfully. 'This must be ... a lot for you to take in. We've been so focused on the numbers ...' that they hadn't factored in the human at the other end, I think. She continues. 'Anyway, there have been a lot of media requests. Harri is in emergency meetings with the press team! They're a bit reluctant because they've got to run everything by America, and Mackenzie is quite cautious. Her attitude is very much "if we're in the news, it's bad news" but I think Harri will persuade her. Hopefully you'll get to go on *Woman's Hour*! *Good Morning Britain*! Maybe even *This Morning*!'

I really, really don't think I want to go on *Good Morning Britain*.

Tabitha has been watching us from her corner of the office. She's like a cat – silent and stealthy, but when she wants to be present, she's really present. 'Won't this all die down in an hour or two? It's not such a big deal, there will be something else coming along in the next day or so. Everything is viral, these days.' She smiles, and there's more than a whisper of cruelty to it. 'I'd hate for poor old Imogen to get her hopes up.'

Gratifyingly, Akila rolls her eyes and smirks. 'Actually, it is such a big deal. It's not 10 o'clock yet, and I've already had calls and enquiries from six brands who have mentioned Imogen's amazing piece. Don't worry, Tab. I'm sure it will be your turn next.' She catches my eye. 'Seriously. Great. Fucking. Job.'

I blush. 'Oh, you know, a lot of it was Harri's idea, and it's just really lucky that Ariana G—' Akila gently places a violet fingernail to my lips. It's a little bit sexy – I must crush that thought before we're both up in front of HR. 'Imogen, I'm only going to say this to you once. Remember it. Claim what's yours. Modesty is not cute. And it's a really obnoxious white woman thing. Everywhere I have ever worked, other people have rushed to take credit for what I have made. Other people have let them. Own your moment, because there are plenty of people prepared to own it for you.' Her glance lands on Tabitha for less than half a second. She gives me a brisk hug, and somehow pops me down at my desk, as if she's going out for the night and leaving me in the care of a babysitter. 'Right gang, let's get to it! Big day! Busy day!' She moves to the grown-up end of the office with a hint of strut, as though it's a catwalk in Milan and not eight feet of wood-effect laminate.

Sitting up a little straighter, I try to attend to the business of writing. The first thing on my to-do list is a round-up of quiet vibrators for people with clitorises who still live with their parents and want to spend twenty pounds or less. (Obviously that's the SEO friendly, Google search-able headline. I'm futzing about with 'Bargain buzz!' or 'Silent delight'. 'Cheap thrills?') But I can't take my eyes off Twitter. People are still reading, sharing, calling me a slut or a hero. Waves of nausea keep rocking and breaking through my body. Surely there is no way my internet-phobic parents could find out about this. Is there? Oh, God.

Louise barrels in, late from the doctor. 'I have no sex life at all, and yet, cystitis!' she announces, quite cheerfully, all things considered. She's clutching a sealed, white paper prescription bag, and she shakes it in my face. 'Oh my goodness, Immo. I saw! I think Busy Philipps just put it on her Insta stories! Should we celebrate? Can we go out for lunch? Pub after work?'

I frown at her bag. 'Don't you have cystitis?'

'Ah, fuck it, I can start the antibiotics tomorrow. For now, I can drink through the pain!'

Harri bursts through the door, her caramel cashmere coat hanging off her shoulders and flying out behind her like a cape. Not all superheroes wear man-made fibres. 'Imogen. Quick word?' She's brusque – no, angry. Why is she angry? Shouldn't she be hugging me, and maybe presenting me with a giant comedy cheque for increasing the ad revenue?

I jump up and follow her to her desk. 'Right. Great news, I've managed to persuade everyone upstairs, you're on *Good Morning Britain* tomorrow, they'll give you a call about getting a car to pick you up. And then we're just confirming with *Woman's Hour*. *Loose Women* is interested too.'

'Ah, right. Harri, you see, the thing is that I don't ... I didn't realise ... this is perhaps not ... I'm not sure ...'

Harri's nostrils flare. I've only ever seen that happen in cartoons.

'Imogen. I have spent – wasted – quite a lot of my morning convincing Mackenzie to sign off on this. You are sure. I am sure. This. Is. An. Opportunity.'

'Do I need to go? Maybe you or Akila could do it?'

I think Harri wants to hit me. 'Imogen, for fuck's sake. You're an ambassador for *The Know*. You're representing the millions of readers,' Probably not millions, Harri, 'who are seeing themselves for the first time. You're disrupting. You have the chance to tell the whole world what we're about, who we're for. Think of The Girl! She's ambitious, she's fearless, she's going head to head with the breakfast Establishment in a T-shirt that says "Fuck the patriarchy". Oh, lord, please, no. 'Anyway, it sounds like you'll be on with Dora Bainbridge. Everyone hates her. It will be an easy win. You're the gorgeous young woman living her life, wittily. And she's the symbol of internalised misogyny. No one will even notice that you're talking about a threesome, they'll be too busy bitching about her wonky Botox.'

'It's true that I have often fantasised about attacking Dora Bainbridge with a big stick. In fact, I imagine that she only bothers bashing out her racist, sexist overpaid nonsense columns because she's waiting to be hit with a big stick.'

'Imogen, you really can't bring a big stick to *Good Morning Bri*— oh, you're joking. Yeah. That's the spirit. Give them hell. You're our Joan of Arc. Ha, or Joan of Snark!'

Does Harri remember what actually happened to Joan of Arc? Am I seriously going to set myself alight to keep *The Know* warm? If this act of public humiliation is for sexual freedom, I think there are hills I would rather die on. Literally die on.

'Tell you what,' says Harri, sounding much friendlier now that she knows I can't say no. 'We'll chat to Tabitha and call in something amazing for you to wear. I bet that if we reached out to some brands, they'd love to gift for this. She can style you! We can do a few videos for Stories, or something.' Oh, no. I think I'd rather go on breakfast telly while wearing no clothes at all.

Chapter Twenty

ImTV

Imogen

I would say the day dawns, but it's still dark when I'm standing outside the flat at 5.15 a.m., with two jumpers under my coat. I don't want to risk the driver ringing the doorbell and waking up Downstairs Colin. I was seized by a strange urge to show off to Gemma and Emma about being on television, but it occurred to me that would definitely jinx things – the universe would punish me for being proud, and my slot would get cancelled and replaced by some actual news. Actually, I would really love that. Maybe I should have gone around bragging to everyone I know.

It's been raining, and the streetlights are still on, their gleam reflected by the puddles and exploding off the wet pavement like fireworks. After a few clashes with Tabitha – mercifully I was able to talk her out of some stripy backless bodycon, on the grounds of possible strobing – she managed to come up with something not too terrible. I'm wearing high waisted, wide legged royal blue Mother of Pearl trousers, and a soft, pale grey jumper with just a hint of pink in the knit. Harri was diplomatic. 'This is a styling challenge, because it's all about messaging. I know you want to put Imogen in something really wild and cool, and I'm sure there will be time for that. But we've got a very clear objective here. She's just a normal young woman. On TV, they'll want her to come across like a mad slut, some kind of cautionary tale. She's really not. She's just every woman who has ever had a sexually confusing experience and wants to wear nice trousers.'

Looking at my phone, I wait for a message saying that the car is going to be late, or that it's actually parked three streets away, but no, a clean, shiny, sober Mercedes is pulling up just as a text arrives to confirm the number plate. Before I can tuck and roll into the back, the driver is out, opening the door with a courteous 'Good morning, Miss!' He does not follow it up, as I fear he might, by squinting at my face and saying *Aren't you that whore from the internet?*

The inside of the car takes me by surprise. I don't know anything about cars at all – I'm aware that Mercedes is a fancy brand, but I have no idea what makes the cars fancy. This is all leather – supple, pale leather, not thick, S&M pleather – with separate chairs and a wide, hollowed-out armrest that has been filled with tiny bottles of water. I find myself thinking of something Harri said the other day, that sat strangely with me. 'The Girl isn't scared of anything'. Sometimes I think I'm scared of *everything,* but maybe life is much less frightening for the people who can take this treatment for granted. This is what true luxury is – not hard and glossy, but soft and welcoming. It's not supposed to shut you out, but usher you in. For the duration of this car ride, I'm allowed to believe that my comfort and safety matter.

Unlike The Girl, I've been feeling sick with fright for about nineteen hours. Yet, a strange calm is slowly descending on my body. Even though I'm convinced that I'm about to shame myself before the nation, a bit of me thinks that they wouldn't bother to send a posh car if they really wanted to make a fool of me. Unless this is to lull me into a false sense of security.

Still, the journey through South London is eerily beautiful. As I watch the sky fade from ink to lilac, I notice some personal landmarks. Here, the pub where I bought a round to celebrate that crappy editorial assistant job and went over my overdraft limit for a month. There, the not-quite-hipsterish cafe where I went on that awful date with the guy from Hinge who kept showing me photos of his mum in a bikini. I want to wave at all of my old ghosts. It's going to be OK, guys! I'm from the future. One day you're going to get a great job and be on telly in some very expensive trousers!

I've been avoiding Twitter as much as possible – partly thanks to Akila's wisdom. 'I've got friends who have been in similar situations,' she'd explained. 'My best mate's boyfriend cheated on her with his Strictly partner – I'll tell you all about that one day but for now, we're not gossiping. You need to mute the conversation. Every time you see the notifications, you'll get a weird burst of adrenaline, and it's worse than cocaine. I can't tell you to stop looking, but you can set it up to make it less horribly addictive. You need a good night's sleep.' For once, I'd slept with my phone beside my bed, instead of in my bed. But it's tempting to tell the world that I'm going to be on TV. It is exciting, I think. I'm a journalist, talking about my work, in front of the country. I should feel proud. Maybe it's a case of mind over matter. On Twitter, I type out ZOMG! On my way to ... as we drive past the Oval. I stare at it for a bit, and then delete it when we reach the Imperial War Museum. I don't need to show off about being on TV, I mean, it's TV! People will see it. Although hopefully no one I actually know. I picture Dad, slumped in front of Sky, Mum whistling and bustling to Motown on Radio 2 before she goes to work. She'll be devastated to miss it. But she might be more devastated if she saw it. Oh, I haven't thought this through. Why couldn't I have said no to Harri? Because she would have fired you, says my brain, unhelpfully.

It's still not quite light when we pull into a car park and drive up to a barrier. My driver says something to a man in a little hut, and we turn and line up behind a row of identical Mercedes. The door is opened, and a smiling woman with a clipboard leans in. 'Imogen? Hello! I'm Carly, we spoke on the phone.'

'HELLO!' I roar. I've been up for over an hour, and I've not spoken a full sentence to anyone. My own voice is a bit of a shock for my ears. Leaping to my feet, I yell 'THANK YOU! THANK YOU SO MUCH!' in the direction of the car's tinted window, windmilling my arms and nearly hitting myself in the face with my bag.

Carly is reassuringly normal. Cropped, coppery hair, jeans that I suspect used to be black, a plain polo neck and what appears to be a tool belt around her waist. 'Follow me,' she says, beckoning me through a doorway. 'I believe it's your first time with us – thanks so much for coming on.

We've got some breakfast bits in the green room, I'll take you through and then we'll bring you into hair and make-up.' Carly is walking fast, fast, fast, and I trot obediently behind her, eyeballing the contents of what appears to be a fabulous showbiz garage. Here a nine foot tall golden candlestick, there a lifesize – double lifesize? – cut-out of a hippo in a Hawaiian shirt, with a speech bubble coming out of its mouth that reads beach bonanza giveaway! I don't know quite what I was expecting, but it wasn't this lightly controlled chaos. Frantically trying to keep up with Carly, I round a corner and bump into a woman who looks vaguely familiar. 'Sorry, love!' she giggles. 'Great trousers!' Where do I know her from? Does she live near me? Was she at *Fizz* mag when I was interning? Oh! *X Factor.* She was a runner-up two or three years ago. I love her. And she loves my trousers! It's going to be fine. Better than fine.

'Here we are. Just grab a seat and I'll get your release forms. Coffee? Anna, get Imogen a coffee,' says Carly, to the air, hurrying off again. I sink into a big, bright purple sofa, and reach for the platter of croissants in front of me. When my mouth is full of delicious almond paste, a dusting of icing sugar covering my chin, like Homer Simpson's beard, I make the mistake of looking up.

Dora Bainbridge is staring at me.

She's much, much thinner in real life. It's not fair, I think, before feeling a strong stab of feminist shame. That was not a body positive thought. I recognise her dress – a bottle green silk shirtwaister that I've seen in the window of LK Bennett – but sexy, stompy, possibly Prada boots are peeping out from under her hem, where her mumsy court shoes should be. How is her hair so bloody shiny? I could probably see my face reflected in it, croissant and all. And the weirdest, weirdest thing is that she's smiling at me with genuine warmth. She's getting to her feet and holding out her hand. She doesn't just look friendly, but properly pleased to see me.

'Hello! You must be Imogen, I'm Dora.' As if she needs to tell me! It's like hearing 'I'm Beyoncé', or 'I'm Barack'. I squeak, clap my hand over my mouth and start to exfoliate my chin with pastry flakes, before squeaking again, wiping my greasy, sugary hand on my borrowed, expensive trousers and shaking hers a little too forcefully. Dora is not perturbed. 'I'm so glad to see you before the debate! Usually, they like to keep us separate, to make sure the sparks fly, but that's not very friendly, is it?'

Feeling a little numb, I shake my head, jaw clamped down to stop any masticated croissant escaping.

'My daughter loved your piece, she's a huge fan. She wanted to come in and meet you, but there's no getting her out of bed before ten in the morning!' Dora giggles, and I remember hate-reading a furious rant that she had written in the *Daily Mail*, criticising new research about the amount of sleep teenagers require. 'My two are up and ready for the day before the sun comes up. It's all about instilling the discipline they need to ensure they become productive, useful adults,' Dora had shouted from the side bar.

Carly appears in the doorway. 'Imogen, they're ready for you in make-up.' She registers Dora's presence, and wags a finger in mock admonishment. 'D, what have I told you about chatting up the guests before a debate? Honestly!' She leads me away, tutting. 'We do try to keep you separate, it makes for better telly, but Dora is a law unto herself. Now, don't forget, it is a debate, you're not to let her get away with anything. She's really going to savage you!' Carly looks up from her clipboard and stares at me, searching for a reaction. I think she wants me to get angry and tell her that I'll savage her right back. Can't I roll over and play dead, instead?

Carly continues. 'She's read your piece, and she's going on the attack. Her daughter is a little bit younger than you, and she's going to focus on that. You're a bad example, a bad influence, where was your mother in all of this, how can you call yourself a feminist when you're not in control of your body, wouldn't the pioneers of the women's liberation movement be heartbroken if they knew this was how you were using your freedom. Et cetera.' She's walking and talking, tapping her clipboard with her pen, punctuating every point of pain. Bad example. Bad daughter. Bad feminist. Bad mistake.

While she has been assassinating my character by proxy, Carly has shepherded me into a chair inside a small, brightly lit, mirrored room. I notice that my skin has turned a very pale shade of grey, and my mouth is hanging wide open. 'Anyway, I'll leave you with Hope, who'll make you look gorgeous. Not that you don't already! See you in a bit.'

Hope is a short, round and smiley woman. She looks at me with such kindness that I long to weep into her soft pink jumper until she feels sorry enough for me to take me home and put me to bed. 'Imogen, haven't you got lovely thick hair? It's all right, sweetie, you can relax. I think I'm going to make you look really glowy! No one likes that Dora, we all call her Dora the Dragon. You can be young and gorgeous, and she can be all scaly!' I giggle, although now that I've seen Dora up close, she's more Dragon's Blood Facial than withered old lizard. Ordinarily, I'd find Hope's patter patronising, but right now, it's strangely soothing. She can call me 'sweetie' – at least *she's* not going to call me a bad feminist.

Facing the mirror, I watch my reflection telling Hope 'I've never done this before, I'm really nervous. In fact, I tried to get out of it, but my boss made me go,' I blurt, before Hope silences me with the tickle of a brush against the corner of my lip. 'Shhh, sorry, I just need you to keep still for a minute. Honestly, it will be over so quickly, these things only go on for five or ten minutes and then the next one will be up.'

Closing my eyes, as Hope applies powder, I sense various brushes being flicked deftly against my face. Her strokes seem fluid and sure, the work of a confident artist, but her stream of chatter never stops, blending with the background burble of the radio. 'I've just blow dried a vegan, and I reckon Chuck will be saving his vitriol for them. We've been watching him on the monitor,' Hope stops brushing. I assume she's pointing at Chuck, live on TV, but I can't actually see. 'He's been pretty mellow with most of the guests today, I don't think you have anything to worry about.'

A tickling sensation against my cheek indicates that Hope is back to work, but she does not stop chatting. 'Seriously, we get so many complaints when Dora is on – not actual complaints but angry tweets, people really hate her. We had that nice girl from *Love Island* on with her, I wasn't sure how it was going to go, but Dora savaged her. Even Chuck said Dora might be The Most Hated Woman in Britain.'

I open my eyes. 'But why does Dora do it? What's the

point of going on and being mean to everyone?' She was so nice to me in the green room, I want to add, but talking is too difficult while Hope is going at me with a mascara brush. I can't manage consonants.

'Keeps her on telly, dunnit?! She's a pantomime villain, like Chuck. She can spout any old bollocks – 'scuse my language! – and as long as she's prepared to be a bit of a cow, people will keep asking her back. There are a few people who love her for telling it like it is, and plenty who just love being horrified by her. But it's all a win for her!'

Hope has been working hard. I'm no longer a grey, lashless thumb. I have cheekbones, a cupid's bow, enormous eyes. This is how you're supposed to use blusher! I don't just look made up, I look like I've been getting nine hours of sleep, every night, for a decade.

'Hope! WOW! Oh my goodness, thank you!'

'Shhh, keep your face still, lovey, just going to do a bit more powder. Now, Lara will be here in a minute for your hair. I'll have a word and make sure she doesn't go too nuts with the tongs.'

After another ten minutes, I'm totally transformed. Lara – bullied nicely by Hope – has given me loose, beachy waves. Without intervention, I daresay I'd look like I was on the brink of being thrown out of a chocolate factory for stealing squirrels. Now I'm waiting in the dark, staring at glimmering silver stretches of duct tape, marking mysterious noughts and crosses on the floor. A mic pack is clipped to my back pocket, and my trousers have been sponged free of sugar. Dora actually giggled when the pale, nervous young man apologised for having to drop hers down her dress. 'Ooooh, most action I've had all week. See, Imogen, that's why I don't wear trousers!' Right. In just moments, she's going to be slut-shaming me before the nation, yet right now she's bragging about forcing the runner to feel her up. Deep breaths. I can do this.

Suddenly Carly looms out of the darkness, a floating head come to impart some last minute advice. 'Remember, it's a debate. Really go for each other! Imogen, don't be polite! Interrupt her!' She steps back into the shadows, and I look sadly at my fingers. I wish I had some nails left to bite. My stomach gurgles, and my whole body tenses. Please don't let the first sound I make on live television be a fart.

The runner returns, and we're led onto the set. Chuck Bloomer and a guest presenter, Amanda someone, are on the comfy sofa, and Dora and I are left to scale some perilously high chairs. Oh, God. We're starting. Help. I can see the autocue, which is quite comforting. Can I please have an autocue?

'Women's website *The Know* is promoting itself as a ground breaking offering for young women – but is it breaking the right sort of ground?' begins Chuck.

'When writer Imogen Mounce wrote an explicit essay about her sexual experiences, the piece went viral, and was shared by celebrities from Emily Ratajkowski to Adele,' adds Amanda. Wow! Adele? I didn't know that!

'However, Imogen has attracted praise and criticism in equal measure, and many people feel that the piece is little more than pornography, encouraging women to take sexual risks, and worse. Well, we're joined today by Imogen, and the columnist and broadcaster Dora Bainbridge. Imogen, why did you write this piece?'

Because Harri made me? Because of the abysmal failure

of Louise's piece about Miss Piggy as a feminist icon? 'Um, well, the thing is I . . . didn't want to encourage anything, as such, *The Know* is about women's honest . . . '

Dora cuts me off. 'I think it's disgusting. As the mother of daughters, young women who are about to start making their way in the world, I am horrified and appalled by *The Know*, and by Imogen's piece. It's cheap pornography masquerading as feminism, and when I think of my sisters at Greenham Common,' What? I've definitely read something Dora has written in which she dismissed the peace protests as 'attention seeking' – 'it's desperately sad to see this generation of so-called feminists squandering their energy on sexual braggadocio!'

Chuck addresses Dora. 'So you think that this generation has lost their way? Or that feminism has gone too far?'

What? How do I come back from that?

'Yes, I do, Chuck. I think women are losing sight of what's important, and this obsession with identity and performance is a real threat to the home, and to the family.' Is that . . . did she just quote Phyllis Schlafly, verbatim? I might cry. I can picture Harri, watching from her monitor in the office, shaking her head. Everyone crowding around, horrified. Harri will be so disappointed in me. And that's the thought that makes me sit up. I've got nothing to lose, now.

'Hold on. This all seems to have very little to do with what I wrote. Most of all, the women who read *The Know* are smart. They are not looking to us for answers. They don't want to be told what to think. They want to see their reality reflected back at them. I wrote an honest, vulnerable piece and I believe it has, um, struck a chord,' I look around wildly, daring someone to challenge me, 'not because our readers want to have a three, ah, the sexual experience that I had' (I'm not sure you can say threesome on telly before breakfast, no one else has, and I'm not brave enough to check,) 'but because the reality of being a woman today is confusing. We don't know what we want. We don't know what we're allowed to want. And that's because of the legacy left by older feminists like Dora,' I catch her eye, and I see a speck of respect.

'We've been sold a lot of confusing problems. Our feminist heroes are the women who fought for our sexual freedom and told us it was what we should want but now they are also the women who are slut-shaming us for sexual exploration. Now, the rug is being pulled out from under us. You told us you broke the rules for us, but in the next breath, you're shaming us for making our own rules. You want to force your experiences upon us without being willing to listen to what we're all going through, right now.'

Dora inhales, poised to interrupt, but I'm determined to keep talking. The rage is cooling in my veins, and I feel good. I feel sure. Finally, I think this is what it feels like to be The Girl. Slowly, clearly, I go on. 'The point of my piece wasn't to brag about a wild night – but to explore the fact that in this millennium, I am living with shame that I shouldn't have to feel. That parts of my encounter did not feel completely consensual. If I'd been raised in a truly supportive feminist culture, I'd probably have had the threesome . . . ' Ha, I said it! 'But I wouldn't be here talking about it because it wouldn't be news. The response simply illustrates that we have a long way to go.' I turn to Dora. 'Now, do you want to help your daughters, or do you want to keep being part of the problem?'

I wish I hadn't given her an opening. My adrenaline comes roaring back. I'm doing a sort of seated *Riverdance*. I'm attempting to stay perfectly still from the waist up, but my legs are vibrating against the metal of the high chair.

Chuck smells blood. 'So, Dora, Imogen says that your generation is complacent. And this is about freedom, right? You can't claim to have fought for their freedom, and then complain that they're using it the wrong way.' Ah, I get it now! He's not an emissary for the end of feminism, he's a pure provocateur.

Dora sniffs. 'Well, I certainly hope that my children don't use their freedom this way. I hope they respect themselves.'

'Don't worry, Dora,' I smile. 'If there's anyone around this table that I do respect, it's myself.'

'Well, fascinating stuff, but that's all we've got time for,' beams Amanda. 'Coming up after the break, we're getting cheesy in the kitchen. That's right, fondue is back – but you'll never guess what we're sticking into it!' The cameras swing away, and a different runner rushes over to unclip our mics as Amanda turns towards us. 'Great debate, guys, lovely stuff. I wish I could have joined in, but I can never interrupt Chuck when he's talking about feminism!'

I stumble out of my chair. 'Imogen, I didn't think you had it in you!' cries Dora. 'I was getting worried. Good job! Well done, darling!' She kisses me on the cheek while simultaneously scooping me up with her left arm and taking a picture with her right hand. Where did that phone come from? 'For my daughter. She'll love this!'

'Right, well, give her my best! I'm just going to ... going to ... going ...' I stumble out of the studio, with no idea where I'm heading. I desperately, urgently need to be outside. I'm not sure where I left my coat, but I'm burning up. I see a door marked Fire Escape, a brick holding it ajar. That will do. The wind is icy, I should be freezing, but sweat is pouring down my face. For a moment, my vision turns Technicolor and then blurs to black. I slide to the ground, gulping at the air, I can't get it into my lungs quickly enough.

I don't understand why this feels so awful. This should be the highlight of my career to date. Dora Bainbridge has been putting herself through this every week for years, and she's not beside me, screaming, crying and sweating through her dress. Technically I think I won the debate, if there was a winner. This does not feel like a prize.

I wonder where my phone is. I think about the thousands of furious faces and voices, locked inside it, shaming me, judging me. Oddly enough, I can't quite connect with the idea of Adele sharing and applauding, but I can feel the strange weight of shame, grey as dishwater, heavy as a tidal wave.

The Girl could handle this. I can't.

Chapter Twenty-One

Maleficent wears a skirt suit

Harri

Harri knows she is a hypocrite. The other day, she delivered what she hoped was a rousing, inspiring speech about fearlessness. But she has never been more frightened in her life. The team has been gathered around her monitor to watch Imogen. It seems to be going well, but Harri can't hear anything that is actually being said, just the sound of her heart roaring in her ears. She's watched friends weep through their children's nativity plays, and she finally understands how they might have been feeling. She does not trust herself to speak.

'Shhh! Chuck just said something nice about Imogen, and we missed it. Oh, she was fantastic! I'm so proud.' Akila bounces on her toes, and fails to suppress a small squeal.

'Were you nervous for her? You cutie!' Kim elbows her in the ribs, and then his face darkens. 'Oh, sorry, I didn't mean – that was a little much, I was nervous for her too.'

'That was so cool!' flutes Louise. 'Go Imogen!'

Akila sighs. 'She did brilliantly. I feel quite emotional.'

Harri places her right hand on the centre of her chest. Her heart is really pulsing. She could swear that it's beating out of her, convex against her ribs, but surely that's biologically impossible.

When Dora started speaking over Imogen, everyone breathed out, an audible expression of collected disappointment. Ohhhhh. It felt like Wimbledon, watching the British hopeful stumble and unravel.

But when Imogen started to sit up a little straighter, and Harri saw the spark in her eye, there was a bang and a blast and a boom, and even before Harri had quite processed what she was saying, she knew, from Dora's face, from the presenters' faces, that her girl – The Girl – was home and dry. She'd won.

Kim is blowing smoke from a finger gun, and saying something about 'Wonder Woman realness', and Louise is squealing, and jumping up and hugging him, and looking like she might be on the brink of a dangerous all office hugging spree, and even Tabitha is saying something nice about trousers, and Akila meets her eyes and nods and Harri feels like running out for a bottle of champagne, but she knows that they need to wait until Imogen is back.

Then, a long shadow is cast from the doorway, the bubbles seep from Harri's soul, bitter bile rises at the back of her throat and coats her tongue. Like the bad fairy at the christening, Mackenzie has arrived, unheralded, in the office.

Harri blinks. Is it her imagination, or is Mackenzie wearing a long, black coat? Is that a scythe? It is her imagination,

142

Mackenzie is in a dull brown skirt suit – a shade known to the designer as 'bracken', and to Harri as 'dead hedge'. She does not harbour a weapon. She's carrying an iPad. Harri does not trust Mackenzie not to use it to harvest any souls, all the same.

'Harriet, I came to talk to you about Imogen's appearance on the talk show ... but what is everyone doing? Why aren't you all at your desks? It's not lunch break, is it?'

The Know team is frozen now, a Hogarthian tableau. Kim is balancing on one leg, just released from Louise's arms. Akila has her hands on her hips, Tabitha's palms are open, to gesture at the monitor. Harri realises she's holding her breath. She feels, and she is startled by the obscurity and specificity of the reference, the way she imagines she might if she were a guerrilla theatre director in the 1600s, and her rehearsal was getting shut down by Oliver Cromwell himself.

'Mackenzie, hello. Good to see you.' Neutralise. Neutralise. As Harri ascended the ranks at *Panache*, she read a lot of books about hostage negotiation. She's calmed the VP of William Morris, she's talked anxious starlets out of the bathrooms of their private jets. She can be a very good horse whisperer. 'We're celebrating Imogen, she was fantastic on *Good Morning Britain*. Very good for team morale.'

The trouble is that Harri knows how to bolster a fragile ego, how to wrangle and manipulate the flighty and frightened. But Mackenzie is immovable, an iron lady. Her anger is solid. 'Imogen has not promoted *The Know* in the way that was discussed. She lost control of the conversation. She barely mentioned the work of the website, or other trade titles in the Hudson portfolio. And I worry that the focus on sexual matters brings the overall brand into disrepute.'

Well, which is it? thinks Harri, angrily. You can't have too much publicity and not enough publicity. And poor Imogen had enough to worry about without bringing up matters of scaffolding. 'Mackenzie, before this happened, we discussed the fact that the British media will be taking a different approach. This sort of slot always runs as a debate. The sort of coverage you're looking for doesn't exist over here. If you want more control over it, you'll need to raise our ad spend.' From nothing. Despite the fact that she has run the numbers, made a watertight case for a proper ad campaign, and more or less been reduced to begging at meetings. Harri has thought about buying a can of paint with her own money and spraying the words 'Read *The Know*!' on bus stops.

Akila has recovered her composure and gestures to her own monitor. 'Mackenzie, if you'd like to come over here and have a look – Imogen's piece quadrupled our overall traffic overnight, and just now – it's blowing up. I can't refresh fast enough. These numbers are insane – I mean, so, so high. People are reading, they are staying on the site. I'm very confident that I can go back to Sales and bring in some serious ad revenue. We've already had a lot of interest from big brands, I've been taking a bit of a risk with some and waiting for the response after Imogen's TV appearance. It looks like it's really going to pay off.'

Kim's raised leg floats back down to earth. Louise's puce face fades to its usual pink.

Mackenzie bristles, but the display of unity seems to have sapped some of her strength. 'Make sure that this revenue actually materialises, and that there is solid evidence that these ... displays are financially viable. Because we can't justify any waste of company resources.' She stops and takes a single step towards the door. Harri wonders where the breeze is coming from – and then realises that every single person in the room has exhaled at the same time. But Mackenzie remains in the office, and gestures towards the whole team. 'You must bear in mind that Imogen – that all of you – are not just representing *The Know*. When we feel that this activity reflects badly on the rest of Hudson, we will be forced to take decisive action.'

When, not if. A curious choice of words. Fighting words. Perhaps Mackenzie expects Harri to surrender. Well, she will go down fighting, if she has to.

She stands up a little straighter and meets Mackenzie's eyes. 'That will be all,' says Mackenzie, dismissively, as if she has the power to eject her team, her gang, from their own space. Harri nods curtly. 'Yeah. I think we're done here'. She will not blink. She stares at the doorway, unflinching and unflickering, until every scrap of brown has vanished from her eyeline.

It's on.

Chapter Twenty-Two

Family stuff

Imogen

I'm the heroine of the hour. The heroine of the office. My phone flashes constantly, hot to the touch.

Even a girl called Gwen, the editor of my old student paper, has texted to congratulate me – I have no idea where she got my number. The only person who is strangely silent is Jen – not only is she supposed to be my best friend, she's the one person I know who would have been at home watching daytime TV. Even Leanne must have heard about it somewhere, she's plastered it all over Facebook, but nothing from the one person I really want to hear from. I want to ring her, but . . . I don't understand how we got here. I don't understand why I keep staring at her name on a screen and sliding my thumb away from the call button.

Eventually I find myself typing, Back for the weekend. Will I see you? Early birthday drinks? X Pressing send. And then, before I give myself any time at all to think it through, I'm ringing Mum.

'I thought I might come home and see you. If that's OK? If you're not busy?' Please be busy.

'Oh, love! That would be nice, just before your birthday, too! We'd really, really like that. I'll make your bed up.'

'Um, Mum, I didn't mention it before in case . . . I wasn't sure . . . anyway, I was on the telly. Just a little thing, in the morning. For work. It really wasn't a big deal, I just thought I'd say, I wasn't sure if you'd seen . . . '

'That's wonderful! Why didn't you say? We could have taped it!'

'It was all a bit last minute, I was . . . covering for someone else?' I have no idea where that lie came from.

'Fancy! My little girl, a famous celebrity.'

'No, Mum, that's not . . . anyway, I'll see you on Friday. Love you.'

Jen doesn't reply until after I've booked my train ticket. Sorry, away, got family stuff. Another time? No kiss.

Chapter Twenty-Three

You can be nice until bedtime

Imogen

Yooooooh-hooooooooh!

I don't know when the hinges of the gate were last oiled. No matter how gently I try to open it, it screeches, loudly, camply and cheerfully, like RuPaul welcoming contestants to the stage. I like to think I have a secret imaginary friend cheering me up the path. Go on girl, you got this! It's the happiest sound I'm going to hear for the next forty-eight hours.

Another thing I don't know is whether the carpet was originally brown with grey swirls, or grey with brown swirls. One colour has always been mutating into the other, and back again. 'At least it doesn't show the dirt,' is one of Mum's catchphrases. One day I'm going to snap and say 'Mum, it only shows the dirt.'

If I did have a secret camp, fabulous, imaginary friend, I suspect they too would emerge regally, from a cloud of smoke. But they would be on a golden throne, not an arm-chair that has yellow sponge bursting out of one side, like a popped pimple. They would be wearing a sequinned jacket, not a vest and a cardigan that appears to be made out of the same fabric as the carpet. And they would say 'Imogen, Babe! You're here!' and not 'Your mother's out.'

'Hi, Dad!' I stoop to kiss him on the cheek, breathing through my mouth. He smells. It makes me feel ashamed of him, and ashamed of myself for minding. 'Do you want a cup of tea?'

'Go on then.'

I drop my rucksack by the foot of the stairs and pad to the kitchen, over shouts of 'I better not trip over that later.' Fat chance. That would require you to get up. I give myself a little shake. Try harder, Imogen. Be nice. You can be nice until bedtime.

Dad is muttering through the hiss of the kettle. 'Heard you were on telly. How much did you get for that, then?'

Fuck's sake. 'I don't get paid, I was promoting the web-site.' Why does Dad have three different golf themed mugs? And one that says Latte All Day? This is a man who once called me a 'stuck-up cow' for drinking a flat white.

'Don't forget, three sugars.'

'But I don't think . . . ' I hold my breath and do the emo-tional maths. Apparently, the doctor said Dad is supposed to cut down on sugar, but I'm not sure I have the energy to explain this, again. Or to cope with the furious fallout when he doesn't get what he wants. 'Coming right up!'

Dad takes his Tee Time mug from me and slurps, word-lessly. This is a compliment. He has found nothing to complain about. A long minute passes. Then another.

'So!' I say brightly. 'Have you ...'

He holds his hand up. 'Shhhh, this is crucial.' He turns up the volume on the TV. Football. His favourite. I think someone is taking a corner for Chelsea. I hold my breath, and he groans. 'Christ! What was he thinking? I could have done better than that.'

Sure, Dad.

We sit in silence. This is OK. It's relaxing. Nothing is expected of me. As long as nothing disturbs the peace ...

Yooooooh-hooooooooh!

'Does that woman have to make so much noise?' mutters Dad, as if he expects Mum to vault over the gate. She opens the door.

'Immy, love! You're here!' I struggle up from the sagging sofa and throw my arms around her. Oh, goodness me, she's getting thin. I breathe in her scent, soapy, antiseptic, the lemon tang of her perfume, Sunflowers. There's more grey in her dark hair than I remember seeing at Christmas.

'Just made a tea for Dad, do you want one?'

'We should be making tea for you, the traveller from London. The TV star!'

'It's really not a big deal, it's only work, you know?'

'Well, everyone at work thought you were wonderful. Nice and clear, you really spoke up. Just like when you were the narrator in the nativity!'

'Everyone ... at ... work?' Oh, God.

'Yes, Andrea found it online, we watched it on her laptop. We all had a little tea break in the staff room. Lovely trousers you had on! And you put that bossy so and so in her place!'

'Ah, and did anyone, say anything about the ... website?'

'The what, love? They all want to know what Chuck is really like – Candace thinks he's really handsome, and she says next time, can you get his autograph? And Andrea wants your autograph!'

Usually, I'm infuriated by my mum's utter inability to comprehend reality. Mum could find a way to look on the bright side during a total solar eclipse. But she appears to have managed the ultimate in compartmentalising. She's thrilled that I was on the telly – but she's somehow been able to blank out the fact that I was talking about my sex life.

I squeeze her again, out of sheer relief, while Dad asks what's for tea.

'Your favourite, love!' says Mum, and for half a second I dare to hope that she has managed to get hold of some bao buns. We have chops, chips and peas, in my honour.

As I'm on my second slice of my other 'favourite', Viennetta (Dad: 'You'll want to watch that, you'll get porky. Men don't like fat girls') Mum makes a suggestion. 'I expect you'll be going out with Jen tonight? Early birthday celebrations?'

I shake my head. 'She's busy.' Sliding a spoon across the bottom of my bowl, I scrape up the last dribble of ice cream.

'There's plenty more, love. Do you want another slice?'

I really don't, and the reason there's plenty more is that my mum hasn't had any. She has always claimed she doesn't 'have a sweet tooth', but I don't believe her.

'Anyway,' Mum adds, 'I saw Su in Tesco and she said Jen was going to the Wheatsheaf tonight, with that other girl from school, Leanne.'

'Oh. Right.' The shock hits my body, before it hits my brain. Leanne. Pain pulses in the pit of my stomach. I will not cry.

'In fact,' says Mum, beaming, 'here's a tenner, buy a round on us! I want you to celebrate your big success.' She's reaching into her pocket. I know that she's in no position to give it – any more than I'm in any position not to take it.

I must tread carefully. 'Mum, that's so generous of you, but honestly, I'm knackered, it's been quite a week. I just wanted to stay in with you and Dad tonight. Maybe see Jen another time,' I finish, lamely. I can't bear to tell her that Jen doesn't want to see me, and I don't know why. Dad leans over and snatches the money from Mum's outstretched hand. Funny how he can move quite fast when he wants to. His face is inches from mine. His breath is hot, and I'm sixteen again, six again, and afraid.

'Imogen.'

He always starts quietly. This is the worst bit. Slowly, slowly creeping up the rollercoaster, before the descent.

'You come here, from London, full of your fucking airs and graces, and you think – YOU THINK – that now you've been on the telly with that rancid old slag, Dora Whatsit . . .' Irrationally I am grateful that in this scenario, Dora is the rancid slag . . . 'that you're too good for your FRIENDS? You're too good for the Wheatsheaf? I'm ashamed of you. I'm ashamed to call you my daughter.' The bowl flies past my right ear, hits the wall, shatters. Mum stares down at the table, where her own ice cream ought to be.

'Dad, I'm . . .'

He takes my hand, squeezing my fingers a little too hard. He has never hit me. I don't think he has ever hit Mum. But he knows exactly how to frighten us. He prises my hand back open. The tenner is now sweaty. He has tried to crumple it into a ball, but it won't retain its shape.

'Imogen, I don't want to see you until tomorrow. Get out!'

I look at Mum, wildly. 'Would you like to come?' I will fail, but I can try.

'No, love, I'd better stay here and clear up, goodness me! Accidents will happen!' She laughs, softly, and I manage to hold my breath, run from the room, grab my coat, make the gate squeal and get all the way around the corner before I sink to my knees and weep.

The Wheatsheaf is an 'old fashioned country pubbe' that is 'proud to be offering fine family fayre'. It was built in 1997. Everything here is wipe clean. If you linger too long, you might get laminated. But you can get a large glass of not entirely terrible red wine for £2.29. I head to the bar first. I need time to work out how to do this, and I need alcohol. I need to blot out the last hour.

I hear Leanne first, '... and if he gets his bonus, that's another 3k, and I've told him we're going to Florida, but he keeps going on about upgrading ... oh. Imogen. Hiya! Long time no see.' She's getting up, she's hugging me, and I'm waiting to feel the sharpness of her acrylic nails, stabbing into my back, but the embrace is painless.

At least Jen looks really, really bored.

'Jen, I didn't think you were around this weekend?' I look at her imploringly. If she had just been on the telly, I'd be hugging her, jumping up and down, squealing, buying her drinks.

'Oh, um, the family stuff got cancelled. How have you been?'

She'd know if she ever picked her phone up.

Leanne has not stopped talking, '... so, work has said

that if we smash our targets, we're doing this champagne tasting up the London Eye, have you been, Imogen? Maybe we can go to some bars, after. You can introduce me to some of your celebrity friends. You're so lucky, I've always wanted to work on a magazine, but you have to live in London and Steve says they're all stuck-up wankers ... you remember Steve? In fact, big news! You didn't like my Facebook post, so I don't know if you saw ...'

Her left hand flies up to my face and I instinctively cower, assuming she's going to make a fist. The nails narrowly miss my eyelids. 'Cost a grand, that did. Well, nearly. Nine hundred quid.'

'It's ... lovely! Congratulations!'

'Do you want to be my bridesmaid? Jen is going to be one.'

'Um, that's so nice of you, but I think I might be away ...' Why am I being polite? Why am I not throwing my wine all over her?

'I must go to the toilet,' I say, getting up, 'and so must you.' I yank Jen's elbow, and march her over to the Ladies.

Over the years, I have been very, very sick in these toilets. But something much worse is threatening to pour out of me – weeks of pent-up rage, fury, fear, bile and hurt.

'You fucking, fucking ... bitch! Why have you been ignoring me? Why are you here with Leanne? Where have you been? What's wrong with you? Have I done something? Oh, yeah, I have done something, I've been making a bloody go of my life, all by myself, while snivelling, shitty ... ex friend ... weasels are weaselling their way into bullies' ... bosoms!' I'm pacing, I'm screaming, I'm crying, all at the same time. I have never, ever argued with Jen, it's all coming out and it won't stop. 'You're being her bridesmaid? She got

Steve to piss in my shoes, Jen. Don't you remember? And then told everyone I stank because I was poor? She made me cry, she made me frightened, and you're going to be her . . . '

I'm crying so hard I can't speak any more. I want to hit Jen, an urge that scares me. My vision is blurring, and I grope for something to throw. There's a roll of toilet paper by the sink. I hurl it at her as hard as I can, but it unfurls from my hand and flutters to the ground. As I watch it settle on the floor, I fail to suppress a sob. I'm no better than Dad.

Jen is indignant. 'Imogen, it's not been easy for me, either.'

'Yeah? Which bit? Lying on the sofa, watching daytime telly, or getting your meals cooked by Su?' In this moment, I'm powerless to stop the poison pouring out of me.

'Fuck you, Imogen!' Jen snaps back. 'You have everything now. Do you think it's been fun for me, being stuck back here, feeling like a failure? Always being second best, since school? It's never my turn! What about what *I* want?'

'You gave up!'

'It's not fair!' Jen is crying too. 'I do the sensible thing, the responsible thing, and where's it getting me? Nowhere. It's you who's got the big break!'

'If this *was* happening to you, I'd be happy for you, Jen! I'd want to celebrate with you. I wouldn't be drinking with someone who tried to ruin your life!'

'Yeah, well.' Jen looks down, and up at me, and down again, weighing her words. 'I wouldn't be putting my sex life out in the open, for everyone to read about, like a . . . slut.'

I do not trust myself to speak. I leave the toilets, and return to the table, where my coat is. Where my wine is.

'Leanne. Lovely to see you, but I've got to go back to

London, Madonna's having a party. Take care!' Can I do this? Can I pull it off? I pull the coat off the back of my chair with a flourish, accidentally on purpose knocking my wine all over Leanne. 'So sorry, clumsy me! Hope it didn't go in your shoes!'

I walk twenty minutes in the opposite direction. I'm too angry to cry. Too confused. The air smells sharp, and slightly sweet. I've missed the stars. I've missed this clean, biting cold, the scent of woodsmoke, the whistles of the early birds predicting spring too soon.

But that's all I've missed.

I don't belong here. I never did.

It's too late to go back to London. I walk up and down and up and down, until I'm too cold to feel my face.

By 10.45, I decide I can risk the wheezing gate. Dad is still up. 'Good night?' he asks, without turning from the TV. I can see a single shard of the shattered bowl still glittering on the carpet.

I wake up just before six, and do not shower. I leave a note. Work emergency, getting the first train. Thanks for a lovely weekend. Lots of love, Imogen. By the time the gate has alerted anyone to my absence, I'm running down the dark road.

Chapter Twenty-Four

Out-out

Harri

Kim puts the idea in her head. Harri is becoming increasingly fond of Kim – like his beloved superheroes, he has an id and an alter ego, and the latter is starting to overshadow the former. By day, he's the quietest, shyest, most humble graphic designer a cost-conscious media company could ever hope to hire. By night – and sometimes by lunchtime, queuing for his sushi, or gossiping with Louise and Imogen, or singing along to Doja Cat when he thinks the office is empty – he's a high energy, high beam force of nature. He has the body of a runway model and the soul of a puppy. Harri has wondered whether there has been a mix-up somewhere in the universe – on another planet, perhaps an adorable dachshund is chain smoking and demanding cases of cocaine and Diet Coke.

Kim has taken an early lunch, and returned from the Supreme store drop in high spirits, laden with red bags.

('Hides the blood,' he jokes. 'It gets violent in there.') 'I've been thinking, we need a night out,' he announces, executing a miniature *jeté* as he drops into his chair. 'It's time.'

Imogen is pragmatic. 'Sure, I can do after work. Were you thinking the Jon Snow or the Coach and Horses?'

Kim pouts. 'No, no, no. Out-out. A proper celebration. All of us.' Harri watches Imogen look at Tabitha, and then look back at Kim. 'Yes. All of us,' he reiterates. Harri feels a brief stab of panic.

Her social map has shrunk, over the years. When she first turned up in the capital, with a carrier filled with knock-off Bodymap dresses and a sleeping bag, the night would usually start in Camden, the Good Mixer or an unoccupied dressing room in the old TV-am building, minesweeping any unattended drinks left by the bands her friend Liv was supposed to be looking after. Then – a blur. (And sometimes, Blur.) She has a vague memory of her early twenties, wide eyed excursions to seedy Soho. Cider and sticky sweet fizzy drinks, dancing and dancing and dancing and never going home, thinking she might be made of magic, feeling that the world was working for her, making a new friend on the dance floor of a warehouse out in Hackney or Clapton or Tottenham, then London's exotic, frightening fringes – and going in to work at that new friend's even newer magazine, seventy-two hours later. An era when luck just kept landing in her lap.

Eventually even Liv left the rackety glamour of MTV for a proper job in A&R at a record company, skirt suits and a six figure salary, with Class As as an occasional birthday treat (although she wasn't fussy about *whose* birthday). And Harri was all too willing to trade every warehouse, every festival, every party in the world for her favourite exclusive Friday night hangout – the sofa, or more specifically the warm gap between Andy's neck and his right shoulder.

Sometimes Harri can't quite work out what happened to her. She doesn't necessarily crave the grand, chaotic social productions of twenty-five years ago. But she's forgotten how to celebrate the end of a solid period of toil by actually leaving the office and going somewhere other than her flat. The Angel does not count.

Louise speaks up – well, she's squeaky and hesitant, but she's trying. 'Um, uckshully ... I've been speaking to some PR contacts who might be able to organise something a bit special. Immo, isn't your birthday coming up soon?'

'Next week. I'll be twenty-seven,' says Imogen, shaking her head in mock horror. 'I didn't want to make a big deal out of it. I was planning an early night at home, thinking morbid thoughts about Kurt Cobain and Amy Winehouse.' Imogen grimaces, and Harri tries to remember being twenty-seven. How did it feel? What was she doing? There is a whole adult person sized gap between them. Oh, God. If Harri thinks about this for too long, she's going to have to retire at the end of the week.

As she walks to the other end of the office, Harri notices that her bones seem heavier than usual, awkward in their sockets. Imagine being twenty-seven! Imagine taking leaps and bounds as you go about your day, without having your right hand drift supportively to the small of your back! These children have no idea how hard it is to try to channel a 'down with the kids' attitude when your vibe is increasingly 'help, I've fallen and I can't get up'.

Harri is saddened when she notices that as she draws

159

nearer, her employees seem to deflate a little. It's barely perceptible, but heads are lowered, sprawled limbs are brought closer to bodies, everything is a fraction of a decibel quieter. Everyone is on their best behaviour. She clears her throat. 'Sorry to interrupt, I just wanted to say – I think a team night out for Imogen's birthday is a really good idea. Send an email round, and we'll get everyone to save the date. Thanks to the birthday girl's brilliant piece, our numbers are looking really good. We've got lots to celebrate. Louise, if you're happy to be social secretary and get us organised, that would be brilliant.' Louise shakes when she hears her name, and then her whole face brightens and blooms. 'You can count on me!' she says solemnly. Did she just ... clasp a fist to her chest? Please don't salute. 'It really doesn't need to be anything too fancy,' says Harri. And then, panicking, 'No, ah, activities or anything. Just a nice bar!' She's pretty sure that she's seen appliquéd cushions and hand-made fascinators gleaming in Louise's eyes.

Chapter Twenty-Five

The Birthday Girl

Imogen

To the surprise of precisely no one, Louise loves a theme. We're ambling towards the Covent Garden piazza while she dances in front of us, skipping backwards so she can face us while telling us that this bar is rilly, rilly great, and we're all going to have a rilly wonderful time. The only thing making it bearable is Tabitha's sulky face. That's my birthday present. 'The last time I came to Covent fucking Garden,' she hisses, 'was on a school trip.' A juggler in a jester's hat beckons at her, shaking his bells. 'Fuck off!' she snarls. It must be my imagination but the points of the hat seem to droop slightly. A woman in a smart navy coat shakes her head and covers her child's ears. Well, you're going to be shocked by Tabitha's vocabulary if you've got this far into adulthood and you're still wearing mittens.

Louise leads us to a large, wooden, prefab structure. The intended effect is clearly 'alpine wonderland' – the reality is much more 'going to see Santa, in a suburban garden centre', which is especially jarring near the end of February. Harri's indulgent smile falls off her face. I had a feeling that her expectations for the evening were pretty low. She wasn't hoping for 'tea at the Ritz' – but she really wasn't prepared for 'booze in a shed'.

Gingerly, I follow Louise down some rickety wooden stairs. The first step seems to buckle beneath me, so I grab the charming, rustic bannister and immediately feel the splinters piercing my palm. When I look around the room, I'm expecting to see barnyard animals, hay, buckets of manure, maybe baby Jesus sleeping in a quiet corner, even though his own birthday is a distant memory now. But the space is beautiful. Pines, ferns, and dark green plants are all hung with warm white lights.

And now that Louise has stopped trilling and skipping, she seems to have grown a foot taller. She's nodding demurely at a beautiful woman in a black cashmere dress and saying 'The reservation is under Cameron, 6 p.m.' Perhaps it's pure professionalism, but the woman seems to acknowledge Louise with something more than respect. Maybe awe.

'Louise, of course. It's wonderful to see you. Please, follow me.'

We're led through the bar. It's quiet – it's pretty early in the evening, and I'm not sure how much call there is for a night out at a festive alpine lodge this close to spring. I see a group of four young women, posh, glossy, but slightly boiled looking, in furry stoles and hats. One touches the top of her head, presumably about to put herself out of her overheated misery – but the other three glare at her, so she scratches her ear instead.

I don't know why we don't just sit at one of the many empty tables, until Cashmere Dress Woman leads us to – well, it's like a woodland clearing. The pines are clustered together to form a secluded space, and they're woven with more white lights. Some of the trees are hung with bronze lanterns, and the table is set in front of another little wooden cabin, only this one seems to have been very thoughtfully designed, with swagged, brocade curtains in the window, and tiny red flowers in the window boxes. Through the doorway, I see a small, fully stocked, wooden bar. Cashmere Dress gestures to the table. 'Will everyone start with a glass of champagne?' I murmur 'That would be lovely,' as Akila says 'Yes please,' a little too emphatically. But not as emphatically as Kim's 'FUCK YES.'

Louise is looking pleased, relieved, a little embarrassed. She touches my arm. 'Happy birthday, Immo! Do you like it? Is it all right?' I'm so touched that my eyes start to prickle, and now I'm embarrassed too. It's easy to be cynical, to pretend not to care, and to make fun of the people who do. Louise didn't have to do any of this. I don't think she organised everything to show off. It's a genuine act of kindness.

Reaching over, I give her hand a squeeze. 'Thank you so much. This is already one of the nicest birthdays I've ever had.' Not that it has much competition. Last year, Jen and I ate an entire Colin the Caterpillar cake in bed. Sam Strong promised he'd take me out to Rules for dinner, but he cancelled just after I emerged from the shower, bleeding, having taken a razor to my pubes because I was too overdrawn for a forty pound Hollywood wax. The year before, a stiff white card came in the post. I assumed it was from Mum, but it was a rejection note from the Wessex-Solent Media Regional Graduate Scheme. I've still not spoken to Mum after the awful weekend, accidentally on purpose missing her calls. And Jen has not spoken to me. I've sent three apology texts, and they have all gone unanswered. Every time I think of our fight, the shame makes me wince. I can understand why she doesn't want to speak to me. But then, shouldn't she be ashamed too? It's too painful. I push the memory away again.

Harri is squinting at the bottle in the ice bucket, looking slightly worried. I squint too. Veuve. Blimey. 'Erm, Louise, I'm sure Hudson can cover a couple of bottles but we might not be able to run to the rest ... ' Louise flushes, and looks straight at the flowers in the window box. 'No, no, honestly don't worry, I've done quite a lot of work for these people with my ... blog. It's, ah, all thrown in.' Kim squeezes her arm. 'You absolute baller, Lou. That's so cool!'

Akila nods. 'That's brilliant. It's so generous of you to share this with us!'

'We should drink a toast!' says Louise, the hoppity-skip returning to her voice. 'Firstly, to Immo, because it's her birthday, and we love her – and not just because she's the filthiest woman on the internet!' My name is called, glasses are chinked, expensive champagne is spilled. 'But I really want to drink a toast to *The Know*! To our readers, to our amazing team, and to amazing women!'

'*The Know*!' we bellow, being slightly more careful with our drinks this time around.

'So, Imogen, you're a Pisces,' says Akila, topping herself up. 'It's the twenty-first today, so you're right on the cusp!'

Louise looks impressed. 'Wow, how did you know that?'

'Because I'm a Leo,' says Akila, grinning. 'No – I am a

164

Leo – but me and my sister Daks – such a Sagittarius, you would not believe, so commitment phobic that she makes me sign her phone contract – when we were kids, we were obsessed. We used to read *Bliss* and *Sugar* and plan our lives around them. A lad in a green jumper will make your day, watch out for crossed wires on the seventeenth, all of that. Daks got into tarot too, more than me, I was a bit spooked by it but it was good fun.'

'Of course you're a Leo,' says Kim. 'Scorpio here, with Aries rising. Your rising sign is important, because some people will not date Scorpios, period. So I have to get the horoscope conversation in early. I've given myself a second birthday in April, just in case.'

I'd expect Harri to roll her eyes at the horoscope chat, but she joins in. 'I'm pretty sceptical, but Akila, you are a total Leo. Imogen, I'm on the cusp too. August the twenty-fourth, which makes me Leo/Virgo.'

'Tabitha, what star sign are you?' asks Louise. 'Obviously it's bullshit and I don't believe in any of it, but Capricorn,' Tabitha says, icily. 'Ah, that must be where you get your sunny, obliging nature!' jokes Harri. It does not land. 'I mean, Capricorns are famous for being quite steady, aren't they? Very hardworking, and diligent. And I really see that.'

'I think there are some really cool Capricorns,' says Kim. 'Dolly Parton. Michelle Obama. Zayn Malik.'

Unexpectedly, Tabitha looks fascinated. 'Is that true? How do you know that?'

Kim looks puzzled. 'Um, I don't know! The internet? It's like knowing your multiplication tables. Although now that I think about it, I'm not absolutely sure that I do know those.'

165

I think about this all the time. 'Why do I know, say, celebrity star signs, and not French? Or why is it that, without thinking, I can remember all of the words to "Don't Stop Believin'" but I couldn't tell you, for definite, when the Second World War ended?'

Louise nods. 'I know absolutely nothing about history, any of it – but I can tell you every single *Bake Off* winner and their winning showstopper.'

Tabitha goes to the loo, Louise goes to the main bar to ask about our 'hot alpine hors d'oeuvres' and Akila asks me if I'm making any birthday resolutions. I smile. 'I love that – a personal new year. Although the actual new year was so recent that I'm not sure I can come up with anything. Did you make any, on your birthday?'

'Of course! Mine was to stop going with the flow so much. Everyone told me that after I turned thirty, I'd really find my confidence, and my voice, and get taken more seriously. But I just felt as though I had less energy to make a fuss. I kept waiting for this magical moment to arrive, I honestly believed that I'd wake up one morning and feel like an adult. After I turned thirty-five, it finally dawned on me that it wouldn't just happen. I'd have to make it happen.'

Akila is looking at me intently, searching my face for a flicker of comprehension. I wince. 'I was kind of hoping for that. I thought that maybe when I was thirty, I'd get there.'

Akila's eyes dart down to the table, then up to the ceiling, as if she's searching for her words. 'It's ... I don't ever want to say it's harder for me, but ... when you're a black woman, working in an overwhelmingly white industry, you realise that you're *constantly* going to be overlooked unless you work out how to advocate for yourself. But it's

166

exhausting. I have to make calculations the whole time, I'm always weighing up the difference between what feels assertive, when I think it, and what might sound aggressive, when I say it.'

I nod, thinking about how calm and balanced Akila is in the office. Always positive, always full of energy, but always sweet and even tempered. It had never occurred to me that she'd had to cultivate her work personality, simply to survive work.

She adds, 'Still, I think all working women have that to some extent. We're told we don't get paid enough because we don't ask enough. As if we're not asking! It's that no one listens, no one takes us seriously.'

I lean closer. Akila is so charismatic and captivating. I cannot imagine anyone *not* taking her seriously. But then I think about the number of offices where I've been stymied by a series of unspoken rules. In bars, in factories, in all of the places where I've been paid by the hour, I've been exhausted and miserable but my duties and expectations were pretty clear. In magazine offices, I've spent days in total silence, unsure of whether or not I was allowed to speak, let alone whether I could expect to be listened to. I'm desperate to know *how* Akila took charge of her career. 'What changed? How did you do it?'

Akila looks thoughtful. 'I think it got better when I did some work in the States. Over there, I was taken more seriously, and because I didn't have to beg for status validation, I could relax a bit. And I think that gave me space to show I was good, without having to tell people, and so more and more work came my way. I'd got so used to being overlooked, ignored and spoken over that I didn't realise there was so much racism in the UK. I thought it was just work.'

Akila sips her drink, and I feel a little awkward, a little ashamed. I can't imagine anyone ignoring her or speaking over her in a meeting. But when I really think, I see Lily and Katie – who are sneery, rude and dismissive of everyone, but sometimes speak to Akila in a way that makes their relationship with Harri look downright deferential. I see my own working history, a sort of living CV flashing before my eyes, and realise that the biggest, most visible difference between working in bars and factories and working in magazines might be my colleagues. In publishing, the world looks overwhelmingly white.

I let myself dream for a minute. 'One day, I'd love to work in the States. Why did you come back? Obviously, I'm thrilled you did, but ...'

She nods. 'Sometimes I wonder! I suppose I was beginning to feel a bit lost. I kept agreeing to things because I thought it proved I was ambitious. I thought I'd keep saying yes until I'd figured out what I really wanted to do, and that was taking me further and further away from working it all out. Then I heard from Harri, and I was intrigued. I loved the idea of *The Know* being a bit of a blank slate. Less money, bit more freedom. I definitely have more autonomy, more creative licence than I have done in a long time.'

I get the impression that Akila is trying to convince herself, as much as me. 'How is it going, though, really? I know our launch was slow, but traffic has really picked up. Everyone must be pleased?'

For the second time, Akila looks as though she's carefully editing herself before she speaks. 'I'm used to Management pushing and pushing, but sometimes it feels as though they really want to hold us back and stop us from growing. But that would be crazy – maybe Mackenzie is taking time to find her feet? Still, early days. I can handle them. It took me a long time to discover that people take you more seriously when you care less.' She points her chin in the direction of Louise, who looks more like she's preparing to give evidence in court than trying to track down sausage rolls. 'Maybe it's a case of giving other people room to make their minds up about you. I work so hard to look like I'm hardly working. When I was much more eager to please, and desperate to show that I had everything under control, I think it was as if I was taking myself so seriously that people could only treat me like a joke. Does that make sense?'

I nod. I think about the early, breathless days doing work experience, especially at *Panache*, when I was so desperate, insecure and keen to be seen that I squeaked when I walked. And that the more time I spent there, as the gleam dulled and I got better at getting my head down – well, that was when Harri started to notice me. Now, even though work is going well, I'm feeling chronically insecure again. I don't know why. If I could come across as being half as confident and capable as Akila, at anything, I'd ... maybe relax is too strong a word, but I might be able to go back to sleep when my pounding heart wakes me up at 4 a.m.

'How do you do it? What would you tell your twenty-seven-year-old self?' *How can I be you?*

She laughs. 'Dunno, you tell me! I think it's a bit of perspective, a bit of practice. And you're a grafter. You're talented.' I mumble a vowelless thanks, while staring at a long, slim patch of spilled champagne. It curves to the right at the bottom and looks a bit like a map of Chile. I trace it with my little finger. 'Imogen. NO! We've talked about this. You look me in the eye and say "thank you". Accept your compliments with grace and sincerity.'

Akila blows an arc of air across the table. I suspect she's enjoying an imaginary, invisible cigarette, that maybe once upon a time every tipsy profundity revealed itself through a rolling Marlboro mist. She adds, 'When I was twenty-seven, I think I just wanted to know that things would eventually work out. I think this is the toughest bit because it feels as though you've been trapped in this awful decade for ever, and it feels much harder before it gets easier.'

It sounds a little too close to home. 'I've got this idea in my head that thirty is the finish line, that if I've not done anything good by then, it's not going to happen for me. And the closer it gets, the harder it is to be inspired and excited and believe I've got a shot at achieving my dreams. In fact, I'm not even sure I could tell you what my dreams are. Until a couple of months ago, everything was so relentlessly disappointing that I was struggling to feel any hope at all. I had so much, but it was almost used up. Even now, I'm holding my breath, waiting for something to go horribly wrong. Every time I've got a proper job, the publication has folded after about six months. I think I might be a jinx.'

Akila laughs. 'Love, that's not you, that's publishing. But – I don't mean to sound condescending – you are young. Some of the best advice I had was "you're going to be thirty anyway". Or forty, or fifty, or whatever. We all give ourselves these arbitrary goals. Sometimes they motivate us, most of the time, we allow them to crush us. Don't not do anything because you're scared that you'll run out of time. We're all constantly running out of time when you think about it. That's a very morbid way of saying Happy Birthday!'

Louise is back, followed by two flustered women, who are both struggling under the weight of a giant wooden tray. 'Which one of you is vegan?' asks the shorter woman aggressively, in the tone another person might use to say 'Which one of you just ran over my mother's dog?' Akila and I exchange a look, each daring the other to mention a dietary requirement. I suppose you could call it Vegan Chicken. I'm ravenous, and my hands hover over – ooooh, a tiny cheese toasty, glistening under the fairy lights.

Instinctively, I look to Louise for permission, and she nods curtly. 'I think you have us confused with a different booking. No one here is vegan.' Where's Kim gone? I think he tried Veganuary for a bit. Except eggs. And KFC.

'Well,' says the taller woman, determined to score some points. 'The herbal puff parcels are vegan, they are made with wheat free almond flour, toasted nutritional yeast, and dandelion protein, and we have lots more in the kitchen if the vegan in the party does arrive. Because. We were told. To Expect. A Vegan. And Chef went to some trouble.' The toastie is in my hand. In order to prevent myself from laughing, I wedge the whole thing in my mouth.

Louise would literally rather die than cause a scene. This isn't hyperbole. It would be an honourable way to go. I've not known her for long, but I know her well enough to realise she is thinking of 'suddenly remembering' a recent conversion to veganism. Eventually she says, brightly, 'Well, I'm sure everyone will enjoy the puffs, anyway. A healthy alternative!' She reaches over and pops one in her mouth.

Her eyeballs seem to bulge slightly. The colour drains from her face. The muscles in her throat are convulsing. Taking Tabitha's abandoned glass of champagne, she drains it and, with great effort, swallows. 'Absolutely delicious!' she trills. 'My compliments to the chef!'

I catch Akila's eye, and she shakes her head at me, mumbling, I think, 'Don't make me laugh' through a mouthful of mini burger. The angry women return to the bar, and Louise coughs into a paper napkin. Unexpectedly, I'm hit by a wave of utter love for them both.

This is the *coup de foudre* – well, it's not love at first sight, exactly, but it feels like a thunderbolt. The start of a real romance. I've never really experienced this with anyone I've been dating. It's always been a case of getting to know someone and watching them become a little less irritating, and then a lot more irritating. Right now, I'm entirely dazzled by these women. I want to hug them hard, which is normal – but I want to smell their hair as well. That's probably a little too much.

Luckily Louise is way ahead of me. 'I just want to say,' she announces, and there's a tremor in her voice, 'I've never had this much fun ... I mean, I know it's early days, we're all getting to know each other, but, I'm really, really happy right now. I'm proud of us.'

'OK, OK, bring it in!' Akila gathers us both into her arms, and everything is as it should be. I don't even have to sniff anyone – hugging Louise is like walking into a tank filled with Miss Dior. 'I'm proud of us too,' she says, releasing us. 'There's a really good vibe here, Harri chose well!' I feel a warm body closing in behind me, as Kim joins the pile, resting his chin on the top of my head. 'You gnnuhhhs,' he says, chewing, then stumbling, choking and doubling over. Minesweeping an unattended glass of champagne, he chugs, swallows, and pats his throat theatrically. 'The fuck was that?'

Spotting a jug on the table, I pour him a glass of water. 'I think they're called vegan puff parcels.'

'Akila, you said my name?' says Harri, returning to the table. 'Oh, God, are we hugging? It's too early!'

'No, it's not!' I say, grinning widely and flinging my arms around her. Looking over her shoulder, I see that Louise and Akila are frozen in horror. This is too much. I've just hugged my boss! I've overstepped. Harri feels stiff, but her shoulders drop, and she squeezes me back. 'Damn, I guess we have a hugging office. This is where I draw the line, though. No team building exercises.' She looks at me sternly, but her mouth is twitching. 'Imogen, I want you to know that if you fall, I will not catch you. I shall leave you on the carpet with your concussion. And I don't know that we have any trained first aiders here.'

Automatically, Akila and I look at Louise. But it's Tabitha who pipes up 'I've got a certificate.' Wait, what? 'It was when I was at art college, I was helping my friend with her degree show and I needed access to a lot of bandages.' I'm overwhelmed with an urge to hug Tabitha too. Fortunately, some instinct for self-preservation stops me. I don't think I understood how lonely I had been before tonight. I only had Jen, really. Being surrounded by so much warmth makes me realise she had been cold for a long time.

Jen might not have a place for me in her life any more. But there could be a place for me, with these people. For over half a decade, I've been writing, commuting, hoping, saying

173

yes, worrying endlessly about money, doing my hobby as an unpaid job, doing a night job as my day job, and trying to make an impression in spaces that seem as scary as school, where people still care about which phone you have, and which bag you have. Until now, I've been very careful about when and where I reveal my secret self.

But I think Louise might be a kindred spirit. I doubt that she's ever pretended to be ill on the day of a school trip, rather than admitting that she can't afford to go. Yet I can sense that she might know the frightened feeling too. I'd been so sure that she was just another posh girl. Well, she is, very much, another posh girl. But maybe a lonely one too? Definitely, in her way, a freak like me. I hug her again, properly, not wanting to be first to break the contact between our bodies, not wanting to do what I instinctively do and pull away as soon as I start to wonder and worry that she might be repelled by me. I have been lonely. For a while, I've had to offer sex every time I've just wanted to be held. Oh, to touch and be touched, to be able to breathe out, in another person's arms, without condition.

'I LOVE YOU,' I mumble into her shoulder.

'What?' Understandably, Louise looks confused.

'I love *this*! Thank you. Best birthday ever!' She leans into the hug, wobbling slightly. I'm so drunk. She's so drunk. I can see Harri, weaving between tables as she comes back from the loo. Is anyone in charge?

Chapter Twenty-Six

Thirtynothing

Harri

Harri's evening is not going to plan. She knows that when you're the boss, there's a strict protocol to be observed on work nights out. You stay for two drinks and pay for all rounds. You drink plenty of water, hoping to encourage your staff to follow your example and stay hydrated. You make sure that no one gets wasted on your watch, and that when your duty of care ends, no later than 9 p.m., everyone is conscious and upright. You leave, you say 'Have fun!' and you bite your lip hard to ensure that it's not followed by 'Don't stay out too late' or 'Busy day tomorrow!'

Trays of drinks have been appearing on the table, heavy tumblers filled with something amber and fizzy, shot glass wells of sticky spirits balanced in this centre. It tastes wintry and warming, slightly herbal, quite delicious! Harri remembers this drink from long ago. Did she have it on holiday? Is it a Christmassy drink?

'Tabitha!' she leans over and prods her sulkiest employee. 'Tabitha! What's the name of this cocktail? It's very good.'

Tabitha looks startled. 'Seriously? Are you kidding? It's a Jägerbomb.'

Oh! Of course it is. 'Sorry, yes, it's been a little while.' Harri giggles and is surprised to discover that she can't stop. 'I'm an old lady, you'll have to excuse me,' she tells the table.

Louise looks panicked. Too late, Harri remembers that you should never describe yourself as 'old' to anyone under thirty. It frightens them. 'No no no no no, you're not old! You're mature. You're experienced!' Experienced is a new one. It makes Harri think of being at school and talking about fingering, which isn't very mature of her at all. She laughs again. Poor Louise. As though ageing is the worst thing that could happen to a person. As though it isn't a privilege. If you get to get old, you're still here.

Harri laughs again, recklessly. 'I am old, young lady! I'm forty-eight! You're, what, I don't know. Twenty-six?'

'Twenty-nine,' replies Louise, her flushed face turning ashen. What's wrong with her?

'And I'm twenty-seven today! Happy birthday to me! Lou, what's up?' says Imogen, who has come back to the bar holding a bottle of prosecco, with a cocktail umbrella tucked behind her ear.

Ah. Louise is a Weeper. Every single office Harri has ever worked in has had one. You blink, and in less than a second they go from zero to sobbing into a paper napkin.

'Um, Harri,' her voice wobbles, and Harri winces. 'Did you think I was twenty-six because I ... I I I, um ...' the tears are shooting down her face now, and she's addressing a decorative tree, 'because I haven't achieved enough? I'm nearly thirty and I haven't, haven't, haven't ...' she sniffs, she presses her forearm against her face, and the sleeve of her jumper sparkles with tears and snot. It reminds Harri of a spider's web, jewelled in dew. It would be quite beautiful if it wasn't so revolting.

'Oh, Louise, love, no! I didn't ...' Louise holds her hand up to stop Harri, and continues. 'Haven't achieved anything worthwhile!' Louise has lost all interest in trying to hold back her tears, she sobs, and sobs, and Imogen cradles her in her arms, murmuring 'But you've achieved loads! You're brilliant!'

Harri is too drunk to operate the heavy emotional machinery she needs to use in order to fix this. The cogs of her brain are rusting, squeaking, crumbling. Harri is trying to remember being twenty-nine, and whether that ever gave her cause to cry in an alpine theme bar. Twenty-nine is shrouded in the mists of time. Harri has a vague memory of doing maternity cover on a glossy Sunday supplement, being surrounded by braying posh girls and losing the will to live. She regards the braying posh girl in front of her with a stab of sympathy. Louise really, really cares. The Cressidas and Henriettas who used to drive her up the wall were mainly killing time, waiting for a Henry or a Hugo to give them permission to give up work and start a gift registry – sorry, family.

Tabitha says, with uncharacteristic sympathy, 'The day after I turned thirty, I nearly had a breakdown, it hit me that I was never going to be on a "30 under 30" list. I spent the afternoon in bed, just – thinking my life was over.'

Harri is confused. '30 under 30 what? The business thing? I thought that was mostly entrepreneurs? Infant coders? Or Kardashian adjacent influencers who have used their inheritance to set up a multi-billion dollar lip gloss empire?'

At least this has distracted Louise from crying. 'No, you know, media movers and shakers. Impressive people. I'm running out of time. Imogen, you'll do it! Do it for all of us!'

Harri privately thinks Louise must definitely be in the country's top percentile for histrionics. 'Look, most people don't do anything interesting before they're thirty! You need to calm down.'

She's got it wrong. Akila gives her a warning look. She knows what to say. 'Louise, you're really, really impressive, you've achieved loads, and I know you're going to go on to even greater things. It's not your fault, we all put ourselves under masses of pressure. When you work in media, it can feel like *The Hunger Games* out there.'

Imogen nods. 'Sometimes literally. Or the Instant Noodle Games, at any rate. But we're here. We're celebrating. And we have tiny cheese toasties!'

As Harri reaches across the table for the snacks, she looks up and makes eye contact with a man. She smiles and waits for him to look away, so she can convey the deep fried item to her mouth as quickly as possible. But he's smiling, and he's walking towards her. Oh, no. Is this – is he interested? Surely not. It's been a while, she's forgotten how to read the signals.

As he approaches, Harri's drunk brain is slowly working out that she might know him from somewhere. Work? Is he a friend of Rosa's? Did he go out with Giles? He looks a little too scruffy for that, most of Giles' boyfriends have been cologne ad glossy. Someone from . . . school?

'Harri, good to see you! It's been a while.'

'Hi! Hi hi hi! Ah, this is … everyone!' She points at Imogen, trying to buy herself time. 'It's Imogen's birthday today, so …'

The man seems to realise that Harri is struggling. 'I'm Tom,' he says. Then, thank goodness, 'I worked with Harri about a thousand years ago on this terrible magazine launch, *Luxus*. It never went anywhere.'

Harri could cry with relief. Yes! *Luxus*. That awful magazine for millionaires! 'How have you been, Tom?'

'Good, really good, dead busy, doing more digital stuff. Listen, I don't think I've seen you since … I'm so sorry, about Andy. He was a great guy. One of the best.'

'Yes, he was … was …'

Harri can't breathe, she needs air, but she can't trust herself to open her mouth in case she's sick, she's definitely going to be sick. She has just enough presence of mind to pull her coat from her seat, did she have a bag, she must have a bag, she's got to get out of here, she thinks she might have leaped over her own chair, clearing it in a single bound, she can't see, she's walking through waitresses, she's oblivious to the people anxiously calling her name, and she's outside, running through the piazza, looking for a taxi, looking for a secret, scarcely lit side street where no one will find her, where she can howl into the darkness.

Chapter Twenty-Seven

Professional widow

Harri

Alone, in the alley, Harri tries to steady her breath, and waits for the pain to subside.

She's been waiting for years.

She can still hear the paramedic. 'Had he experienced any shortness of breath? Any palpitations? Chest pain? Fainting episodes?'

No, no, no, no. Unless she hadn't been paying enough attention. Unless Andy, noticing the grey shadows, the later nights, the earlier mornings, the missed weekends, hadn't wanted to give her anything more to worry about. 'Was he a smoker?' No. He hated it. She'd given up for him, more or less.

Apparently sometimes, hearts just stop. Literally and otherwise.

Harri needs to centre herself, regroup. She's OK. She's alive. She's got through winter. She's had a little too much to drink, but she's a relatively solvent adult woman, in the twenty-first century. She can press a button on her phone and someone will take her home. She rewinds through the evening. What was happening, before Tom arrived? Imogen. Birthday. *The Know*. All of those young women, under her care, talking – moaning – about their bloody careers, their insecurities, their anxieties and fears. Something weird had shifted. Youth was supposed to mean confidence. Being a go-getter, untouched by tragedy, feeling as though you had nothing to lose. Harri had lost everything, and she was supposed to sympathise with people who were sad because some boring business website hadn't put their name on a list?

But a memory, a feeling, has been knocked loose. Harri hasn't wanted to remember the end of her twenties for a reason. Now, she realises how vulnerable she was. How naive. Lit up by hope, soaring, untouchable. Most of the time, her career had seemed to be running itself, carrying her along with it. She felt sure of herself. Her anxieties and insecurities came from a different place. From the back of a Prius, Harri thinks about her twenty-seven-year-old self, and twenty-seven-year-old Imogen, and composes a speech she will never be able to give to either of them:

You will meet people who promise everything, people who seem to flood you with love, who drown you with it, and then kill you with contempt. You will meet people who claim that they want someone to complete them, when they mean that they are so frightened that they are missing something that they're too scared to give any of themselves away. You will meet people who are so fucked up and angry that they will make it their mission to tarnish your shine.

But if you're incredibly lucky, you'll meet someone who is kind and decent. They will want you to grow strong and sure. They will let you build your home with them, inside them. They will never make their own not-enoughness into an excuse to use you up. They will fill your life with joyful noise, the sound of their footsteps in the hall will become the beat of your heart. And all they will ever ask of you is that you love them and let them love you back. THAT'S what matters. That is happiness. And nearly everything else you think you want is bullshit.

Chapter Twenty-Eight

A love story

Harri

When Andy arrived, Harri was in no fit spiritual condition for anything. It had taken her several long, bleak weeks to get over The Bad Man. And that's using 'over' in its most generous sense.

TBM was very much her type, at the time. He was six and a half feet tall, eyes like the centre of the molten chocolate lava cake in Scott's, shoulders you could take a camping trip on. He was the epitome of gracious living. He looked and talked as though he had fallen out of a catalogue. (One of those smart interiors catalogues that Harri sometimes still gets sent by mistake. Not the Argos catalogue.) TBM did not have a car stereo, he had a Blaupunkt. He did not make coffee in the morning, he fired up his Keurig. And when she spilled it on his sheets, he'd whimper 'My Pratesi!' as opposed to saying 'Hey, don't worry about it!' Well-meaning friends kept asking Harri if she'd read *American*

Psycho. Of course she had. She was trying very hard not to think about it.

The trouble was – one of the troubles, it was a troubling time – the awful love affair? Dalliance? Ruinous and soul crushing obsession? – coincided with the Year Of Anal. Every single women's magazine was claiming, audaciously, that today's cool, confident woman loved it up the ass. If you did not do butt stuff, you were a pussy, in every sense. Harri has since spoken to the people who would have been responsible for this. They deny it emphatically, but she would swear on a stack of bibles that *Glossy* ran, as a coverline, 'First date anal: It's the new shaking hands.'

Harri was secretly convinced that TBM was constantly on the brink of leaving her for a yachtful of supermodels, and that the way to keep him in her life was to keep letting him go around the back. No, not letting him. Begging him. Telling him it was her absolute all-time favourite thing. Her head kept telling her that TBM's perfect magazine lifestyle was based on bollocks. She knew this, because she made the magazines. But in her heart, she believed that only TBM's endorsement could make her life truly magazine worthy.

Harri was haunted by a book even more frightening than *American Psycho*. It was called *The Rules*, and it was filled with demands that were as confusing and arbitrary as a maths exam. 'If he calls you on Tuesday and asks you out on a Friday, you may say yes! But if he calls on a Thursday and asks you out on a Saturday, don't go! Say no!' There may have also been a very specific way of preparing a chicken that somehow forced the eater to propose marriage. Maybe the chicken had tequila in it. It was a black and white, aggressively heterosexual world in which, if the magazines were to be believed, women only loved men, and men could only be persuaded to love women back if they learned the dating version of close-up magic. 'Was this your card? The one that says we're registered at John Lewis and that guests must RSVP by the twenty-fifth?'

Out loud, Harri and her friends noisily mocked *The Rules*. Still, they made up their own set. Any sexual hang-up was forbidden. To be a modern, open minded woman, you had to put out and shut up about any misgivings you might have about, say, the pop music videos that looked like pornography, or the expression 'post feminism', or paying strangers vast sums of money to pour hot wax on one's labia. (It was a great period for lazy journalists and magazine staffers, because every week, they could commission a debate about waxing. 'It's reductive, it's creepy, it's antifeminist!' 'It's ironic, it makes me feel more confident, for another twenty quid they'll stick on a sparkly butterfly!')

For Harri, the main rule was about wanting. She wasn't allowed to want because she was a woman who had everything. A great career, sex on tap, the Atkins diet and a very cold, hair-free vulva. Her sex life was a free for all. The only love that dared not speak its name was the romantic kind, which was to be sneered at. Every other week, whichever magazine Harri happened to be working on would run a piece assassinating the (fictional) character of Bridget Jones. Professionally, she lived and breathed freedom, sashimi, seventeen speed vibrators. Privately, secretly, she wanted someone to stay in with, someone to come home to. Someone kind who smelled nice and wore lovely jumpers. The opposite of TBM.

Harri had been helping out on a doomed project, *Luxus*,

Hudson's failed magazine for millionaires. She staggered into the boardroom on a Monday morning, hungover from a christening, of all things, wheelie case creaking, mascara on her chin. She decided to sit beside the one guy who looked rougher than her. His jacket looked as though it used to belong to an Edwardian undertaker. His hair hadn't just been blow dried, but blow dried, apparently, by Frank Lloyd Wright. His trainers would suggest recent, major orthopaedic surgery, or significant prowess on the basketball court. He eyed her with interest, which was fair, because she had been squinting at him, baffled, for a good three minutes. As he told her his name, he nodded, as though thinking, 'Yeah, that's what I'm called. Sounds good.'

For twenty minutes, a table filled with overpaid thirty-something men named Tom and Matt compared their hangovers. Then one of the Toms suggested that the *Luxus* meeting be moved to its natural environment, the pub. 'We'll catch up with you. I need to discuss the flatplan with Harri,' said TBM. Harri was about to protest, in the strongest possible terms. She needed to be sitting in a place where she could order something that had melted cheese on it. Then, she looked into his eyes. Oh. Oh, yes. Oh, no. Oh, fuck.

The hottest, and most shocking thing he did was listen. 'Tell me everything,' he said. So she did. 'I was thinking about a series with leading architects writing profiles of the artists they love. I've been reading about Santiago Calatrava, and I think he'd write something brilliant on Calder. And instead of standard celeb interviews, what about calling it a "conversation between creatives". Leo DiCaprio is in that Scorsese film coming out next year, we could get them to interview each other. And I think it would be fun to have a really retro, smart, funny gossip column. I'm sure we could get a big designer to write it – well, obviously I'd probably end up ghosting it.'

TBM did not look away. Every few seconds, Harri would feel painfully self-conscious and uncomfortable, and drop her gaze down to the table, but when she forced herself to come up again, there he was, unmoving. He wasn't undressing her with his eyes. He was taking her flesh off the bone. The waves of lust were so sharp, so acute, that she had to shuffle around in her chair in order to ease them. Touch me, she thought, while her tongue flapped frantically in her mouth and flung out professional sounding thoughts about fine art and fast cars and whether sherry was the new cognac. For goodness' sake, please touch me. I'll give you money.

She was speaking too quickly, hands spinning and flying, desperately trying to disguise her wanting. When he interrupted her, he spoke slowly. His eyes moved to her neck, her collarbone, her right hand. 'Oh. You have a cut on your little finger.'

She did. Right below her cuticle, a comma, not a millimetre long, in gleaming crimson. That was the part of her that he was prepared to touch. Shame pulsed in the pit of her stomach and bloomed through her body. She was repulsive, sticky. She wanted him. How could he possibly want her?

'Sorry.' Why was she sorry? 'I must have caught myself on a nail, I move my hands a lot when I talk.'

She realised later that his next words were straight from the TBM playbook. 'It's because you have an intensely passionate nature.' He traced her tiny wound, with his own little finger.

At first, when his lips were on hers, the gesture was solemn, chaste. Harri was not chaste. She groaned, she squirmed, she pushed her tongue against his. He withdrew. 'We have to leave.'

He stood up, and Harri trailed behind him, looking mournfully at her wheelie case. I'll come back and pick it up tomorrow, it will be fine, I can buy another toothbrush. He was silent in the corridor, silent in the elevator. Did he really, really want her? Would she get a call from a PA in a couple of days, a humourless woman saying 'He has requested that you be taken off the project,' the exasperated note in her voice making it painfully clear that Harri was the latest in a long line of foolish girls to throw themselves at her boldly dressed boss?

The taxi appeared as soon as TBM extended his elbow, because the universe ensured nothing was ever permitted to keep him waiting. He moved like a leading man and smelled like big tips. He leaned back into his seat and stared at her, and studied her, and did not kiss her.

The day was dull, the traffic heavy, grubby, flashing rubies muted by the mist. In other cities, every horn, every puddle, every stale croissant feels like it could mark the start of an *MGM Parade*. In London, especially in Soho, Harri could have been on her way to do a murder, and the city would have remained indifferent. It was a shabby, patterned carpet, entirely oblivious to the party on it, raging, spilling, staining. She picked at her scab and blotted the blood on her hem.

Harri was not surprised when the taxi pulled in front of a familiar hotel, a place she went often for press junkets, preview screenings. Neither was she surprised when the receptionist greeted him warmly, and by name. Still, he stared at her in the lift without blinking, even when Meryl Streep got in. And when they reached their door, and Harri said 'Oh my God did you see ...' he held his index finger to her lips but did not touch them. And when he opened the door, he told her to stand in front of the window.

Where? One wall of the room was all window, broken into squares by a heavy iron framing. From here, Harri could see Old Soho in surprising detail. A venerable deli, tubes of cannoli stacked into pastry pyramids on the counter, old neon blinking and crackling overhead. She saw a door left ajar, a 'Models Upstairs' sign written in Sharpie marker.

'The straps of your dress – do they untie? Are they real bows, or ... no, don't turn around. Keep looking out of the window.'

Harri could have walked away. Perhaps she should not have reached up to tug the bow. It came undone in her hand, like a boot lace. She didn't know it would yield to her touch so quickly.

The bodice of the dress fell away to her waist, exposing her bare back. Soho moved silently, below her, as TBM's breathing became more laboured. As instructed, she waited, listening to the sound of his stare. Then she reached for her zip and released the rest of her dress.

In that moment, she felt like a Model, Upstairs. In the full beam of his wanting, she was briefly able to escape herself. Harri knew he was objectifying her. It was reductive. Yet, she felt magnified, a moth made enormous in the projector light of his gaze.

Briefly, it crossed her mind that she really wasn't wearing

the right knickers for this. But if TBM wanted a lingerie model in silks, he could have summoned one in seconds. Sir was welcome to inspect the goods, but the final sale had already been agreed upon. He'd chosen grubby, hungover Harri, unshowered and bleeding. She felt feral. She could have pissed on him, bitten him.

Harri took three certain steps across the hardwood floor, but when she reached the rug, her confidence had failed her. 'Changed your mind?' he asked, as she stood beside the bed, and it sounded like a challenge, so she threw herself on top of him and kissed him hard, pushing her lips against his, like a teenager trying to win a dare.

For a moment, he let her, then he kissed back, just as ferociously, rolling over and pushing his full weight on top of her. She wrapped both of her bare legs around one of his denim clad calves, squeezing him tightly between her thighs. She wanted to use him, rocking against him, rubbing and rubbing, until she had erased his essence from the room, escaping into a space where there was nothing but the heat and throb of her body, the flashing lights behind her eyes, everything swelling and swelling before it broke and burst. She heard a distant, animal grunt. When she blinked her eyes open, she realised it had come from her own throat.

Later, TBM would tell her that he'd been very upset about her orgasm, because she had soaked his Evisu jeans, and he'd had them imported specially from Japan. At the time, he rested his palm heavily against the curve of her belly, barely above the pubic bone. I am formulated, sprawling on a pin, when I am pinned and wriggling on the wall, she thought, as he touched her very slowly with his other hand, running an index finger from the lowest, wettest part of her, all the way up to her clit. It was too sensitive, too much, and Harri tried to squirm away, but he pressed his palm down harder and kept stroking her, testing her, exploring a part of her body that she barely knew. She felt powerless now, vulnerable and peeled. He stroked and circled and pushed, gentle but relentless, until she felt the swelling start again, and pour out of her.

When she opened her eyes, the reason for TBM's unearned confidence was springing up proudly, at a 135 degree angle. She rolled a condom down to the base, registering the textbook perfection of his penis. It could have been a teaching penis. Kneeling, she positioned herself on top of him and looked him directly in the eye again, without smiling. Pinned and wriggling once more. Leaning back on her palms, to better angle herself for her own selfish needs. This time the waves of pleasure were inside and outside, over her head, drowning her even before the full tsunami hit.

TBM touched her forehead, and looked at his fingertips with surprise, and some distaste. 'You're very sweaty,' he told her.

They ordered room service, they drank beers from the minibar, they fucked again, they watched the snooker. Well, he put it on and she pretended to be interested. By 10 p.m., he had somewhere to be, and Harri refused to ask him for any further details. By 10.32 p.m., Harri was still in the suite, and wondering what he was doing, and who he was with. By 10.47 p.m. she was obsessed and she already hated herself for it. Eventually, she fell asleep with all the lights on, the words 'you're very sweaty' playing on a loop in her brain.

Like *Luxus* itself, the entanglement went on for much, much longer than it should have done.

Sometimes TBM would praise Harri extravagantly, sometimes he would ignore her, and sometimes he would put her down, quite cruelly. She'd vow that she was never going to speak to him, see him, or look at him outside work, then she would blink and be in a black cab gazing at the streetlights gleaming gold against the water of the Thames, on her way to his Docklands flat, where they would fuck like people in a play. She always felt like the understudy. Everything about his life was arranged for performance, which meant there was no intimacy left for her. Harri spent a lot of time telling people she was fine. She lost a stone in weight. The scratch on her little finger never healed, not properly.

But in the final days of *Luxus*, when she was pinned, not wriggling any more, trapped under the weight of her own heavy heart, who should turn up but dear old Andy, daft Andy, geeky Andy, Andy who Harri hadn't seen since graduation, Andy who Harri hadn't known all that well, but who once missed an entire Depeche Mode gig and stood outside the G-Mex centre with her, in the cold, because Harri was convinced that she had just taken some dodgy Ecstasy and might need a lift to hospital, imminently.

Andy's work in the art department was so strong that it meant *Luxus* limped along for an extra couple of months. Over cheesy baked potatoes in the caff on the corner, Harri and Andy discovered they lived about fifteen minutes' walk from each other in Camden, and that they had both just been to the same screening of *The Leopard* at the Curzon, and that they both had tickets for Depeche Mode at Wembley. She thought he'd married his old girlfriend from

Manchester, a Laura or a Lara? She was Laura, they had not got married, she was now living in California with a computer genius and had three children. Andy had been the drunkest person at their very glamorous wedding. Not, he stressed, that he'd been drowning his sorrows, but because he was quite jetlagged, and Californians are weird. And the wedding breakfast had been very salady.

After work, Harri and Andy would travel back to Camden together, and usually have a quick half at the Elephant's Head, then another, then a curry. Sometimes Harri might say 'I really need a quiet night, I've got to put some laundry on, I haven't spoken to my mother for a fortnight and she's furious with me,' but within five minutes of closing her door, Harri would be reaching for the phone, or hearing its ring, and the voice on the other end would make her think *I don't ever want to be away from you.*

The Matts and Toms teased her. At first, Harri wasn't upset or offended. Just baffled. 'Andy? My old mucker, Andy? Known him for years! What are you talking about?' It was TBM who realised she was in love with him. He sent flowers. A lavish, phallic, red, pointy, hedge sized bouquet. She read the card and assumed the florist had made a mistake and meant to send them to some other girl. He called and called, and Harri would be laughing at something Andy was saying, oblivious to the phone buzzing in her bag. Eventually TBM confronted Harri at her desk. It took her a moment to tune into what he was saying, because she was trying to recognise the rock star on his shirt.

'Is it serious . . . ' he hissed, 'actually serious, between you and that . . . spod?'

Oh! It was Chairman Mao! A man responsible for the

persecution of tens of millions of people, now an ironic, expensive fashion joke on TBM's chest.

'Who? Andy?' She smiled sweetly. She wasn't sure that she could have told him, even if she wanted to. But she didn't want to. 'Why?'

When TBM became angry, which was often, his rage came from sheer confusion. Why isn't the world working for me? Why am I not getting exactly what I want, when I want it? He had arranged his life so carefully, for the complete avoidance of disappointment and pain, and so he had no emotional processing facilities. In that moment, Harri realised he was a human show home. He'd seemed gleaming, and perfect, but the cupboards were empty, glued shut. Nothing would happen if you tried to turn a tap on. What you saw was what you got. All along, he had been telling Harri who he was. Finally, she believed him.

Why Andy? Because he was profoundly, shockingly kind and decent. Because in the past, even Harri had written him off for being too boring, too nice, and he had sensed that she needed a friend, and been that friend, without ever once attempting to get into her knickers. In fact, Harri had caught herself having knicker removal related thoughts about him and felt embarrassed, ashamed. Andy probably didn't think of her in that way, at all. Was she even his type?

But then, she thought her type was a chiselled, chilly designer outfit addict, a misogynist who could validate her by hating her less than the other girls. It turned out Harri's type was a man who could never walk past a dog without petting it, someone who frequently gave away all of their loose change to anyone who asked for it, who sang his own words to the *Countdown* theme, who let her eat egg and

194

chips on her knees on his sofa and laughed when she got ketchup on the carpet.

TBM wouldn't have understood any of this. But Harri knew how to salt his wound.

'The thing about Andy is that he's very cool, very secure in himself. He's not one of those men who tries too hard,' she said, slowly and meaningfully. She hadn't made such prolonged eye contact with TBM since they'd had sex for the very first time. 'And,' it was cheap, but she couldn't resist. 'He has the biggest penis I have ever seen.'

The universe should have punished her for such an audacious invention. But her lie turned out to be true.

Chapter Twenty-Nine

Imposter syndrome

Imogen

It's been a weird couple of weeks. Things in the office have been a little strained since Harri ran away from my birthday party. Allegedly, her occasional irritable bowel syndrome flared up and got the better of her – she fell victim to stress, strong alcohol and deep fried cheese. Louise was especially concerned and offered to make a formal complaint to the bar, but Harri has told her, quite tersely, to drop it.

Harri's mood is puzzling, because *The Know* appears to be doing really well. Our numbers keep going up, Akila is constantly meeting with new advertisers, and most tellingly of all, Lily and Katie are only coming in for a couple of hours a week, and they always look exhausted, and pissed off. Usually, they circle with a sort of dark energy, like vultures who suspect they can smell future carrion.

I rewrote an unpublished blog about wanking when lonely, framing it as a celebration of the joys of self love. I was asked to go on *Woman's Hour* to talk about masturbation and the Millennial Woman. The presenter was very open minded and kind, and we spent so much time trying to work out who or what the Millennial Woman might be that I wasn't forced to really get into things, as it were. I only spent one night wide awake with a pounding heart, and I threw up all of my morning coffee in a very roomy BBC Broadcasting House toilet cubicle, but I felt fine for the rest of the day. A handful of men called me a whore on Twitter, but only one could spell it correctly.

Still, there is An Atmosphere in the office, and we are all sensitive to it. I'm starting to realise that Akila is very good at keeping Harri mellow and balanced. It's Akila who says 'well done' and 'this is great' and 'thank you'. Harri used to do this, but increasingly she seems to prefer 'this isn't aspirational enough' and 'where's that piece?' and 'I wanted this an hour ago'.

'She's very stressed,' I said, trying to comfort Kim when Harri told him his illustration for my piece on ethical non monogamy looked like a logo from a public information film about nuclear war. (Once we'd googled it, we all spent the afternoon worrying about nuclear war instead, which made a change.)

Louise has taken to starting every pitch suggestion by whispering 'You're going to hate this, but . . .' I think she'd annoy Harri less if she was writing directly onto a blackboard with her nails. Tabitha is building herself a protective exoskeleton out of a series of increasingly elaborate capes. She had a screaming stand-up fight with Harri yesterday, I wasn't entirely paying attention but it seemed to end with Tabitha flouncing out at 11 a.m. to go to the British

Museum to look at bugs 'for research'. Any questions that any of us might have had were halted by Harri, who looked at us with an expression that could have curdled gin. I am still the golden girl, and my pieces about waterproof vibrators, sexy bits in books and vulval ejaculation have all 'done numbers' – but Harri will not give me permission to write any piece that does not require an anecdote about something that happened in, on or around my vagina. I am also drinking a small bottle of Pepto-Bismol every day, but that may be unrelated.

I need to ask Louise for an email for the Disney+ publicist, but the thought of putting it in the loathed Slack channel makes my intercostal muscles twang with anxiety, so I decide to do something radical. I stand up, shaking out my poor, crumpled heap of bones and stretching myself into the approximate shape of a human being, and move my body by a bare 12 inches in order to position myself behind Louise's desk. 'Oi oi! I have a question for you.'

Louise looks flustered. 'Immo! Hello! Hi! What's up?' She has spun around quickly – very, very dangerous in these chairs – in order to face me in a casual, friendly, natural way, with her back to her monitor. There is nothing casual or natural about this, I know. There is a protocol if someone approaches you directly while you're at your desk. You grunt 'WHAT?' without letting your eyes leave your screen. There is also nothing casual or natural about the way that Lou is moving her mouse behind her. She's trying and failing to shut down her browser.

'Everything OK?' I say, eyeing her screen.

'Yeah, yeah, good, so good. I've been looking for case studies for that new party drugs piece we're doing, and I'm interviewing this dominatrix about her Only Fans . . . what? What are you looking at? What have you seen?'

Nearly every browser tab on Louise's screen is open on the Good Food website. I can see a recipe for Chicken With Borlotti Beans and Cavolo Nero. I think I can make out a Google search for Homemade Cardamon Marmalade. 'Is that what you're having for tea?' I ask, gesturing behind her.

'Shhh! Shut up! Sorry, but *shut up.*' Louise has become very flushed. I know she's upset, because her fringe has separated, and a tuft of hair is pointing at the ceiling. This is how her body responds to professional stress. It tries to signal to potential predators that she is daffy, flaky and not worth attacking.

'Dude! Are you OK? It's just some chicken.'

Louise is now puce. Most of her hair is now springing up from her scalp, turning ginger under moonbeams of pink neon. She looks like she's been forced, reluctantly, to have a go on the Van De Graaff generator on the school trip to the Science Museum. Is she crying?

'Immo . . .' She is crying. It sounds as though she is addressing me as 'Bumhole'. 'Immo, I, I, don't belong here. OK? I can't do . . . it. I'm. big . . . big failure.'

'Louise . . . love. It's OK. You'll be OK. Let's get out of here. Let's get you some air.'

Louise looks panicked, and gestures to the office. 'Will we get in trouble?' She sounds so plaintive that my heart breaks. For a moment, I'm back at primary school. Anyway, we won't get in trouble. Harri is out at a meeting, Kim says he's at the dentist – but he winked as he said it, which makes me think he may just have taken the afternoon off to hoof nitrous at some sort of day rave. Tabitha is reading her WhatsApp, and all I can see on her computer is a screen filled with Saint Laurent handbags. Even the intern is skiving. She's supposed to be transcribing an interview but I can hear from here that she is listening to 'A Whole New World' from *Aladdin*. Bloody hell. And we're the sharpest minds to disrupt new media, apparently.

With a jerk of my chin, I gesture to Tabitha and her scrolling. 'I reckon we're fine. Harri can't tell us not to take a mental health break.' Louise looks a bit panicky, so I add 'If you like, I'll tell her that I started crying over chicken and you took me out for a few deep breaths and a glass of wine.' Louise is solemn. 'I don't think we should have wine.' So, trying to be as low key as possible, I gather our coats and settle her in the nearest Pret with a hot chocolate and a Love Bar.

'We don't have to talk about anything if you don't want to,' I say. I might not be able to talk about anything at all, as I've just burned my tongue. Luckily with Louise it doesn't take much to start her off.

'So I've been reading about this thing called imposter syndrome. And I think I have it ... only the opposite. Because I hate *The Know*. I shouldn't be here. But nowhere else will hire me. I just want Harri to like me, and I keep letting her down. And Tabitha is so mean!'

'Really mean. But she's awful to everyone, it's definitely not just you.'

'I didn't tell you this. A couple of days ago, I pitched this idea to Harri. I wanted to do a recipe section. You know my blog?'

I do know about Louise's blog. It's called Truly Scrumptious, and it mostly features pictures of Lou holding pale pistachio macarons next to her pink, smiling face. She has recipes for Victorious Sponge, 'to celebrate life's little wins' and Marry A Millionaire shortbread. Sometimes there are photos of her friends trying her recipes. They all dress as though they're on their way to a wedding on the outskirts of Oxford.

The thing is that while Lou's blog is very much not for me, I'm sure it's for someone. She's executing a much-loved aesthetic, and she does it well. If there are nine million branches of Oliver Bonas between Westminster and Marble Arch, there must be a billion people who want to make Victorious Sponge. It's certainly well produced. You can tell that she puts the hours in.

'I love your blog!' I beam, ignoring the rising wave of nausea brought about by an easy lie.

'Well, Harri doesn't. She said "Food isn't really our thing," and I tried to tell her that I love it. I live for it! She sighed and told me to go back and read Our Bible, and that The Girl, you know, our target audience, is spending all of her money on vintage vinyl and zodiac readings, and she won't be,' here, Louise leans forward on her elbows to make air quotes and knocks her hot chocolate all over the table. '"Fucking about with a savarin mould."' This triggers a fresh batch of tears. 'I just – look, Imm, I know what Harri means, but – am I not The Girl too? Aren't you? We can't pour our whole lives and all of our energy into making something for … for … for … I don't know, TABITHA?'

I reach for Lou's hands, and then drop the left in order to grab a napkin and mop up the hot chocolate with my right.

'Maybe we can change Harri's mind? I'm sure that over time, we can persuade her to let you do some food stuff.

And if not – well, you know, the blog is great! Couldn't you do that full time? It would be a bit risky, I know, but maybe you could find a part time job, and I'm sure ...' Louise cuts me off. 'My dad would be furious. He'd probably stop paying my rent. He paid for Leith's, for the MA in Medieval Literature that I didn't finish, because bloody hell, Imogen, Medieval Literature? Have you ever tried to read any? I mean, no one should have taken me seriously, you shouldn't be allowed to attempt it. Anyway, he called me a dilettante. And when I got this job he said this was my last chance and if I quit I'd have to do a law conversion.'

I drop Louise's other hand. Her dad pays her rent? His solution to his daughter's career crisis would be to pay for her to do another degree? These are Louise's problems? Not, say, a father who says things like 'Well, if these magazines aren't paying you, why should I give you any money? It should be coming out of their pockets, not mine.' Not that he has any money to give me.

I'm torn between shame and fury, maddened by Louise's entitlement, her cluelessness. Can't she suck it up and make it work? I've made it work – I think of the places I've lived and worked, the weeks when I've eaten nothing but tuna and rice. Louise can afford to fuck up, over and over again. She can wear her fear and insecurity weepily and volubly and know that someone else will rush to rescue her, and shore her up. I do not have the luxury of expressing this much self-doubt, out loud. And she's just learned about imposter syndrome?

Louise's tear-stained face, her visible fragility, is infuriating. I burn through so much energy trying to hide my own brokenness. Yet when you're wealthy, when you grow up believing that the world wants you to be safe and happy, you can just dump your pain on the table of a cafe and wait for someone else to clear it up.

I've had desperate moments when I've combed some of the darkest corners of the internet to find ways of making money. I don't think Louise has ever gone on Craigslist and come close to selling sex to keep a roof over her head – but her accommodation is still paid for subject to the whims of a manipulative man. She's just as frightened and unhappy as I have been, when I didn't know how I would pay for food. Her problems might not seem real, but she can't see a way out of them, either. And this is Louise, lovely kind Louise. Her head is in her hands. 'I'm so sorry,' she says, quietly. 'I don't know why I'm like this. I've always been like this. I'm just not ... good enough.'

It occurs to me that anyone walking past our table might assume that Louise has just been dumped or been cheated on. Tears, chocolate, a crumpled pile of paper napkins, all universal symbols of hurt and heartbreak. I think of being a woman weeping, and of hearing women weeping, sometimes over a sandwich, sometimes in the street, and usually outside offices, behind cubicle doors. As secretly and silently as we are able. Because we're just not good enough. Because we're only ever one mistake away from catastrophe and collapse. Because we have too many feelings, and too many ways to fail.

'Imogen? What am I going to do?'

'I don't know, love. I suppose – well, what do you want to do? If Harri was a little nicer, and let you write about food, would you stay?'

'I guess, for now. I need to get promoted before the end of the year, according to my Five Year Plan.'

'You have a five year plan? Like Stalin? What else is on there?'

'What you'd expect, really. Either become editor-in-chief somewhere or turn my blog into a destination website, grow my social following, get a book deal ... don't you have a plan?'

What do you mean, get a book deal? Where's the part where you write the book? 'Not really, I'd like to live in a less awful flat, pay off my credit card debt, stay employed. But I've never been a big planner. I mean, I've worked on two magazines that shut down overnight – one where senior management did a midnight flit with everyone's money. I've done shifts in a brewery where I've picked up trench foot. It really keeps your ambitions in check, getting trench foot in the twenty-first century.'

'But you're ambitious, obviously. Have you tried bullet journalling?'

'I don't know. No, not the bullet journalling – I don't think that's for me,' I say, shaking my head and hands as Louise starts to pull a rose gold notebook from her bag, 'but ambition, it confuses me. If you'd asked me a few years ago, I'd have said that I was extremely ambitious. I think I had a lot more self-belief, and I'm not sure why, or where it came from. Now, I've spent so much time trying and failing that I'm not sure what I'm allowed to want. I love being at *The Know*. Well, I don't hate it.'

'Well, of course you love it. You've got this massive following now, you get to go on TV. You're growing your profile.'

I grimace, a little, thinking of my nascent media career and the fear/relief cycle I'm stuck in. 'Well, I love writing.

All I want is to get paid to write all day, and ideally not get trench foot again. Oh, Louise, I don't know what to tell you. I don't think I have any good advice. Just, maybe, give it another month? I'm sure this part is the most stressful bit. Maybe when we're a little bit more established, Harri will give us some more freedom.'

'You might be right. Thanks Immo, it's been good to get it off my chest, anyway. Shall we go back?'

We amble back to the office, me making neutral noises as Louise tries to sell me on the virtues of bullet journals. Am I ambitious? Can I make a place for myself in the world, without pushing anyone out of my way? I think of what Louise might do if she left *The Know*, her privilege, the power she holds by way of default, the back-up plans she has. I couldn't leave if I wanted to. I have nowhere else to go.

Chapter Thirty

Cachet

Imogen

Back at my desk, I'm staring down the barrel of a hundred Slack notifications when something – someone – makes me jump. Harri.

'Imogen? Quick chat?'

Instinctively I flinch. A 'quick chat' means I must have done something wrong.

I follow her to her desk where she sits down – I stand – and yet she retains all power.

'So, Imogen, what are you going to do for us next?'

'Well, I'm setting up some interviews with those feminist porn directors, and I've got . . . '

'The threesome piece did brilliantly but we need to beat it. Our traffic needs to keep growing. And the numbers on your latest pieces haven't been so strong.'

'Well, I don't think they were ever going to be as . . . you know, clicky . . . '

'That's exactly the problem. We need clicky. You need to keep capturing people's attention. This well-meaning, earnest feminist stuff you keep pitching won't bring enough people to the table. What else have you got for me?'

I think my CV might claim that I thrive under pressure. Now, the pressure is making me nauseous. The air seems thinner, my ears might pop. Harri is both shoutingly near, and far away.

'Harri, I ... I ... I'm really sorry ... I don't know.' What's wrong with me? I must have at least fifty blog posts I could recycle, other pitches I could tweak, angles I could add. But fear has descended like rolling fog, I can't seem to see my own thoughts. It's as though Louise has infected me with some sort of emotional flu.

Harri sighs and seems to soften a little. 'Basically, Upstairs – management – have decided we're the victims of our own success. The threesome performed so brilliantly for us, so early, that now everything else needs to do twice or three times as brilliantly.' Harri looks at me, earnestly – as if she's asking for something entirely sensible, logical, reasonable. What's three times as brilliant as a threesome? A ninesome?

What can I do? 'Maybe I could try to get an interview with that revenge porn campaigner ...'

Harri cuts me off. 'I'm thinking we want a personal angle. That's what worked so well. The Girl really responds to it. We'll have a think – but you do need to come up with something. You couldn't have another threesome, could you? Ha, I'm joking. But bring something good to the features meeting tomorrow.'

Or else.

'Hahahaha. Another threesome! I'm on it!' I smile, and my vision swims again. As I walk back to my desk, I have to concentrate very hard in order to move in a straight line.

Some hours later, Sam Strong is reaching a juddering conclusion, and I am screaming, primally, into a pillow.

'Ahhhhhhhhhh!' I think I might hate my job. My dream job.

'Ahhhhhhhhhh!' Is there some way I could spend two weeks in hospital, in a safe, relaxing coma? Is there any way I could get knocked down by a bus, and not die, or break any limbs, but just be taken out for a bit? And I'd still get paid, and everyone would have to be nice to me?

'Ahhhhhhhhhh!' What am I going to do?

'Oh, yeah, you really loved that, didn't you? Dirty girl.' I get up to pee, and he hands me the used condom – making exactly the same 'helpful' face as a customer in a bar, handing me an empty pint glass.

When I come back from the bathroom, he's mid-sentence, '... reckon I must be responsible for half your traffic, I sent it to everyone I know! Very, ah, entertaining. You should get into erotica. Bounce with Mounce! Imogen ... in-me-again.'

'You are so full of shit.' I pick up a pillow and throw it at him.

'Seriously, it was impressive. You're a very talented writer.' Oh, how I love hearing that from Sam Strong – and how I hate myself for it.

'The trouble is,' I say, absent-mindedly picking up the pillow, patting it for feather points to pluck, 'I have to write another one.'

'Imogen, don't do that. They get in the bed and they

208

scratch. What do you mean, another one? They want you to be some sort of threesome columnist? A ménage monthly? Hey, if ever you want to bring a friend ...'

'SAM. No, it's just ... I'm worried that it might be a one-time deal. I'm only ever going to be as good as my last piece, and that might be it. I can't connect with the writing, like I used to, because I'm so overwhelmed by the other stuff. It was fine when I was just a blogger, and you were the only person who read it, but ... I feel as though I've accidentally told all of these lies, and misled people, and I'm wrong for *The Know*. I'm a fluke. I'm going to get caught out. But I'm so, so lucky. I'm finally getting paid to write. I'm starting to think there might be something wrong with me.' Why am I telling him all this? Oh, yeah. I don't have anyone else to tell any more.

'What are they paying you?' I don't know why I tell him the truth, but I do, and he shakes his head. 'That can't be market rate. How do you live? I'm about to do some editor-at-large stuff at *The Gentleman*, I'm sure they'd give you a decent staffer salary.'

'You have offered me – what – three, four jobs over the last couple of years? And the offers have come to liter-ally nothing.'

'Yeah, it's different now, though. You have cachet.'

And that is the word I eventually come to nuzzle against, cling to, and self-soothe with, as I drift off to sleep in a bad man's feather-filled bed.

Chapter Thirty-One

The Fear

Harri

Harri is starting to feel The Fear. It's almost March. Is time too fast, or is *The Know* too slow? Her one real inheritance from *Panache* is that she can think across multiple time-lines – for her, autumn begins immediately after Christmas, and if someone asks her what day it is, she has a tendency to ask 'Do you mean the on-sale date, or the civilian one?' But *The Know* doesn't follow the old publishing calendar, or even the Gregorian one. Does a firefighter care what time it is, when the flames are licking the side of the building and they appear to be the only person who bothered to learn how to work the hose?

That's not fair, Harri thinks, catching herself. For the most part, her team are really trying – even though they can be really trying. And Harri likes to stay late, and work, and go home, and do some more. She likes finding solutions to pressing problems. It's a form of insulation. It stops the loneliness from seeping up from under the skirting boards, through the gap in the door jamb.

Today, she's up early, in order to ambush March. March has got to be better than February. She's going to make March her bitch. She's got her excellent new trousers on, wide legged and high waisted, the brightest colour she can countenance. 'French denim', they said in the shop, but her brain prefers 'funereal cobalt'. She has a venti black Americano, in a cup slightly longer than the length between her forehead and her chin. She's eating a small plasticky poached egg, with a scrap of smoked salmon, and a Trivial Pursuit pie sized slice of avocado, and she's making up for her miniature first course with what Giles calls 'a fuck-off croissant' for pudding.

Once Harri turns on all of the neon, she is queen of all she surveys. She sits and takes her ease. The smooth hush and whirr of her computer fan coming to life is as soothing as the sound of the sea. She's doing something small, but significant. She's a farmer. Soon she will be surrounded by her chickens, clucking, fussing, scattering seed. She must gently but firmly encourage them to lay.

Harri is attempting to remove a flake of croissant from the crease between her thigh and her crotch when her second-in-command arrives. 'Akila! You always cheer me up! How was your evening?'

'It was pretty good. My mate just had a baby, so I popped over to see her ... cute as all get out, but her sister, who I'd never met before, was asking me about when I was going to have kids! I'm laughing and saying "Oh, you know, soon!" not "Are you kidding me? Why do you need to know? Shall I get knocked up and bring them to yours for Christmas?"

Anyway, I felt so free and single and pathetically rebellious that I went out afterwards. I've had Red Coke and three Nurofen for breakfast.'

'I know that feeling,' says Harri, even though Akila *looks* radiant, and she has a suspicion that her hangovers are cheery Beatrix Potter stories, when compared with Harri's own worsening thousand-page Gothic tragedies. 'Anyway, can I grab you for a bit of planning? We need to think of something huge. I've just been going over Mackenzie's targets for us. Because of Imogen's bloody threesome – I shouldn't complain, I know – but the traffic spike has actually thrown our figures out, we need to do something enormous to beat it.'

Akila looks nervous. 'Do you think we can?'

Harri nods. 'She's made it clear that we have to. It's weird, you'd think she'd be throwing parties for us, but she's throwing around phrases like "if you continue to fail to meet new targets" and "inevitable consequences".'

Akila frowns. 'I wanted to ask you about something, actually. I don't want to be whiny, but I'm really confused. Every time I try to meet with senior management to give them a progress update, they either never get back to me, or they fob me off and say something about doing it later. There have been a few big things that we really needed to respond to quite urgently – and you know that with stuff around ads and money, we usually need their sign off, we can't authorise it alone.'

She looks up at the ceiling, down at the floor, and takes a breath. 'I wasn't sure whether to mention this, but Lily actually scheduled a meeting with me on February the thirty-first. I felt like such a dick, I wasn't really concentrating until I went to put it in my diary. She was all "Ooooh, sorry, is it not a leap year?" which doesn't make any sense! It's breaking my brain. Our stats, our analytics, our uniques – everything is way, way, way over target. I was under the impression that I would have to beg and plead for ads, but big brands are coming to us proposing partnerships. And upstairs, they don't want to know!'

Now Harri is looking at the floor. She has worked at Hudson long enough to know that the company cogs move in a manner so protracted and convoluted that the business might as well have been founded by Heath Robinson. It would be senior management's style to wait until The Girl was well into her eighties before they were ready to declare the new venture a success. Even so, they have been unusually obstructive.

'Do we think it's maybe Mackenzie's old company culture? The American way?'

Akila shakes her head. 'Nah, I'm not sure that makes any sense. You know I've worked in the States, and certain stuff, when you get really granular, is a bit slow – everything has to be signed off twelve times – but nothing like this. In the grand scheme of things, Hudson isn't even that big. It's making me anxious. And we shouldn't be anxious. We should be giddy.'

Harri feels her optimism vanishing, her soul slumping. If she's a human soufflé, the oven door has been opened, and the dinner party is ruined. 'But, I think we can be a bit giddy, you know? If you take Imogen's threesome out of the equation, we've got a good, strong, steady amount of growth, definitely better than I would have predicted for the first month.'

Akila walks over to look at Harri's computer screen and frowns. 'They have doubled down. I thought I saw the numbers a few days ago, how can they have increased them already? I mean – these just aren't achievable. *Panache* couldn't pull these figures.'

Harri will have to go and talk to Mackenzie about this, and she'd rather have a root canal. Through her eyelids. She's really living the dream. People think that the life of an editor is a riot of free shoes and private jets to Paris. The reality is that at least half the time, you're craven, missing most of your fingernails and envying people with proper power careers, like traffic wardens.

'Nil desperandum,' says Akila. 'Before we really fall into the gloom pit, I've had a very interesting pitch this morning. We might have some super lucrative sponcon coming our way. I think that as long as you and Imogen go for it, we can get it signed off straight away. Have you come across Fallen Angels? The sex party people?'

Harri runs a quick mental Google search. 'Yes! I've never been, I was always a bit spooked by their screening process, but I have a few glamorous friends who like to get a bit *Eyes Wide Shut* ...'

'They are very, very keen for Imogen to go along and do a piece. I'm trying to negotiate so it's not just a one off – that it would lead to some regular advertising – but their marketing budget is nuts. I think they just got bought out, or something. It might cover most of our operating costs, and any other ad revenue would be profit. Even Mackenzie would have to go for it, it's a no brainer.'

It's a long time since Harri felt her sap rising, but she feels her spine uncurling, her shoulders descending from underneath her ears. 'Akila, you superstar. You genius! This is brilliant news!'

'Well … unofficially, shucks, it was nothing. Officially – yes, I am a genius! You're very lucky to have me, and don't you forget it.'

'Spoken like a true hashtag girl boss.'

Akila grimaces. 'Harri … promise me you'll never use that expression ever again.'

Chapter Thirty-Two

The Art of War

Imogen

I can do this. The last six weeks have been a blip. I just needed a decent night's sleep, and a proper cup of coffee. Now, I am properly caffeinated, courtesy of Sam Strong's Keurig, armed with a page of ideas, and fortified by a cursory glimpse at *Make Big Business Work For You!* and *The Art Of War.* (His library is pretty limited.)

It's simple. I just need to focus on my goals, dreams and aims, while . . . subduing the enemy, without fighting. I will not rise to Tabitha's constant needling, I will smile and nod and say 'sounds interesting' while pretending that I'm interviewing her for a piece on being a massive bitch. And with Harri, I'm going to . . . power pose? Was that it? I think I have to stand in the doorway with my hands on my hips, and speak in a low voice, because women betray themselves by using too many upward inflections, and that's why we don't get pay rises. Anyway, I have ideas. Good ideas. Pieces

I'd be really excited to write. I've been thinking about The Girl, too. The Girl is ambitious, and in control. The Girl pleases herself, she isn't obsessed with pleasing her boss, as though she's constantly trying to placate a bad boyfriend.

Opening my notebook, I feel very pleased with myself. Staying at Sam Strong's cuts my commute by almost 70 per cent, and I have used the time wisely.

1. Slow dating, and the new intimacy. Emails and DMs from our readers indicate that they are burned out, bewildered and exhausted from the effort of trying to maintain modern love and sex lives – and the gulf between single and attached women is growing. This would be a call for slow dating, a celebration of tenderness and a validating rally cry, letting our readers – The Girls – know that they are not alone in their craving for intimacy, and that there is an Industrial Dating Complex which is profiting from their alienation. It will include tips and advice about how to embrace emotional needs and date in an empowered way, but ultimately liberate the reader by showing them that they are not alone.

2. An absolute beginner's guide to masturbation. We've assumed The Girl is a confident masturbator and sex tech spender – reader comments indicate a split. We get many queries from readers who are anxious about spending a lot of money on a vibrator and don't know where to begin. This would frame masturbation as a confidence boosting, joyous aspect of our relationship with ourselves. It would be a chance for us to talk about how orgasms don't have to be

the ultimate goal – I think some of our readers have orgasm anxiety, and we need to speak to that.

3. Listicle – Cluedo – What to make of the items you find – and don't find – in your partner's bedroom. John Waters said, If you go home with somebody, and they don't have books, don't fuck 'em. If they own the *The Art Of War* ... (I don't know? Have a word with yourself? Oh, bugger.)

Today, I am confident and calm; today, I am confident and calm. I repeat this to myself as I practise my box breathing. Through the tube doors, in for four. Squashed into the corner, hold for four. Actually, this is a scenario in which holding my breath has multiple advantages. Breathe, breathe, breathe. Don't forget to breathe. And if you can call yourself a guru and make a multi million pound fortune from telling people that, I never need to worry that any of my pitch ideas are ever stupid or ridiculous. Out for four. I am confident and calm on the escalator, on the pavement, and even when I collide with Tabitha as I trip over her tiered skirt, while trying to stride, confidently and calmly, into the building. 'Fuck's sake, please, I really don't – look, I gotta go,' she hangs up her phone and scowls at me. 'What did you hear?' She sounds ... almost frightened. Is there something different about her voice? I can't put my finger on it. 'Um, what? Sorry, I wasn't paying attention.' As always, I'm distracted by her outfit – the yellow taffeta is topped by a velvet jacket, a ruffled silk blouse – half Beauty, half Beast, very Austin Powers. Meanly, I think it would be a lot of fun to watch her attempt the revolving doors. I'm not sure she could even get through the emergency exit, to be honest.

'Well, I'm sure no one told you that it's rude to eavesdrop, and I know it's too much to expect you to walk with any grace or decorum, but will you mind my Molly Goddard?' Her face shifts, from snarl to sneer, and she picks up her phone and walks away from the office. What was that?

In for four. Confident and calm carries me to Harri's desk. Make a statement. Show you're in control, said the Sam Strong books. 'Good morning! I've been working on some ideas and I can't wait to present them in the meeting. I've been looking at all the responses we're getting on social and it's so interesting to see how we're being read, who The Girl is actually . . . '

'No need!' Harri holds her hands up. Her eyes are glittering.

'Imogen, we've got a brilliant assignment for you! You're off to an orgy!'

Pardon?

'Oh, but . . . ' I clutch the notebook. In for four. Hold for one. In for one. Out for one. In for half. 'I really wanted to . . . I thought . . . I worked so hard . . . '

'You know Fallen Angels? They've asked for you, especially. Check your emails, you need to contact the PR and sort out the details, it's a bit last minute but they're just checking to see whether they can squeeze you in tomorrow night. Really excited for this one, Imogen. Make it bold, make it hot, make it wild. Go get some, for The Girl!'

I think about the actual Girls, and their anxious emails. Does The Girl want this, really? But then – right now, I'm tired of The Girl. What do *I* want to do? Briefly, I allow myself to recall an old forgotten fantasy, and shiver with lust. I suppose I have always been quite curious about the Fallen Angels parties . . .

Chapter Thirty-Three

No Wallflower at the Orgy

Imogen

Writer Imogen Mounce goes deep undercover at the hottest sex party in the capital

Fallen Angels, the notorious and 'exclusive' sex party organisation – or, according to its website, 'the Capital's premier erotic event' – has deemed me fit enough – in every sense – to go to one of their parties. They talk a good game. 'This is where the most beautiful people in the world get to know each other intimately.' And the only time I've ever been called beautiful is on Brick Lane, by the maître'd's who are standing on the pavement persuading passers-by to come into their curry houses. ('Hey gorgeous! You look like you can put away a lot of sag paneer!') Still, I upload a headshot and a full length photo, and even though the site warns me to wait a week, I've had my 'exclusive' e-vite within twenty-four hours. I suspect that in this context 'beautiful' might simply mean 'has own teeth, is not standing in front of a windowless van.'

Clothes wise, I try and reject a pile of Primark party dresses before deciding to play it safe – black slip dress, black bra, black high waisted knickers, black hold-ups, black coat – and I Uber straight from The Know offices to a mews building tucked a few streets behind Berkeley Square. I'm expecting a burly bouncer, but I see two women clutching clipboards. Like me, they are both wearing long black coats. Unlike me, they both have astonishingly shiny hair. The light from the street lamps really bounces off it – I feel less like I'm entering a den of iniquity, and more as though I'm in a football stadium, about to run onto the pitch. If you were an interior design expert, you'd get one of them to permanently stand at the end of your hall in order to make the space look bigger. I feel slightly intimidated. OK, really intimidated. But they're much friendlier and more smiley than the average PR girl guarding the W1 doors. Giving them my name, I walk up the stairs to the cloakroom. My heart is pounding so hard that I think it's creating electricity and conducting it through the underwire of my bra. Which, incidentally, might not be the best place for my cloakroom ticket this evening.

At first, the 'party' looks like any old posh press launch. Everyone is mingling in a huge, main room. The ceilings are high, the lighting is low (thankfully), soft and neon pink. The heating is set to Bikram Yoga. To my left, there's a semi-circular mirrored bar, tucked into the corner. The barman is setting out trays of pink drinks in champagne flutes – at least, I think they're pink, it might just be the lighting.

I'm transported straight back to a Year 9 disco. Everyone is older, and better dressed, but the vibe is the same. Nervous and giggly, with boys on the right and girls on the left. I'm terrified – but there is a generalised sense of terror in the air. Not Mad Max debauch, just edginess, and twitchiness. I need a drink before I can talk to anyone, and I ask the barman if it's OK to take one from the tray. 'I suppose,' he sighs, huffily, as his quiff collapses and he blows it back into place. I was expecting 'Help yourself!' with a wink, a twinkle. The cocktail is just a little too warm. It tastes of sugary prosecco and – I struggle to place it for a moment, it is literally on the tip of my tongue – peach dish soap.

Who are my fellow orgy-goers? Every single one of the women looks like they work in PR. Yet more black dresses, a ratio of three parts satin to two parts lace. In the near-dark, I can't quite work out who looks genuinely scared, and who is trying to look bored. There's the odd very young, very tall outlier. It's possible that they are models, but I suppose they might be here with someone who has hired them for the occasion. Laughing in the middle of the room is one truly stunning woman, in nothing but a white lace thong that glows in the dark. Objectively beautiful, but really too perfect to be my type. Any lust I feel is overpowered by another sin, envy for her flawless, butterscotch body. Her hair glows even more fiercely than her knickers, not blonde but yellow gold, glossy badonkadonk curls undulating in waves that hit her shoulders and break across her back. I tug at my frizz despondently. An hour with a BaByliss Big Hair and nothing to show for it but an aching right elbow. Who is she laughing with? Well, I hate to be heightist but it's a man who is not only half her size but reminds me of Vizzini in The Princess Bride. *There is a lesson here.*

I knock back my horrible peach drink and grab another while the sulky barman is looking at his phone. For a second, I worry about the tastes I haven't detected, and whether I'm going to wake up naked and tied up in a skip in ten hours. Then I realise that if the organisers wanted to drug us all, they would make more effort to a) serve the drinks and b) make them taste good.

Forcing my face into a looming, unsexy smile, I look around and make eye contact with another girl. 'Hello, I'm Imogen,' I announce, and she looks startled, as well she might. I sound as though I'm about to try to sell tickets for the Church Heating Fund tombola. 'How are you doing? I've never been to one of these before, how does it work?'

'I'm ... Carlotta! Hello!' she shrieks. Blimey, I sound quite sultry in comparison. I mean, it's a relief to learn that I might not be the uncoolest person here, but I'm not sure I want to start flirting with someone who talks like Mickey Mouse. 'Actually, Carlotta isn't my real name. This is my first time too. My boyfriend really wanted to come, and I liked the idea of it, but ...' I follow 'Carlotta's' gaze and see a group of three men, standing about ten feet away, chuckling together. I squint at them. If one of these guys turned out to be my Tinder date, I'd give it a go, but the idea of having anonymous sex with any of them in about half an hour doesn't make me feel quite as thrilled as it should.

'He always bloody does this,' she hisses.

'I thought this was your first time?' I reply, surprised.

223

'Yes, no, I mean ... at weddings, in the pub, you know. We go out together, he just manages to make fucking friends with everyone, he tells me he's getting our drinks in and suddenly it's "Oh, you're Ben's brother, I think we met once, weren't you at Bristol, and did you see the rugby?" and I'm in the corner, again. We've not had sex in weeks. He keeps coming home pissed! I honestly thought this would be hot, that he'd see me in a wild new light, we'd do something a bit different and he wouldn't be able to take his hands off me, but once again, it's a fucking university reunion.'

Poor 'Carlotta' is quite flushed, now. Her nose is glowing through her Double Wear. Honestly, I'm not overwhelmed with an urge to drag her into a 'party room' and suggest I make her forget about her terrible boyfriend. Still. Courage! Clear eyes, full hearts, nice shoes? Sort of. She's in Valentino Rockstuds – or good copies – and they make her feet look like toddlers strapped into car seats.

Praying the alcohol will soon work its magic, I decide to seize the initiative. As huskily as I can manage, I murmur 'Well, why don't we ... make out a little, and I'm sure he'll come running over as soon as he sees what you're doing.' I seize the mettle. I'm a little taller than 'Carlotta', even though she has a Rockstud advantage, so I take her into my arms. My right hand is chilly from clutching my drink, and I'm worried that she'll wince at the sensation on her bare back. But unexpectedly, Carlotta yields. Her lips are on mine, soft, soft, soft. She's wearing, I think, Angel by Thierry Mugler – a perfume that I've tried, and makes me smell like one of those special Yankee Candle fresheners you get for your car. But Carlotta smells of honey, vanilla, treacle – sexy cake.

She leans back a little, pulling me towards her, and I'm into it all – her scent, her soft skin. I can feel my nipples hardening against the silky fabric of her dress. Suddenly she pulls away and looks back at the three men. They are still laughing, matily. They've even acquired pints! Where did they get pints from? How come they don't have to put up with the revolting peach drink?

Even though the room is barely lit, I can see the storm clouds gathering across her face. She flings her arms to her sides and shrieks, in her Mickey Mouse voice, 'FUCK HIM. Fuck you, Matt!' She looks around wildly and sees my glass on the floor, which has maybe an inch of liquid left in it. She moves to grab it, and, knowing what's coming, I mutter 'Not that. Take his pint.'

She marches into the middle of the cluster of men, squaring up to the paler, bespectacled ginger one. So that's Matt. 'Oh, sausage, what's wrong? Come and meet the chaps! Peter was at college with ...' We will never know. Carlotta/Sausage has grasped Matt's glass and upended it all over his head. 'And just so you know,' she squeals, sounding like air escaping from a balloon, 'I never. Came. Once. And last Christmas I got so bored that I fucked your uncle in the cellar! I'm going home. Alone!'

Turning to me, she adopts the Church Tombola register. 'Imogen, it was nice to meet you,' she says loudly, and flounces out, which is a challenge for the spike heels.

The room has fallen silent. Worryingly, I notice that Vizzini is eyeing me with interest. He nudges his fabulous girlfriend, grazing her thigh. She looks me up and down, sighs, and walks up to me.

'Would you care to join me and my husband? 'Husband'

is the first shock, and the accent is the second – I thought she might be Russian or Brazilian, but she sounds more Cockney than Dick Van Dyke in Mary Poppins. *(Mind you, I sound more Cockney than that.) This is very much in the spirit of the event – and I guess there is a first time for everything. I'm attracted to women, but I mostly date men – and I've never been with a couple before.*

Honestly? I don't know. On any normal night, no, not really. But this isn't a normal night and this isn't exactly something I'm doing for fun. It's an experiment. I'm Louis Theroux. And that kiss might have meant less than nothing to Carlotta, but it's stirred something up for me. I'm feeling louche, wild, daring.

'I'm Michelle,' says the goddess, 'Are you having a good night? I don't think we've seen you here before, have we?' My hand slots very neatly into hers – she feels firm but soft, and warm. Honestly, this is worth the price of admission – a good hand hold is better than a weighted blanket. Still, I notice her taupe acrylic nails with alarm. I do not want to end the evening in A&E, improvising a story about an awkward fall in a salon while a sceptical nurse goes in with a torch and a pair of tweezers.

I follow Michelle out onto a landing, up a set of stairs and into a room that could be described as an ante-chamber, if you were feeling generous, and a large cupboard if you were being realistic. Vizzini follows close behind, presumably panting. The room looks as though it has been papered with the wrapping from fancy Easter eggs. The walls are foiled in dark bronze, and the only furniture I can see is a black leather couch, something between a sofa and a day bed. I'm relieved to see a large glass jar filled with condoms. It looks like it came from an old-fashioned sweet shop.

What do I do with myself? Gingerly, I sit on the edge of the couch, hoping Michelle will give me some instructions. Ideally, she'll whip a tiny projector out of her thong, and give a PowerPoint presentation. 'Your first orgy. Dos and don'ts.' Instead, in one impressive movement – like a magician with a tablecloth – she lifts my dress off, over my head, and throws it into a corner before straddling me. She presses her lips against mine, and it doesn't feel as good as it did with Carlotta. They are a little rubbery, reptilian, slick with gloss.

'You're such a good kisser,' I lie.

Moving my head to the right, ostensibly so that Michelle can kiss my neck, I peer into the darkness, curious – and a little nervous – about what Vizzini might be doing. (I must find out his name before I call him that.) Oh, God. His black suit trousers are concertina'd into pleated puddles around his ankles. Three shirt buttons are open, his bow tie – bow tie? How did I not notice a bow bloody tie? – is loose around his neck. His underwear is black, short, plain, inoffensive – but he's really getting stuck into it. Even though I can barely see, I'm aware of pale flesh being pumped furiously, a grunting metronome. Maybe this is all he needs. We'll manufacture a few moments of real-life girl on girl, he'll come, and I'll be back on the bus and on my way to a deliciously greasy takeaway before you can say 'cheesy chips with doner meat'.

Michelle is kissing my mouth again, tensing her tongue and pushing it into mine, with a rapid, stabbing motion. Why? Also, she seems to be stroking my back in a strange and uncomfortable way. It takes me slow seconds to *realise she's trying to undo my bra and struggling. Out of politeness, I reach and pop the clasp open. Which was silly, because when I had my bra on, I could escape with a little dignity. There is a tiny angel Imogen on my shoulder, shrieking 'Make it stop! Make it stop!' Not for any kind of moral reason, just a generalised horror response. It knows about the very bad sex I am definitely about to have in the name of journalism.*

Even though my eyes are shut tight, I'm aware that Vizzini has moved towards us. Michelle is pinching my nipples as forcefully as a spiteful child. I don't not like it. It's sort of thrillingly horrible, strangely centring, forcing me into the moment. Michelle's bare breasts feel fascinating, warm, yet immoveable. Obviously fake – but so upright, buoyant, unignorable that they might be the most authentic thing in the building. I don't usually hate my breasts, but they wobble, they slope a little when unfettered – to her, they must look and feel like ghosts.

Michelle clambers off me, and a now naked Vizzini looms behind her, about to take her place at my crotch. Thinking fast, I stand up. 'I'd love to watch you ... together,' I say, very quietly. I'm holding my breath, expecting one of them to say 'No, wench, it's pillaging season! Get back on the couch!' but Michelle shimmies out of her thong and lies down, her legs open almost 180 degrees. Vizzini leaps between them and goes to work. Light bounces against his bald spot, as he licks and licks while Michelle arches her back theatrically, crying 'Oh God, oh God, oh God!' Oh God that feels so good, or oh God please call a chiropractor, I have a twenty-four hour clinic on speed dial because this happens to me a lot?

Every so often, one of them looks up and over at me, to check that I'm enjoying myself. 'Oh, wow, so hot,' I say, prodding a nipple that is still slightly sore to the touch. 'Just going to the loo, but I'll be right back!' Shit! Where's my dress? Never mind. I pick up my bra, realising, with a sinking heart, that my cloakroom ticket is no longer in it, and I'll have to use my limited descriptive powers in order to get the attendant to pick out my black coat from a line-up of a hundred identical black coats. I can leave without a dress or without a coat but it's not warm enough or safe enough to go outside in my knickers. Not even in Mayfair.

Vizzini and Michelle are now engaged in full congress. Now it's his pale buttocks that are bobbing up and down and catching the light. There's a weird mark on his arse. It looks like a lizard scale. Even though every instinct for self-preservation that I have is screaming at me to run out of the room, I pause, and squint. Almost moaning with relief, I realise what it is. A pink paper rectangle, inked boldly with the number 194. Snatching at it, I cry out 'Um ... lovely to meet you!' and run away into the night. Well, the night bus. The cloakroom lady does not seem fazed that I'm standing in front of her in my underwear, even though I later realise at home that I put my bra on inside out. 'Am I the first to leave?' I ask her. 'Oh, no, love, not at all, we've had a few heading off early. It's a shame though, you're all missing the hot nibbles in the break.'

If any of this has piqued your curiosity, I want to make this clear: The website sounds quite intimidating, but you don't need to worry about their 'exclusive' policy. I was convinced that I'd be the heaviest, un-hottest girl there, surrounded by supermodels and feeling awful and insecure.

But the breadth of bodies and faces represented really did range from A to Vizzini. The FA website prominently positions black and brown faces and bodies in its gallery of former guests and flags up a Diversity and Inclusion policy – however, on the night I attended the guests were overwhelmingly, if not exclusively, white. I think about how nervous and awkward I felt – and how much harder the experience would have been if I was even more anxious about feeling welcomed and included.

Ultimately it doesn't really matter what you wear to an orgy, as long as you don't mind leaving it behind. I'd love to see the Fallen Angels lost property box – maybe I'd find Carlotta's boyfriend in there, trying to organise a pub golf session. The event I attended was one of their larger gatherings – 'perfect for curious new Angels and experienced, wicked ones'. I wouldn't completely rule out another visit, but I'd look for something a little bit smaller, and I'd bring my own wine.

Chapter Thirty-Four

*'Five hundred words – you could make
it a thousand if the muse descends'*

Imogen

'It's brilliant. It's utterly, completely brilliant.'

Louise sounds solemn, almost as if she's contemplating a holy text. 'Immo, the jokes are so good, but you're in there. I can see these people. I can smell it.' She wrinkles her straight, narrow nose, and her face shifts from pointer to pug. 'It's a really good, honest, funny, real piece of writing. I don't get the title though. What's a wallflower?'

I do love Louise but I sometimes wonder about the odd gaps in her knowledge. Maybe she accidentally neuralyzed herself playing laser tag at a hen do. 'A wallflower is an introvert, a shy person, someone who doesn't do well at parties. Nora Ephron – you know, *When Harry Met Sally* – a collection of her journalism was published in a book called *Wallflower at the Orgy*. The idea being that she went to all of these wild, thrilling events and observed them from the sidelines, without getting involved. And I've done the very opposite.'

Louise giggles. 'I would have given anything to see it slowly dawning on Vizzini that you weren't coming back. Was your ticket really stuck to his bum?'

I nod. 'It sounds funny now, but ... I was hoping that the vigorous pumping would dislodge it, and it would flutter to the floor without me having to touch his arse. I think the sweat made sure that it really stuck on.'

She shudders. 'Still, such a good detail! I think Harri will love it.'

'I hope so. I've been feeling so ... nervous, about work, at the moment. As though I need to prove myself all over again. I don't know, maybe it's all in my head.'

Louise nods. 'I don't think you have anything to worry about, this is excellent.'

Cheered up by Louise's encouragement, I read my piece again, and – quaking slightly – I email it to Harri. It is good. It's a bit long, she might want me to cut the Carlotta stuff, but I think it's funny and relatable. I'm convinced that The Girl will love it. So I'm not prepared for the icy chill that descends in the office when Harri returns after lunch and stops by my desk, frowning. 'Imogen? Quick word?'

This is definitely not a woman who is about to congratulate her star writer and tell her she's done it again. She's so cross she looks like a cartoon. I can detect the invisible, squiggly anger lines, furious epaulettes hovering above her shoulders. Wordlessly, she sits down in her ergonomic chair. (Harri, I note resentfully, never, ever has to gingerly lower herself into her office chair because there's a chance it will collapse from under her and throw her to the floor.) 'Your piece,' she says, staring straight ahead at her screen. 'What happened?'

What happened? I went to an orgy, because you made me, it was awful, I wrote about it, now I'm worried about how long it's going to take Accounts to put the expenses through and whether they'll make a fuss about paying for the Uber.

'Um,' I stare at my toes. How do my shoes always get so scuffed? Anyone would think I spent hours a day running around playing Red Rover.

'Imogen, I'm concerned that you have spent a lot of time working on something that just falls short of our standards. We can't run this. You know what *The Know* is. This isn't for The Girl.'

Harri, who is The Girl? I want to scream. Because the women, the typical readers who message all day long, are just like me – over their overdraft limits, at the beginning of a kidney infection, with bosses who are somehow able to define and dictate their entire emotional state.

'I thought it was funny,' I tell my toes. 'And it's what happened.'

Harri frowns. 'There's the title, for starters. No one is going to get that Nora Ephron reference – and if they do, they'll be, well, startled, to say the least, that a twenty-seven-year-old sex writer has taken it upon herself to compare herself with one of the greatest journalistic talents of all time.'

I daren't look up, because I'm on the brink of tears. That really isn't what I meant at all. 'Harri, I just thought it was fun, and that anyone who knew it would love it, and that anyone who didn't would get the meaning ... '

She flashes a palm, stopping me mid-sentence. 'It just isn't sexy. It's long, it's laboured. It starts off like reportage, but it just turns into this rambling mess. I mean, most of the piece is about some girl having a fight with her boyfriend. How is that sexy?'

Sticky, creeping tendrils of shame shoot up from my churning bowels, down from my burning cheeks, and meet in the middle to flood my whole body with poison. I'm crying now. I look to the right, all the way down the office to my desk. Louise meets my eyes and mimes a hug. Her sweetness wilts the scrap of steel that was holding back most of my tears. I won't let Harri see that she's made me cry, but I can't shake the sob from my voice.

'Would. You. Like me to. Rewriiiiiiiiiiite – it?'

Harri sighs so forcefully that it probably counts as cardio. 'Yeah. Cut that Carlotta stuff right down, just keep the kiss and that thing with the couple at the end. Could you make it a bit sexier? It just all sounds so negative, right now. It needs to sell the orgy more. You were supposed to be excited about this! It isn't very aspirational, and that's what The Girl likes, remember? She's confident. She's glamorous. You come across as being about as confident as day old wet toast, here.'

I'm so lit up with indignation that it takes me a moment to work out what Harri might mean by 'selling the orgy more'.

'You want me to make it up?' I'm incredulous.

For the first time in our conversation, Harri looks up and makes proper eye contact with me. She does not look as defensive as I think she should. 'No, no, absolutely not! Not exactly. Just … this is about creative licence. Use the facts of the experience, but also, configure them with what you think The Girl really wants to read. You have a following – we have a following – because you write sex so well. There's no desire here, in your piece. That bit about kissing Carlotta, that was good. And maybe – no one wants to read about the *Princess Bride* man, but you could sort of recast it, a bit. There must have been some hot guys you could write about?'

I'm speechless. And because I don't say no, she assumes it's a yes from me. The rules of the orgy make it clear that consent must be explicit; it turns out that when you're writing about the orgy, anything bloody goes.

Harri continues. 'So send me two or three sexy paras for first thing tomorrow morning. We can go a bit longer here, and stretch to another five hundred words. You could make it a thousand if the muse descends, I'll cut more of the original.' She actually winks at me. 'You got this, Imogen! Impress me!' Sliding my phone out of my pocket, I see that it's 5.58 p.m. I hate her. I hate her so much.

Chapter Thirty-Five

Feelings aren't facts

Harri

Sometimes Harri really, really, really hates her job.

In the past, she had worked for editors who took a sado-masochistic pleasure in humiliating their juniors but that wasn't her vibe at all. And yet, here she was, itching with the shame of having broken Imogen's heart.

It wasn't a bad piece, at all. It just didn't fit the brief. And that was Harri's fault, sort of. She and Akila had decided to tell Imogen to make it 'sexy, glamorous, aspirational' but they hadn't mentioned that *The Know*'s financial future was resting on the work. 'Good sponcon never sounds too spon, I think Imogen's writing will lose its freshness and funniness if she feels like she's doing an advertorial,' said Akila, and Harri agreed.

Matters were not helped by the fact that Harri had just emerged, dazed, from a surprise 'performance review' with Mackenzie, Lily and Katie. She was feeling freaked out and overwhelmed, and she might have taken it out on Imogen. No, there was no 'might have' about it. And she hated herself for it. She ambushed Imogen, because she had herself been ambushed.

'This should have been in your diary,' frowned Katie, tapping her own notebook with a heavy ballpoint pen, as though she were using it to rap Harri's knuckles.

Harri had tried, and failed, to exert some kind of editorial authority. 'I think this must be an error. We've not been up and running for the full month yet, I think that it's too soon to have any kind of meaningful review ...'

'No, we're acting in our human resources capacity today. This is about your performance as a Hudson employee,' sneered Lily, who appeared to be shivering with vicarious pleasure. Harri was about to be bollocked, and she wanted to watch.

Mackenzie warmed up with a few digs at *Panache*. 'I'm very concerned about the culture of complacency on the magazine, and how you left things when you moved over. Morale seems low, there's little appetite for innovation amongst your former staff.' Technically, Mackenzie was not wrong. Giles' updates had started to sound like war reportage. 'I spend most of my time encouraging everyone out from under their desks, because they duck for cover whenever she comes in. There's always a huge line out of the door for the Ladies, because everyone wants to go for a big cry at lunchtime.'

Harri knows the rule – never apologise, never explain. Always offer a solution, even if you have no intention of executing it. 'I'm sure they're just getting used to the change.

I'll look into it.' But Mackenzie's real wrath was reserved for *The Know*. Of course it was.

'I'm concerned the explicit content has alienated your international audience.' Never 'our' audience. If it's negative, it's Harri's fault. 'You're getting plenty of media attention' – somehow Mackenzie made 'media attention' sound like 'chlamydia' or 'tax fraud' – 'but I'm concerned the core product isn't strong enough. And it's not glossy. At Hudson, we have a reputation, a certain standard.' Only now would Mackenzie deign to use the first person. What was this 'we'? She just got here.

Harri took a deep breath. 'Our star writer, Imogen Mounce, is doing an investigative piece, attending a Fallen Angels party, and we expect it to be our traffic leader for the month. Imogen's pieces are consistently huge traffic drivers for us. US readers are making up a quarter of our readership, and a third of all shares. So they're not just reading, they're the ones sending these to their friends, posting them on social, making our audience grow beyond all projections.' Harri is hoping that if she focuses on the numbers, she can impress the Trio of Terror and distract them from asking any awkward questions about what Fallen Angels actually is. Against every bit of her better judgement, Harri starts to think about what it might be like to encounter Mackenzie at an orgy. She'd almost certainly be smooth and cold, like Barbie, only with cashmere nipple covers, and a tweed crotch, a forbidding triangle of Burberry check. Do not enter without a handwritten letter of introduction, in black ink on monogrammed stationery.

Most surprisingly, Mackenzie looked not displeased. Even Lily murmured 'A very upmarket brand.' Interestingly,

Katie's cheeks bloomed bright red, and her gimlet gaze fell to the floor.

'Just make sure the content reflects a certain level of quality. Imogen's pieces have been rather too,' she paused meaningfully and menacingly, looking at Harri with some disgust, '... too ... Lena Dunham for my liking.' Harri's response time is hampered by shock. There's something strange and startling about Mackenzie making any kind of vaguely contemporary reference. Still perhaps it isn't sex itself that bothers Mackenzie, just the sex enjoyed by anyone who had not attended a Swiss finishing school in 1958. If there is any known orgy etiquette, Mackenzie probably owns the Emily Post guide. 'The most important penis must be placed to the right of the hostess.'

Harri stumbled out of the meeting feeling confused and disorientated.

She definitely isn't the sort of person who uses slogans such as 'I speak as I find', mostly because that's usually an excuse to bludgeon vulnerable people in their softest places, without apology. But she's straightforward. She's no dissembler. And that has always worked in her favour, in the past. Her instincts, her integrity, mean she is not often subject to the machinations and manipulations of others. She's never been a victim of office politics, simply because most people feel that they couldn't hide anything from her if they wanted to.

But for the first time, Harri feels unmoored. She senses she is being deceived and disorientated, spun around in the dark, and when she looks up and regains focus, there is a chance that everyone and everything will have vanished.

Still, feelings aren't facts, are they?

Chapter Thirty-Six

This is what you get

Imogen

I'll show her.

I'm going to stay up all night writing the most devastatingly sexy, explicit, meltingly hot piece of prose my brain is capable of. And I'll have to stay in the office, and she'll come in, and she'll notice that I'm in last night's clothes, and that I have massive shadows under my eyes, and she'll be sorry. And I'm going to order Uber Eats on the company credit card, which is in her desk drawer, and dare her to object when the bill comes in. 'Oh, because I was working through the night I thought it would be OK to have something hot and nutritious delivered to the office,' I'll say. 'Maybe next time I should just eat some of the leftover stale cookies from the M&M World PR.'

I'm so tired. I'm always so desperately tired. Ever since I started, I've been muddling through, thinking I'll be able to get to the end of the day, or the end of the week, and sort my life out. Or rather, construct a life. Everything begins and ends with *The Know*. I crawl to work, I stare at my screen, I do whatever I have to do for work, after work, I crawl home, I close my eyes and I get up and do it all over again. The only thing I do that could count as a hobby is Sam Strong. When did I last have a hot meal, eaten with metal cutlery? When did I last do any actual exercise, if I don't count running up the escalator at Tottenham Court Road?

This is what you wanted, says my brain. You're success-ful. You're ambitious.

This is what you get.

Harri could probably replace me tomorrow, probably for half my salary. This is everyone's dream job. When I think of the trail of nightmare jobs that led me here – how can I possibly complain?

I have read maybe a hundred blog posts and comment pieces about 'entitled millennials' and wept with frustration over the idea that I take anything for granted or believe that the world owes me a living. I know, better than anyone, that a career like this isn't a right. It's a prize to be won, through late nights, and extreme tiredness, and fear and vulnerabil-ity and humiliation. Being a good writer isn't good enough.

The office is warm, and quiet. At least Harri didn't make me go back to a different orgy. At least I'm getting paid to sit and think, and I'm not staggering between work experi-ence and a ten hour factory night shift. This really isn't so bad, it could be so much worse.

The piece needs to be sexier. How could last night have been different, in my imagination? What would I write if I were blogging about my ideal orgy?

Louise's voice floats through me. *I've been reading*

about this thing called imposter syndrome. Yeah, well, talk to me when you're a professional orgy-goer whose wildest bedroom urges involve seventy-two hours of uninterrupted sleep.

Sex used to be my constant craving, my release. When the world was really weighing down on me, orgasms were all I had. That was why I started my own blog – I felt compelled to write, and to make myself come. Work and worry burned me out, but sex brought me back to my body. Touch has always been my love language, and instinctively, I've touched myself when I have not felt loved enough. It has nourished me, and as well as bringing me peace, rest and freedom, it opened up a creative space.

Now, I've sold something sacred, and private, and made it public. I don't feel ashamed of who I am, and what I want. But I realise that the magic has been compromised. Now that sex is work, my mind has nowhere else to go. And it needs a special space.

I revisit a favourite old fantasy. I used to dream of having an anonymous lover. After hearing too many of Sam Strong's inanities, I decided that my fantasy lover is French, and that his English is very limited. There are specific, recurring broad brush strokes. For my fantasy to work, first I must mentally move house, to a thirties, art deco wedding cake apartment on the edge of Hampstead Heath, with wooden shutters and white sheets. The hasty reinvention of myself and my life, liberating myself from the constant, nagging cramping sense of self-doubt. The main difference is in work and money. Fantasy Me is solvent and secure, a woman in a position to pursue all of her passions. Sex aside, it's my favourite daydream. I live alone, I write, and I can make choices about clothes, meals and journeys, not compromises born out of necessity.

Imaginary Imogen is a woman who has the headspace for lust, a woman who can breathe out. Already, I feel different in my body, a little more luscious and feminine because I'm not so cramped and slumped.

Sexy, confident Imaginary Imogen has just kissed Carlotta, who has not then stormed off into the night screaming about her awful boyfriend. I'm drinking champagne, not Horrible Lukewarm Peach Drink. I'm a sex goddess, we're all immortal, and a golden girl looks over and asks me if I'll join her, and her husband ...

Her partner, a ripped, six foot Adonis ...

No, an Adonis sounds too hard and pointy. I want a little bit of yield.

Michelle points at her partner, who looks at me, appraisingly. His hair is long, and messy, a wavy lion's mane of dark gold that almost falls to his shoulders, which are as broad as his eyes are narrow. He looks as though he fell out of the Viper Room in 1992. He has Big Cat Energy – he's gazing at me as though he wants to eat me. 'Good to meet you ... I'm ... ' Dave. NO. Keith. Imogen, what is wrong with you? Paul. That will do. 'Will you join us?' he asks. Michelle takes my left hand, and Paul my right. Everyone in the room is staring at us, lustfully and enviously. I feel a little nervous, a little self-conscious, but I follow Michelle's lead. She moves slowly, confidently, as though she's used to being admired. She's putting on a show. Her body seems to glow under the collective gaze of the guests. The three of us find ourselves in a little anteroom. Michelle elegantly steps out of her white lace, and now she's in nothing but her hold-up stockings. Her body is flawless. 'Your turn,' she says, lifting the black satin over my head before I can protest. And now this imaginary woman can see the weird mole by my belly button, the bits I missed when I was shaving, the ... no! Confident! No wet toast!

Michelle gasps, and Paul purrs with pleasure. The sheer mesh of my black bra accentuates the curve of my breasts, my swollen nipples push against the tight fabric. My high-waisted knickers outline my hourglass figure. I feel like a pin-up girl. Michelle cups my breasts, pinching my nipples tightly between finger and thumb, while Paul deftly unhooks my bra. Softly pressing her lips against mine, Michelle pulls me down to the couch in the corner of the room. I can feel the heat of her body warming mine, it feels like sunshine on my skin. She reaches between my legs and moving the fabric of my underwear to one side, starts to stroke me, softly. I wriggle and writhe against her, desperate to feel her pushing her fingers inside me, but she arches her back. I slide my right hand between her legs, and she's soaking wet, all the way to the top of her thighs. Slowly, with a little trepidation, I slide a finger inside her. I want to make her feel good. I imagine telling my French lover ... No, no one needs the back story. Focus up! Michelle moans so deeply that I'm worried I've hurt her, but she grinds her hips and squeezes my fingers further inside her. I'm lost in her world, desperate to draw those sounds out from her, so I'm briefly confused when I feel a warm hand on the small of my back, more soft lips against my neck. Wordlessly, Paul pulls me away. He's naked now and seems more like a wolf than a lion. His body is tight, but lean, a little spare flesh on his abdomen indicating that he's a man who always puts pleasure first. He places his hands so that they span the space between my breasts and my belly button. 'Now I've got you,' he grins. 'What am I going to do with you?'

He pushes his face against the plane of skin where my neck meets my shoulder, and inhales deeply. I feel his tongue – no, his teeth, grazing the curved flesh, and I feel terrified, but turned on. He's shifted, so I'm on his lap, I feel his cock – too rude? Dick? No. Penis? Noooooooo – stiffening against my skin. He slides his huge hands down my body, his fingers brushing my pussy for less than a second, before he starts to stroke my inner thighs. I squirm against him, desperate to bring his touch higher, but his whole body turns rigid. He grabs my soft skin, slightly too hard, and pushes my legs apart.

He makes eye contact with Michelle, who crawls towards us on her hands and knees – where am I getting this from? – and kneels between my legs. She's breathing rapidly, raggedly, and I can feel the heat of her breath against the most sensitive part of my body, before she even touches me. She kisses me, with agonising slowness. No one has ever made me wait like this, or made me want them so badly. I realise I'm also breathing through my mouth, too fast, gasping and trembling. When I feel the tip of Michelle's tongue against my clit, I start to come. Barely daring to believe what I'm doing, I cup the back of her head in my hands – even her hair feels like thick satin – and tilt my hips towards her, so she has to take more of my body into her mouth. It makes me think of every time some terrible boyfriend has pushed my head against his crotch, and I'm overwhelmed with feelings – I'm guilty, angry, ashamed, powerful. I pull back a little bit, trying to give Michelle room to breathe

245

properly, to move away. But she moves closer to me, as if she's trying to breathe me in. Her fingernails dig sharply into my flesh, and I cry out, I can't control how loud I am and I don't care who hears me.

Steadying herself by holding onto my thighs, Michelle gets off the floor, stooping to kiss me, softly. I can taste myself on her. It's warm, slightly spicy, undeniably human. And when she takes both of my hands in hers, and pulls me up, so that I'm standing, facing her, and says 'my turn', I can't wait to get on my hands and knees. Tentatively, using my left hand for balance, I use my right hand to stroke her clit. It feels enormous against my fingertips, hot, and soaking wet. Closing my eyes, I push my lips, then my tongue, against her. She gasps again, and growls. The sound is shocking, it's raw. Now she's got her hands in my hair, and she's pulling me into her, and I can't breathe but it feels right, I feel completely lost in her.

I stop writing and drum my fingers against the desk. What next? Even though this is pure invention, my breathing is getting a little laboured. My heart is pounding, and my right hand is creeping away from my keyboard, down towards the crotch of my jeans. Looking down, I can clearly see the outline of my nipples through the wool of my jumper – even though I'm wearing a T-shirt underneath, and a very solid bra ... Michelle's whole body is shaking, and she moves against me, wanting more. Still on my hands and knees, I'm aware of two warm hands behind me, against my bare skin, and I moan into Michelle as Paul pushes his cock – Harri will probably change it to penis anyway but I can't do it, it's just too clinical – inside me. He's gripping my hips so tightly that I think his fingertips are going to leave marks against my skin, he bites my neck and murmurs my name – did I even introduce myself to him? Never mind – and thrusts, and thrusts, and I start coming and can't stop. Every cell of my skin is singing with desire, with lust, I'm crying out, I don't know what I'm saying, I can only feel Paul inside me as Michelle quakes against me. Paul cries out and leans back, and Michelle and I fall to the floor. For a moment we lie there, panting and gasping. Seeing my silk slip, I give Michelle one last, lingering kiss, and shake the dress back over my head. 'Enjoy the rest of the party,' I smile. 'Maybe I'll see you again some time.' Without looking behind me, I know they're watching me walk out of the room. Collecting my coat, I find myself welcoming the chill of the evening air, cooling my flushed skin. It's late, but London is still full of tourists, revellers, explorers, people who are only just finishing their work and people who are only just arriving. I wonder if any of them have been on adventures like mine – and whether they'd be shocked to discover my sexy secret.

I'm not sure about the last line. Fallen Bloody Angels could use that as promotional copy in their brochure, but it's purple prose, definitely a little bit flowery, too slick. Still, it's what she asked for. If I copy over my original closing paragraph, it sounds slightly less saccharine. It was deliciously fun to write. I was so angry and anxious when I sat down. Now I feel calm, strangely sated. I could experience pleasure, but at a safe remove. It was as though I was using a completely different part of my brain when I allowed myself to fantasise fully. I feel almost ... cleansed. My breath is getting slower, deeper.

Is this what The Girl wants to read? I'm honestly not

sure. Because when Harri talks about The Girl, it's not a woman I recognise. We all seem to be writing for a young woman who seems sneery, stuck-up, difficult to impress.

I know how magazines work. We need to make out that we're writing for this glossy, confident audience, because glossy, confident people like buying things. Even so, I believe The Girl is much more vulnerable and uncertain than Harri thinks she is, and that's the reader I want to speak to. The reader who needs us the most. The messages are becoming increasingly alarming. '*Hi Imogen, I loved your piece about festival sex – but I'm not body confident. How can I go to outdoor events and feel sexy when I'm so ashamed of the size of my thighs?*'

'*This is for Imogen – could she write back and tell me how she manages to be confident on TV? I'm giving a presentation at work, and I'm so scared, I haven't been sleeping. Hoping she has some tips!*'

'*Dear Imogen, I've tried everything in your dating profile feature but I'm still not getting any matches, can you reply and tell me what I'm doing wrong? I think lip fillers might help?*' Then there are the ones – hundreds of them, every week – who think that all they want is to come and work at The Know. '*I know I don't have much experience, but I'm really organised and passionate,*' or '*Ever since I was little, I've dreamed about writing, and at the moment, the only chance I have to be creative is when I write the company newsletter.*' '*I've applied for so many jobs, and I never even get an email of acknowledgement.*' '*I know twenty-eight seems a bit too old to do work experience but I've been saving my holiday allowance, and I really think . . .*'

It's heartbreaking. Some days, I wish we could give them

all jobs. Some days, I feel like weeping with rage. It took me years, and years, to get here, and I never sent emails like this. I've worked to work, taking on as many minimum wage night jobs as I could, in order to pay for the privilege of working for free. Even so, I'm in debt. I've slept on so many floors that I have permanently twisted a nerve behind one of my shoulder blades. I've been treated like shit, and I've cried, and I've felt very, very hungry.

It has to be worth it. I can't afford to admit that any of this might have been a mistake. The odds have always been stacked against me, but I've always believed – or wanted to believe – that I could earn my dream job, simply by being willing to put up with enough pain. It's worked. Finally, I'm doing something where I'm envied, not pitied. None of these women are writing to tell me to quit, and become a teacher or a recruitment consultant, so that I can buy a house.

They're not happy, though. They're restless, they're not getting the recognition they deserve, they are spending their lives feeling trapped, frightened, unfulfilled, unable to reconcile their ambitions, and their sense of who they are and where they're going with the person they have to turn up and try to be for eight hours a day. These women want to be me. They write to tell me so. I can't quite bring myself to believe that I'm not happy with all of this. And yet. And yet and yet and yet and yet and yet ...

After saving, saving again and saving a third time, I decide that I need a break from my screen. I'll take a quick look in the morning, before sending it to Harri, but every bit of my body is aching. I'm struggling to keep my eyes open. There's no question of me leaving the office. I can barely face leaving this chair. It could easily take me two hours to get home – and there's nothing homey about the dark, damp, chilly flat.

Foraging under Louise's desk, I discover a neat pile of blankets, called in from her 'Hygge is back!' piece (spiked by Harri who claimed that there were only about five people in the world who cared about Hygge first time around, and they all worked at *Good Housekeeping*). Shivering a little, already very much wanting to be under the blankets, I make myself a nest. I take off my boots, and unhook my bra, sliding the straps down, wiggling an elbow and whipping it off through my jumper with a flourish. I could take my jeans off, but ... oh, I'll just close my eyes for a moment, I'd really like to brush my teeth, but sleep is too delicious, the lust for utter stillness floods my body, and I wrap my arms around my chest, and rub my right toes against my left instep. I am confident, I am calm, I have cachet.

Just as sleep creeps up on me, I have a final, unwelcome thought. Harri wants me to be The Girl. The Girl wants to be Imogen Mounce.

But who do I want to be?

Chapter Thirty-Seven

'There's a dildo-making
workshop in Norwich ...'

Harri

'Imogen, this is much better. Thanks for doing this so quickly. This is just what I had in mind.'

Harri is feeling tense, twitchy, not as centred as she'd like to be. She should be relieved. Imogen has done excellent work, and turned it around so fast. Fallen Angels will love it. Even Mackenzie should love it, or at least, love the result. This should save *The Know* for now, or at least grant it a stay of execution. Still, Harri knows she's contravened her own moral code. Putting Imogen through all of this stress is definitely a Mackenzie move. It's grubby, not telling her about the sponsored element. Still, the copy is perfect, so the end has justified the means.

'I'm glad you like it, ' says Imogen, sounding flat. Is she upset about something else? She seems very tired.

'We'll get Kim to do the illustration, he'll do a fantastic

job on this. Everyone's going to be so pleased. Even management – Akila has already lined up some serious advertising on the back of this, so ... '

Harri spots something unsettling flashing across Imogen's face. Anger? Resentment?

'I guess that's good, that Hudson can make some money out of my—'

'What?'

'No, nothing, sorry. I'm really pleased. Just a bit tired. I've had a few late nights!'

Harri notices the dark circles under Imogen's eyes, and winces with guilt. Come on! She's twenty-seven! She should have limitless energy and peachy skin! Harri has two whole extra decades of tiredness to deal with! *When they make you the editor, when you're up all night frowning at Mackenzie's impossible pie charts, then, by all means, come back and yawn in my face.*

'Well, there might be more late nights to come! I've got plans for you! I think we could maybe do a series on the sexiest nights in the capital. Maybe send you all over the country on exciting trips! That would be fun, wouldn't it? Akila was just telling me about a dildo making workshop in Norwich ... '

Imogen does not look too thrilled about this. 'Harri, I was wondering ... I think I might be coming down with something. Could I maybe ... go home? It feels like a bug, hopefully if I can catch it now, I can sleep it off.'

Harri realises this is an opportunity for her to be magnanimous. She can afford to be. The poor girl does look like shit. Maybe it is a bug. 'Oh, love, of course, go. Get some rest. Do you want me to get you a taxi? I'd treat myself to a black cab if I were you, you don't want to be thrown around in the back of an Uber if you're feeling poorly.'

Did Imogen just roll her eyes? 'Um, no, I'll walk. I could probably use the fresh air.'

Chapter Thirty-Eight

The great affair is to move

Imogen

While Sam Strong is an unequivocal creep, I have a theory that he doesn't just date much younger women because he craves our firm young flesh. I strongly suspect it's because we're mostly low maintenance, and we hardly ever bother him with phone calls. Actually ringing him indicates a Defcon 1 emergency. So he picks up in two seconds. 'Imogen! What's happened? What's wrong?' Half a beat. 'You're not pregnant, are you?'

'No, no, nothing like that. Having a bit of a weird time at work, and I was hoping to take advantage of your wisdom and experience ...'

Sam Strong is vain, and I can sometimes use that to my advantage. He chuckles. 'I see. I'm in the office but I can probably be home in an hour or so. See you at my place?'

'We could just go somewhere for lunch? Or coffee?'

'Ah, it's been a while. I'm in the mood for a nooner.'

Dammit. This means a thirty quid trip to Boots the Chemist, and toothpaste and deodorant and everything else it takes to remove every trace of my night in the office.

When he opens his apartment door, he's in a white towelling dressing gown.

'Did you nick that from a hotel?'

'Hello to you too.' He lunges at my mouth. 'Mmmm, minty fresh. Actually, Miss Smarty Pants, I think you'll find that I designed them for a hotel! There's one for you too, if you want. A branding thing I did for *The Gentleman*.'

'How do you even design a dressing gown?'

'Robe.'

'Robe, then? It's only marginally harder than designing a tea towel. You can hardly put a bonus sleeve in.'

Sam looks exasperated. 'Do you want one, or not?'

It does look cosy. Usually, I attempt to undress with intent, but I'm so tired that I peel down my underwear with my jeans, pull off my jumper, and leave my boots at the bottom of a puddle of clothes on the floor. The robe is heavy, and blissfully thick. I could wrap it all the way around me, twice over. It's made for a man. Of course it is, I think resentfully, even though it's a delicious novelty to feel fragile, to feel enveloped by the too muchness of something.

'What's this?' I've spotted a brown splodge on the breast pocket. 'I hope that's chocolate ... oh, it's embroidered. It's ... is that supposed to be a pair of poo emojis?' One poo is balanced on top of the other.

'What? My logo? We had it designed, it's a double S, in dark bronze! We commissioned Design Lab, it cost twenty grand.'

'It's a double poo, Sam.'

255

Sam Strong frowns, and stares at me for a second. 'Shit. Oh, shit, oh shit, oh shit.'

'Exactly.'

'Give me a minute, I need to make some calls.'

Fine, fine. 'I'm just going to lie down and close my eyes for a second ...'

I come to, feeling much better, if slightly disorientated. Where am I? What's happening? Oh, Sam Strong is at the end of the bed, reading a magazine. I squint at it. Protein, Prada, Power Posing – are you a luxury gym bro? Right. I know exactly where I am. 'Are you OK?' Sam asks. 'You've been out for the count for about three hours.'

I yawn. 'Much better, thank you. I pulled an all-nighter in the office last night.' Better to put it in language that Sam Strong will understand. 'Pulled an all-nighter' sounds much more hardcore and more glamorous than 'I couldn't face going home so I made a nest from blankets and bean bags'.

'You said it wasn't going well? I've been hearing rumours about Hudson. Apparently that American, what's her name, is making a big investment in the trade titles, so they're pulling the plug on most of the mags.'

More Sam nonsense, surely. 'We only just launched, and they'd never close *Panache*. Anyway, yeah, I'm not sure ... it's really demanding, and fast paced. And it's a lot of fun, but I just did a piece about Fallen Angels, you know, the sex parties ...'

He suddenly seems a little more interested. 'Ah, tell me more!'

'Honestly, it wasn't great. Not that sexy. But Harri made me rewrite it, I had to make it sound sexier than it was, and then I found out that it's being used to pull in a lot of ad revenue, and I was wondering – please can you tell me, honestly, as a man who has done it – how do I get them to pay me more? I've only just started, and I think I'm technically still on probation, I'm not sure that the timing is right to demand more money just yet. But – when? And how?'

Sam Strong is scrolling through his phone. 'Oi, stop that! I'm asking for some advice.' I poke him with my toe.

He raises an eyebrow. 'I can do better than advice. John at *The Gentleman* was very interested when I told him you were the one who raised the alarm about the robes.'

'You didn't tell him I was in your bed, did you?'

'Of course not!' He is smirking, and I am not convinced.

'How does he know about me?'

'Your media career has been raising some eyebrows. And probably some other things, let's be real. He sounded very keen to meet you, and he was saying that they're under some, ah, pressure, to get more women in there and writing. It's Marker Media, so they've got cash. Just think about the pay rise you'd want from Hudson, add ten grand to it, and ask for that.'

'Ten grand?' He looks at me. 'Maybe five grand. Anyway, it puts the ball in your court. You go, or you stay. Here's the thing, Imogen. No one ever gives you a pay rise because you actually deserve one. You move – or you threaten to move. That's all the power you ever have, as an employee. The great affair is to move.'

'Diana Vreeland?'

'Well done, good girl.' He is unbelievable. Six months ago, Sam Strong didn't know who Diana Vreeland was, and had to borrow my copy of her memoir in order to give a talk at an Esquire party at the V&A. I look pointedly at his protein article, but he does not register my sarcasm. He's texting someone. 'Right. You're on. John will see you tomorrow. You know Marker? That massive office near London Bridge.'

'What will I tell Harri?'

'Whatever you told her that made you available this afternoon. Now, take that terrible robe off and tell me all about Fallen Angels.'

Chapter Thirty-Nine

Perfect Gentleman

Imogen

Things are very different at *The Gentleman*. The building is opposite London Bridge station, but for a moment, I'm worried that I've taken a wrong turn and gone back inside a new part of the tube. Hundreds of people – OK, maybe not hundreds, but lots – are scurrying. Everyone looks sour and serious, and packed with purpose. Everyone seems to be wearing grey or black. Focus fills their handbags, their briefcases. Believe me, it's a briefcase sort of place.

Even though I have applied for every single internship, placement and editorial assistant job I have ever seen advertised by Marker Media, this is the first time that I've been invited inside. I did not think this door would ever open for me, no matter how politely I knocked, or powerfully I pushed. *The Gentleman* exerts a strange pull on me.

Even though all I want is a job offer, a bargaining

chip, I start daydreaming about seeing the words 'Imogen Mounce: *The Gentleman*' on a business card. It sounds like titanium. No one bullies a girl who knows her way around a single malt whisky, or a Louis Vuitton monogram. I'm trying not to think about the seedy, depressing rumours. That they only hire interns from model agencies. That their Christmas party has a cocaine budget. That someone in their ad team had been fired for 'using' an inflatable doll in a stationery cupboard.

Foolishly, I have decided to wear a black satin pencil skirt. I still remember its origin story. Maybe three years ago, I got really into *Mad Men* on Netflix. Just like every other woman in the world who has ever gazed down at her thighs and felt disappointed, I decided that if I really tried, I could look like Joan Holloway. Around that time, I was sifting through the dregs of the sale at Topshop and couldn't believe my eyes when I found a Joan skirt, my size, 80 per cent off. I rushed home with it, without trying it on and decided that I'd make it fit. Even if I had to give up bread for a week.

I'm reluctant to admit this, even silently, to myself, but in front of the mirror, the skirt looks good. It's twenty-first century miracle-corsetry, squeezing me in at the waist and making everything else appear swollen, but smooth.

Once I'd tapped my card, gone through the station barriers and yanked the stupid skirt down for the fortieth time since I'd left the house, I realised I'd made a big – huge – mistake. The fatal, flattering flaw of the skirt is that it's so tight, it's impossible to move any joint connected to my hips. It binds my knees together so that my only option, for progress, is to take a series of miniature kicks with straightened calves, allowing me to cover the tiniest sips of ground. Or, I suppose, to hover. My journey would have been easier if I'd done it as a sack race.

Fortunately, my coat covers me from nose to knee. After some slow, frustrating waddling, I rolled the skirt right up and wore it as a pool ring. The good news is that this means I'm on time. The bad news is that I'm boiling hot, my white shirt is soaked with sweat and I have no idea how to hoik everything into place without being escorted out of the building for public indecency. Also, there's the matter of my own knock-off Louboutins, which are currently nestled in the grubby cotton tote bag hanging off my wrist. Experimentally, I try to pull the skirt down with a short, sharp tug. Nothing doing. I dump the tote and try to use both hands. It won't budge.

I'm about to step outside and try to sort myself out around the back of the building, away from the eyes of the world's press, when one of the receptionists catches my eye. She asks if I have an appointment. Isn't the English language a complex, powerful tool? It's interesting that in the wrong hands 'Can I help you?' becomes the cruellest, least generous question in the world.

She is predictably, obnoxiously glossy. Her hair is swept up, smooth at the top, ornate at the back, thick and bountiful. It could be used as a display model in the window of a Parisian patisserie. Her lips are carmine – a word I did not realise I knew until I saw it, staring me in the face. Are those perfect false eyelashes, or her own perfect eyelashes? She has clearly never given herself conjunctivitis by faffing about with tweezers and old glue during a last minute panic on New Year's Eve.

'Yes, I'm Imogen Mounce, here to see ...' Oh, bloody hell, what is he called? 'Tom Johnson, at *The Gentleman*.'

She keeps a straight face, but her eyelashes seem to laugh at me. 'Do you mean John Thompson?'

I do mean John Thompson. What a stuck-up bitch, knowing the names of the people who work in the building. I try to inject a little *froideur* into my voice. It's like dropping a very small ice cube into a cup of steaming hot tea. 'Yes, that's what I said, John Thompson,' I gurgle.

'OK, I need you to look into this camera, and I'll print your security pass,' says The Girl With The Croissant Updo. Right – professional, polished, poised. Come on. Making a claw with my thumb and forefinger, I smooth my eyebrows, which are damp to the touch. Some of the dark brown pencil has come off on my fingers, and it looks like ... oh no. No. How can I fix this? Just in time, I stretch my neck up and suck my cheeks in. At least I won't have a moon face. 'Here you go,' says the receptionist, smirking as she hands me a metal clip, affixed to a small plastic wallet that appears to contain a picture of E.T.

I'm exiled to a metal bench, and attempt to discreetly slip on my Interview Shoes. They are very plain, black leather, with a sort of stiletto heel, from a department store that claims its 'airsole' is the last word in 'shoe comfort technology'. Airsole also being the perfect insult for the lying marketing strategy that tricked me into this particular purchase.

As I slip off my Converse, I detect the faint but unmistakable stale scent of my own feet. I can't bring smelly shoes to *The Gentleman*. But I can't leave them here, crammed in the tote bag. Someone will think it's a bomb scare, they will get blown up and I will have to hobble home in my stupid high heels. My toes are slightly too long for my smart shoes, and the little toe of my right foot is bent and twisted. I try, and fail to wriggle it, which makes me gasp in agony and screw my face up like a gargoyle's.

'Imogen? Imogen Mounce?'

When I look up, I discover the voice is coming through a set of very small, very white, very even teeth. He smells oddly familiar. Slightly fruity, slightly cake-y. Oh! That's not perfect skin, that's NARS Pure Radiant Tinted Moisturiser, my most prized beauty cupboard freebie. Aha! Ahahahahaha.

I beam at him, and then clamp my lips shut to hide my own entirely normal, serviceable teeth. Speaking out of the side of my mouth like a gangster, I offer 'Hello! You must be John?'

'Ah, no. No, no no. John wouldn't come down to meet you, he's upstairs. I'm Bradley, I'm here to take you to John, for your interview.'

Never in my life have I felt more like a shambling, homeless person. The grotty bag. The awkward walk in unfamiliar shoes, made weirder and wobblier by the skirt still rolled around my middle. The enormous coat that I can't take off. The shameful and unshakeable conviction that I smell. 'So, Bradley, have you worked here long?' I am taking some comfort from the fact that, in spite of his access to spendy skincare, Bradley is clearly twelve and must be quite junior.

'I've been features director at *The Gentleman* for five years now. I'm surprised you didn't know that.'

Somehow, I manage to humiliate myself even more on

the slow, slow escalator ride to the first floor. 'It's a beautiful building, isn't it?' I beam to Bradley's back. 'Very airy!' Hours, days, weeks pass. Governments fall. The sea level rises. 'Do you, um ... have any pets?' What is he, my German pen pal? 'No,' smirks Bradley, and as he leads me through his office, I work out why. He does not need any extra animals in his life, because he works for an actual walrus.

'Ah hum hum hum!' says the walrus, his neck rolls a-quiver, and it takes me a moment to translate this as 'Imogen'. 'Yes!' I cry. 'The time has come to talk of many things ... sorry, I mean hello! You must be John.' John takes my slightly damp hand in his actually slippery one, and pumps vigorously. Forgetting myself, I stare at him, fascinated. Every part of his body, as far as I can tell, is in perpetual motion, with the exception of a greying, waxed and curled moustache, solid and still as compass North.

'Sit ye down,' says John, with a little menace, as if I've threatened to climb on the table and perform a collection of madrigals. Out of habit, I squat, not quite resting my weight on the chair he is indicating just in case it immediately collapses beneath me. But I'm not in the Hudson Media Offices anymore. I have no reason to suspect that someone rescued this chair from a skip. Money has been spent. A lot of money, I think, as I feel an ornamental button digging through my coat, straight into my spine.

'Now, Imogen,' says John, just as my eyes land on a crusty patch on his waistcoat. Please, be egg. 'Imogen, we've been watching your career with, ah, great interest, we saw you with Chuck Whatsit on the TV, and we thought "girl's a tonic!"'

Bradley chips in. 'So, Dora Bainbridge called you a slut! She's so outrageous, I love her. She's hilarious,' he says, snidely. He doesn't sound as though he's ever laughed in his life.

'Um, did she actually call me a slut? I don't think ...'

'We're longing to hear more of your ... erotic adventures,' says John, wiping his palms on his thighs. 'We're hoping you could give us a little preview!'

I must pull this back. 'Actually, I had a few ideas I'd love to explore with you.' My notebook is also in the tote bag, but I can't bend down and pull it out. My skirt has graduated to my nipples, and now it has my entire torso in its evil grip. Maybe if I sort of ... kick the bag? Prodding it with toes, I get the straps caught in a stiletto heel.

'OK, so ideas. I'd love to write about fragrances worn by pop culture icons. Ian Fleming wore Floris 89, and suggested that Bond did too, and when he made *Alfie* Michael Caine was wearing Guerlain Vetiver ...'

John looks through me, smirking at Bradley. 'Actually, darling, we're much more interested in something along the lines of your recent efforts.'

Bradley opens a navy blue leather Smythson notebook. It brings me some pleasure to note that it appears to be monogrammed, and his initials, picked out in gold, are 'BS'. He clears his throat. 'Why Don't You: A Guide to Morning Masturbation, by Imogen Mounce. Ladies, let's be real. No one wants to get out of bed on a cold morning. So what if I told you there was a sure fire way to get yourself up, in every sense? We all deserve to go out into the world with a smile on our face. Let's stop hitting the snooze button, and start hitting the other button ...' He looks straight at me.

He does not deserve to have a smile on his face. His delivery is camp, and cruel. He isn't even trying to conceal a sneer. However, John's expression is even more upsetting. I think he's openly leering at me, breathing through his mouth, rapidly and noisily. His neck – or the place where his neck should be – is all a-quiver, wobbling and undulating like the crowd at a music festival.

'Go on,' breathes John. 'Imogen, do you really ... do that first thing in the morning?' Well, I used to. After this, I don't think I'll be able to do it ever again.

I have to take control of the situation. Maybe it's a test! John is just being a little bit ... old school. I'm not an idiot, I know that *The Gentleman* is not exactly marketed as a crucial feminist text. But it's an iconic title and working for them would mean forcing myself to get used to this. Whatever this is.

John's got to be closer to fifty than forty, but he's not the urbane, sophisticated media star I believed him to be. He's more like a twelve-year-old boy, convinced the best day of his life is the one when he almost saw a single nipple.

If I don't rise to it, I can get this back on track. It's so weird here. I imagine sitting at a desk in a room as elegant as this one, with its gleaming, dark wooden table, the soft, Scotch Mist blues warmed by bronze lamplight. And in the middle of it all, John, poking my forearm, showing me a scribbled picture of a spurting penis, or getting hold of an old-fashioned Casio calculator just so he can write BOOBIES upside down.

I try to smile, drawing on my final reserves of nerve. 'We can definitely talk about content that's a little closer to what we're doing at *The Know*, although I think my tone there is very different. I'd love to hear your thoughts about what your readers are looking for. One thing that consistently performs well for us is our sex toy pieces. That sits really well with our demographic, but maybe there's a way of covering it for an olde— I mean, slightly more mature male audience? And the advertising potential is huge, of course!'

That was magnificent. I wish I had a microphone, so I could drop it hard onto the polished tabletop. Advertising potential! Tone! Demographic! I actually sounded like a grown-up.

John strokes a tusk, I mean, his nose. He breathes in, he breathes out. He rattles. Is he dying? Is he about to tell me that he will bequeath me a column as long as I respect his final wish and spend the night at a haunted house?

'And have you, ah, um, have you had any more three-somes lately?'

Oh, for fuck's sake.

Did Harri put them up to this? I'm genuinely starting to wonder whether this is a prank, and she's about to jump out from behind a potted plant and say 'Ahahahaha! Caught you! I knew you didn't have a stomach bug!'

I look at Bradley, expecting to see contempt, but he's staring at his Smythson and furiously crosshatching with a Biro. He's a little flushed, under the NARS, and I think – I hope – he's feeling slightly embarrassed. I'm trying to catch his eye, wanting him to see my fury, my indignation. He won't look up. And that's when I have to bite hard on my lip to stop it wobbling. How very bleak. How desperately sad. No wonder Bradley is such a knob. He has to deal with this all day long.

However, I will get on my knees and suck John's dick

under the table before I allow him to see a single tear on my face. So I blink very hard and spend the last of my confidence currency. 'I have to get to another meeting, but it's been great to meet you both. And if you want to discuss those ideas further, you have my email. Hope to see you both soon.' I do! Ideally, in a big picture on the front of a newspaper, arrested for being a sex offender, and an accomplice to a sex offender. Standing up, I offer John my hand, even though my brain is screaming 'Don't touch him! You don't know where he's been!' Unfortunately, the stiff wool of my coat has bunched, and it buckles under the strain of the sudden movement. The button has not been properly secured in its hole. My coat falls open, exposing not delectable, voluptuous, satin clad thigh, but my black cotton crotch, sandwiched between a thick wad of skirt and a bobbly roll of 100 denier tights.

John's face is so red that he's turned neon. You could hang him on the wall of a bar and stick a pool table underneath. I'm genuinely concerned that he might die, or at the very least, fall into a coma, but that's Bradley's problem. Making no attempt to conceal my underwear, I hook my thumb over John's pudgy one, and touch him for the very last time before heading towards the door.

Fuck him! I hope he has nightmares about my crotch. Let him masturbate over that, if he wants to! I wish him lots of luck! Now I'm breathing in a ludicrous, laboured way, like a pervert in an alley, because I know that if I'm not careful I'll start laughing and crying at the same time. As I pick my way along the corridor, I'm emitting bat-like squeaks, until I start giggling, and start roaring, and I'm weeping with hysterical relief. Poor, poor Bradley! Poor

John, even! I can just imagine him turning up to the cover shoots while supermodels run for cover, locking themselves in the toilet and begging for mercy. I think about all of the film premieres that *The Gentleman* has sponsored over the years. I can picture John, so sweaty and excited that he's in danger of sliding out of his seat, popcorn stuck to his moustache, while the space beside him remains empty, while A-list actresses call their managers and sob 'Tell him I've had to leave because I have diarrhoea! Tell him I've gone to hospital with it.'

When I reach the top of the escalator, I pause. This is where the dream dies, really, isn't it? Back down the moving staircase to real life, Harri's moods, Louise's freak-outs, too many late nights and not quite enough money. I really hoped that I'd come back down as someone who belonged, that being in this gilded world would allow me to shed my scalier self and discover something fresh and smooth beneath. I thought I just wanted a way of strengthening my position at *The Know*. Now, I'm forced to admit to myself that I wanted to be wanted. As a *writer*, not as a cheap laugh for a middle-aged man.

But then, I realise with shame, *The Gentleman* has always made me feel rejected and excluded – even more than any fashion magazine. I've been waiting for so long to be invited in that it never occurred to me that I might want to walk straight out again. Did I think John might validate me? Did I hope he'd make me feel like a supermodel? I'm pretty sure he makes the supermodels feel like shit. Does John feel like he belongs anywhere? Well, he hardly seems awash with self-awareness. But how lonely, desperate and mad do you need to be to summon a woman to your office just to get her to talk about her sex life, especially when you can read about it for free, on the internet? I wonder how much Bradley gets paid. Whatever they give him, it can't be enough.

The interview was humiliating, but I'm not ashamed, and I'm not embarrassed. I'm furious. I thought that ambition meant trying for trying's sake, pushing myself beyond the point of pain, desperately grasping at the next rung on the ladder, no matter what it costs me. Since I left that room, I'm not sure that makes any sense to me, any more. I want to have choices. Under no circumstances would I choose to work at *The Gentleman*. I'm shocked to realise that I no longer need these people to validate me. That that feels liberating.

Maybe there would be more money, but I might be even more stressed, burned out and exhausted. I'd be choosing between a boss who makes me go to sex parties and write about it, and a boss who might make me go to a sex party as his date. Perversely, this feels like ambition. Putting my own happiness and wellbeing before some obscure, arbitrary definition of success. I don't know who said 'Dress for the job you want, not the job you have', but I think they should change it. 'If you go to the interview in an outfit that feels like fancy dress, you really don't want the job.' I can't wait to take my shoes off.

As I totter out of the building, into the cold, I realise that my trainers are in my tote bag. In the boardroom. Under John Thompson's chair.

Chapter Forty

You can never be bigger than the building

Harri

'They're firing me.'

'Fuck! NO. Giles! Oh my God, I'm so sorry. Fuck. Fuck.'

Harri is choking on her white wine, gulping for air, frantically waving away her concerned friend's administrations and scissoring the air in front of her as she struggles for oxygen. Giles hands Harri a pint glass filled with water, and equilibrium is momentarily restored.

'I'm sorry, that was ... oh, Giles. How can they? I mean, can we sue them?'

Giles smiles, ruefully. 'Redundancy. Fucking Katie and Lily have recommended that fashion be folded into advertising, so everything will be a bastard advertorial, organised by some twelve year olds from a call centre in Reading. In three months, my job stops existing.'

Harri frowns, and gulps some more. She doesn't want to pull focus, but she fears she might be sick. 'That makes

271

no sense. Without a fashion editor, *Panache* is just … a catalogue with some features in it.'

'Right. I mean – Harri, honestly, it's been awful. It's not been *Panache* since you and Rosa went. It feels like a ghost town. It's almost a relief. But … but … '

Harri has never seen Giles cry before. She takes his hands in hers.

'We'll work something out. We will. And if it's redundancy, you must get a decent pay off?'

Giles is sobbing now. 'No, not really. It's almost funny, how ingeniously evil it is. You know I was doing a few consultancy bits, here and there, a few years ago? They took me off my staff contract and made me a contractor? The day rate seemed too good to resist – well, it means that legally, they can give me bugger all. I've got savings … '

For long, long seconds, Giles cries silently. His shoulders rise, and fall, and rise again. Harri squeezes his hands as tightly as she can, and then gets up from the table and takes him in her arms.

'Oh, Harri, I'm sorry. I'm so sorry.'

'Shhh, love. It's OK. It's OK.' It's not OK, at all.

This bold, bright, brilliant man has been broken by a business operating system. Giles – who seemed so dazzling, bitchy, quick witted and glib when Harri met him over a decade ago – but who has also revealed himself to be tender-hearted, wise, profoundly loving. Giles, who turned up and was simply kind to her, day by day, hour by hour, when she thought her own world had ended.

'It's just so undignified,' he says, extracting himself from her body, pressing a crimson cashmere-clad forearm against his temple. 'I'm forty-nine, Harri! As we all know, that makes me about seven hundred and three, in gay years. Where will I go? What will I do? No one else is going to hire me. I'm too old, I'm not relevant anywhere.'

Harri shakes her head. 'That's crazy, any magazine would be lucky to have you! You're too talented not to be snapped up. We'll fix this, together. We'll make it work!'

Giles sighs. 'I feel like I lost my instincts. I should have seen this coming. I should have gone with you and Rosa, but I felt too old and tired and scared. You know, for a long time, the job was hard, but it was so much fun. I loved the jetlag, the panic, even the sodding models! Do you remember when we made the fake Hollywood sign for that shoot at Pinewood Studios, and we had to get Cara Delevingne to sit in the Y? And every year, it got a little more miserable, a little more pinched, but I was so proud. Together, on a page, we could make every fifty quid in the budget do five grand's worth of work. And now ... '

Giles looks up at the ceiling and blinks. Harri knows this trick can temporarily staunch a flow of tears. 'Now, well. What does redundant mean? It's not just a word for laid off. It means I'm useless. My job at *Panache* is going to stop existing, but my job doesn't really exist anywhere. If this is happening at Hudson, it's happening all over publishing. I feel a bit like the inventor of the Betamax video. I've dedicated my life to building a talent, a skill that nobody wants!'

'For what it's worth, things obviously didn't go that well for the inventor of VHS in the end ... '

Giles sips his white wine and gathers his thoughts. 'Harri, there were so many times that I wanted to leave. Every so often I thought "I'll give it another year, then I'll go and work as a stylist, or see if I can get something going with

273

a designer". You know what stopped me? It was the mast-head. I loved telling people I worked at *Panache*.' He digs into his pocket, pulls out his Thom Browne grained leather wallet, and holds up a creased, yellowed rectangle, about two inches long. Time has drained almost all colour from the logo on the back, but Harri recognises it instantly. 'I was so proud when I got my first business cards. Giles Robinson, *Panache*, could go anywhere. But Giles Robinson, freelance stylist, is no one. *Panache* swallows up your identity. I could never be bigger than that building. I couldn't bear ...' the tears begin again, '... couldn't bear the thought of talking to people about my job, and having them say "but didn't you use to work at *Panache*?" And that was when I was thinking about doing it on my own terms!'

Harri gets it. She isn't just thinking of her own sudden ejection from the hallowed halls of *Panache*, months ago. Giles' pain evokes a memory of a different period of grief. She tries to remember something comforting, anything the counsellor might have told her that made some sem-blance of sense as she howled her way through the shock and the pain.

What can she tell him? She should have seen this coming. She should have intuited it, fought harder, planned a coun-ter attack. There must have been something she could have done. Now, all she has for him are platitudes.

'This feels like the worst thing that could possibly happen. It feels like the end of hope – the end of who you are and who you were going to be. But you will muddle through it.' She thinks, hard. What does she wish she had known? What does she still want to believe most?

She looks at her friend. 'At the moment, you feel as

though you'll never be happy again. The pain will never pass, completely. You will know moments of joy, moments of peace. Right now, you feel entirely buried by the weight of this. But I promise you shall find yourself again.'

Giles shakes his head. He drains his white wine, rests his head against the sticky table, and cries, and cries, and cries.

Harri is starting to realise she may have underestimated Mackenzie. She better not have overestimated herself.

Chapter Forty-One

Breathless

Imogen

The day after the interview, I'm all better from my 'bug' and heading back to work, restored by a very early night, and a very big pizza. Still, I've been avoiding my emails, scared of what I might find. A telling off from Harri, a telling off from Sam Strong, a photo of John Thompson masturbating into one of my abandoned trainers. On the journey to the office, I reach the point of realising that I have nothing to fear but fear itself – or rather, not looking seems slightly more anxiety inducing than looking, so I take a deep, dread filled breath and check my inbox.

At first, I assume the message is junk, and my spam filter is not working correctly.

FW: Naked speed dating
Think we need to cover this. Can you sign up? Hx

I stop suddenly on the steps, and five furious people pile up behind me. 'Fucking tourist,' mutters a man in a be kind T-shirt. He accidentally-on-purpose treads on my toes as he pushes past.

If I can come up with something else – anything at all – in the eight minutes before Conference starts, I might be able to get out of it. I squint at my phone notes, hoping that Past Me had some amazing idea that can be repurposed. Surprisingly sexy films? Tried it, Harri gave it to Louise and killed it after Louise refused to back down on her conviction that the sexiest film of all time is *The Piano*. What is Bacterial Vaginosis? Oh, yeah. Not aspirational enough, according to Harri.

My brain is working so furiously – and hopelessly – that I don't really register the rest of the journey to the office until I'm in the meeting sitting on a wobbly chair, telling Harri that I saw her email and I've signed up. Akila is beaming. 'We've got a meeting with Rimmel later, they're big fans of yours.'

'Mmmm,' I say, staring at the grain of the fake wood. I know I should use this to my advantage – maybe next week I'll feel brave enough to ask for a raise. Right now, if I look up, I know that Tabitha will be staring at me so furiously that I will turn, instantly and irreversibly, to stone.

My first match is Geoff, a 33-year-old vet. He has a nice smile, and ... neatly trimmed pubes. For all I know, Geoff exists and is out there meeting some other naked Imogen right now, in a smart Mayfair hotel. But I am in Mitcham, alone in bed, writing on my phone with my head under the duvet. Geoff is very friendly, and ... I can't do this.

I want to cry. I want to quit. I want to call Louise. I've deliberately been very vague with her about the naked speed dating – well, about the fact that I had no intention of going.

'Maybe you'll meet the love of your life?' she'd said, hopefully. 'Maybe this is the answer we've all been waiting for!'

'Yeah ... no. I don't think that's likely.'

'You know what they say. You'll find him when you're not looking!' Louise looked so dreamy and excited that I briefly thought I might have found a solution to my woes.

'Why don't you go? Who knows – *you* might meet the one.'

Louise shook her head violently. 'No way am I brave enough for naked speed dating. And I don't like dating, you know that.'

I didn't, actually. 'But don't you want to meet someone eventually?'

'Not now. My twenties are all about establishing my career and meeting my professional goals. I told you about my five year plan! I've got to be an editor by the time I'm thirty, and then I can date.'

When Louise once told me her dream man was Eric from *The Little Mermaid*, I thought she was joking. But maybe she just doesn't do men in 3D. I didn't know what to say.

'But you're already an editor. You're our entertainment editor.'

'Not just a section editor! Editor in Chief. Not of *The Know*, necessarily, but somewhere.'

'By the time you're thirty?' I didn't want to say it out loud, but Lou's goal meant being promoted about nine times in roughly six months.

'That's why I don't date! No time,' said Louise, as though

she was explaining to me why she didn't walk on railway lines or eat from dustbins.

Sometimes I think that the only people who are actually dating are journalists desperate for something to write about. But the data claims that The Girl dates, cheerfully and fearlessly. According to the media pack, The Girl is a bloody nymphomaniac. I don't believe Harri, or even Akila. If The Girl is real, she isn't out there, confidently and dispassionately inspecting testicles. She's probably in a single bed, like me, with her head under the duvet, certain that everyone else in the world is out having fun without her.

I write directly to her. 798 words intended to cheer her up, make her laugh, and try to make her believe that she's cool enough and hot enough to go naked speed dating too, if she really wants to. But she doesn't have to.

I draw my own conclusions. Ultimately, naked speed dating might just be the perfect antidote to twenty-first century dissembling. If you're fed up with finding false friends on the internet, you might want to look for a partner in a place where no one has anything to hide. What you see is what you get. However, I'm starting to wonder whether the pursuit of modern love really just leaves us all with a yearning for old fashioned romance. This simply made me miss the longing, dreaming, waiting and craving you feel on a perfect first date. I want the connection and intimacy that comes from a slow reveal. And I don't know why I can't wear my heart on my sleeve when I know there are so many testicles under the table.

Harri will hate that. But I think she needs to hear it. I'm offering her some market research. The Girl wants true love, lust and longing, I'm sure of it. I do.

I put the copy in a draft email to Harri. I decide that I don't want to send it – but maybe I can revisit it, and use some of the jokes, if I reschedule and go to the next one. If Harri isn't too furious with me.

As I start to drift off to sleep, with my phone in my hand, my pounding heart keeps jerking me awake. I'm so tired, and so wired. Fragments of bad dreams loop and flicker. I have a nightmare that I suddenly panic about the deadline, send the email, then I am naked, and Harri is chasing me through the traffic on Shaftesbury Avenue. Every time she catches me, I wiggle, sweatily, from her grasp. I'm ducking behind bushes, into side streets, and there is nowhere to hide. She finds me every time.

Screaming, I wake myself up. I'm weeping, clawing the air, trying to catch my breath. My mouth doesn't work, my nose doesn't work, the world is separated from me by invisible straws, all clogged with lemon pips. The sheet beneath me is cold, and sodden. I can't stop crying. Is this a heart attack? Am I going to die?

I think about calling an ambulance, but then, if this isn't a heart attack, will I get into trouble? Do women in their twenties have heart attacks? I can't call Mum, she'll worry. Obviously I can't call Jen. I have a vague memory of a conversation with Kim about cholesterol. 'I'm super careful, most of the time, my dad had a cardiac episode last year, he's fine now, but ...'

It's late – well, early. But this is an emergency. Kim it is.

'Im, oh my God, are you OK? It's 5 a.m.'

'Sorry ... think I'm dying ... am I having a ... heart attack?' I don't think I've ever cried like this.

'It's OK, you're OK, deep breaths if you can. Where are

you? At home? I think you're having a panic attack. Do you have any intense shooting pain in your chest or arms?'

'A little ... my chest ...'

'Hon, can you breathe with me? In, count to four ... You're doing so well. Go slow, as slow as you can. You feel like you're dying, you're not dying, I promise! I used to get these doing exams.'

Miraculously, I feel a bit better. 'Have you been out tonight?' asks Kim. 'Have you had any drugs or alcohol? I'm not judging, but if you've had an adverse reaction to anything we need to get you to the hospital.'

'No, no. I've just been at home in bed.'

'OK, that's great, that's really good news. Let's do some more breathing. In, two, three, four ...' Kim's kindness makes me want to cry all over again, but I feel a lot better. 'Did anything bring this on, or did it just happen?'

'I woke up like this!' I say, and Kim laughs. I laugh too.

'OK, good girl. It sounds like you're on the mend.'

'Kim, I don't want to sound dramatic, but I honestly felt as though I might be dying, just then. It's not the first time I've had something like that but ... it was definitely the most severe. The most frightening. What do I do if it happens again? I can't keep having these attacks, out of nowhere.' But as my heartbeat starts to slow down, I think about that phrase. It did not come out of nowhere. This wasn't a total shock. It felt more like a manifestation, a boiling over. Something I've been on the brink of for some time.

'Anyone can see you're stressed. When did you last see a doctor?'

I frown. 'Maybe just before Christmas, I was working a lot, and I kept crying for no reason.' That feels like a strange thing to share with Kim, but it's slipped out now. I'd picked up some extra bar shifts, and it was hard to fit them in with the factory. I went to an emergency walk-in clinic, hoping for a magic prescription to get me through the month. The doctor rolled his eyes and suggested that I try a yoga class.

Kim pauses. 'You could probably do with some time off,' he says, finally.

'But I just had that, er ... bug,' I say, guiltily. I'm sure I could have told Kim about *The Gentleman*, but I think I've left it too late. The lie is left to fester. 'Harri has sent me a huge list of features, she's said it's our priority to maintain the traffic numbers. But next month ... I just need to get through this, and then I'm sure things will slow down.'

'At least you sound calmer now,' says Kim, relieved. 'Do you want me to stay on the line, or do you think you can go back to sleep?'

'I think I'm OK now. Thank you. Thank you so much. Did I wake you?'

'Nah, I was just on my way to the gym.'

'You're so committed.'

'There's a hell of an incentive.'

'The swimmer?'

'Yeah. Although I think we're on the outs. There's this new guy who dominates the battle ropes ... '

Chapter Forty-Two

The Sense of an Ending

Imogen

I sleep fitfully, and within moments of waking, the panic is back. This is all such a mess.

Why didn't I just go naked speed dating? What will Harri say when I tell her I just didn't turn up? I've failed. I've fucked up. I'm getting fired. A few days ago, I was trying to counsel Louise through her imposter syndrome. Now I'm an actual imposter.

I cry in the shower. I cry while I'm trying to put mascara on. I cry too hard to see my shoelaces, and have to tie them using guesswork. I can't catch my breath or stop myself. I think about staying at home and hiding, but I think the fear of being caught out skiving, on top of everything else, would finish me off.

There is no way I'm going to get away with this. I'm sure that before I've got to work, the publicist will have spoken to Harri, or Akila, and wonder why I wasn't there.

Although there is nothing that Harri could say to me that could make me feel worse. I hate myself for doing this. I lied. If I'd had this opportunity a year ago, or even a couple of months ago, I would have felt like a competition winner. I have been striving for a chance like this, for years of my working life. And I've thrown it all away, because I'm lazy and cowardly. I don't deserve this job.

The only way to stop the tears is to try to come up with a plan. I think of all the bars, all the agencies, every single place I have worked that might take me back . . . round and round and round my brain goes, until I come to in the lift. I've got all the way into the Hudson building on autopilot. Harri sees me before I see her. As soon as she says my name, I take a deep breath. 'I've got something I need . . .'

'Excellent news!' she interrupts me. 'The Fallen Angels piece is flying. Flying. It was in *New York Mag*'s newsletter, and *Vogue Italia* want to syndicate it! Akila and I are just off upstairs to get it all signed off now.' She lowers her voice to a whisper. 'Don't want to jinx it but it looks like it's about to overtake your threesome piece. Brilliant, brilliant, brilliant!' She gathers me into a strange hug, for a moment it's as though we're slow dancing. Harri releases me, awkwardly. 'Sorry, sorry, not a hugger, just . . . between us, we needed a massive win. And we have one. Well done! And thanks so much for filing speed dating so, ha, speedily. Can't wait to read!'

Filing. It was in my drafts. On my phone. I thought I'd simply saved the email. I feel very hot, then very, very cold. 'But Harri . . .' *what* can I tell her now? She gathers up her notebooks to go, and that's when I notice Tabitha staring at both of us from the doorway. She waits for Harri to pass, which takes a while because Harri wants to admire her lucite heeled cowboy boots.

'So. Naked speed dating. A good time had by all? Meet anyone ... interesting?'

This is weird. Tabitha always sounds strange, and slightly strangulated, but I've not heard this before. There's a raw, bitter note in her voice. If I didn't know better, I'd think she'd been crying too. This is it. This is the end. This is where I give myself up. But my mouth starts before my brain can stop it.

'Oh, you know! All a bit gimmicky, really. Very *Naked Attraction*. You don't really see anything because we were all behind tables!'

'Interesting.' Tabitha raises her right eyebrow. A perfect, flipped-up tick. The square root of evil. There is a single flake of glitter clinging to one of the hairs. On any other day, at any other moment, this would fill me with schadenfreude. But every bit of my body is now screaming Run. My stomach gurgles violently. My bowels are always a pretty reliable barometer when it comes to terror. They want me to take flight and hide in the toilet.

What does she know?

Tabitha picks her phone up from the desk. She scrolls her screen with a slow, stroking motion. Too late, I realise she's Blofeld. The phone is the cat.

'Funny,' she drawls. 'Because I used to work with Libby at *Tatler* – Elizabeth Watson Hughes, who runs the naked speed dating events. And I just so happened to notice that she posted something on Instagram about it being cancelled last minute, due to unforeseen circumstances.' Tabitha smiles at me, almost affectionately. 'Between us, I happen to know that "unforeseen circumstances" is code for pubic lice. She'd brought in a load of rugger boys to make up the numbers – Jonno, Jonty and Jon – all riddled! So, I was quite surprised when I overheard Harri thanking you for filing your piece.' The eyebrow is soaring higher and higher, like a carrier bag tossed to the trees on the wind, up into the undergrowth of Tabitha's multicoloured fringe. Are her roots ... pink? Is *Miami Vice* the hair trend of the moment? 'But, you know, maybe there was some other naked speed dating event going on.'

I stick my chin out. 'Um, yes! I remember, there were two. There was Libby's, and the ... other one. Which is the one I went to.' Tabitha looks me in the eye. I'm on the table. The laser is heading for my crotch. 'Why are you lying, Imogen?'

I look past her shoulder, at the create your own reality sign. The first 'a' is unlit. Crete. It's a sign I should flee to Crete. 'I ... I don't know.'

'I wonder what Harri would do if she found out her star journalist was veering quite so far from fact. I was talking to Harri earlier. She is very excited about your piece appearing in *Vogue Italia*. It would be quite embarrassing, wouldn't it, for *Vogue Italia* to be syndicating the work of a liar? *The Know* – and Hudson – certainly wouldn't want to keep employing someone who had embarrassed them so badly.'

'Look, Tabitha ... I made a mistake. I don't ... I didn't ... anyway, why do you care? What's it to you?' Does she want to blackmail me? I don't have any money.

The last trace of unhappiness leaves Tabitha's face and

she smiles, properly. It's dazzling. She's quite beautiful. It's very unfair.

'I just thought you should know what I know.' She picks up her phone and turns to leave the office, swinging her black, buckled Balenciaga over her shoulder. It's a metronome. Counting down the seconds until the end of my career.

Chapter Forty-Three

A law unto herself

Harri

'No.'

Harri barks out a laugh, assuming Mackenzie is having a go at British sarcasm. Akila yelps an incredulous 'PARDON? I'm sorry, but why not?'

Mackenzie shakes her head and folds her arms. 'This simply isn't a priority for us right now. Hudson are focusing on the new trade title launches, this is a diversion of resources and focus.'

Akila is scrambling for her notes. 'I've been working up some new projections, pitches – this is beyond any of the targets you gave us, on the basis of this traffic we can rewrite the rate card . . . ' Mackenzie speaks over her. 'Harri, this goes against everything we covered in our initial discussion. You know this.'

Harri must stay calm, she must not give into her instincts and hit Mackenzie or threaten to sit on her until she reinstates Giles. She wants this for *The Know* – and she *really* wants it for Imogen.

'Mackenzie, syndication is really straightforward. The fee is considerable, and it would be a wonderful bonus for Imogen, and Hudson would stand to benefit from reprinting rights. I used to handle syndication requests for *Panache* all the time . . . ' As the words fall out of Harri's mouth, desperately, uselessly, she begins to realise what she has resisted. Mackenzie isn't slow, or old fashioned, or following peculiar practice, is she? She is deliberately blocking Harri.

'But if you're concerned about the . . . complications . . . ' Harri keeps talking. She wants to believe she can fix it still, stumble upon some magical combination of words that will cast the right spell, ' . . . we could just think of this as a PR exercise. It's a huge coup. We don't have to do anything, they sort the translation, all of it.'

'I said no.' Mackenzie speaks in a perfect monotone.

'But perhaps . . . ' tries Akila, her voice cracking with false hope. Mackenzie ignores her entirely. Addressing only Harri she says, 'I have a meeting. I trust we're finished here.' It's really odd to watch Mackenzie doing anything as human as walking. She looks as though she should be carried everywhere by sedan chair. Or coffin.

Harri and Akila look at each other for a long minute before Akila notices the stack of papers on the table. 'Mackenzie! I think you forgot your . . . '

'Fuck her,' Harri says. 'Fuck her, fuck her, fuck her. She'll come back. Let's not do her any favours. It doesn't look that important, anyway, it's just some sort of brochure. Whittaker-Chambers media pack.' She reads, upside down. 'Akila, can you pass that over?'

Harri scans. 'Weird, *Construction & Scaffolding Weekly* is one of ours, but I don't recognise most of these titles. All building, all property.'

Akila sighs. 'Ain't no party like a *Construction & Scaffolding Weekly* party 'cos ... oh, I can't be bothered. I hate it here. Let's go back downstairs, where our people are.'

'You mean, where Tabitha is dressed as a space cowboy and Imogen is writing about ... I don't know, golden showers?'

'Yeah. Those are our Girls.'

Chapter Forty-Four

Not Found

Harri

Harri is working her croissant like a worry bead. Kim is sitting on the edge of her desk, while she rips up flakes of cold dough. Stella Luna, *Panache*'s syndicated psychic (real name Beverly Fowler) would say their energies are not aligned. Harri knows her body is in the building, but her soul, her spirit, keeps getting up to stretch its legs, popping out for a flat white. Whittaker-Chambers media. Whittaker-Chambers. She's tried to google, there's a website, but it keeps leading her to a 404 page. She's feeling jarred. Mackenzie isn't just intransigent. She's unfathomable. Or she's up to something. And Harri doesn't know how the hell she's going to break the bad news to Imogen. She should never have mentioned anything about *Vogue*. But then, Harri never, ever dreamed Mackenzie would do this. She genuinely thought this might mark the start of The Thawing, the point where Mackenzie picked her up, twirled

her around the room and said 'I'm sorry I ever doubted you.'
'We want to keep things classy, yeah? I think dicks and titties is too Robert Crumb. I was thinking of a swirl of pink and purple, a lifted curtain, something to evoke the boudoir?'

'Right, right.' She's not being fair to Kim, she needs to focus. She brought him in on little more than a hunch, and he's surprised her. He's bloomed and flourished before her eyes, like a flower in a nature documentary, revealing its secrets at high speed. He's so like Giles was, at the beginning, it makes her want to weep. All of that untrammelled passion and enthusiasm. She's been hoping that Giles will start to rally, to start to see the crisis as an opportunity, but he's fading to grey. She must be able to do something, talk to someone.

'Of course,' Kim continues, 'it will be easier when Imogen has been, and filed copy. I'll have a chat with her – do you know when it's happening?'

Harri thinks for a minute. Her head is far too full. Oh, God, flatplan, flatplan, where are they ... 'Naked speed dating was ... last night.'

Kim shakes his head. 'No, I think she was at home last night, she had a pan— I mean, she was sick. She called me.'

Harri stares at Kim, confused. Kim stares back. His expression shifts, from confusion to comprehension. His pupils dilate.

'Oh, no. Maybe I am ... thinking of something else. Someone else. I got up early, so I'm a bit ... ' he smacks his wrist against his forehead. 'Cool, cool, well, it would be great if I could have a read soon. I think it'll be amazing!'

He springs up and bounces back to his desk, a handsome

ball of happy collagen and functioning knees. He makes Harri feel like a Ford Model A at the Grand Prix.

Right now, Harri is not ultra-alert. There is too much on her plate. *The Know* has been demanding more and more of her. If anyone has made a mistake, she's entirely prepared to put her hands up and say it's probably her. Did she dream that Imogen filed copy? Has she got the day wrong? No, it's definitely here, filed at 2.42 a.m. last night.

Now, it's not beyond the realms of possibility that Imogen left the naked speed dating event at midnight and stayed up writing while the whole thing was fresh in her memory. But it seems unlikely.

Once Kim's gone, Harri opens Imogen's latest piece, and reads it again. Well, for the very first time, really. She realises that the sense didn't sink in before, she was simply skimming for typos.

She'd hoped, so hard, that it couldn't be true, but her heart is sinking. It's fine. If it had come from a freelancer, she wouldn't question a word of it. But she knows it doesn't sound like Imogen. It sounds like a press release. Until the final paragraph.

Harri's eyes alight on 'Longing, dreaming, waiting, craving ... connection and intimacy. I don't know why I can't wear my heart on my sleeve ...'

How dare she? How fucking dare she? Rounding off a load of lies with talk of intimacy, of hearts. This is utterly unbelievable. Everyone betrays Harri. Everyone leaves her, or lets her down, and she thought her staff at least could show some fucking integrity ... Harri is shaking, her joints are jerking, she can't even plant the soles of her feet on the floor and steady herself. She'll have to fire Imogen. At least that will save Harri from having to explain that Imogen won't be in *Vogue Italia* after all. She has let The Girl down. What's *wrong* with Imogen? The piece isn't confident, or aspirational. It's the work of a desperate, vulnerable, struggling woman. It reads like a cry for help.

Oh.

It is a cry for help, isn't it?

Still vibrating, Harri removes herself from the office. She has failed her Girls. All of them. She simply had to keep a cool head, and a warm heart, and get to work. But she got it wrong. She got lost. *The Know* isn't reflecting its readers. It's becoming just another media monster.

If Mackenzie wants to destroy it, maybe Harri should stand back and let her. She is so, so tired.

She takes herself for a brisk cry in the furthest Pret she knows.

Chapter Forty-Five

Something Else Has Happened

Harri

After a night spent worrying and wondering about Imogen, and Mackenzie's mysterious brochure, Harri has come to no useful conclusions. She starts the day feeling especially sad and slow. Something is off. Something is about to go wrong. But she does not suspect that Something will start with Akila, approaching her desk. 'Harri, can I talk to you about something?' The cadence is painfully familiar. The measured tone, the minor key. Someone is getting dumped. *No, Akila, you absolutely can't, I already know that I don't want to hear it.* 'Sure! Absolutely. Of course.'

'I think we should maybe do this outside the office?' *NO! Let's stay here, where it's safe! You wouldn't quit on me in the office, would you?*

Harri's thoughts go unvoiced, her mouth is running operations. 'OK, I'm free now, if you are? Soho House?' Harri has a funny feeling that whatever Akila has to say will hurt less if she finds it out in a safe space, with table service. She does not want to get her heart broken, and then have to fetch her own coffee.

Harri is frightened further by Akila's reluctance to talk shop on the way over. Usually she's a font of figures, prospective glossy business, power, positivity, profile boosting. But Akila comes up with startling revelations along the lines of 'I'm so fed up with the cold, but at least it's getting lighter' and 'the clocks will be going forward before we know it!' and the classic 'I never feel like I've nailed the spring coat, you know? By the time I've really thought about it, and found one I like, it's practically summer, and it seems pointless! Mind you, I've known it to be cold enough for a coat in June ...' Is she trying to bore me into firing her? wonders Harri, miserably.

The coffee is cooling by the time Akila comes out with it. 'I have to hand in my notice. My contract says a month, I can make it six weeks if that would help, but ...'

'No. You can't. We need you. I can get you more money, I'm sure I can.'

Akila looks at Harri with sadness, as though Harri is a child, and needs to have bad news broken to her with great gentleness. 'No, Harri. I tried. I tried everything. I'm so sorry. I've loved,' past tense, bad sign, 'working for you, but I can't work for Mackenzie and her team. It's just not possible. It's so frustrating. There's so much talent and potential in our little office, and it's just stuck in a bottleneck. We've missed out on more than one major revenue stream, because management won't meet with me, they won't sign anything off, they won't get back to me in a timely way. The syndication thing was the last straw. They won't listen to me, or

to you. Katie and Lily are downright hostile. Mackenzie ...
well, you know. You've seen. I've met Will several times
now. More than once, he's called me Rachel.'

'Rachel?'

'I asked around. Rachel Adamson. She left Hudson in
2017. She was in internal comms. We had very little in
common professionally – but she's another black woman.'

'God, Akila, that's fucking horrendous, I'm so sorry.
That's outrageous. We can make a formal complaint, I'm
sure there's a ...'

Akila opens her mouth to speak, closes it, pauses, waits,
thinks. Opens it again. 'Harri, it's not – how do I put this?
You know I love you, you know I think you're brilliant,
but I don't have the energy for your outrage. Of course
you're appalled, but I live this. Not just at Hudson. I really
believed in *The Know*, but I came here because I thought
there would be opportunities for me to put my mark on the
project. And it doesn't make any sense for me to sacrifice
money, structure, the perks I could get elsewhere when I
can't flourish here.'

'I understand. I really do. Do you know what you'll do
next?' Harri's mouth is going off on its own again, on
autopilot now, while her soul screams 'NO! There must be
some way to change your mind!' All this time, Harri has
wanted to believe she was driving The Little Engine That
Could. But she can no longer ignore the fact that she's the
captain of the Titanic.

Akila talks about freelancing, about a friend of a friend,
setting up a beauty brand in the States, about considering
consultancy. 'It's sad, in a way. I always loved the idea of
being part of a company, of belonging, of everyone coming

together to meet the same goal. And I thought that was what we had. It's taken me all of my working life to realise that you don't get any points for loyalty. The more 'you' that you bring to work, the easier it is for the people in charge to exploit you. I'm going to be dealing with the same shit everywhere I go. If I'm going in as a consultant, or a project manager, at least I'm not emotionally investing in my work.'

Harri thinks of Giles, and every single hope and dream he'd been bringing to the office, over the last few years. Of everything he'd lost by believing in a company before he believed in himself. Of all the compromises he made, of all the opportunities he never took because he was scared of what he might lose, how he believed he was doing the safe thing, the sensible thing. And how Hudson took and took and took from him, then fucked him over.

Harri throws her hands out in front of her. 'I kind of feel like you're divorcing me. Which I know you're not,' she says, hurriedly. 'I know you have to do what's right for you. But all this time, I thought I was keeping myself, my personal life, and my emotions out of the office. Instead, work just took over the space where the rest of my life should have been. I think I'm only just starting to realise what you mean by emotional investment ...'

'Harri, you must know you're a bloody workaholic. We both are. The reason I wanted to come and work with you was that I could see *The Know* soaring. It has soared. You're obsessive, you love a challenge, you have vision and insight and flair. You inspire me,' says Akila, dabbing at her right eye with a paper napkin. 'And it's maddening because *The Know* is doing so well, in spite of these circumstances.'

Harri looks at her beloved colleague, and sighs. 'It's just a shame we can't just leave Hudson and do it by ourselves.'

Yet, as the words leave her mouth, Harri feels a prickle of hope, a shot of adrenaline, a restlessness, a giddiness that tingles in her calves, her abdomen, and the tips of her ears. Or can we?

Chapter Forty-Six

The Fulham flit

Imogen

I make it to the weekend without being found out. Or rather, I'm convinced that I'm living on borrowed time.

In the office, Harri seemed frighteningly distant and distracted. What does she know? Does she know? She went out for a long meeting with Akila, and they both came back looking stressed and sad. I'm certain that they must have been discussing me, and how they will formally fire me. The fact that she hasn't shouted at me yet makes me think that she's already made her decision. I'm gone. She just has to get around to telling me.

Still, I've been watching Tabitha intently, obsessively – as though I can prevent her from having any interaction with Harri, simply by being in the room. Friday was awful – my palms are still stinging, because I dug my nails into them every time Tabitha got up from her desk. And I didn't dare leave to go to the loo, unless Tabitha did too. Which was not the best way to ingratiate myself with her.

My worries have a weight and a roundness, I'm sliding them up and down an invisible string, searching for solutions. Could I afford to rent a bedsit in some distant town, and get a job in a supermarket? I remember a news story I read, just before Christmas, about how nearly three thousand people had applied for twenty casual, seasonal staff roles in Morrisons. And if I stay in London ... well. What would be the point?

I'm trapped. If I'm fired, I can keep looking for bar work, and factory work, and do as many minimum wage jobs as I can find, to just about manage to pay the rent on this horrible room. And I can try to find another job on a magazine, but I'd be competing with three thousand Tabithas and Louises – and that's assuming that my mistake stays secret, and I don't get on an industry-wide blacklist. Maybe ... PR? Every PR I've ever met has told me that they desperately wanted to work for a magazine, but got utterly fed up of being treated like shit, and earning no money. But even those women all seem to be West London girls who went to school with each other.

Who is stupid enough to get themselves fired from their dream job?

Funny dream, though. Being stressed, anxious and frightened all the time. Dreams aren't supposed to cause chest pains. Dreams shouldn't make you sick.

Pulling my duvet over my head, I wonder how I'm going to get through the next forty-eight hours. The easiest thing to do would be to stay here in the dark, torturing myself with my thoughts until I start hyperventilating again.

But maybe I can save that as a treat for tomorrow. I need company, and fresh air. That can't make things any worse. Maybe Louise fancies an afternoon drink. If anything is going to distract me from my troubles, it will be throwing myself on the mercy of the various rail replacement bus services that lie between here and Fulham.

I send her a message, and she replies with heartwarming, if terrifying alacrity. Come over!!! XXX Imogen is going West.

I'm so excited that the nice man in Gail's gets to hear all of my plans in great detail. 'An afternoon tea?' he smiles. 'That sounds delightful. But, croissants – that's an unconventional choice! We do some scones, if you'd rather ...'

As soon as he mentions it, I can feel my cheeks getting hotter. I can feel what Robert Browning described as 'that faint half-flush that dies along her throat' – or rather, the luminous red blotch that flares up on my neck when I feel especially awkward. (It's clashing magnificently with my vintage pink Laura Ashley stripy dress, £12.99 at the Notting Hill British Heart Foundation, purchased after reading four different magazine articles about Cottagecore.)

'Um, scones sound good, why not? I'll take six of those too! And maybe the croissants will keep for breakfast, or something.' These are croissants unlike any that I have ever met before, gleaming spirals embellished with flaked almonds, mirror-shiny with apricot jam. If I'd seen them anywhere but a bakery counter, I'd have assumed that they were going to have their picture taken for *Architectural Digest*. I thought They look posh, Louise will like them, I'll take six of those. It turns out that each croissant costs nearly two pounds. The man has already put them in a glossy white box.

Fulham is fairyland. Right down to the tiny, warm-white sparkling lights, threaded through the trees. It has its own seasons. In Mitcham, the only sign of spring is that the streets seem to have a slightly higher ratio of brown to grey. (You won't hear the sweet sound of the first cuckoo, but I have seen a pigeon doing battle with a Cornetto wrapper.) Here, nature is blushing even harder than I am. Every shop doorway is framed by pink and white petals. Nearly everyone is dressed to match the pastel macarons, piled up in every shop window. Even the key cutting and shoe repair place has a cake stand filled with lilac macarons, flanking a display of Kiwi Colour Shine Leather Polish.

It's otherworldly enough to make me feel as though I'm on holiday, which may go some way to explaining why and how I have managed to spend over sixty pounds on my credit card on nonsense food – as though I have failed to understand an obscure exchange rate. As well as the baked goods, I have acquired two cartons of Kermit-green gobstopper olives, a tub of Extra Velvety Organic Hummus, champagne-pomegranate jam, some crystallised ginger 'Luxuriously Enrobed in Dark Chocolate' and three bottles of prosecco. (The third bottle was to compensate for the family sized trifle I abandoned at the checkout.) To be honest, I'm genuinely surprised the authorities let me through the tube barriers without patting me down to make sure that I already had some prosecco on my person. Surely it is the petrol on which the district runs. Unless there's so much here already that it's all a bit coals-to-Newcastle. I had imagined the streets were literally awash with it,

Fulham as Venice, Audis and Pashleys floating along a sea of sweet, fizzy white wine.

I'm late, and I know my White Rabbit is behind one of these windows, hopping about impatiently and frowning at her graduation Cartier. Number 28. The door is painted a pretty pastel green, intended, I suppose, to evoke Mediterranean holidays and pistachio gelato – unfortunately it's also exactly the same colour as the waiting room of the Thornton Heath Sexual Health Clinic. I try the knocker, a pale gold metal wreath of delicately intertwined flowers and branches. It makes no sound. I try it again. It comes off in my hand.

'Imogen! Thank God,' cries Louise, opening the door so quickly that I trip through it, throwing my pricey groceries down the hall, almost face planting into the hummus.

'Louise, I'm so sorry, I'll replace ...' She snatches the knocker from my hand. 'Don't worry, don't worry, it always does that. To be honest, it's no bad thing if we don't have a knocker this afternoon, far too many people are turning up as it is. It's all a disaster, a fucking disaster.'

My hostess sighs heavily, and even though I've already bought her the best part of a supermarket, I realise there's a much more useful gift I can offer her. 'Do you want me to go? I can just ...' I gesture to the door.

'You have to stay, for the sake of my sanity! It was just supposed to be the girls, but bloody Muffy told Hugo, and apparently the "lads" were all drinking in the Pear Tree, and of course Hugo is friends with Willo – I told you about Willo?'

'Willow? Like the tree? Willow the Wisp?'

'Willo my fucking ex!' When upset, Louise sounds like posh Yoda. What is a farkingeggs, anyway? Perhaps it's a mystery word, like "quadrangle" or "martingale" – maybe a special piece of cutlery used to eat sorbet between courses? Oh. Oh, no. Poor Louise.

'It's OK! Do not worry. Is he here yet? I have many, many edible things. And enough prosecco to fill an aquarium. It's going to be fine.'

Louise looks a little more cheerful, which is gratifying, if scary. Don't take my word for it, on the 'fineness' front! I'm hardly a credible source! But she gathers my many bags and tells me to 'go on through to the drawing room'.

I hear three women laughing almost harmonically. The laughter stops abruptly as the door swings open. They stare. They do not smile, or say anything that sounds like a greeting, or make the sort of gestures that would suggest they are finding space for me on the sofa.

'Is this your new housekeeper, Louise?' says a fourth person, a man in white chinos, wearing a navy blazer with brass buttons. I do a double take – yes, I imagined the captain's hat.

It's a shame that these women are looking at me as though I just crawled up from a hole in the skirting board, because I'm longing to ask them about their tans. Over the years, I have experimented with fake tan in all of its forms. I have buffed and shaved and exfoliated and moisturised and not moisturised and patted and dabbed and blotted and waited. And every single time, the same predictable thing has happened. No, that's not true. There was one occasion when I didn't go orange. I turned green.

These women have bathed in butterscotch. Every inch of exposed skin – and I can see two pairs of knickers – looks lickable, even and gleaming. How do they do it? Is there a descendent of Leonardo da Vinci working at a local salon? Maybe the sun in Barbados is somehow superior to the regular old sun that shines in the park.

Louise announces me. 'Everyone, this is Imogen, I work with her at *The Know*. Imogen, this is everyone: Buffy, Amelia, Muffy and Plum.'

Well, that's no help whatsoever. Louise gestures to the hatless man. 'Plum is short for Ronald, but we don't bother with that. I'd better get back to my millefeuille.' No! Don't leave me! I feel as though I'm being abandoned at the school gates. I'd quite like to burst into tears, throw myself on the floor and hold onto her ankles.

Instead, I creep into the room and look for somewhere to sit. I don't know why Plum is perching on the arm of the sofa, with the girls – there's an unoccupied chair that looks incredibly comfy. Everything else in the room is repro mid-century velvet, straight from the West Elm catalogue – but this looks soft, old and cosy, covered in a charmingly tatty floral patchwork quilt. 'So!' I say, beaming, dropping into the cushions and anticipating a soft embrace. My knees hit my chin, and I hear a quiet crack. Was that the chair, or my jaw? I prod my face, checking for blood, while Plum, Muffy, Buffy and Amelia titter.

'I see you're making yourself at home on the family heirloom. You and our Louise must be very close,' says Plum, implying, in three syllables, that we're running drugs and guns together, or maybe we share a dark secret concerning a winter's night and a body found in a lake. 'How do you all know Louise?' I ask. Socially, this is much, much more difficult and exhausting than trying to make small talk at an orgy.

'Oh, school,' says the one brunette, who I think might be Amelia. 'Well, obviously not Plum! He could hardly be a Dolphin, could he?' I'm none the wiser, but Louise's squeaky tendencies are starting to make sense.

The blonde on the far right – Muffy, maybe? – has been looking through me, as though she is waiting for me to go away. But suddenly she snaps to attention. 'Oh, you were the one on TV. The slut! Yeah, I've had loads of threesomes, but I thought you were really ...' I tilt my head, waiting to hear the word 'brave'. Strangers are always telling me about how brave I am, and I don't believe it, or agree, but I've prepared a good 'gracious' face, '... weird. Dora Bainbridge has been for supper a few times. She used to be my mum's decorator.' Muffy sniffs, and her eyes turn opaque once more.

There is a moment's silence.

'I am just. Going to see. If Louise wants some help,' I say.

'Figures,' says Plum, and I'm aware of more smirking and sniggering. Oh, if only I had enough core strength to get out of this chair! I pitch forward and roll onto the balls of my feet, arms outstretched, bottom up like a duck diving into a pond, my momentum propelling me perilously close to the sofa. The girls recoil. 'Just something I learned in yoga!' I lie.

Louise is bent over a plate, doing something fiddly with a toothpick. 'May I grab a glass?' I ask, opening up cupboard doors and looking for glasses before she replies. After the chair affair, I am heirloom wary. I don't dare to touch the heavy, crystal flutes – presumably they were a wedding gift to Louise's grandmother from Princess Margaret or Genghis Khan or someone. I shall have to drink from

307

the novelty goblet emblazoned with the legend 'So many shoes, so little time'. Still, you can probably get a whole bottle in there.

I need all of the Dutch courage that I can get my hands on before I return to that room. To be honest, I'd really like some Russian courage, or Mexican courage, but I can hardly start demanding shots while Louise prepares an afternoon tea. Louise is talking at me, and I'm drifting in and out. 'I was up at 5 a.m., it's not even a rough puff, it's proper puff pastry. I don't know why I bother. Plum never eats after midday, Buffy is doing some sort of intuitive fast and Amelia claims to be doing plant based paleo although ...' Louise lowers her voice. 'Muffy claims that she saw a KFC bag in her glove compartment.'

I drain my glass and refill it. I'm feeling slightly more cheerful. 'Fuck them! We'll eat them, they will be delicious! The most important thing is that we get a great picture for Instagram.' I am very proud of myself for remembering this.

Louise produces an eau de Nil cake stand, some eerily convincing artificial peonies, and a ring light. I help. Which means that I must stand on a kitchen chair, light in one hand, and glass in the other, drinking and hovering until Louise has taken seventy-four different photographs, and found one to be acceptable. 'Let me give you a hand,' she offers, as I sway slightly unsteadily. Oh, there's the floor.

The millefeuille are a work of art. Somehow Louise has etched the icing on the top to look like a water scene in a Watteau painting, albeit rendered in chocolate and vanilla. We form a two person procession, and I concentrate very hard on holding the tray, walking in a straight line and not spilling any alcohol.

We enter, and Plum leads the sneering. 'Oh, cute! Another one of Lou's little DIY projects! I'm sure they're quaking in their boots at Patisserie Valerie! No, not for me.' Only the quieter blonde takes a cake. She holds it in her palm and stares at it balefully, as if she is reluctantly taking part in a TV segment where guests have to overcome their fear of baked goods in front of a live studio audience. I've seen people look at poisonous spiders with more enthusiasm.

'I wonder how many calories are in a tarantula?'

The prosecco is driving my train of thought right off the rails.

'What?' Even Louise looks a little taken aback.

'Nothing, nothing! These are so delicious!' I'm talking through a mouthful of custard and crumbs. I swallow and take another slice. Plum gasps, audibly.

Then, I am ignored. Amelia complains at length about her parents, taking her to 'fucking Verbier again' at Easter, and it's going to be so very dull, and no one even goes there any more, it's over, why can't she go to Courchevel, she's twenty-eight and what's the big deal about a family holiday? Plum says it could be much worse, his family are forcing him to come to Florence, where there is nothing to do 'and the apartment is ridiculously small'. Buffy – I assume it's Buffy – bravely breaks her silence to deliver a nine minute monologue about suitcases. 'And if you don't bother with the USB port and the monogramming, the carry-on is under a grand!' she finishes, breathlessly.

I drink more prosecco.

'No monogramming? I'm not an animal!' howls Plum, slapping a chinoed thigh.

I drink more prosecco.

Slowly, the conversation becomes much more interesting, as the assembled guests assassinate the character of a woman called Caroline – did she catch chlamydia from Eddie, or did Eddie catch chlamydia from her? Louise occasionally attempts to join in, but mostly gets talked over, by Plum. Every so often, she mutters 'anyway, I'll just ...' and gets up, and returns with a platter piled with golden, miniature sausage rolls, or luscious, fudgy brownies, and at one point, a medium sized, tiered sponge cake adorned with spun sugar butterflies. Louise and her food is ignored. As am I. How dare these awful people treat her like that? In her own home? I'm trying to come up with something blisteringly, incisively crushing to say to Plum. The trouble is that I've drunk a whole bottle of prosecco.

Is that the door? 'I'll get it!' Oh, that came out much more loudly than I was expecting. I try to jump up from the heirloom, fall onto the floor, leap up, brush my dress down, catch a melting chocolate chip brownie crumb and paint a brown streak from my arse to my thigh.

Deep breaths. I can recover my composure, sober up in the hallway and then hide in the kitchen and drink a lot of water until it's OK to go home.

I open the door. I can do this! I am the gracious Deputy Hostess!

'Hello! I'm Imogen, I'm a friend of ...'

The gracious Deputy Hostess is drowned in vowels. A stadium roar from a cheering crowd. I hear a 'waheeeeeeeeeeey!' and a 'whoooooooooo' and an 'oi oi oi!' The sound of thousands is being made by four very drunk men. I thought I was pissed, but ... 'Louise, Louise Louise Louise!' sing the men, surprisingly melodically, pushing past me, and changing tunes. 'Where's Louise? Where's Louise? Where's Louiiiiii-ise?'

The door opens. Plum can be heard saying 'And if I were her, I simply wouldn't bother to show my face in Hertford Street, ever again . . . ' Two beats of ominous silence, then . . .

'Willo! You came!' Louise's voice.

'Oh, God, Lou, I just had to say I love . . . I really love . . . ' Standing outside the door, I hear a violent and unmistakable sound. My own stomach gurgles in sympathy and threatens to violently eject the prosecco and millefeuille.

The voice is now drained of all its fanfare. And, I suspect, solids. 'I'm so sorry. Could I possibly have a glass of water?'

The only vessel I can find in the kitchen that is definitely not priceless and inherited is bright yellow and has Bart Simpson's buttocks on it, but at least it's big. I return to the drawing room, where Louise is gazing reverentially at a pile of puke, as though she can see the Virgin Mary's face within it. Willo, I assume, is sitting beside it, looking contrite. The other members of his choir are, if not exactly sobered by the change in circumstances, briefly silenced by them.

Of course, Plum is not silenced. Plum is apoplectic. 'All! Over! The Aubusson!' he hisses. 'We were having a pleasant afternoon tea, and you came in and heaved right beside me! You nearly ruined my—'

He's just a bully. I know exactly what to expect from a bully.

'Plum. Be quiet.' I sound low, loud and clear, summoning the same energy I used to defeat Dora. 'You have been rude to Louise all afternoon. I've watched you. She has gone out of her way to make you happy and comfortable. She has made all of this food by hand. And you have ignored her,

311

you have sneered and bitched and been cruel and I think you should leave.'

Muffy and Amelia look down at their Ferragamo flats. The brass logo on Muffy's left shoe appears to be adorned with a small chunk of carrot. Only Buffy catches my eye and gives me the most luminous smile.

Plum opens his mouth and makes another series of dolphin squeaks. 'I . . . I . . . I . . . how dare . . . how very . . . you uncouth . . . anyway, we were just leaving!'

I'd braced myself for Plum to have a lacerating, vicious comeback, but he's deflated. It's almost as if no one has ever interrupted him or criticised him in his life before.

As subtly as a drunk girl can, I manoeuvre myself towards Louise, away from Willo, so that Plum is unable to leave the drawing room without walking through the vomit. I move back just in time to allow Buffy to find a puke-free path.

Willo is still a very pale shade of grey. He looks up at me from the floor, very slowly. Oh, I hope he's not going to be sick again. 'Well done. I've been waiting . . . urghhh, sorry . . . waiting for someone to tell Plum off for years. I'm Willo – William.' Raising himself up on an elbow, he offers me a hand. Instinctively, I reach for it, and then decline just in time. I am sobering up by the second. 'Sorry, I think you're still a bit – maybe a shower, or a bath would help? Louise, do you have a bath?'

She laughs. 'Of course! Who doesn't have a bath? That's like not having a downstairs loo.' I let it go. 'Right, Willo, do you think you can face a bath? Louise, if you can run it, maybe, I'll clear up here.'

'Me and the chaps will give you a hand, if you like. Sorry, we didn't – I'm Tristan, this is Hugo, that's Benners.' I have never seen two more identical looking men than Hugo and Benners. They are both in quilted black leather jackets, and black jeans. They are wearing a collection of silver necklaces, and black desert boots. They both have blond hair, coaxed into a quiff, reminding me a tiny bit of Tintin, and a lot of an old fashioned meringue. Benners is maybe half an inch taller – I could think of him as Big Benners? I'll never be able to tell the difference, I'll just have to call them both 'you!' and smile a lot. Is there a way I can get one of them to put on a hat?

Tristan is much easier to tell apart – good – because he is wearing red trousers – bad.

'I'm Imogen, I work with Louise. This is the first time I've been to her house, so I'm not sure where she keeps her cleaning stuff. I assume under the sink?'

In under ten minutes, Tristan has sourced rubber gloves for all. 'The great thing about this happening at Louise's is that she has a metric tonne of baking soda on hand at any given moment. Benners, don't forget the baking soda! You need to make sure all the puke is cleaned up before you sprinkle it on; if you can't find any newspaper just use a kitchen towel. We just need to limit the damage before it goes to the cleaners.' He smiles. 'Benners is an expert at sick. He's usually the puker.'

We get into a rhythm, side by side at the sink, I wash while Tristan dries. It's odd that people make such a fuss about the importance of eye contact, when there is some-thing so disinhibiting about simply being next to someone. It makes it far easier to ask, and answer, big questions. For example, 'Louise hasn't really mentioned Willo to me, but I get the impression that she has strong feelings for him. Do you think they'd get back together?'

Tristan wipes some foam from his cheek. 'To be honest with you, I reckon that's up to Lou! They have been on again, off again for years. Mostly off, lately. He does love her, I know he does. But he's not prepared to stop ... you know.' Tristan takes the damp glass he is holding and gestures to the empty air. I don't know. Stop gambling? Stop his weekly visits to BDSM sex dungeons?

'Stop what?'

'Drinking himself insensible and getting off with other girls. And occasionally, chundering.'

'To be fair, I didn't think Willo's card was any more marked than yours when you all came in. It could have been any of you.'

Tristan flushes. 'I'd hope that at this point in my life, I'm past chundering. I'm an old man!'

'How old?'

'Thirty-two. And unlike most of my reprobate friends, I'm not knocking five years off, and telling people I'm a "DJ" or an "influencer". I have a proper job!'

'What do you do?' I brace myself for something horrific, he's a trader, a broker, he goes around the city buying up orphanages and selling them for parts.

'I'm an English teacher. I'm guiding the teens of Tower Hamlets through their GCSEs. Oh, hold on ... I've just realised. You're *that* Imogen!' Somehow, I don't think Tristan is going to tell me how brave I am – but I don't think he's going to call me a slut, either. 'My girls love you. They think you're sick. I'm given to understand that's a good thing, hopefully they don't labour under the misapprehension that you are, in fact, contagious.' I should be annoyed by Tristan's faux Dickensian syllable stacking, but it's strangely endearing.

'I don't suppose you'd want to come in and do a Careers talk?'

Oh, no. For the past few hours, I'd let myself forget about my career, and its imminent death. Tristan misinterprets my look of horror. 'We could pay you, of course! It's a small budget, but ...'

'No, no, it's ... honestly, I did something really stupid, and I'm not sure I'm going to be at *The Know* for much longer.'

'I'm sorry. What happened?'

I tell him everything. I clean a pile of delicate blue and white china plates, while I explain about skipping naked speed dating, accidentally sending the email, and letting myself get caught in my own lie. I clean a spring-bottomed tin while telling him about the first big piece, going on TV, being called a whore on social media, feeling as though my life was spinning out from under me. I clean a hand-held blender, and explain about the orgy, the way Harri's criticism was even more stinging and humiliating than almost having horrible sex with horrible strangers, the lying, the anxiety. I clean a set of cake forks, and tell him about *The Gentleman*, about feeling so crushed and trapped, about being exhausted from constantly having my hopes dashed, that if – when – I get fired from *The Know*, there will be nowhere for me to go. I clean a baking sheet, accidentally scratching off the protective coating with a wire brush, when I tell him about Devon, my family, the fight with Jen, my horrible flat, the panic attacks, how work is the only thing that has made me feel like I have any worth, how I feel so desperate and scared that I don't feel capable of making a rational decision.

Tristan listens. He does not interrupt. He does not make

315

any suggestions. Finally, he puts a dry hand on my wet arm and says 'You poor thing. That sounds shit.'

And I cry into the washing-up bowl, tears landing on the surface of the foamy water like rainfall, soft on a lake. And then, he takes me into his arms, and I cry in the crook of his shoulder, against his neck. His body is warm, solid, soap-scented. His hands are firm, both on my shoulder blades, never creeping downwards or sideways. Sam Strong would have had my bra off in seconds.

I don't know if I'm there for ten minutes, or for an hour, but when every bit of moisture from my body has been absorbed by Tristan's jumper, I let go of him and take a deep breath. 'Thank you. I feel much better now.'

'Please don't feel obliged to take my unsolicited advice. But honestly – just talk to Harri. I don't think you can be alone, in any of this. I know that's how it feels. But it's clear that you're really talented, she must value you enormously, and you're human. Everyone is allowed to make a mistake, and be properly sorry, and get a second chance. Everyone. No exceptions. You've been under a huge amount of stress. My Year Elevens genuinely think you're better than Shakespeare.' I sniff a bit, and it turns into a snort. Well done, Imogen. How attractive.

'Maybe I should be a teacher?! I bet you're really good at it. You must enjoy it?'

Tristan smiles – but it's tinged with the merest, merest hint of longing, or sadness, or something. 'I have occasional, wonderful days when something unexpected happens, and I feel as though I'm helping. I couldn't love the kids more, they're so funny and fierce. But they can be little shits. It's tough.'

He looks into the middle distance and sighs, twisting a tea towel around his forearm like a tourniquet. 'Every Monday morning, it seems that some initiative has been brought in that means I will spend less time in the classroom doing the work, and more time filling in forms. But – it's my life. You have to really love it, and really want to do it, it's all you have when you're muddling through the really grim bits.'

You have to really love it, and really want to do it. Oh. I look at Tristan, and my face flushes. He's seen my secret, he knows. I look away, and fiddle with the damp cuff of my dress. It's not just about *The Know*. It's writing. In the event of an apocalypse, I will be writing, scrawling thoughts with a stick in a muddy ditch if I have to.

Tristan untwirls his tea towel. 'I've seen colleagues come and go, people who have given up on what they really wanted to do, and thought teaching would be safe, straightforward. It isn't, at all. And you're already doing plenty for young minds, without having to supervise anyone's detention.'

We're interrupted by Louise, pinkly naked under a white dressing gown. Her mascara is smudged, and her tell-tale hair tuft is sticking up, but I don't think it's an anxiety signal this time. 'Um, is everyone still here? I thought you would have gone home! Perhaps, ah, would you all mind going home?'

Tristan looks at me and raises his eyebrows, and I try not to giggle. 'Roger Roger. I'll gather the chaps. Imogen, we're just going to walk home, but can I drop you off anywhere? Find you a taxi? Chaps! Come on, get up, time to go!' The three of us walk to the drawing room and find Hugo and Benners on the sofa. They are watching, improbably, a programme featuring a number of people in a field, with easels, and Sandi Toksvig sitting on a horse. 'Good, you've got your coats on!'

'Lovely to see you, Tristan,' Louise says. 'Thanks for, for ... you know. Thanks! And Immo, I'll see you Monday. Thank you so much for coming all this way!' Louise kisses me on the cheek, and kisses Tristan on the chin, and blows kisses to Hugo and Benners before giggling and running up the stairs. Hugo and Benners mumble something about pubs as they heave themselves off the sofa, and shuffle down the hall. They do not wait for Tristan, who waits for me.

I stand on the doormat, not sure how to say goodbye. 'Sorry ... and thank you. Thanks for being so kind.'

'Of course, any time. I really enjoyed meeting you.' Tristan looks through the open door. He starts to descend the steps. He looks back at me, turns around, and joins me on the doormat. 'I like you, Imogen Mounce.'

He kisses me on the lips, softly. He does not open his mouth. He pulls away, looking slightly shocked, and confused, as though the kiss had been my idea. Then he grins and bounds back down the steps.

The clouds are edged in old gold, and even though the sky is turning darker and deeper, I feel a lightness inside that I have not known for a long time.

Chapter Forty-Seven

Our doubts are traitors

Harri

'Harri, are you free for a quick chat?'

'Now?' No, not you too. I know the ship is sinking, but I'm building a raft. Trust me. 'Actually, Imogen, I was hoping to grab you too, why don't we go out to lunch?' Harri had been excited about drawing Imogen into her conspiracy – now, she's feeling anxious and wrong-footed. Is bad news about to trump good?

Imogen looks panicked. 'Lunch, lovely! Where were you thinking? Cafe Cucina? Pret?'

Harri can do better than that. 'What about Soho House? My treat, of course. I've got a meeting at twelve, meet me there at half one? Just give them my name at reception and they'll send you through.' Usually, Harri finds it's an invitation that never fails to impress and excite a member of the media who has yet to see their thirtieth birthday. But Imogen barely flickers. She smiles weakly, and Harri watches the nation's hottest, most audacious young sex writer shuffle back to her desk, back hunched, shoulders slumped. This is not encouraging.

Still, Harri has enough edgy energy for both of them. *I bet this is what an affair feels like.* Harri has a secret and she can't quite decide whether she feels elated, or just paranoid. She has not slept for days. Her eyes are glittering, her hands are aching and her right index finger is slightly swollen, from obsessive scribbling. She has been plotting, and she's afraid that it shows. Part of her research involved reading Imogen's blog, from the beginning. Maybe Imogen has seen her analytics, she knows that some obsessive fan from north London has been bingeing her old posts and that's why she's treating Harri with suspicion.

Giles thinks she's crazy, and even Akila wasn't quite as enthusiastic as she'd hoped, when Harri pitched her the idea that morning, over the office kitchen kettle. 'You definitely have something, but I'm not sure you can make a publication so similar without running the risk that Hudson might sue you. And you've got to think about investors, advertisers, backing. People want to give *The Know* money because it's part of a publishing company they're very familiar with. I think you can raise the funds, but it's going to be really, really hard.'

Harri was on a charm offensive. 'And that's exactly why I want you on board! You're brilliant, and so well connected.'

Akila frowned. 'Well, I'm still on duty here for the next few weeks, seeing out my notice. I've already got a bit of consultancy booked in, while I get myself set up. Right now, I'm looking for lucrative, boring work. What you're suggesting is the complete opposite.'

'I know, but ... think about it? Please?'

Harri knew Akila's concerns were entirely legitimate – but there was a tiny part of her that had expected Akila to say 'Great idea boss! I'll make some calls,' and then Harri's head cut to a montage of newspaper headlines that read PUBLISHING VISIONARY HARRIET KEMP DOES IT AGAIN! Even though she still wasn't entirely sure what 'it' might be.

Sex was *The Know*'s most contentious content, and by far the best performing too. Given the fact that Mackenzie constantly – if unsuccessfully – objected to the sex on *The Know*, surely she couldn't object to Harri setting up her own site and taking the sex elsewhere? She wants to make a space that feels smarter, but softer. Something with sensitivity, and a sense of humour at its core. A place where the erotic imagination is cultivated, a place to play, where storytelling is as revered as experience. A place for curiosity and questions. Really, something with great graphics, and a good editorial budget, that feels like Imogen's blog.

Which means that at the centre of this project is Imogen.

The blog has not been updated for months, since *The Know* went live. When Harri noticed the date of the last post, she felt a little guilty, a little defensive. She knows she has claimed most of Imogen's waking hours. But Imogen is ambitious! That's why she's here. Surely she wouldn't be working for a paltry wage, staying up late, going to events after hours, commuting into central London if she wasn't ambitious. Will she be ambitious enough for *this*? Ambitious enough to help Harri work out just what 'this' could become?

If not, Harri was – as sleep tugged its heavy blanket up

and over her consciousness, the more poetic word eluded her – fucked.

On Sunday night, Harri had dreamed of Andy. She often does. But this time, she did not wake weeping, or pawing the space beside her in the bed.

'Our doubts are traitors, and make us lose the good we oft might win, by fearing to attempt,' said Andy, in the dream.

'You old ham!' said Harri. 'When did you learn that?'

'Am dram!' said Andy. 'I was Lucio in *Measure For Measure*! Epping Forest *Summer Stock*, 1988! You knew that.'

'Did I?'

'I'm sure I told you!'

'What else did you tell me?'

'Don't lose the good. Don't ...'

Harri is ambivalent about religion, and she'd eat a bag of crystals before she entertained the notion that she might be a spiritual person. But for once, she didn't feel bereft, betrayed, abandoned all over again. It was more as though her subconscious had given Harri, and her idea, a benediction. Now, as she stares at her screen, pretending to work, and hugging her secret hard, Harri realises that convincing Imogen to join her might be the toughest challenge she faces. But if she can get Imogen to come on board, she can do anything.

Chapter Forty-Eight

The start of another love story

Imogen

I guess that's it. Harri has made up her mind. She's planned it. She is going to take me out of the office, to spare my feelings, buy me a luxury lunch to soften the blow, and then – that will be the end of my journalism career.

Tristan's kind counsel made me believe that I could go out fighting. I spent the whole of Sunday planning and plotting my argument, working out how I might advocate for my worth. Surprisingly, it was a life affirming exercise. They say – and by 'they', I mean 'Google' – that the key to managing any kind of difficult talk, and getting your desired outcome, lies in visualisation. You're supposed to imagine the conversation and work out how you would like it to go, and how you can take control of any negativity by anticipating it and practising your response.

Initially, all I could visualise was Harri standing over me and calling me a 'disgrace to journalism' as I cried into my sleeve while mumbling 'Please, please don't fire me'. But I've done some research. I have solid evidence of how I've boosted the profile of *The Know*. My pieces have grown the site's social media following by over 30 per cent (I'm underestimating, because I'm not wildly confident about my maths) and they make up over 75 per cent of the site's shares. I'm not going to mention this to Harri, but if they need to fire anyone, Tabitha really does not give much bang for her buck. My bang is as figurative as it is literal.

Then, there is my secret CV. After I gave myself a performance evaluation, I started to think about every single step I have taken to get here. About what I've endured, and what I have learned.

I didn't go back home when *StarLook* Magazine closed, the week before Christmas 2016, and the day before payday. I went to Craigslist and Gumtree, and I hostessed and waitressed for men who were far creepier and skeevier than John from *The Gentleman*, and I paid my rent. I have also paid my rent selling 'used' underwear on Craigslist. In an hour, with a cheap multi pack of knickers from the market, and a pot of yoghurt, I could make more money than I'd earn in a whole shift at the Sports Grill, including tips. Although I was quite relieved when Craigslist shut me down, once and for all. I think the staff at the post office knew I was up to something, and I was starting to feel sick whenever I smelled yoghurt.

I will never, ever be glossy. I will never feel like a person who doesn't have to work for her place in the world. But maybe my worth is in the work. Not that anyone should have to sell their underwear to collectors in order to keep a roof over their head, but I have proved, over and over again, that I can cope. 'You got this!' claims my least favourite meme, usually proffered when something terrible happens concerning something I have demonstrably not got, like work, or rent money. 'You got this!' means 'Sort yourself out, I'm not getting involved'.

I believed this job would transform me, validate me, turn me into a person of worth. That I was finally allowed to think of myself as a 'real' writer, with permission from my payslip, christened by an email signature. But I'm an asset to *The Know* because of everything I learned before I arrived. Not because of what they have conferred upon me. They can take the job title away from me. But they can't steal anything else. I think of Louise, who feels hopeless because she feels so helpless. I'd swap flats with her, in half a heartbeat – but not lives.

I arrive at Soho House. As I climb the stairs, I think of the years I've wasted, dreaming of what it would be like to come here for an important meeting with an editor. Past Imogen was an idiot. The receptionist tells me to 'go on through', indicating a 270 degree radius, and I worry that I'm doomed to a Sisyphean search, trawling the endless luxury lounges, the Great Firing hanging over my head for ever. But I see Harri as soon as I walk through the doorway. I'm also delighted to see that she has made a cosy nest amidst the mid century *objets d'art*. The Coat is half rolled, half thrown over a velvet banquet. She's chewing a cheap Biro. A second Biro is behind her ear.

'Imogen, thank God! Can you help me find my pen? I don't know what I've done with it.'

'Uh, have you tried your ... ear? And hand?'

She looks down, and sighs softly. 'Anyway, glad you're here. What I'm about to ask you might seem like it's coming out of the blue, but I really hope . . . '

'Are you going to fire me? Please don't fire me.'

'What?' Her pen falls from her hand, into her coffee cup.

'Naked speed dating. I don't know if Tabitha told you but I didn't go. I lied. I'm so sorry. I don't want to make any excuses about what I did. It was unforgivable. But I really hope I can persuade you to give me another chance.' I scrabble for my notebook. It would be so nice if I could reach into the air and pull out, say, a pie chart, or a compelling power point presentation. 'I put some figures together, and it turns out I'm responsible for 75 per cent of all thirds . . . no, sorry, that's wrong . . . '

'Imogen, what are you talking about?'

I hang my head. 'I know you probably need to fire me. But I was hoping that you might be able to consider it in . . . in the context of my . . . my . . . ' Shit. I really didn't want to cry.

'Oh, Imogen. It's OK. I know you didn't go. And I understand. You fucked up. And I put you under so much stress that it was probably inevitable. Thank you for apologising. I'm really sorry too. But that's not why I invited you out to lunch.'

'Then . . . what have I done?' I must have done something. My heart starts to pound faster. This is even worse than I thought.

But Harri doesn't look as though she's about to tell me off. She seems nervous, vulnerable. Hopeful. 'I want to leave Hudson and set up my own women's website. And I'm hoping you'll come with me.'

'What?' I'm not being fired! The relief courses through me, draining the tension from my body. I might slide off my chair. This is a second chance! Away from *The Know*, I can wipe my slate clean. Start over. But how can Harri leave Hudson? Harri *is* Hudson.

Harri is also looking relieved. 'I need to tell you that this is very, very new, and I've got lots of details to work out. This is far from being any kind of done deal. But I have a feeling there might be some big changes at Hudson, and I think that it's going to get harder to keep the spirit of *The Know* intact. I want to take everything I love about our work – mostly sex – and make a dedicated space for that. It was the last part of your naked speed dating piece that really inspired me. You write so beautifully about sex and bodies in terms of curiosity, experimentation, thinking, feeling and dreaming.'

I open my mouth to respond, but I'm not sure what to say. Harri continues. 'I've been rereading your blog, I miss it! And I think there's something at its core that we could recreate, we could get all of that raw magic and make it into something huge. And I've been so impressed by your, ah, creative writing.' I blush. 'No, honestly, you have a real talent there, and we might have found an unorthodox home for it at the moment – but I want to celebrate it, really give you a space for it. You're such a good storyteller.'

I'm struck dumb, so Harri continues. 'At *The Know*, I've had to be so wholly focused on traffic that I've lost sight of what it's all for – who it's for. And I don't think I can carry on working with Hudson's management changes. There have always been rumours that *Panache* is on the brink of folding, and I usually laugh them off, but with some of the recent changes, even I can't see how it can carry on for much longer.'

I think of Sam Strong, and his rumours. 'But *Panache* is a proper institution,' my voice starts to wobble. 'I've wanted to work there since I was twelve,' I say, quietly. 'Does this mean I never will?' I think about Louise's five year plan, and my own secret, buried dream. I always wanted to be a columnist at *Panache*. I knew it would never, ever happen. But then, even though I know I'll probably never write a screenplay that wins an Oscar, on bad days, that's the crazy hope that sometimes sustains me. I'd still grieve for my silly fantasy if someone decided there were going to be no more Oscars.

Harri responds gently. '*Panache* is very expensive to run. It's always been a prestige title – ten years ago, the ad revenue was enormous, but the profit margins were narrow. The awful thing is that we made it easy for them. The company culture at Hudson has always been bleak, management constantly demanding the impossible, and when you deliver, demanding that you deliver doubly the next day. When Rosa announced she was leaving, I think Will saw his big chance. It's like Jenga. They're sneakily sliding the magazines out, one by one.'

It's hard to get my head around. '*The Know* only just launched. It can't cost that much to run,' I say, thinking of my paltry pay.

Harri shrugs. 'If they can set it up to fail, they can use it as evidence that their consumer titles are struggling and ditch them quietly. In the meantime, they can force everyone out, and hope to make conditions so unbearable that everyone quits. I don't get redundancy because I've signed a brand new contract. None of you get redundancy because you've been here for less than a year. I know it's a lot to get your head around, but it's not uncommon. I've seen it happen with other publishers. That's why I want to set up on my own – and bring you with me! If you'll have me.'

I have been so naive. I've always understood that, on some level, glossy magazines are full of nonsense. But solid gold, million dollar, all powerful nonsense. I didn't know that Hudson is all flimsy facade, cheap people in cheap suits running numbers, and finding them wanting. I've spent so many years watching Harri, wanting to be her, believing that with just enough hard work, I could belong in her shiny Technicolor world. Now she's pulled back the curtain and I feel disorientated. It's one thing to work, and worry, and never get what you want. It's another to realise you've been worrying and working for a lie.

'Why did you stay here? Why didn't you set up on your own before, or work for another magazine?'

Harri looks thoughtful. 'I'm starting to wish I'd done it a long, long time ago. I came close, a couple of times. But then Andy – my husband – died.'

Of course.

Because I was the indentured work experience at *Panache*. The most junior, least important person in the office, forced to pretend to know nothing. But I saw everything.

And I remember Harri, subdued, paler than usual, the whispering, 'she's come back too early,' Giles protective, tender, defending her from all real and imaginary threats. Agonising over what to say, and never saying anything. Accidentally wiping the information from my own memory, for fear of intruding on hers. Doing nothing, and doing it wrong.

But I can say something now. 'I really am sorry. You must miss him very much.'

Harri pauses and presses her fingertips to her eyelids for three seconds, before speaking. 'Every single day. He was the best, Imogen. He was sweet and kind and funny and decent and, just ... my favourite. Way back when, *Panache* used to send me out to fashion week. Front row shows. Endless free stuff. Hot and cold running taxis, I'm not sure my feet ever touched a Parisian pavement. Anyway, I'd be alone in these hotels, hotels we'd run big pieces on, claiming that they were the sexiest, most desirable, most luxurious vacation destinations in the world. Every night, I'd be miserable and lonely, counting down the seconds until I was back with Andy in our tiny flat in Archway. I remember it so vividly, being almost sexually desperate to feel my key in the lock, and then ... the yearning. The dreaming. Of my dear old husband, in his joggers! It was like being a teenager, all over again. Sorry, I'm going on.'

'Not at all, I'm very, very touched that you want to tell me.'

'I want to tell everyone. All the time. But when I start, I can't stop, and I can't bear ...' she pauses, and looks away. 'Distract me. Tell me about you – I know I've been using up all of your evenings and sending you off to orgies, but are you seeing anyone at the moment? Any gossip?'

'It's silly, really.' That kiss, on the step – what did it mean? And why does that feel more intimate than, say, telling the nation about who has been sucking my nipples? 'I don't know, I met someone at the weekend, I'm not sure if I'm interested. Probably nothing. Oh, but there is this guy I see sometimes, Sam Strong, I don't know why I always use his surname ...'

The colour has drained from Harri's face. 'You have got to be fucking kidding me. I know him. Know him, know him. From way back.'

Oh. Oh no. 'Is that a, er, problem?' If bloody Sam Strong ruins one more job for me ...

'No, no, we're not in touch any more, ancient history. But you're still seeing him?'

Harri's voice is cautious, and I detect a note of alarm. I get the impression that 'yes' is the wrong answer. And I know 'ancient history' can mean anything from 'I hadn't thought about him in years' to 'I still sleep in his old T-shirt'.

'It's very, very casual. I'm not very invested in it.' In fact, I realise, it's embarrassing to talk about. Not the casual part, but the whole, sordid relationship. Maybe Sam Strong does like me, in his way. But I hate admitting to Harri that I've settled for what he has offered me. Here we are, talking about our careers, and our futures. My passion for writing, and my need to write about passion. Sam Strong isn't the bad man of my fantasies, he's a sad man, alone, cynical and unwilling to let anyone in.

He made me feel safe. I'm used to being with people who don't think I'm worth very much, people who don't want to give anything away. I don't think I realised quite how low my self-esteem was until now, as I feel it rise. *Bring you with me! If you'll have me.* Harri Kemp, industry legend, thinks I'm worth something. This might be the biggest gamble of her career, and she wants me by her side.

This realisation forces me to ask an awkward question. 'How will I get paid? *Will* I get paid?'

Harri screws her face up. 'That's the plan. Hopefully sooner rather than later. But I need to be very honest and clear with you – I don't have any investors yet. So I'm going to be spending every spare minute I have over the next few weeks planning everything out, and I really, really hope you'll join me. I know it's a lot to ask. You might not want to do it. ' Harri tents her fingers, and rests her chin on her knuckles.

'This would be a full collaboration. Ultimately, we'd be running a business together. I hope that would, in time, lead to big rewards for both of us. If that's not for you, I'd love to bring you in later, as a staff writer, when we have investors and budget – but I really, really want your ideas, and your brilliance from the start. I don't want to be your boss. I want to be your partner.' She's declaring herself, and there's only one way to respond. I know it's impulsive, I know it's impetuous, and I'm still filled with doubt – but I can't help myself. I take her hand. 'I'm in.'

Chapter Forty-Nine

Pretending

Imogen

Harri has sent me back to the office, alone. 'Right now, we have to be very careful,' she explained. 'I'm being extra paranoid, but this needs to be super, super secret. You can't even tell Louise just yet.'

I'm so excited – and I'm *so* scared. It's as though every cell in my body has been renewed. It's not logical. To have a tiny bit of security for the first time in my life, and then even think about giving it up, basically to run a fancy version of my poor, neglected blog – there's no way that can work. I'd be mad. Harri must be mad. But she isn't mad. She knows what she's doing. Is the little voice in my head ... encouraging me, for once? The fear is tempered by a curious joy. This feels like the opposite of a panic attack. A sense of space. My own business. I could create my own role, on my own terms. Harri and I, in it together. No one to fire me, shame me, or tell me off.

It's as though winter has finally ended inside me – and outside, too. Nature's confetti cannon has exploded, and the parts of Shaftesbury Avenue that aren't covered in old McDonald's wrappers are carpeted in pink. I feel like singing! In fact, as I approach the Hudson Media building, I can hear someone singing. No, it's crying. Violent scream-sobs are coming from the stone stairwell on the corner.

The Londoner in me wants to keep walking and give the weeper their privacy. But the cries sound so vulnerable, so wretched, that I can't. Cautiously, I call out 'Hello! Are you OK? Would you like me to call someone?'

I descend the steps. In the shadows, I can just about make out a pair of gold, glittering brogues. A familiar pink fringe. Tabitha.

'Are you OK?' Stupid question, the woman is weeping as though she's watching Leonardo DiCaprio sinking to the bottom of the ocean. 'Have you hurt yourself? What happened?'

'Like you care.' She won't look at me.

'Tabitha . . .'

'Fuck off. Don't forget what I know. Don't forget how miserable I can make things for you. Now leave me alone.'

She sounds so vicious that I instinctively turn around to scuttle back to the office. But then I think No. I can stand up to bullies. I can stand up to you. I have nothing to lose any more. I take a deep breath. 'I don't know what your problem is but you have to stop giving me shit, Tabitha. I've talked to Harri, I know I shouldn't have lied – but you can't hold it over me.' Waves of rage are rolling and breaking. I'm not afraid, but I am filled with fury. 'I don't know why you think you're special. You're no different from any of the other stuck-up bitches that have made my life a misery. A good fashion editor is unique. A visionary.' I want to be cruel. I want to wound. 'Well, you're just a type. Another posh girl. You come to work looking like a space cadet, or a bee keeper, sneering at everything, like you're special. You think you're Isabella Blow when you have the soul of a ... gilet with a pashmina on top.'

I've wanted to make that speech a thousand times – and not just to Tabitha. Yet, I don't feel exonerated. Her eyes are narrow, glittering, but she looks broken. I have hurt her. I'm ashamed of myself. 'You don't know me at all.'

'Tabitha, I'm sorry, I ...'

'It isn't Tabitha, all right? It's Tanya. Go and tell your mates that I'm a big fake. Just like you. I'm probably quitting, anyway.' She sniffs. 'I finally got my *Vogue* interview, and I don't think I can go. I can't stay here, either. I'll probably have to move back to Tottenham ...' She starts crying again. 'It's easy for you! You can just be yourself. My whole life is lies.'

'What are you talking about?'

Tabitha shows me her phone screen. There's yesterday's #OOTD picture – bright blue silk pyjamas, white backless loafers, inflatable handbag. Odd, but not unusual. 'Look at the comments.' I scan. I recognise a few publicists, media names – but not the anonymous accounts. *'Is that Tanya Pollard? She looks like an actual clown.' 'What an embarrassment – but she looked like shit at college too.'* The words I'm reading are vicious, violent. I don't understand.

'But what ...' She registers my confusion and takes her phone. She scrolls, and hands it back to me.

'I just got tagged in this.'

The girl in the photo is young, with lank, mousy hair, a spot on her chin, a very short tie, a button missing from her shirt. But the oval jawline, the flipped-tick brows, the defiant glare-to-camera show that it's clearly Tabitha. Or Tanya, I guess.

'Now she's a fashion editor at a slag mag – never would have predicted THAT at college.' The account handle is @BitchesOfHaringey.

'This is your fault,' she whimpers. 'None of these people would have even heard of *The Know*, if you weren't on telly. I thought I'd left all of this behind me. And it was finally going to come together, and ... I'm exhausted. I'm so tired. I thought, if I got to *Vogue*, I could finally leave Tanya behind for ever.'

I'm puzzled. 'Why does this matter? Why can't you just be Tanya?'

'Tanya is a nobody. Tanya could barely get a fortnight's work experience on a home shopping catalogue. But as soon as I changed my name, I started to get jobs. I started to be seen. I know that Condé look at everyone's socials. They're going to see this. They'll probably cancel my interview.'

Good. Serves her right.

Does it?

Cautiously, I rest a palm on her shoulder. 'I don't want to give you advice, and I don't think you'll take it, anyway. But tell them. Own it. I don't think *Vogue* will care if you're Tabitha or Tanya. Still, you might feel better if you open up. We're all pretending, one way or another.' I take another good look at her shoes. 'In fact, tell them it was all performance art. They'll probably ask you to run the magazine.'

Chapter Fifty

The lines are warped

Harri

Never, ever, ever have 'one last look' at your emails. It's 8.03 p.m., and Harri is on the brink of calling it a night when she makes the mistake of refreshing. At 7.59 p.m., Mackenzie emailed her. Mackenzie wants to set up an appointment to 'formally discuss the future of *The Know*' with regards to 'a failure to meet targets consistently' and 'the publication of explicit content' which is 'bringing the brand into disrepute'. She has attached graphs. She has gone to the trouble of manipulating the figures – so rather than focusing on the highest highs, Imogen's huge hitters, those which have brought untold traffic, and glory – the lines are warped. It looks like *The Know* has had a couple of OK days, and barely half a reader. Harri knew Mackenzie was touted as some sort of financial genius – she didn't realise she could use maths to lie. 'You have two weeks to make significant improvements, otherwise there will be serious consequences for you and your team, with a view to termination.' It makes no sense at all.

Harri writes five furious half sentences before giving up and gathering her notebooks together. She'd forgotten about the Whittaker-Chambers media pack. She'd been using it as a bookmark. She's on the brink of binning it, but she feels compelled to try Google again.

The 404 error message has been replaced with 'Coming soon'. She tries 'Mackenzie Whittaker'. Harri is familiar with the first few results – 'publishing maven', with years of experience in something called 'luxury outdoor pursuits', who has recently moved to the UK for a new challenge.

Scrolling down the page, she sees results for a Mackenzie Whittaker-Chambers, an heiress worth forty-eight million dollars. Ah! Mackenzie isn't good with money. She just has lots of it. And if Harri thinks she's a financial genius for weaseling a few grand here and there out of the ad men, the Whittaker-Chambers family is a brains trust. Mr Whittaker-Chambers Senior is the head of a luxury property empire. Mr Whittaker-Chambers Senior has been accused, according to the *Wall Street Journal* (a site where Harri is surprised to find herself using up her free article limit) of pledging to build affordable housing, taking government money to buy land, then selling the land back to himself for buttons and building compounds with swimming pools for fellow billionaires. Mr Whittaker-Chambers Senior 'gifted' Mackenzie Whittaker-Chambers 'an undisclosed sum' before her move to the UK, to 'set up a charitable foundation'. Court proceedings are ongoing.

Only now does Harri realise she had been nursing a secret hope that she was wrong. She wanted her instincts to be off. She wanted Mackenzie's villainous carapace to melt away, revealing a silly misunderstanding, a person she could grudgingly respect, a secret nice girl underneath. She had been holding her breath, waiting for the plot twist. She believed Mackenzie *must* have hidden depths – and that they would become unlikely friends at the eleventh hour. She knew Mackenzie was ruthless. She had pushed away the most alarming thought, and now it has been proven incorrigibly true. Mackenzie is corrupt.

Snakes, all the way down. *I have got to get out.*

Harri is old enough and tired enough to know this won't end well. Something seriously sketchy is happening at Hudson, worse than she'd feared. And if she was the true heroine of her own life, she'd stop the rot, reverse the wrongdoing, seek justice for her friends and save the day. But she knows that people who are prepared to manipulate, sneak and dissemble in order to accumulate that much money cannot be vanquished by something as basic as the truth. Here, morals are meaningless. She feels a bit sick. She can't do nothing, but she knows she can't really do anything, either. She had been thinking of her escape plan as a hope, a dream, a way to create some breathing space in her head. Now she *knows* she has no other option. It's not just her career at stake, but Imogen's, too. Forewarned is forearmed, they say. But Harri's googling has not helped her to feel prepared. She's in a state of panic. Now, more than ever, she needs to feel solid, certain, sure-footed. She needs to ignore her sense that life as she knows it is about to descend into freefall.

She wishes she'd never seen that bloody brochure.

Chapter Fifty-One

There's more than one way to be exploited

Imogen

'Imogen, can I ask you a weird question?' Harri looks tentative. 'I hope you don't mind. I've been thinking about you and Sam Strong. Has he ever . . . hurt you? Has he ever done anything to make you feel uncomfortable?'

Harri is, I'm learning, much chattier when it's just the two of us in the office. We've been staying late and plotting for almost a fortnight. It's thrilling, it's exciting, it's inspiring. I'm exhausted.

'No . . . maybe . . . I'm not sure.' I'm slightly cagey. I don't really want to think about it too hard.

'When did you last see him?' Harri asks gently.

'It's been a while. There was,' I think about mentioning *The Gentleman* and decide that it might be a story for another time, 'a moment when I met some of his awful friends, and I've pretty much ignored his messages since. Not completely ignored them, I've just told him I'm busy.

And I *am* busy,' I say, failing to keep the defensive note out of my voice. Harri looks thoughtful. 'I bet that makes him even keener. The dickhead. Sorry, I know you're still involved. Honestly, I'd not thought about him for years. I make sure I avoid his part of the paper on Saturdays but when I do, I get flashes of rage. He made me very unhappy, but maybe he's changed?'

Harri sounds hopeful, desperate even. What can I tell her? I think about the very first time we had sex, the third bottle of wine, the ease with which we somehow ended up in a hotel room, the blacking out. Why have I kept going back? How many girls have there been? 'Honestly, there's nothing I wouldn't suspect him of – but I suppose it's been easier for me to tell myself that I was seeing him on my own terms. He's dangled various jobs in front of me, and that was a bit manipulative, but I'm making it work for me by eating my way through his fridge.'

Harri snorts. 'He must have changed a bit if there's anything to actually eat in there. It used to be all fancy mineral water. But you don't feel exploited, or anything? Sam Strong was – is – notorious for being *the worst,* and I'm pretty sure that he has slept with every woman who has ever worked on a London magazine. He goes around like the flu. But sometimes, when I think about some of the stories, the rumours, what we put up with, what we laughed off ... I wish I'd challenged him. I wish I'd called him out. I wish I knew how to fix it.'

I'm touched by Harri's words, but they really are just words. She wants to help – but what could she do, really? And there's more than one way to be exploited, I think, crossly. I wonder how many hours I have spent in this building, working and not getting paid. I know that what I'm doing with Harri is different. It's a collaboration. The work itself is exciting, absorbing. But part of me wants to kick myself for coming back and doing it *again*. My face must betray me, as Harri frowns. 'Look, I know this isn't ideal, all of this extra work. I do appreciate it, really. We've done so much, we've got loads to show to potential investors – I think we'll be ready soon.'

'I'm enjoying it, really.' I am! Harri has pulled back a curtain, and I'm starting to understand how her world works. My brain is pulsating with the effort of keeping up, as I learn how to link my wildest, weirdest ideas with the evidence that will make them commercially viable. 'Always think like a trickster,' Harri had said. 'We won't get anywhere if we think of the money people as Dickensian villains, getting between us and our art. We must be prepared to meet them at their level.'

For a few moments, we work in companionable silence, until I hear Harri saying 'Huh. That's strange.' I wonder if it would be rude to put some earphones in for a bit.

'This came in with the weekly mags.' She waves a crappy magazine, more of a pamphlet really. 'Luxury' something. Developer?

So? 'Is it not just a crappy leaflet? With the ones for giant garden gnomes, and elasticated trousers in fifty shades of beige?'

Harri shakes her head. 'I assumed so, but I saw that it has a Hudson logo on it, which is a bit weird. No one mentioned anything about a new magazine. Usually a new title is launched with a bit of noise and fuss, we all have to go and drink warm cava and eat Caterpillar cake in the boardroom.' She flicks through the flimsy pages. 'Most of this appears to be an ad for something called the Whittaker Complex.'

'What's that?'

'A big housing development. Apartments starting at 4.5 million. Whittaker, presumably as in ... '

'Oh yeah, our Mackenzie! Well, you know. Hardly our Mackenzie, but ... '

'Yeah. It's odd.'

Chapter Fifty-Two

Lazarus

Harri

Mackenzie had promised – or threatened – two weeks for Harri to make 'significant changes'. But ten days after her email, she bursts into the office just as Harri is removing her coat, and resting her coffee on her desk. Uninvited, unannounced, almost cheerful.

'I'm going to advise the board that we close *The Know* down with immediate effect,' says Mackenzie. Harri almost respects her for not bothering with a hello, or a how-are-you. 'Legally, apparently, we're obliged to give you a month. The law, in this country.' Mackenzie rolls her eyes, for once, almost friendly, inviting Harri to join her in cocking a snook at the absurdity of a system that forces an employer to prevent their staff from becoming immediately homeless.

At this point, Harri could almost laugh.

'I see.'

'There has been a failure to establish consistent audience

and advertising targets, various content issues, budget mis-
management, and our server monitoring system has found
evidence that the office space was being used out of hours,
for unauthorised purposes. I'm sure you know that *Panache*
will be closed in the coming months too, although I'd appreciate your discretion there, as it has yet to be announced.'
It's such an obvious, wicked trick, such a lazy way of
wrongfooting your enemies. How has Harri allowed herself
to fall for it? '*The Know* was always a secondary product,
to support *Panache*, so there's really no point carrying on.'
Mackenzie's laugh is a staccato burst of sharps and flats,
the sound of glass shattering against the wall.

There's really no point carrying on. Harri remembers
having that thought twenty-four hours after the conversation with the coroner, when the ambulance had come and
gone. Briefly, it had calmed and comforted her. But she
had carried on, and maybe the worst of the pain was in
the plodding. She'd wept, she'd screamed, she had felt so
wretched and wrong in her own body that she had prayed
for the skin to fall from her skeleton, she'd begged the universe to vaporise her, to turn her to dust. Since then, she'd
measured out her life in a thousand cups of undrunk coffee,
she had made toothmarks in her toast, she had bathed, and
slept, and woken up and come in and turned her computer
on and made scores of tiny scratches that amounted to an
existence. Harri is Lazarus, she is the walking dead. She's
been keeping a foot in the surface world while secretly,
silently, loving a ghost. What the fuck can this white collar
criminal robot do to her, really?

'OK. I will be launching an investigation of my own,
but my immediate concern is for my staff.' Harri must go

out fighting. She's got to say something. She might want to run out into the streets and never look back, but she has hungry mouths to feed. What about Imogen? What about Kim, and Louise? Even Tabitha, who clearly does not want to be there, should be allowed to leave on her own terms. Harri needs to come up with something, for their sakes. 'Presumably, it will be possible to find jobs for *The Know* team in other areas of the organisation? I understand that is a legal obligation for Hudson.'

Mackenzie actually laughs at this. A real mean girl titter. 'We'll see, shall we?'

Before she turns to leave, Mackenzie has one last gift to give. 'We know you're up to something. Management have been monitoring you closely. You will be punished for it.'

If I had forty-eight million dollars, I'd be at home, drinking champagne in my swimming pool, thinks Harri. *Not hanging out in a crappy office, taking jobs away from people who have next to nothing in the first place.*

The summons comes much later, at the very end of the day. Harri's presence is requested by the board at 10 o'clock in the morning. She scans the email for suspicious phrases. No 'disciplinary hearing'. No 'redundancy negotiation'. No clues. She thinks about calling Giles. She thinks about calling Akila. She thinks about calling a lawyer. She goes home, gets her Erdem dress out of the wardrobe, and waits.

Chapter Fifty-Three

DRAMA

Imogen

It's not unusual to see swarms of police cars converging on Soho, so I don't look up when I hear the first siren. Or the second one. But the noise is getting nearer. Then there's the muffled squawk of a megaphone. 'Oh my God, DRAMA!' yells Kim. Then he turns pale.

'I might have the tiniest bit of MDMA in a baggie in my jacket. Do you think this is it? Am I getting busted?'

'Yeah, sure. They are sending most of the Met to arrest you for that. We will visit you in prison,' I say, solemnly. 'Although – who knows? I might be in the next cell! I'm always convinced that I might have broken some obscure law, without knowing it. You know, they will suddenly decide to enforce something from the fourteenth century about women wearing hats every third Wednesday. Lou, have you ever broken the law?'

'Look at her! Louise hasn't ever broken a New Year's resolution!' says Kim, ruffling her hair.

'Well,' says Louise, flushing, 'I did eat swan once.'

'What? When? How?' This is not the answer I was expecting.

'It was at university, I'm not proud of it. Some boys found one and barbecued it, I think it died of natural causes, but ... I was quite ill, afterwards.'

Kim clutches his chest. 'Oh, sweet Louise, you're breaking my heart! This is like something out of Little House On The Prairie, desperate homesteaders, trying to stop yourself from starving, in the English wilderness ... '

Louise looks confused. 'Well, Jamie, who cooked the swan, his dad is the earl of—'

'Oh my GOD! Have they come for her? What is going on? What is happening?' Kim has spotted something. Through the window, if I bend down, I can just about see a policeman, a policewoman and a familiar figure between them. Fawn tweed, glossy, glossy hair, a brown furry coat draped over her shoulders. She is being led into the Cleveland van that is parked on the pavement. Is this what Harri was going on about the other night? I did not see this coming.

Kim whistles. 'Damn, that woman gives good felon. Very Anna Delvey. That coat!' He kisses his fingers. 'So they weren't after my stash after all! We could have a quick celebratory breakfast ... no?'

'Dude, you're halfway through a kale smoothie. Is your body a temple, or is it Disney World?' I snap, feeling slightly aggrieved. Kim keeps telling me that the sugar in my pain au chocolat is another panic attack waiting to happen.

'Can't it be both? Anyway, what the hell is happening? Does anyone know?'

Louise turns to me. 'Immo, you seem to have been spending a lot of time with Harri lately, has she mentioned anything?'

'Um, well ...' What can I tell them? We think Senior Management is going to shut us down, and we'll all be unemployed, but not to worry, I'm starting up a small business with our boss! No idea what you'll do, sorry! I choose my words carefully.

'Harri hasn't told me anything, but I think Hudson might be in trouble. And I've seen Lily and Katie coming in and out of the *Panache* offices, and they never turn up when things are going well.'

Tabitha takes her headphones off. I didn't realise she was listening. 'Mackenzie's dad is George Whittaker-Chambers. He's on trial in America and being investigated by the FBI for securities fraud. So it's probably to do with that. I can't believe none of you knew.' She rolls her eyes and puts her headphones back on.

There is a long pause. I daren't say what I'm thinking out loud because I'm frightened of sounding stupid. So I look over Louise's shoulder. Sure enough, she's on Wikipedia, reading the page about Securities Fraud.

I pick up my phone to see what I can find online – I decide I don't want to use my work computer to search for stories about my boss's boss, *even though* it seems silly to worry when she's the one going to actual prison. Then a name appears on my screen and I gasp. I blink. I feel sick. I don't know whether to shriek with joy or burst into tears. Jen. Jen who has ignored every single frantic, craven, beseeching message of apology that I have sent her since I went to Devon. I was starting to wonder whether she had blocked my number.

Her message makes no reference to any of that.

OMG Imogen heard about your boss. Just saw her on the news. Is she going to jail? Have you lost ur job? Leanne says they'll shut down The Know AND Panache. So sad. Call me ☺ xx

And for a pathetic second, I nearly do. I'm on the brink of ringing her, weeping, begging her to take me back, just because she has finally deigned to get in touch.

It's funny that she has been discussing this with Leanne before she tried to talk to me. It's funny, really, that she has any kind of relationship with Leanne, a woman who used to abuse me for fun.

Funniest of all is the fact that a long time ago, Jen was my cheerleader. But now, I only hear from her when things appear to be going badly. I know she can see me when I do well. But she chooses to ignore it. As soon as disaster seems to be looming, she wants to be back in my life. She will share my grief, but she wants no part in my joy.

I think about replying and telling her that *the* Harri Kemp has just asked me to be her business partner, actually. Instead, I delete Jen's message, and grin at Louise and Kim, and tell them I love them in the most work-appropriate way I know. 'Who wants a tea?'

Chapter Fifty-Four

Everything she wants

Harri

Harri is back where it all began, the boardroom where Will first summoned her forth to issue the world's worst early Christmas present. It's weird that Will isn't here. No Lily or Katie, either. No Mackenzie. None of her enemies, which is strange. In a way, it's nice not to see them – but perhaps this means Harri won't have the opportunity to argue her case. If she has one. Maybe whatever Mackenzie has already said about her is so damning that she doesn't need to be there to reiterate it? For half a second, Harri wonders whether she is even in the right room. Perhaps the stress of the last few months has led to some sort of breakdown. Has she appeared in someone else's job, someone else's life, someone else's firing? She can count twelve faces, all vaguely familiar from Christmas parties past. She thinks one of the men is called Martin – a red face, a red tie, and a recollection of an alarmingly ... *thrusty* dance to 'Get Lucky'. None of them are unfriendly – in fact, they look downright welcoming. Maybe that's just the blood lust. Maybe firing people is their favourite thing.

'Harriet? I'm Linda Morris. We're delighted to see you, please take a seat.' Harri doesn't remember meeting this woman before, but there's something reassuringly familiar about her. A warmth. A sense of purpose. Linda must be in her early fifties, but she seems centuries older than Harri, the polish, the poise, the low voice, the round vowels. Her steel grey blouse has a pussy bow. Harri has tried similar blouses, and she has always looked like a joke shop fancy dress secretary. On this woman, the blouse somehow implies she's a person whose secretary has a secretary. Harri suspects that this woman has also never sniggered at the word 'pussy'.

'Now, the last few months must have been very tough for you.' Ah, here it comes, the letting me down gently. 'I'd like to make a sincere and heartfelt apology on behalf of the entire board,' and we're obliged to offer you, to thank you for your years of loyal service, three days' severance pay, and an attractive carriage clock, perfect for the mantlepiece of the home you will have to sell in order to … 'and assure you that we were misled as to what was going on within the company, and we're committed to rectifying it.'

'What are you talking about?' The words leave Harri's mouth before she has a chance to edit them.

'I'm sure you're aware that Mackenzie Whittaker is about to go on trial in the US; she has been advised to tender her resignation with immediate effect.'

'Oh. No. I didn't know. Is this connected with the new magazines? Or her property interests?'

Linda wrinkles her nose. 'Oh, we're just becoming aware

of the extra titles she was trying to launch, but that's the tip of the iceberg, really.'

'I don't understand. Mackenzie told me yesterday that she was shutting *The Know*, and eventually, *Panache*. Because we hadn't met our targets.' Harri is horrified, furious with herself. Why would she say that, in front of the board? In front of Linda Morris, who seems to be, to all intents and purposes, the Head Prefect of Hudson Media? Is Harri going to confess to stealing sweets from the tuck shop, too?

Linda speaks gently. 'Harriet, a lot of this is on a need to know basis, and we're still getting to the bottom of most of it. It's complicated, there's a lot of legal back and forth between here and the US. The authorities are working out where she will face trial, and for which offences. But here is what we know. Mackenzie used Hudson as a front to launder a substantial sum of money. As she had a background in magazines, Hudson was chosen as a target. We think that she was trying to close the expensive consumer titles, while creating a range of trade titles, that are cheap to produce, in order to make it look like her appointment led to an implausible bump in profit margins, and a greater company valuation. Her multi million-dollar investment appeared to be revenue, and did not get traced back to the States. We think she was supported by some members of staff, who had been promised substantial payouts, when the consumer titles folded.'

'What, Will, Katie and Lily?'

Linda's face does not flicker. 'That's confidential.'

'Have they been fired?' Do they have families? She knows Will has a family. She suspects Katie lives behind a mossy boulder, or amongst a clan of hyenas.

'For the time being, those members of staff have been relocated to our payroll and administration centre in Reading, with salary freezes, pending further investigation.'

This, Harri knows, is a fate worse than firing.

'So . . . what does this mean? For *The Know*?' And for me?

'Harri, we've asked you here because we want to fully reinstate you at *Panache*. As editor-in-chief.'

Black spots appear before Harri's eyes. She clutches the table in front of her. Linda's carefully modulated voice suddenly sounds very loud.

'Oh. I see.'

'We're able to retain a chunk of Mackenzie's "invest-ment",' Harri is surprised to note that Linda is not above making air quotes with her fingers. 'We want to divert the funds back into *Panache*. The magazine is part of Hudson's heritage, it's one of the most beloved brands in the UK, it's part of our legacy as a publisher, and it's one we want to maintain. And we've been so impressed by you and your team at *The Know*. We hope you'll bring them with you, to the magazine. We want to invest in *Panache*. Significantly.'

Harri weighs up the word. She could hire Giles back! She might even be able to persuade Akila to come and freelance! Shoots! Shows!

Linda misinterprets her silence. 'Obviously, we can start salary negotiations immediately but we'd be looking to give you a significant increase. Better stock options, too.' She gestures to the rest of the room. 'We need to give Ms Kemp some time to consider her demands. But our legal team will be in touch about the package. And, ah . . . ' for the first time, Linda looks a little uncertain. 'Our conversation, just now. With regards to Mackenzie. We'd appreciate your utmost discretion there. We'll definitely bear the brunt of some industry gossip, which we will ride out in due course. But for legal reasons, what was mentioned cannot leave this room.'

But Harri can. She floats out. Her lucky dress finally delivered. Editor-in-chief. *Are you proud of me?* she asks the air, out of habit, listening for an answer.

Always, my love. But are you proud of you? Are you sure this is what you want?

Chapter Fifty-Five

*A missed call from a withheld
number. And a voicemail*

Harri

Harri's nerves are shot. She knows it's her job to soothe her disrupted staff. She understands they must be unsettled by the events of the morning, and she has a duty of care towards them. She realises that although she has been forbidden from revealing any explicit details, she needs to share some of the story, if only to contain it. But sound is too loud, light is too bright, her brain is broken glass and her skin is paper. Even Akila's curiosity is too much to bear. And if Kim says 'dra-ma!' one more time, she is going to throw him out of the tiny window.

Her phone shakes, and she shrieks. Her strange, dream-like day has been punctured. It's jarring. A missed call from a withheld number is always alarming. A missed call from a withheld number and a voicemail is an invitation to assume that something unimaginably dreadful has happened.

Harri spends fifteen seconds mentally rehearsing every single scenario. It's a call to say Management meant to offer the job to someone else. No, worse! Mackenzie has, from prison, implicated Harri in her wrongdoing, there is a warrant out for Harri's arrest, or Lily and Katie are armed and roaming the corridors. Harri's panic rises with every syllable of 'One. New. Mess-age . . .'

'Hi, this is Erin Faulkner. I'm trying to speak to Harri Kemp, thank you so much for your email. I'm looking at investment opportunities and I'm very keen, I'd love to talk to you about the new project – ah, can you give me a call back? Thanks.'

The new project. Harri's parachute. Her escape route. Twenty-four hours ago it was all she could think about, but it's funny how things slip your mind when you watch a woman who has been psychologically torturing you being taken away in a police van. Harri has a decision to make. She doesn't need to run away any more. But will she walk?

Chapter Fifty-Six

Can your boss break your heart?

Imogen

I panicked, and said I'd have the same as Harri, so I'm eating a Caesar salad. As far as I can tell, the only Caesar-ish aspect of it is that it looks and tastes as though it were made by an angry Roman general, thousands of years ago. I've had chewing gum crispier than this lettuce.

'Why do we keep coming here?'

'The burger is nice,' says Harri, defensively.

'Why didn't we get burgers, then?'

'You ask a wise question, grasshopper.' Harri puts her fork down and catches the eye of the waitress. 'Could we order two burgers?' I look at her expectantly and she sighs. 'And a side order of the triple cooked chips.'

Harri seems preoccupied. She's staring at her hands, which are busily shredding her paper napkin. 'Imogen, I have some news. I've been asked to come back to *Panache*. As editor-in-chief.'

'Shit! Sorry, I mean, brilliant! But what does that mean for us?'

Harri picks at her napkin. 'They want you, too,' she says quietly. 'They're really keen. There's talk of a relaunch. With you as a lead columnist. They're already planning a podcast that they want you to host too.'

'What about Emily Forge?' *Panache* already has a lead columnist, long term object of my professional jealousy. Harri is still picking. 'Dunno. I think she might have gone, to be honest, Mackenzie forced her to take a massive pay cut, I could rehire her but I'm not sure I'd bother.'

'This is … good news?' Isn't it? It's better than good, it's an impossible dream come true. I'd still get to work with Harri – and for *Panache*! This is everything I've ever wanted. Why does Harri look like she wants to cry?

'The other big news is that we have a potential investor for our site. Well, one investor who is pretty much committed, a couple who are extremely interested and a few more possibilities.'

'That's fantastic. Get yourself a woman who can do it all, I say!' Harri does not laugh. She has started on my napkin.

'Look, I haven't said yes to *Panache*. I don't know what I'm going to do.'

It's obvious, isn't it? 'Surely we can go to *Panache* and launch our new business as a side project?'

Harri shakes her head. 'Imogen, *Panache* wants all of us. It wouldn't be a 9–5 job. Look at your blog – you haven't been writing it because I've taken up all of your free time, and *Panache* would be even worse. And even if there was time, for either of us – we'd be expected to live the brand.

There are all kinds of contractual clauses about who else we're allowed to work for, and how.'

I have a brainwave. 'Maybe we could come to *Panache* as freelancers?'

Harri frowns. 'The business plan I've produced is contingent on the two of us working full time. If we're doing this as a hobby, our investors pull out. Imogen, I can't keep you from *Panache*. I know exactly what that job would mean to you. I know what it used to mean to me. Although I'm not sure what it means any more.'

I think about the unpaid hours I have spent at *Panache*. The coffee runs, and every suspicious 'is this definitely soy milk?' instead of 'thank you'. The time I was asked to assist on a shoot and spent most of the day on my hands and knees, cleaning up after the model's dog, and sponging actual shit off her shoes. And the even more miserable minimum wage hours I've worked in order to be able to pay for the privilege of cleaning up dogshit for free. I did all of that, hoping and praying that I might be noticed. Longing to be taken on as the lowliest, most poorly paid assistant, just for permission to belong in that world. Until I started at *The Know*, I wished for a job at *Panache* on every loose eyelash and blown-out birthday candle. This isn't just what I wanted – it's what I was scared to dare to dream of, coming true. I should feel elated.

I prod my salad. I hope the chips come soon. 'But what's going to happen to *The Know*? What about Louise and Kim?'

Harri frowns. 'They'll definitely have jobs at *Panache*, if they want them, I'll make sure of it. I'm going to see if Akila will take the reins and freelance for them for six months.

She's not editorial, of course, but she's brilliant. And I'll suggest she gets an eye-watering, ruinously expensive day rate, too!'

It's as though Harri is acting. She doesn't sound convinced of her own words. She isn't convincing me.

'What do you want. Really?' I ask Harri.

Her reply is simply 'I want to be my own boss.'

I nod and open my mouth but Harri interrupts me.

'Still, this is a huge opportunity for you. It's not fair for me to force my agenda on you. Sixty per cent of new businesses go bust in the first three years – there would be no one to bail us out. Don't forget, I'm able to take bigger risks. I'm older and uglier and I've already got a mortgage.' Her laugh is flat.

Cold, spidery dread creeps across my torso. Was this always Harri's plan? 'So ... what? I go to *Panache*, you set this company up, you take my ideas, get all the glory and recognition? What if I want to be my own boss too?'

'Imogen, please!' Harri has the decency to look embarrassed. Good. 'Of course that's not what I want. That's not what I meant. I'm giving you a more secure option. I'm trying, desperately, to be fair to you. I'm trying to be a good friend.'

Giving me a more secure option? Who does that remind me of? I thought Harri believed in me and wanted to work with me. I feel tender, raw. This *hurts*. I lift my chin. 'You're not my friend, Harri. Friends don't constantly remind you about what's going to go wrong. Friends don't make you play it safe. They give you room to dream of impossible things. Friends are supposed to make you bolder and braver.' My tears become thicker, viscous, almost opaque, and I run, stumbling, following the faint impression of light until I'm outside on the pavement. I have to get back to the office. I don't have anywhere else to go.

Chapter Fifty-Seven

Only a job

Imogen

I've worked in more than thirty different office buildings, and every single one comes with its own version of a padded cell. Sometimes, it's a cupboard. Usually, it's a toilet. But it's the very first thing to suss out when you start at a new place. Glossy companies boast about their amenities, and the way they promote the mental wellness of their employees by providing toiletries, tampons, top of the range snacks and table football. But I have yet to see the HR orientation pack that reads 'Welcome to the company. Glad to have you on board. Just so you know, when you have your inevitable breakdowns, there's a weird underground gym you can use. Just a treadmill, an exercise ball, very low ceiling, no windows. The light only works occasionally. When people just can't bear to be here, they go and sit on the end of the treadmill and bawl their eyes out. Please don't leave any food down there, we've had problems with rats.'

Hudson – possibly owing to some confusion around being American owned – has two ground floors. There's the 'first' ground floor, where Reception is, and the ground-ground floor, which is technically a basement. It's where our office is, and where you go to the post room and suck up to the surly deliveries team when your ASOS package has gone missing. Then, there's the actual basement. You have to take the stairs. The neon strip lights are neither on nor off, they flash suddenly and erratically in the stairwell. (Akila christened the basement Studio Epilepsy.) There is a dark, dark passage, a shower, and a single disabled toilet. Your phone won't work but take it anyway. You will need the torch.

With one hand feeling the wall for balance, you must try not to think about mice or spiders. Or worse. You'll remember a rumour that ten or fifteen years ago, a *Football Fever* staffer found a dead homeless person down there, and you will mentally have to put your fingers in your ears and sing 'la la la, I'm not listening!' Do not actually put your fingers in your ears, the darkness will overwhelm you, and you'll lose your balance. It will be freezing cold, nipples-out-through-your-bra cold, seeing-your-breath-like-cigarette-smoke cold (once your eyes have adjusted to the dark, it will just be visible). But you won't mind, because the world is cold, and cruel, and inhospitable, and that's why you have ended up in the basement.

As I descend the stairs, the wall feels slightly damp beneath my palm. I'm certain that out of the corner of my eye, I can detect something scurrying. It's just my imagination. It's a floater, it's dust, I'm paranoid, and surely I can cope with a mouse?

But not a rat. Not, under any circumstances, a rat.

Still, as I feel my way to the cubicle and shut the door, I feel my spine slumping, and my head growing heavy. It's only a job. Who cares?

And that's the thought that flattens me, crumples me, that wrenches the sobs from my body. Here, no one can hear me scream, so I'm screaming, weeping. Crying for my life. Ugly crying. Orgiastic crying.

Only a job.

It has been my life, my identity, my ability to feel happiness, my entire sense of self-worth and self-esteem. And it's only a job. And yet, because of our jobs – or maybe, the way we feel about them – I've broken up with my best friend, Louise is having a breakdown, Tabitha has effectively put herself under her own witness protection programme, and Harri – Harri wants to leave. Harri has given the best and worst years of her life to Hudson and being offered the ultimate prestige job – the job she has been working towards for so long – isn't enough of a reward. She wants out.

Six months ago, I believed that if I had a full time job at *Panache*, I would feel safe and happy. But Harri wasn't happy. She wasn't safe, either. But no one ever is. I think of her grief, the secret, silent weight of it, the numbness of it. I think of my own mother, the living grief she endures, the way compromises can stack up, and mutate and turn into something that looks like giving up.

I can't blame Harri for refusing to compromise any more. But I can't really blame her for wanting me to play it safe, either. It's exactly what my mother would tell me to do.

Maybe I should call her.

Coming out of the basement, I feel as trepidatious as I did going in. Calling Mum is always an ordeal, but it's been extra stressful ever since that last, hideous visit home. As I lean against the wall of the Hudson building, I realise I'm shaking. I'm feeling more strained with every ring of the phone. Mum picks up in seconds.

'Imogen! Love! I've been worrying! We saw your company, whatsit, Hudson, on the news! That awful woman, stealing all of your money! Are you OK? Do you need anything?' It's as though she's been biding her time, waiting for everything to go wrong.

Sighing heavily, I start to wonder whether I've made a mistake. 'Yeah, that was a shock. But it's OK, really. How's Dad?' I ask brightly, and again, curse myself immediately. 'Keeping well? Looking after himself? What's the latest?' I feel like a bloody magician; every time I open my mouth, a stream of uncontrolled, primary coloured nonsense shoots out.

'Actually, he's not too bad. He's been cutting down on sugar, although he does hate being nagged about it. He's even been going for the odd walk! Apparently someone in the pub was teasing him about his glamorous daughter, on TV, and said he needed to start sorting himself out.

'He's very proud of you. We both are. I know he doesn't always tell you ... '

'He doesn't ever tell me, Mum.'

Silence. I'm losing control of the call – and I don't want to put Mum in the middle of this again. She has to live with it. I take a deep breath.

'Um, with everything happening at Hudson, there are some big changes. I've been offered a job at *Panache*, the magazine I've always dreamed of working for. More money, more security. But ... '

'But what?'

'I've been talking to my boss, and we're thinking about setting up a brand new website together, having our own business. There would be more storytelling, more personal stuff, I guess. We started developing the idea together, she's found some investors. But it's probably ridiculous, it might not work out, it wouldn't be ... secure.'

'Investors?' I can hear Mum smiling down the phone. 'You're making something people want to invest in? Oh, Imogen, that's brilliant!'

'But ... if there's a chance for a bit more money and more security, you'd tell me to take it, right?'

There's a pause on the line. 'Imogen, security isn't the be all and end all. I've done things ... made decisions ... I suppose I've always felt that it was my job to keep you safe. And I've worried, because I couldn't do anything else. I thought that I was obliged to keep your life risk free. But I think there's much more out there for you.'

'But you didn't – would you – oh, I wish you'd take some risks, Mum.' Like leaving Dad. Which will never happen.

'Imogen, the best and worst thing about being your mother is I've never really been able to give you anything. Not just because we don't have much, and because I've been looking after your dad, but – you've always been so restless, and curious and determined. I don't know where you get it from. I suppose I always thought you were in your own world, but you're not a dreamer, you're a doer. Not like anyone else I've ever known.'

'Mum!' I am absolutely, utterly floored. 'So – even you don't think I should necessarily take the proper job? Do the sensible thing?'

'Why would you start now? I've been telling you that for years and you haven't taken a scrap of notice. Besides, if it doesn't work out . . . '

Oh, don't say it, don't say it.

' . . . You can always come home.'

'Thanks, Mum. I'm going to go now. Love you.'

Chapter Fifty-Eight

Like family

Harri

Linda Morris is becoming increasingly impatient to get Harri back inside the Hudson boardroom. It's not quite 8 a.m., and she has just sent an email asking if Harri got the three voicemails she has left over the last twenty-four hours. The longer Harri waits, the bigger the *Panache* offer becomes. She's scared to listen and hear what she's thinking of turning down now. Linda has probably offered her the lease of the building, and a quick go on any Hemsworth brother profiled by the magazine. She's in limbo, really. There have been days – well, weeks and months – when she's stared at the walls that surround her, or felt the life force drain from her as she's passed between floors in the lift. She's got stuck in the automatic doors, she's breathed through her mouth while she opened the tiny kitchen microwave, she's stared at the post and packages and piles of press releases and thought oh, to be anywhere but here.

It has been her crucible, placing her under improbable pressure – but it has protected her too.

She thinks of what Giles said. For Harri, the glamour and status has been incidental. She loves an upgrade, a canapé, a free handbag, as much as the next person, but that isn't what Hudson means to her. It's been her safe space. Every day, she's had somewhere to go. She belongs. 'We're like a family!' Will had said once, years ago, and Harri gave him a sharp look, and worried and wondered about his actual family. But he was not wrong. Families are dysfunctional, or rather, they function awkwardly, unfairly and chaotically – but they do somehow function. There's love there too – if love really means never having to say you're sorry. But no matter how broken, cold, manipulative or overbearing your workplace family can be, they keep a roof over your head. They give you somewhere to go at Christmas – even if you work for a magazine and Christmas takes place in July. They can define you, even if you never stop feeling like a rebellious teenager, determined to be the opposite of who they say you are. If she walks away from all of this, who will she be?

Thinking of teenage rebellion seems to summon her sulkiest staffer. Tabitha's scowl can be decidedly adolescent – but not only is she first in, she's *smiling*. Harri has observed that the least likely people seem to control the temperature in the office. Even though Rosa's mood swings were occasionally operatic, they never seemed to have much of an impact on the *Panache* ecosystem. Yet she has known sour, set-faced interns who have changed the psychogeography of a room before they've put their bags on their desks. Anna 'Nuclear' Wintour has much to answer for. Her dedicated followers laboured under the misapprehension that the first rule of fashion was to inflict chill.

So it is with Tabitha. She thought Tabitha's perpetual bad mood was an immovable part of the furniture, the grubby rug they were all stepping around. It turns out that Tabitha is capable of radiating joy, light, and actual warmth, and she is bearing down upon her. Oh, no. Has she accepted the Lord Jesus Christ as her personal saviour? Because, in Harri's experience, those who do like to lead communal, celebratory singing and Harri's alto is so flat and scratchy that she has to mime whenever there is an office birthday cake.

'I don't know if I have to put it in writing? Probably, but, anyway, I quit! I'm going to Condé. To *Vogue*!'

'Ah! Congratulations!' And phew. Because when all the puzzle pieces were thrown up in the air, she wasn't sure where Tabitha would land – she did not tessellate well with others. Harri knew she'd be happier at *Panache* than *The Know* – if Tabitha could be happy, anywhere. But she didn't want to inflict her sulkiest, grumpiest employee on the shiny new team. 'Is that with Elsa? Is Diana still there?'

Tabitha beams. 'I'm not sure, I'll be assistant deputy demi-fine timepieces editor.' Harri isn't quite sure what to say. 'Gosh! Timepieces? Is that, um, pocket watches and things?'

'It really is everything I've ever wanted. And, I'm sorry, I know I've not been the best fashion editor, for you. It's been hard, especially with, you know,' she waves her hand in the direction of Imogen and Louise's desks. 'I've always felt a bit left out, I suppose. Anyway, do I need a written letter, or will an email do?'

'Email is probably fine.' Harri thinks for a minute. 'Although, listen – between us, I think an announcement is coming soon. There might be some big changes on the way, so I don't know if you want to wait to see what happens before you make anything official.'

Tabitha rolls her eyes, just like old times. 'I can't believe it. Mackenzie and her dad are all over every news channel, and we've not had so much as an email about it.'

Harri nods. 'Trust me, that's company policy. In 2004, *Panache* did a big interview with Madonna, and a small pro war group got the idea that she must be in the building. This was over a week after the interview came out. I like the idea that Madge would have just wanted to hang out here, drinking our crappy coffee – anyway, obviously no Madonna. But we didn't realise that a group of gun wielding maniacs had taken control of the building. The only people who knew were the ones who happened to watch BBC Breakfast before coming into work. And even then, the only thing that happened was a company-wide email, a week later. "Owing to the unprecedented events of last week, all non-staff visitors to Hudson Media will be required to wear a security pass for the duration of their visit."' *Why do I still work here, again? Remind me?*

This is the first time Harri has seen Tabitha expressing an interest in anything she has said. 'What happened? How did they get them out?'

Harri shakes her head. 'I've never got to the bottom of it. There is a rumour – almost certainly not true – that Geoff from Maintenance tried his hand at a bit of amateur hostage negotiation.'

She has Tabitha's full attention. 'What did he do?'

Harri wishes the truth were a bit more exciting. 'Well, I think he asked if they wanted to see the new disabled loo with the double flush, then he offered the leader a bite of his Ginsters pasty. At that point the group fled in terror. Anyway – sit tight for a minute, if you can, just in case you can squeeze any extra cash out of Hudson before you go.' She thinks for a moment. 'Let's not make it easy for them.' *And I really ought to take my own advice.*

'Make it easy for who?' Louise has arrived and is beginning to embark upon the tortuous daily process of untangling herself from the straps of various tote bags. Some are slung across her body, like ammo belts. Some are tightly wedged over the arms of her coat, garrotting her armpits. Ladymag Rambo, thinks Harri, ready to fight her way out of a publicity junket at a moment's notice, with an arsenal of sweaty sports kit, used tissues and unwashed keep cups. Kim walks in behind her, with a single, sleek, small rucksack. Being a working woman, with lipstick and laptops to carry, is essentially being condemned to spend your waking life trapped in an escape room of your own making.

'I was just saying to Tabitha that the last few days have been quite unsettling. Officially we're waiting for news. Unofficially, I can tell you that Mackenzie has gone, and no one seems to know quite what's going to happen next. But I promise that there isn't anything to worry about, and I'll keep you as informed as I possibly can.'

Imogen arrives in time to catch the last part, and Harri feels her breath catch in the back of her throat. She smiles – is Imogen avoiding her eyes, or does she always make a beeline for Louise? What can she say to her? Please? I'm sorry? Harri's dilemma feels heavy in her chest, sharp cornered. If she leaves, she'll lose everything. Yet it's the thought of staying that seems like a gradual death. Imogen is her Thelma, and in her heart, all Harri wants is for the pair of them to drive off the edge of the cliff together. But it's easy for her to prepare to lose everything when she doesn't really believe she has anything to lose, any longer. It's different for Imogen.

If a decision is difficult, it usually means there is no right answer. There is no safe option. Whatever you pick will inevitably lead to gains and losses. All anyone can do is focus on those gains, and not what they might regret.

Harri hoped that by this point in her life, she'd finally feel wise enough to choose confidently, and well. Hadn't she learned anything? Take the money, you can always quit. That didn't feel right. Harri wasn't a quitter. She was too proud. Even when she was drained, anxious, too tired to close her own eyes. Quitters never win. She was brave. She was famous for it. No matter how vulnerable and broken she felt, she kept showing up.

Had she? Or had she just been turning up, and staying numb? Was she fearless, courageous – or just trading her own happiness to stay safe, to maintain a broader status quo?

That wasn't brave at all.

While Harri grapples with her conscience and wonders whether she can be as brave as Susan Sarandon, the real Louise is finally free, and able to start unbuttoning her coat. 'Imogen! Guess who has been asking about you? You remember my friend Tristan ...' Harri feels herself zoning out. She mimes busyness. She tries not to think about anything. She'll delete her junk mail. She'll change her screensaver. She'll avoid all human interaction for the rest of the morning, and then ...

'HARRI! Harri! Can I talk to you?'

Imogen is standing by Harri's desk, hopping from foot to foot. For a minute, Harri wonders whether she has come to ask permission to go to the toilet.

'Sure, of course, what's up?'

'I want to do it. I really, really want to do it.' The intensity is alarming – Louise and Tabitha are looking over surreptitiously, and Kim isn't even pretending to be subtle. He's got his palms on his knees, and he's leaning forward in his chair as though he's watching a particularly shocking edition of *Police Camera Action!* Is Imogen propositioning her? 'I've been thinking, and I had a long chat with my mum, and I just this minute thought of a good name. *Touch.com.* Because that's what this is. That's what's missing. We're inviting people to feel.'

Harri blinks, trying to catch up with Imogen's words, which are being issued at triple speed. She's still talking. '... and I know it's a big risk, a huge risk really. But maybe staying at *Panache* would be the bigger risk, because I know I'd keep having to compromise. And right now, they love us, but they will only love us for as long as we keep making money for them. This is a chance to do the thing that I really believe in. I think we've already done the difficult, scary bit, really. I believe in it. The investors believe in it. If you believe in it, then we're in business.'

When Harri and Imogen find Linda in an office on the top floor, it takes Harri a moment to notice that she's holding

Imogen's hand. Also, doing so while saying 'We have something that we really need to tell you' to an expert in employment law, is an ill-advised move. The pair just about manage to compose themselves, although Harri can't stop grinning, as she starts to tell Linda 'it is with the deepest regret that I am tendering my resignation.'

'We understand we need to put it in writing ...'

'A new opportunity has presented itself ...'

'More than happy to serve a notice period ...'

Linda rolls her eyes. 'Stop! Stop talking like that. I'm surrounded by HR robots, all sodding day long, I do understand the Queen's English, you know. Just what is it that you two are going to do? I am agog!'

Imogen Mounce, sex writer, broadcaster and – not that she knows it yet – one of the most influential women in media, under thirty, looks at the floor and sketches a small circle with her toes. 'Um, it's for storytelling ... erotic ... empowerment ... sexual ...'

Linda looks approving. 'YES! That's what I like to hear, women's pleasure, front and centre. Massive market too, up for grabs, you're going to make a killing. I really wanted Hudson to move more explicitly into that area but they wouldn't listen. You did it so well at *The Know*, we wanted more. I'm assuming you have investment, but so long as there's no conflict of interest, I'd certainly be keen to have a conversation about it. And I can put you in touch with some other potential investors too.'

Harri speaks hesitantly. 'On that theme – legally, I was a little concerned that Hudson might argue that we were setting up a rival product, and I wanted to make sure ...'

Linda waves a hand, airily. 'Oh, I wouldn't worry about

that. Firstly, I think you can technically argue that yours is a health site, not a woman's lifestyle site. Different category. Secondly, and most importantly, after all you've been through with this company, Hudson are lucky that you're not suing them into oblivion.' She sniffs, making it very clear that she's slightly cross that Harri hasn't already launched a lawsuit.

'Anyway, congratulations! Officially, I'm very ... what's the word? Pissed off. *Entre nous*? I think this is a brilliant, brilliant move! Sisters doing it for themselves. Although,' Linda's face darkens, a thought only just occurring to her. 'Who in the name of fuckery is going to edit *Panache*, now? We have big plans.'

Harri has an answer prepared. 'I always thought that Giles Robinson, editor-in-chief of *Panache*, had a nice ring to it.'

Chapter Fifty-Nine

It's not a dream job.
My dreams are bigger than that

Imogen

Please not the bank. Please do not be the bank.

I hold my phone at arm's length. Withheld. Is it withheld or unknown that's bad?

I was on such a high after the conversation with Linda Morris. It would be so typical if, the moment that I decided to follow my heart, my heart was stopped in its tracks by my overdraft. Again. It's beating a violent and erratic tattoo. Quitting your job was a bad idea! Bad idea! Bad idea! Ah, fuck it. I'm going in. Death before dishonour. Bankruptcy before prison. I slide my thumb across the screen.

'Hello?'

'Hello? Am I speaking to Imogen? Imogen Mounce?'

'Ah, may I ask who is calling?' Imogen has run away to Brazil. To Beirut. To Barry Island! That's impossible,

Imogen Mounce died ten years ago! Sorry, wrong number, this is Mimogen Ounce!

'This is Ruby Kahn, I'm the editor of *Guardian Weekend*.'

'Oh? Hello? Do I . . .'

'We haven't spoken before, Harri Kemp passed your details on. I've known her for a while, and I've been really enjoying your pieces for *The Know*. We're aware of the, ah, ongoing situation there, and I was wondering whether you might be available to come and do some work for us. We're looking for a new freelance weekly columnist, someone young, frank and funny. I think you'd be perfect.'

Is this a practical joke? Is this a very elaborate ruse for the bank to check up on me?

'Oh. Wow. Right, I'd love to! Is there a theme?' Do I have to write about sex for the *Guardian*? I should probably go and have some, soon.

I can hear Ruby smiling through the phone. 'Oh, excellent! I thought you might take some persuading. Obviously, I'm very keen for something sexy but we're open to ideas. Did you ever read the Sam Strong column? That's the spot we're looking to fill. As long as it's entertaining, and it's not a litany of B-list celebrities assembled to launch the latest crappy car, we're up for anything.'

'Oh.' I let this sink in. 'Sam's been doing that column for years!'

'Exactly!' Ruby laughs again. 'He's a bit pale, male and stale for us. It's definitely time for a shake up. Anyway, give me your email, we'll get a coffee in the diary, can you do early next week? We'll get a contract sorted too. I'm so excited about this, Imogen. I think you're just right for us.'

*

379

Girls in books pinch themselves. I hold my hand out in front of my face and wiggle my fingers experimentally.

My dream job. No. I check myself. That thought doesn't quite fit, any more. My dreams are bigger than that.

It's a job I have dreamed about. A job I'm excited about. Not a job that is going to define me. Or fix me.

For a long time, I confused success with self-esteem. I was constantly prepared to give all of my power away. I thought it was up to someone else to allocate a status to me. I have let my employers decide how I was allowed to feel about myself. Whether or not I was allowed to like myself.

Soon, I will be Imogen Mounce, *Guardian* columnist. And Imogen Mounce, founding editor of *Touch.com*. I'm so proud of that. But that will never be all that I am. I was just as worthy, and just as deserving of love and respect, as when I worked in the pen factory.

I'm the one who has been finding my own way. I'm not here to serve someone else's story.

This is the thought that will anchor me, for months and years to come. It will bring me security and peace. It will stop me from feeling as though I'm constantly, frantically chasing validation, and careering out of control.

It is the thought that makes me realise I am writing my own happy beginning.

Epilogue

It's a wrap

Tonight, the roof will be raised, and *The Know* will be toasted, before it goes offline. The content will be absorbed into the shiny new *Panache* website, and Harri is preparing to waive her no crying at work rule. She's going to miss everyone very much. Even Tabitha.

Touch.com is still an exasperating embryo. Harri can't wait until she and Imogen are able to spend their nine to five writing and scheming – instead of fitting it in after hours, and wrestling for room for their creative vision. For every ten minutes she spends doing the work she loves, Harri must spend a full and frustrating day with an investor, slowly and patiently explaining how the internet works.

She spent a few sleepless nights worrying about what might become of the gang. Happily, Kim was thrilled to be part of the glossy new *Panache* redesign, and even more thrilled to work with Giles, who he has chosen to be his new spiritual mentor. (Giles is less than thrilled about the fact that Kim calls him Yoda.) Akila has said she'll consult for *Touch,* for mates' rates, in addition to consulting for

Panache for a fee that means that she only has to work four months of the year, if she wants to. And sweet, neurotic, arch-worrier Louise might have the happiest ending of all. She has just found out that she's been selected for the next series of *The Great British Bake Off.*

And yet – this does not feel like an ending, at all. This is the first day of the future. Harri wants to shudder at the aphorism, but it seems so apt.

Tonight will be chaotic, but this morning feels calm. Harri is lying in bed. She has not yet opened her eyes. She is waiting for the sun to rise and listening to the skylarks. At least – she hopes she hears skylarks, they are one of the few songbirds she can name. She can only confidently identify the sound of a blackbird, and she secretly thinks of everything else as not-a-blackbird. In north London, the noise is homogenous, anyway. All birds copy car alarms. Art imitates life and improves upon it. In the unlikely event of a robot uprising, would there be a musical mirror bounce, with the cars singing along with their avian imitators? This is very silly, thinks Harri. But she feels silly. Or rather – expansive. New. Free. It is as though someone did a loft conversion in her mind, in the night. Something has gone. A heaviness. She did not know the weight of the heaviness until she felt this lightness.

Harri idly rubs her thumb along her bare collarbone. Behind her eyelids, behind her curtains, a cloud rolls and parts.

I'm alone, here. But not all alone. Not by myself. With my self.

Harri's thumb dips and circles her breastplate. Her skin, she notes, approvingly, feels smooth, firm. Far firmer than she deserves – a pale Yorkshire woman with almost five decades of beer gardens, and cavalier sunscreen use behind her.

Her thumb slides a little further down.

Oh.

The curvature of her breast surprises her. She's made of slopes, bends, undulations. She cannot remember when she last touched herself. In the shower she's brisk, perfunctory, and yet trepidatious, grabbing bits of her body and patting herself down for bad news. Now, with her index and middle finger, she traces a shell spiral all the way to her nipple.

Oh.

Harri's vagina, her vulva, really, her cunt, no, she can't; she supposes, exasperated, her pussy – is present.

What would it be like to touch, to trace, to follow this pulsing and swelling? She daren't. She won't. It is too tender. Too much love has been left there. She can't open up again, she might have to close for ever.

And yet.

She can take her fingers and draw a soft line up her inner thigh. Harri does not, at this juncture, wish to think about Imogen. But she does.

'I want to write about desire. Not vibrators that cost a hundred pounds. I want to write about women wanting themselves, on their own terms,' Imogen had told Linda Morris, who had nodded approvingly, and signed a sizeable investment deal.

Masturbation was her feminist duty, probably. Sexual self-sufficiency made sense. Heaven knows Harri was hardly ready to enjoy sex as a contact sport. When she had a free weekend, she would have a really good go at masturbating. But first, she would get those prints to the framers, and replace her pans, and do something about that damp spot on the ceiling in the hall.

Still, she remembers the giddiness. She remembers, with great clarity, a holiday in Greece, tipsy touching and kissing and working herself into such a state that she was left bent over a ferry rail, breathing through her mouth and shifting from foot to foot, while Andy said, in wonder, 'Your eyes are all pupil' and asked if she'd got hold of an E while they were in the Customs queue.

Harri is breathing through her mouth right now, fast and shallow. She is, she realises, licking her lips.

Her thumb slides a little further up.

She has lived through many winters. Winter is treacherous. It is not just the length, the darkness, the bitter, numbing iciness of it – it's the way the cold kills hope. It makes us push our tenderness and vulnerability far out of reach. It makes spring seem illogical, impossible.

But the earth is moving, the ice is melting, and spring is coming. And Harri's memories are joyful, now. She touches, and touches, and remembers how magical and mysterious it is that this tiny button buzzes her toes, her neck, her nipples. And love breaks over her body in great waves, and just when she reaches the point of glorious unbearability, she feels a great soaring, a surging, a release.

This is love, she realises. Now, this is enough for me. She opens her eyes. The sun has come up.

Acknowledgements

All books are born through acts of creative collaboration; I have never been more aware of that, nor more grateful for that, than when writing *Careering*. Working on this book during 2020 and 2021 was a challenge, but it was a joy and a privilege too, thanks to the excellent team at Sphere and Little, Brown. It's because of the kindness, encouragement and talent of my brilliant editor Darcy Nicholson that I could take refuge in Imogen and Harri's world when the real one became especially difficult to bear.

I'd like to also give enormous thanks to Millie Seaward and Brionee Fenlon – whose hard work, skill and imagination are responsible for getting this book into readers' hands. Thanks to Thalia Proctor and Vanessa Neuling for their brilliant editing skills and making the text as fresh and sharp as it could possibly be. Thanks to the magnificent Bekki Guyatt for her truly fabulous cover design – I'm so, so lucky to work with her.

I'd also like to thank my adored agent Diana Beaumont, whose insight, talent and support are invaluable, I could not ask for a better advocate or friend. I also send my love and thanks to her colleagues at Marjacq Scripts: Guy,

Leah, Phil, Imogen and Sandra. A huge, huge thank you to independent booksellers everywhere, especially Fran at The Margate Bookshop, Gayle at the LRB Bookshop, Gem at The Deal Bookshop, Chrissy at Bookbar, Simon at The Big Green Bookshop, Jo at Red Lion Books, Clare at Harbour Books, the team at Bookish in Crickhowell and the team at Fox Lane Books. It's an honour and a privilege to have your support as a writer. As a reader – thank you, with all my heart, for all of the brilliant stories you have brought into my life.

Much, much love and thanks to Lauren Bravo, Lucy Vine, Sophie Morris, Grace Plant and Jo West, the darling brave souls who dared to read this when the manuscript – and I – were in pieces. Your insight has shaped this book, and I'm so lucky to have such generous and encouraging friends. Also, a huge thank you to my kind, supportive friend Sheryl Garratt, who, among so many other brilliant things, was the one to introduce me to the London Writers' Salon. Thanks to Parul, Matt and everyone who wrote this book with me, over Zoom, on dark winter mornings. It's a pleasure and a privilege to write alongside you, and I think of you all as beloved colleagues.

As always, all my love and thanks to my sisters and my parents, for reading books, sharing books and teaching me everything I know about how to tell stories. Thank you to everyone who read and supported *Insatiable,* and who listened to *You're Booked* and *Daisy Is Insatiable* (and a huge thank you to all of our wonderful guests).

Enormous thanks to Quince Tree Press and the Carr Estate for so generously allowing me to use a line from JL Carr's novel, *A Month In The Country,* as an epigraph.

Being married to a fellow writer can spell disaster, or bliss. I got enormously lucky. 'Producer' Dale Shaw, I love you, thank you for your constant sweetness, generosity and empathy, for being the best and wisest comrade, for being prepared to discuss the rhythm of a joke or a line on the sofa, after dinner, when we're watching *Taskmaster*. Thank you for letting Harri borrow your birthday.

Finally, this book is partly inspired by the earliest days of my career. So many of my colleagues were so kind, encouraging, inspiring and funny. I think of you all often, and I miss you. And everyone who has ever written for me, feeling lost, and seeking career advice, I think of you often, too, and wish you all the love and luck I can. I hope you get what you really want – and that you're as ambitious for your happiness as you are for your careers.